Me Since You

Also by Laura Wiess

Such a Pretty Girl
Leftovers
How It Ends
Ordinary Beauty

Me Since You

Laura Wiess

GALLERY BOOKS MTV BOOKS

New York London Toronto Sydney New Delhi

Gallery Books
A Division of Simon & Schuster, Inc.
1230 Avenue of the Americas
New York, NY 10020

MTV Music Television and all related titles, logos, and characters are trademarks of MTV Networks, a division of Viacom International Inc.

First MTV Books/Gallery Books trade paperback edition February 2014

GALLERY BOOKS and colophon are registered trademarks of Simon & Schuster, Inc.

For information about special discounts for bulk purchases, please contact Simon & Schuster Special Sales at 1-866-506-1949 or business@simonandschuster.com

The Simon & Schuster Speakers Bureau can bring authors to your live event. For more information or to book an event contact the Simon & Schuster Speakers Bureau at 1-866-248-3049 or visit our website at www.simonspeakers.com.

Designed by Aline C. Pace

Manufactured in the United States of America

10 9 8 7 6 5 4 3 2 1

Library of Congress Cataloging-in-Publication Data is available.

ISBN 978-1-4391-9397-6
ISBN 978-1-4391-9399-0 (ebook)

For my parents
Geza William and Barbara Sellner Battyanyi,
who have always gone above and beyond for their family,
for Scott and Suzanne,
who make me so proud to be their sister
and
for Bernie,
who is always in my heart

Me Since You

Acknowledgments

Sincere thanks to my editor, Abby Zidle, for her enthusiasm, insight and wonderful, thought-provoking questions, and to Louise Burke, Jen Bergstrom, Parisa Zolfaghari, John Paul Jones, Jillian Vandall and Anna Dorfman at Simon & Schuster for lending their considerable skill, talent and expertise to *Me Since You.*

It's always a pleasure to thank my agent, Barry Goldblatt, for his advice, encouragement, support and belief in my work.

Heartfelt thanks go out to retired Franklin Township Police Department Sergeant Rich Recine for answering my questions with patience, humor and grace. He was trained by the best and is one of the best, so any narrative license taken or errors regarding police procedure in *Me Since You* are all mine. Next time, Rich, the coffee's on me.

Much love to the incomparable Bonnie Goodwin Verrico, who gently told me to *Just keep breathing and the answers will come* when I was certain they wouldn't. Thank you, kindred spirit. You were right.

I'm very thankful for dear friends and virtual diner talks that ease my writing angst.

I owe a debt of gratitude to wildlife rehabber Terri Coppersmith, and to Drs. Michele Zajac, Audrey Zajac, Denise Hardisky and the wonderful staff at Bunker Hill Veterinary Hospital—Mark, Leslie, Sarah, Sherry, Kelsey, Sandy, Jackie, Karla, Lisa, Sue, Trish,

Susie, Cindy and Garrett—for their generosity, compassion and the invaluable care they give the animals. I admire them greatly for it.

Thanks to Wendy Gloffke for her friendship and support, our excellent adventures and for being the gamest, most intrepid person I know. I count myself lucky to be your friend.

To the beloved Petose and Wiess families, Stew Russell, Jane Russell Mowry and John Verrico, who always listened, opined and supported even when I became truly tiresome. You're the best, and I'm forever grateful.

Me Since You is a story of hope, love and family, and so to Bill and Barbara, Scott, Rose, Sue, and Paul . . . thank you. You guys are my heart, my joy and my home base, and I love you madly.

There are two ways to be fooled:
One is to believe what isn't so;
the other is to refuse to believe what is so.

—Søren Kierkegaard

The Last Friday in March

Nadia and I scramble down the hill at the edge of school property right as the morning's final late bell rings behind us.

"Come on, hurry," I say, passing her and leaping across the little creek that divides the school from the back of the businesses on Main Street. "We can't get caught."

"Relax, will you?" she says, stepping neatly across the creek and stopping beside me. "This is an adventure, Rowan. It's supposed to be fun."

"Yeah, well, we have to get there first," I say, because we've cut school twice before and crossing this flat, empty lot stretched out before us is always the most nerve-wracking part. *Stay alert. Always be aware of your surroundings.* How bizarre that I'm pretty much using the key points from my father's personal-safety lecture against him. "All right, let's go. And try to act casual."

"Whatever you say," Nadia says with laughter in her voice.

And maybe I'm just all tensed up, knowing there's no turning back now, but the moment I step out of the sparse trees and onto the open lot my back gets twitchy, like the entire school faculty is watching us ditch and the principal has my father on speed dial.

I break into a jog, heading for the back of the row of businesses.

"Panic is not casual," Nadia calls from somewhere behind me.

"Run, will you?" I yell, speeding up.

"No," she says amiably. "They're not going to see us and even if they do, so what?"

"Easy for you to say," I mutter, hurling myself into the shadows behind the bank. High drama maybe, but too bad. This is serious stuff for me. My parents are *way* stricter than Nadia's, so if we do get caught all she'll get is a resigned sigh and a slap on the wrist while I'll get lectures, grounding, no computer and even worse, no phone.

This had so better be worth it.

I press myself against the cold brick wall and watch Nadia's easy, ambling approach. Her jacket's open and her white top is cut in a low V. Her jeans hug her legs and disappear into a pair of her mother's over-the-knee, black stiletto-heeled boots. Her long hair, twenty shades of rippling, layered blond highlights, makes her recognizable at least a mile away, and my parents *know* that wherever the social butterfly Nadia is I usually am too, so—

"Could you maybe even *try* to hide?" I say, scowling.

"No. It's Senior Cut Day," she says, sauntering up. "That's the whole point, isn't it?"

"Well, it *would* be if we were seniors," I snap, grabbing her arm and pulling her against the building beside me.

"So? We're sophomores *hanging out* with seniors," she says mischievously, and pulls out her phone to check messages. "Text from Brett: 'Still waiting. Where are you?'"

I snort and give her a speaking look because Brett would know *exactly* where we were if he and Justin had just picked us up at the corner fifteen minutes ago like they said they would instead of going straight to McDonald's and then texting us to meet them there. I don't say it though because Nadia really likes Brett *and* she says Justin thinks I'm hot. This morning's rendezvous is the farthest we've ever gotten with them and so for now we're willing to overlook their bad behavior, or justify it, or whatever kinds of deals girls make with themselves just so they can stay in the game.

"Tell them we're on our way," I say, sidling along the brick wall to the corner and stopping.

"Mmm-hmm," Nadia says distractedly, texting away.

I take a deep breath and release it.

Stay alert. Always be aware of your surroundings.

Right.

I inch forward and peer around the corner to Main Street, to Dunkin' Donuts, where yes, of course, there is a local cop car parked right up front in the lot. "Damn." I pull back, heart pounding. "He has to get coffee now? I can't believe this."

"Is it your dad?" Nadia says, sighing and leaning against the brick.

"I don't know," I say, rubbing my forehead. "He's on duty this morning but I don't know which patrol area he has, so yeah, it could be him." I peek around the corner again in time to see a very tall, solid, stern-looking cop with mirrored sunglasses and iron-gray hair step out the door and head for the patrol car. "Shit!" I whip back out of sight, praying he hasn't seen me. "It's Lieutenant Walters."

"Did he see you?" Nadia asks, finally sounding concerned. "Here, let me look." She starts to step around me. "He might not recognize——"

"No!" I hustle her toward the back of the building and we stand for a moment, listening for footsteps and hearing nothing but sirens in the distance. This is bad. He could be sitting there waiting till we come out or walking right up on us. "Forget Main Street. We'll go the back way and come out down by McDonald's."

"That's going to take longer," Nadia says, frowning.

"Don't care," I say in a singsong voice, and take off across the back of the buildings. "Watch for white cars pulling up to corners," I say, cutting down a side street. "And keep checking behind you, too. He's good at sneaking up on people." My tone is grim because Lieutenant Walters and I have a history, part of which Nadia already knows but part I will never tell her because it's just too humiliating to ever say aloud.

It happened three years ago, during the annual PBA picnic. I'd been spending every day at Nadia's that summer watching all the trashy reality show reruns I wasn't allowed to watch at home, and on the day of the picnic I was thirteen, trying hard to look eighteen. I'd been sent storming back to my room to change my clothes three times before my appalled father, calling the rejected outfits "middle school stripper" and asking where in the almighty hell I'd gotten them ("borrowed" from Nadia's mom's drawers), decided my lame, midthigh white shorts and stupid turquoise tank were respectable enough for me to set foot out the door.

Ugh.

I'd been allowed to bring Nadia as my guest though, and when we stopped to pick her up she came sauntering out of her house in almost the exact same outfit I'd had on—tiny black boy shorts and a black halter (mine had been red)—smiling and waving good-bye to her mom standing at the pool gate, who waved benignly back and hitched up the strap of her little black bikini with the thong bottoms.

"It's not fair. I look stupid and Nadia looks hot," I said from the backseat, where I'd been working up a mighty case of outrage. "And I swear, Dad, if you tell her to go back and change I'm gonna—"

"Hey, watch your tone," my father said, frowning at me in the rearview mirror. "Who do you think you're talking to?"

"He's not going to say anything," my mother said at the same time, giving him a smile and her peacemaking look. "It's the style, Nicky, and she's not your daughter. If Nadia's mother thinks that outfit is appropriate for a thirteen-year-old child—"

"Thirteen isn't a *child*," I cried, highly insulted. "How can you say that? She looks like she's at least sixteen!"

"Physically, in those clothes, yes," my mother said, shifting and glancing over her shoulder at me. "But her emotions and logic, Rowan, and her decision-making capabilities . . . no. There's still a thirteen-year-old brain controlling that body."

"So, what's wrong with that?" I said, scowling.

My mother, ever the librarian, hesitated as if searching for just the right words.

"Nothing, if you've got a good head on your shoulders and aren't trying to grow up too fast," my father said as Nadia opened the back door and plopped onto the seat beside me. "Hi, Mr. Areno. Hi, Mrs. Areno. Hey, Rowan." She shook back her blond mane and her dancing gaze took in my outfit. "Um, cute top. Is it new?"

I gave her a black look. "Right."

"Hi, Nadia," my father said, glancing at her in the rearview mirror. "You bringing a jacket? It might get chilly later."

"Oh, c'mon," Nadia burbled, leaning forward and poking his shoulder. "It's like a hundred degrees, Mr. Areno. You're so funny." She sat back and buckled her seat belt.

"So like, are they going to have all kinds of food there or what? Because I'm starving."

My father glanced over at my mother, mustache twitching. "Butter wouldn't melt in her mouth."

"Ah, the peril and glory of youth," she said, and, smiling, turned up the CD player to drown us in some ancient Isley Brothers tunes.

Nadia and I glanced sideways at each other and cracked up.

And it wasn't until dusk, after we'd been good long enough for my parents to relax their vigilance, after my father and his best cop buddy, Vinnie, joined the softball game and my mother was lounging on the bleachers cheering with the other cops' wives, that Nadia finally nudged me and nodded toward the two guys hanging out near the tree line past the bathrooms.

"They've been watching us," she said, lifting up her hair and fanning the back of her neck. "Want to take a walk to the bathroom?"

"Uh . . ." I sneaked a peek and even from here, I could tell two things: One, they were definitely not part of the PBA picnic, and two, they were cute. And older. Like, "out of high school" older. Like "facial hair, college and real muscles" older. A thrill ran through me. "Okay, I guess."

And so we eased away from the picnic table with studied casualness, taking our time smoothing our shorts and acting like we were totally bored and in absolutely no hurry to go anywhere for any reason. Nadia whispered updates as we strolled across the lawn toward them—"The one in the green T-shirt just smiled and said something to FUBU T-shirt and they both kind of turned toward us like they're waiting. I want FUBU and you can have green T-shirt, okay?"—but I felt awkward and obvious, like my whole body was a neon sign flashing our intent to my parents.

I kept expecting to hear my father's voice stopping us but it didn't happen, and every step screwed the tension in my stomach tighter. Moths fluttered around the bare bulb lighting the girls' room door. Peepers sang in the deepening shadows. The heat coming off Nadia was scorching, my was heart pounding so loud I could barely think and suddenly we were there. The guys were lounging against the side of the cinder-block building, smiling, gazes smoky with the kind of dazzling, open appreciation that seventh-grade boys wouldn't master for years. They asked if we wanted to hang out, drink a few beers and smoke a little, exchanging mocking grins and saying what a farce it was, partying in the middle of East Mills's finest. I didn't like the tone in FUBU's voice but green tee was staring at me like I was the best thing he'd ever seen, handing me a beer and easing back into the shadows while FUBU lit up and passed Nadia the joint.

I'd never really partied before—my father ran the DARE program from middle school up through junior high and was always on the lookout for deviants—but when Nadia handed me the weed, her gaze brimming with dark excitement, I took it without hesitation.

This was an adventure and we were in it together.

I don't know whether it was the weed, beer or desire that made me so woozy; I don't know how I went from laughing and giddy at flirting with college guys, smoking a joint, draining a beer and feeling green tee's sinewy arm claiming me, his hot breath in my ear, to melting against him weak-kneed and wanting, feeling an insistent tug at my waist and then hands on my bare skin, sliding high, leaving a shivery trail of ripples in their wake, prying up my bra and closing around—

A burst of light blinded me. "Okay, come on, break it up."

"Shit," green T-shirt muttered against my mouth, and suddenly his groping hands were replaced with a cool wash of air and emptiness. I stood there blinking and confused until the dim realization that my boobs were exposed penetrated the slow fog in my brain. Belatedly, I folded my arms across my bare chest.

"Stay where you are," a stern voice said, and then, "Fix your clothes, young lady."

I drew a deep, hitching breath and, mortified, wrestled down my bra and tank top.

There was a sharp snort from behind the flashlight. "Jesus Christ, you've got to be kidding me. Nick's kid?"

I squinted in the direction of the light, recognized the tall, forbidding-looking man behind it and burst into tears.

Lieutenant Walters, my father's by-the-book, hardass training officer—and boss.

The flashlight beam did a quick sweep of the area, over green tee lounging against the wall, and returned to me. "Where's your friend?"

As if by magic, Nadia appeared out of the girls' room door behind Lieutenant Walters. "Rowan?" she said, rushing over in concern. "What's wrong? What happened?"

I gazed at her, bewildered. Her eyes were bloodshot and her breath sour but her clothes were in place and other than her puffy lips and missing gloss, she looked totally normal.

There was no sign of FUBU, and nobody mentioned him.

The next ten minutes were torture: The look in Lieutenant Walters's eyes, reminding me of what he'd seen; the sick knot of real terror that he would tell my parents in horrifying, irreversible detail; the weight of Nadia's arm around my shoulders as if in comfort but actually making me feel like a stupid, pathetic baby, a victim instead of a hot girl who knew how to party and not get caught.

Like her.

But the worst was when Lieutenant Walters flagged down my father and drew him aside, and they spoke quietly for a moment. I saw the relaxed good humor in my father's face tighten to anger, saw Walters's gesture at the empty beer bottles, heard him say, "... caught your daughter and this guy getting a little too friendly ...," and when my father glanced over at me with a look of disbelief and, worse, disappointment, I hated Lieutenant Walters like I'd never hated anybody.

I hated Nadia for a minute too, because somehow she'd ended up the innocent one.

The rest was a humiliating blur of green tee going into shock when he found out I was only thirteen and babbling that he didn't know, didn't even know my name, that we were just hanging out, no big deal, and of me nodding tearfully when my father glanced at me for confirmation— I lied, yes, but I was willing to agree to anything just to get it over with.

I didn't dare look at Walters.

I never told Nadia what he'd caught me doing and I guess he never told my father the details either, because the questions, lecture, grounding and forced return of Nadia's mother's clothes were nowhere near as bad as they would have been had my parents known what really happ—

"Row, c'mon," Nadia says, hip-bumping me and, since I'm not paying attention, almost knocking me off the curb. "Whoa." She catches my arm, keeps me from falling and grins. "Nice save, huh?"

"What would I ever do without you?" I joke, bumping her back, because the McDonald's is there right across the street and so is Brett's car, parked in the lot and waiting.

The Big Plan is that the four of us will head to an out-of-town diner (where my father won't catch me) and then go back to either Brett's or Justin's empty house to hang out until three o'clock, when I have to be at work.

"Told you we'd make it," she says with a cocky smile.

"*Now* I can relax," I say, and, laughing, look both ways and then step into the street, heading straight for the golden arches.

The Last Friday in March

8:49 A.M.

I follow Nadia into McDonald's.

Justin and Brett are sprawled at a table by the window, and judging by the crumpled food wrappers, they've already had first breakfast. Brett sees us, smiles and waves, but Justin is busy texting and doesn't look up.

I smile anyway, just in case he does.

Brett sends Nadia a mock-chiding, "Hey, you finally made it."

"Yeah, lucky you," she drawls, laughing and flicking back her hair.

"Hi," I say, but they're too busy flirting to notice and Justin is still hunched over his phone, thumbs flying. I clear my throat and shift close enough to see the new pimple forming on the back of his neck. "Um, hi."

Still nothing.

I shoot Nadia a sideways look.

"So, diner time," she says brightly. "Are we ready or what?"

"Yes!" Justin crows, lifting his head in sudden triumph. "Brett, man, it's *on*. Shane got the keys! Party at the shore house. *Score*." He stands, stretches his meaty arms up over his head and finally notices me. "Hey. How you doing?" Turns to Brett. "Let's get moving. Fun in the sun, bonfire on the beach tonight. Half the class is heading down there."

Brett glances at Nadia. "You good with the shore?"

"Always," Nadia says, eyes sparkling.

"Okay then, let's——" Justin says.

"Wait," I blurt, trying not to panic, and when everyone looks at me, I blush and say, "It's already, um"——I glance at my watch——"five to nine. Can't we just go to the diner?"

"Why?" Justin says, looking at me like I'm an imbecile.

Why? Because I risked a lot for a chance to hang out with you; am missing a history test; bought a new shirt; spent hours last night waxing, plucking, shaving, whitening, painting my nails, practicing my smile. Because I need you to do what you said you were going to do, what we planned to do, what I've been counting on. Because there is no way in hell I can go all the way down the shore, party and still find a way home in time to get to work at three. But all I say is, "Because I'm, uh, hungry."

"So get something here and eat it on the way," Justin says impatiently, falling back a step. "Come on."

"Row?" Nadia says, and the question in her gaze is about way more than food.

You know I can't, I tell her with a desperate look.

Brett jingles his car keys, slings an arm around her shoulders and starts steering her toward the door.

She resists for a moment, glances back at me, pleading, frustrated, and when I don't move to follow, expecting her to pull away, she mouths, *I'm sorry. Don't be mad,* flashes me a lame, apologetic smile and trails Brett out the door.

Wait . . . what?

Brett unlocks his car.

Nadia slides into the front passenger seat.

"You can't be serious," I say to no one, and plop down at the deserted table.

Justin pauses and glances back. Spots me sitting there, shrugs and lifts a hand. Climbs into the backseat and slams the door.

I gaze in disbelief at the crumpled, grease-stained napkins and Egg McMuffin wrappers littering the table. Squeezed-out ketchup packets leave bloody smears across the bright laminate and salt is strewn everywhere. It's wreckage, ruins spread out before me, and when I look up again, the three of them are gone.

And they left me their garbage.

I stare at it for a moment, then shove it away across the table. Why should I get stuck cleaning up their mess? I'm not even supposed to *be* here right now. I'm supposed to be on my way to the diner with my best friend and two cute seniors, one of whom supposedly likes me, talking, laughing and having a blast, because *that* was the plan.

That's what we *said* we were going to do, and I believed it. Stupid.

I scrub a frustrated hand across my forehead, totally at a loss. Sit back and look around the place. It's nearly empty, only me and a couple of senior citizens across the room in a booth in the corner.

Great. Now what?

Glance at my watch.

Nine oh one.

Only six hours to kill till work.

My stomach growls.

I dig around in my jeans pocket for my money.

Two dollars and thirty-eight cents.

Stupid me again, I actually thought they'd treat us to breakfast.

Well, at least Brett will still treat Nadia.

To breakfast, lunch *and* dinner around the bonfire.

Right.

She's going to owe me big-time for this one.

I shake my head in disgust and glance out the window, look right at the patrol car pulled up to the curb beside me, at the unsmiling, weary-looking cop staring back, badge number 23, Patrolman Nick Areno, my father, who is talking into his radio mike and motioning for me to come out.

Shit.

I gather the garbage, shove it into a can and trudge toward the door.

The life I touch for good or ill
will touch another life,
and that in turn another,
until who knows where the trembling stops
or in what far place my touch will be felt.
—FREDERICK BUECHNER

The Last Friday in March

9:26 A.M.

She's lying, and he knows it.

Impatient, he rests his hands on the gun belt at his waist and says, "All right, Rowan, let's try it again, and this time, how about telling me the truth?" He tempers his voice, keeps it calm and cool to mask his disappointment and stares down at the sixteen-year-old girl sulking on the bed. "How many times have you done this?"

"I already *told* you." She lifts her head, flicks a long strand of hair from her eyes and glares up at him, her dark gaze bitter with all the resentment a thwarted daughter can summon against the father who has ruined her fun. And then she looks past him, making certain the accusation spills over to her mother, too. "Only once. Today."

"Only once," he repeats, and in his measured tone is the same polite disbelief the tired answer *Just a coupla beers, Officer* always earns. "I see." He nods, thoughtful. "So if I check your attendance record with the school, they're going to confirm only one unexcused absence."

"Check my attendance record? Oh my *God*, are you *kidding?*" She bounds off the bed, an explosion of dramatic outrage, and storms around the cluttered bedroom.

"I told you I only cut once! Why can't you just believe me and let it go already? Why do you always have to make everything into such a big deal? I'm not a criminal, you know!"

"I know," he says, resisting the urge to add *but this is how it starts and I'm not letting it happen.* "You're too smart to go down that road. And I *will* believe you, when you tell me the truth."

"But, Dad, I *swear* I didn't—"

"Don't." He holds up a hand, stopping her. "I get it all day, every day from the general public. I don't need it here, too." He only has another minute or two, no more. "I'm not your enemy, Row. Just be honest. Talk to me. How many times have you cut out of school so far this year? Two? Three?"

"*Three?* Oh my God, Dad, come on," she says, but her eyes are too wide, her tone too quick. "You must think I'm a real degenerate."

No, he doesn't, and if he didn't have to call out on a break and leave his assigned patrol area on the other side of town just to bring her home, if he was free to parent and not police right now, then he would sit on the edge of her bed, not caring if Stripe's wispy black and gray cat hair clung to his uniform pants, and invite her to sit down next to him like a daughter, not a suspect, and talk.

If his shift didn't start with an adrenaline-spiked nightmare of domestic horror, then maybe he'd have more patience, but it's hard to ramp down to teen truancy after being the first car on the scene of this morning's brutal assault, after following the frantic, sobbing mother into the bedroom to check the vitals of little Carrie Connolly, a limp, unresponsive three-year-old clad only in a pair of pink underpants and suffering a half-dozen savage, crushing head wounds.

Her eyes were rolled back and her pulse weak. Her skull was misshapen, her blond hair matted, stained a sticky maroon-black from the frenzied blows . . . but it was the position of her body that pierced him, the sight of her chubby, outstretched arm, fingers dug into the rug in a last desperate attempt to escape the attack and . . .

Crawl under the bed to hide.

He'd always been calm and capable during crises, trained to keep an emotional distance, remain in control, to assess the situation and do what needed to be done. He did it this time too, swallowed the despair and, with sirens growing closer, surveyed the scene. The bedroom windows were closed and locked, with no signs of forced entry. Blood drenched the pillow and splattered a floppy-eared stuffed rabbit lying nearby. Reeking, urine-soaked Little Princess sheets had been half wrenched off the mattress, leaving it askew, and trailed across the floor next to Carrie's body.

Blood on the bedroom doorknob and tracks down the hall to the kitchen.

The detectives arrived and he briefed them. They split up, questioning the distraught mother and her live-in boyfriend separately. The mother said she'd kissed her sleeping daughter good-bye and left for work. Halfway there she realized she'd forgotten her cell phone and raced home to get it, walking in to find her boyfriend with a blood-smeared arm plunged deep into the kitchen garbage can and the house eerily silent. She'd run into Carrie's room and found . . . and found . . .

No, he was not Carrie's biological father. They'd only been together for five months. He was a laid-off carpet installer who watched Carrie while she worked. No, Carrie wasn't a chronic bed wetter; she'd actually stopped when she was two years old. This was something new, happening three, maybe four times a week now. Yes, it created stress between her and her boyfriend because for some reason he took it as a personal insult. No, she didn't understand it either.

EMS rolled in and moments later, Carrie, her mother and one of the detectives were gone.

There were bloody prints all over the black plastic kitchen garbage can, a pair of stained men's slippers and strands of Carrie's hair on the tack hammer shoved inside.

And on, and on.

The lying sack-of-shit boyfriend was read his rights. He was a talker though, wanting them to hear his side and denying ever touching Carrie even as dried blood spatter freckled his T-shirt, his neck, his hairline, and congealed beneath his fingernails. He swore he'd gone into the bedroom to wake her up and found her that way, suggesting she'd probably wet the bed again and tried to crawl out of it, fallen and hit her head on the floor . . .

Yeah. Six separate, skull-fracturing times, not counting the smashed fingers on the tiny hand she'd lifted to try to shield herself from the blows.

Right.

It sickened him, knowing she wasn't the first and wouldn't be the last kid he was too late to save, that this little girl could have been anyone's little girl, *his* little girl . . .

No matter how hard he tried he could never protect them enough.

He rarely gave voice to how futile it felt sometimes, trying to stop people from destroying themselves or each other, never discussed the most brutal parts of the job with his wife or daughter. No, for that he had his partner, Vinnie, or, more often, just pushed the scenes away into the back of his mind and tried to forget.

Sometimes when he was tired though, and his defenses were low, the ones he'd failed returned to haunt him: The first person he'd ever lost, a seventeen-year-old car-crash victim hopelessly pinned in the wreck, conscious, mangled and bleeding out, clutching his hand and begging him not to let her die. Even with police, fire rescue, EMS and the Jaws of Life working to free her, they had not been in time.

The bruised and battered baby with the beseeching blackened eyes, who, despite evidence of chronic abuse, was returned to the parents, and then four days later arrived at the morgue with third-degree burns charring over 90 percent of her body.

The elderly man on his way to the hospice to sit with his dying wife, driving too slowly for the asshole behind him, who, in a fit of rage, cut him off, stormed his car, grabbed the couple's blind, arthritic Scottie dog from the seat beside him and threw it into traffic, where it was immediately hit and killed by a car that never even stopped. When he arrived at the scene the old man stood stunned and weeping, the dead dog cradled in his arms, and couldn't give a detailed description of either vehicle.

Nineteen years' worth of senseless tragedies, some more memorable than others.

He wants to explain this to his daughter, to tell her that if he is sometimes too strict or overprotective it's because he's seen what can go wrong, knows that her standard, scoffing *Oh, c'mon, Dad, nothing's gonna happen* is sometimes true but other times not, and you don't get to choose when it fails.

He wants to talk until her attitude seeps away and she confesses why, when he pulled up to the McDonald's drive-through earlier for coffee, she was sitting inside, alone and miserable, when she should have been in class.

But he can't because his break is over.

Keying the radio, he says, "Eight oh one central, ten-eight Victory Lane," calling himself back into service. He glances up, meets his daughter's stony gaze. "Never mind. I'll just stop by the school." Sees the flurry of guilt and panic flash across the face he used to know by heart, and suddenly he would give anything to go back in time, back to the days when she ran *to* him instead of away, when she would get home from school and skip right out to see him in his wood shop, telling him everything she'd learned while he sanded and stained, smiled and listened. Back to when leaving for work meant kissing *both* his girls good-bye, a ritual never sacrificed because they were his reason for vigilance on the job, for never getting sloppy or lazy or taking anything for granted, because that was the fastest way to get himself killed.

Now though, to kiss his daughter good-bye he has to tiptoe in and do it while she's sleeping, or he can't do it at all. Those same pink cheeks he kissed a thousand times when she was little are off-limits to him and her mother now, personal, private property reserved for whichever scruffy, slouchy, text-happy slug she was cutting school to see, and it reminds him—

"Mom," she wails, abandoning anger for misery. "Oh my God, I can't believe you're gonna let him do this to me!"

It reminds him that although he's her father, he's no longer her hero.

His wife, Rachel, gives him a commiserating look over the top of their daughter's head, and he's about to tell Rowan she's grounded when his radio squawks and the dispatcher says, "Eight oh one central."

He keys the radio. "Eight oh one. Go ahead."

"Eight oh one, Victory Bridge, possible ten-ninety-six, man with child climbing over wall."

Ten-ninety-six. An emotionally disturbed individual.

With a kid.

Jesus Christ.

"Eight oh one copy." He turns to leave. "I have to go."

"What did they say about the bridge?" his wife says, sounding surprised.

"What's a ten-ninety-six?" Rowan says at the same time, her voice bright with undisguised relief at the sudden reprieve.

"Tell you later," he says, and in seconds is thundering down the stairs, striding through the living room and kitchen and out the sunporch door to the patrol car he's left running and parked in the driveway alongside of the house.

| | |

At 9:26 that same morning, while Rowan Areno is up in her bedroom being questioned by her father, a husky, twenty-three-year-old man in jeans and a khaki jacket trudges past her house on Victory Lane and up the sidewalk of the Victory Bridge, a rural, rarely used overpass stretched high across the busy four-lane highway below.

The man's bottom lip is chewed and chapped, his gaze glazed, detached, his hair uncombed and his cheeks rough with stubble, but his hands are scrubbed clean, the nails trimmed painfully short so as not to accidentally scratch the sleeping three-month-old baby, the son he has finally gotten for the weekend and now carries in a sling under his jacket, on his chest, nestled against his heart.

The boy is his pride, his legacy, the best and only thing he feels he has ever done right.

And he has failed him.

He stops and rests his hands on the flat, gritty top of the waist-high cement wall, closes his aching, red-rimmed eyes and, for a moment, turns his face to the early spring sun.

"Great day, huh?"

Startled, the man turns to see a kid sauntering up the overpass sidewalk toward him, a tall, wiry teen with sleek black hair pulled back in a ponytail, a smudge of soul patch under his bottom lip and a large, shaggy German shepherd padding along at the end of a leash.

"She's friendly," the kid says with a slight drawl as, fringed tail wagging, the dog stops and sniffs his shoes. "You mind?"

The man shakes his head but slides protective arms around his son. "Don't let her jump. I got my kid here." He turns slightly, allowing the boy a glimpse of the baby's pink forehead and the wisp of unruly, ginger-brown hair, so like his own, that just won't stay tucked up under the knitted hat. "Nice dog."

"Thanks," the kid says, reaching down and affectionately rumpling her furry, black and tan head. "She's a good girl." The shepherd looks up at him, tongue lolling, and leans her bulk against his leg. "Yeah, I know. We're going to get you some water." He glances at the man. "Something's up with her. She's been drinking a lot lately. We're going to the vet's this afternoon." A shadow crosses his face. "It's probably nothing but I don't want to take the chance, you know? I mean, she was born in an Iraqi war zone. She's already been through hell."

The man grunts, not wanting to encourage him.

"I know, pretty amazing, right?" He shakes his head, scratches the smooth hollow between the dog's eyes. "My dad found her and her sister starving when they were just like, six-week-old pups, and his unit adopted them. He busted his ass to get her out of there and shipped back to me before——" He stops as if he's just remembered something crucial, averts his dark gaze, and it's only then that the man notices the circles under the kid's eyes, the tautness of the pale skin drawn across his cheekbones. "Anyway." He shrugs and gives the dog's leash a gentle tug. "Come on, Daisy." But as they start past the kid hesitates, searching the man's haggard face. He opens his mouth to speak, then shuts it again. "Enjoy the day."

"Yeah," the man says, but he isn't watching the kid leave, he's checking the sidewalk for others because streams of joggers, dog-walkers, foot traffic on this lonely overpass never occurred to him. Finding it empty, he puts his hands back on the cement wall.

His son squirms, hiccups and starts to cry.

The thin wail echoes out over the breeze.

"Shh." The man pats the baby. Rubs his back. "It's all right. We're here now." Brushes away the tears gathered in his eyes, tears that seem to come and go at will these days, and with a grunt of effort, slings his right leg up and over the wall.

"Whoa, hey!"

The man freezes.

"That's dangerous. What're you doing?"

The man turns his head, only his head, because he is straddling the wall, the baby is fretting and his fingertips burn from his grip on the rough cement surface. "Don't," he says, catching sight of the kid with the dog from the corner of his eye. They've stopped and turned back to him, standing maybe fifteen feet away. "This has nothing to do with you."

"But—"

"Just keep walking," the man says.

"Okay, but I don't . . . You shouldn't . . . Holy shit, wait, you're not gonna . . . ?" the kid blurts, and then the man hears quick, musical beeping and the kid's talking again, low and urgent.

The man wishes he could turn his head farther to see more but he's dizzy, and he didn't expect that, either.

Heights have never bothered him but now, half over the edge, he dares not look down. He sits a moment, absently listening to the kid babble, gaze fixed on the crisp, blue sky, breathing deep to quell the sickening lurch of vertigo, and when it passes, he shifts his butt and swings his other leg over the wall.

Both feet dangle in the air.

"Oh, no way," the kid says, his voice tight and shaking. "C'mon, man, don't do this. Seriously."

The man doesn't answer. His heart is pounding too hard, his breath too scarce.

It's the most alive he's felt in months.

"Think of your kid," the kid says. "Jesus Christ, it's just a baby."

"He," the man says, looking at him. "Sam. My son, Sammy." The man stops, not knowing why he feels compelled to set that straight.

"Sam, okay, yeah, good," the kid says, glancing worriedly back over his shoulder.

The road is empty.

The baby whimpers.

"Shh," the man says soothingly, patting him. "I'm here."

A horn blares somewhere down below on the highway, and the baby starts to cry.

"Hey, uh, look, it sounds like he's not too cool with heights," the kid says with false brightness. "What if I hold him or something for you? See if he'll calm down."

"No. He's shy with strangers." Dimly, over the thundering of his heart and the baby's fussing, the man hears brakes squeal and an engine roar to a stop, the kid babbling, his frantic voice loud and loose now, charged with adrenaline and fear.

He hears the officer speaking, calm and controlled, hears the recited, "Eight oh one central, be advised I have a white male, early twenties, brown hair, jeans, tan jacket, sitting on the Victory overpass wall with an infant . . . ," condensing him into an efficient, emotionless, no-frills dilemma, then going on to request backup, an emergency response team and traffic control both at the bridge and on the highway below. He stops listening, looks up instead and sees the police car parked at the curb, the solemn, uniformed cop and the kid, eyes huge, face filled with disbelief, the dog poised and watching, red lights spinning . . .

It disturbs him.

This moment was supposed to be peaceful, just the two of them, a permanent bonding of him and his son, the one thing they could have that no one could ever take away, but now, thanks to his poor planning, even that is slipping out of his grasp.

He tightens his grip on the baby.

The cop approaches, talking low and reassuringly, taking deliberate steps toward him, telling him everything will be all right, that his name is Officer Areno, Nick for short, and he's just there to listen to whatever the man has to say and make sure everybody stays safe. The cop, Nick, is older, middle-aged and worn looking, not cocky, beefed up and bald but with a slight paunch and worry lines, dark salt-and-pepper hair sticking out from under his hat and one of those classic, old-fashioned cop mustaches.

His gaze is steady with purpose. Steadier, the man fears, than his own.

"We can work this out," the cop says firmly, and then, into the radio pinned to his shirt, adds something in a low voice about getting the crisis negotiator here. "Come on down, sir, so we can talk. There's nothing here that can't be fixed."

The man stares at him, unmoving.

"Do you have any weapons on you? Any knives, guns, explosives . . . ?"

"No," the man says, offended.

"Okay, good. And I see you have your son with you," the cop says, nodding at the baby held against the man's chest. "Sam, right? How's he doing? Mind if I take a look at him?"

The man hesitates, then, keeping one hand on the bridge, pulls back the edge of his jacket, the edge of the sling, and caresses the baby's damp, ruddy cheek with a gentle thumb. The baby gurgles and beams up at him.

"Good-looking boy," the cop says, nodding. "What is he, four, five months old?"

"Three," the man says absently, lost for a heartbeat in the pure, hypnotic sweetness of his son's smile. "He's big for his age."

"That's good," Nick says, ambling forward another several steps. "Good, strong, healthy boy. You two have a lot to look forward to. First birthday, teaching him how to swing a bat, ride a bike—"

"Stop," the man says, dropping his hand and letting his jacket swing back into place. "I know what you're doing."

"Hey, just talking one father to another," Nick says, and his voice is casual but there's a watchful light in his eyes that the man doesn't trust.

"Don't come any closer," he says, shifting forward on the wall.

"No problem," Nick says, halting his advance. "So, what did you say your name was?"

"Corey," the man says after a moment.

"What's your last name, Corey?"

The man remains silent.

"How about Sammy? What's his last name?"

The man's mouth tightens and he doesn't answer.

"Does anyone know you're here?"

"No," Corey says flatly.

"Is there someone we can call for you, a family member maybe, bring them down here to talk? Best friend, parent, girlfriend . . . ?"

"No," he says again after a long moment.

"Well, if you change your mind, the offer's open," Nick says, his gaze never leaving the man's face. "So are you from East Mills, Corey?"

He doesn't answer.

Nick keys his radio and says in a low voice, "Eight oh one central, be advised subject's first name is Corey, three-month-old male is his son, first name Sam. DOB and birth mother's name unknown. Check Mercy General." Dispatch acknowledges, and he says to Corey, "I don't know about you but I could sure use a cup of coffee right now. Or maybe a nice, cold soda." A bead of sweat trickles down past the cop's ear. "What do you say you, me and Sam go grab something to drink and work this out together?"

"No," the man says, forgetting his vertigo and shaking his head. The sky rises and dips, his stomach lurches and he gasps, fingers digging into the cement. "Just leave us alone." The man tightens his jaw and his son, perhaps sensing the tension, lets out a whimper.

"Look, I can see you love your son," Nick says, sweat darkening the armpits of his blue uniform shirt. "And right now you're just sitting on a bridge with your boy, enjoying the day. Nothing's happened and nobody's been hurt, so let's keep things safe, okay?"

The man is silent a moment. "Life is what's gonna hurt him, not me," he says finally, stroking the baby's back.

"Yeah, sometimes it feels that way," Nick says, resting a white-knuckled hand on the cement wall. "I have a kid, too. A daughter. She's sixteen. She's a great kid, really smart, but I still worry about her and want to protect her.

That's what fathers do. I know it's not always easy, but it's worth it. So what do you say, Corey?"

The man gazes past the cop at the kid with the dog. Somehow, in these last few moments the kid has aged and doesn't look so young anymore. "Your father's dead, right? Isn't that what you meant before?"

The kid blinks, taken aback, and glances at the cop, uncertain.

"Come on, now, this isn't about him," Nick says, motioning the kid back a few steps. "Let's——"

"Your father put himself in harm's way to protect you, and when he died they told you he was a hero and that you should always be proud of him," the man says, holding the younger guy's stricken gaze. "Right?"

"Don't t-talk about my f-father," he stammers, his eyes welling up.

Corey ignores him. "Well, I'm putting myself in harm's way too, but you know what they'll tell my son when *I'm* gone?" He lowers his head, keeping his gaze on them, and kisses the top of the baby's head. "That I was a coward and a loser who didn't give a shit about anybody but himself, and how they're all better off without me."

"They're wrong, Corey," Nick says. "Come on down and we'll talk."

"They'll poison my own son against me. He won't understand, he'll never forgive me and I can't have that." He is careful not to glance down at the highway below. "A kid shouldn't grow up thinking his father didn't care about him." He looks into Nick's eyes, letting him see all that's left. "It screws him up inside."

"Easy," Nick says, and the tension in his voice is obvious. "We'll get you through this; you have my word on it. If you come down from there we can sort this out and——"

"He didn't ask to be born, and he doesn't deserve all

the miserable, rotten shit that's gonna be dumped all over him because of me." The man can't even see them now; the sudden spark of anger has flared and died, and despair stains his vision a dense, opaque red, blotting out all but futility. "And it will." His voice is thick, dull to his own ears. "It will."

"Corey, listen, it doesn't have to be that way." Nick keys his radio. "Eight oh one central, requesting ETA on county crisis ERT." The words are sharp, tight, and the radio squawks in return but for Corey it all fades and is finally gone.

Only the pain remains, overwhelming and unbearable, conquering him in what feels like an hour but is actually only seconds. It blinds and deafens him to all but the rumbling landslide of hopelessness and helplessness, drowns him in the unchecked misery flooding his brain, cutting off any chance of survival. He surrenders, beaten, exhausted from waging this brutal battle with himself every day, forcing his leaden limbs out of bed, tormented by the constant, bitter burden of unanswered prayers, the wanting, waiting, hoping to feel something better than desolation, sweeter than doubt, something kinder than the relentless, razor-sharp shredding of his own tortured thoughts twisting him up inside, fueling the hemorrhage of all he ever was, hoped for, would be.

A sudden, whispered thought—*You can go now*—twines through his mind, and, grateful, he accepts it.

"I love you, Samster," he murmurs, tears streaking his face. "Close your eyes."

"No," Nick says, stepping closer. "Corey, wait. *Please* let me help you."

"You can't," he says simply, and as the cop lunges the last few yards the man pushes off of the wall and, tipping forward into empty space, plummets out of sight.

"No!" Nick yells, and peers over the wall, shouting into his radio.

Eli Gage, the guy with the dog, stands forgotten, staring in stunned shock at the spot where the man and his son went over. Their plunge sends ripples through the air, and shuddering, he retreats a step, then another, but there is no escape. They widen, spread, and break over him. He is awash in it now, a part of it, and will be forever.

The cop stands, chest heaving, his face raw with anguish.

He is a part of it now, too.

Trembling, Eli pulls a pack of Marlboros from his T-shirt pocket, lights one and, knees weak, sinks down on the curb, head in his hands, dog at his side.

In the distance, someone is screaming.

But when I looked for good, evil came;
And when I waited for light, darkness came.
My lyre is turned to mourning,
And my pipe to the voice
Of those who weep.

—JOB

Chapter 1

Does bad news come in threes, the way dead people are supposed to?

Because it feels that way today, like something else is going to go wrong but I have no idea what, so all I can do is wait for it on this hot, hazy April Thursday when the air is hushed, heavy and strangely silver, the phones are silent and storm clouds bank in the distance.

I have the door propped open and am working alone for the first time in the month since I started here, standing behind the front counter of the dry cleaner's trying not to worry about what's happening at home and digging forgotten change from the pockets of old Mr. Hanson's damp, ugly polyester slacks before pinning an ID tag on the waistband and tossing them in the bin scheduled for Friday cleaning.

I put the coins on the counter.

We're supposed to return anything of value we find in our customers' pockets, put it in an envelope and staple it to the ticket on their hanger, but my boss, Eva, left early to take her car to the shop and it's only twenty-seven cents, so I drop the pennies in the *Need one? Take one!* bowl by the register and pocket the quarter.

I'm saving for a car and I figure anything under a dollar is fair game.

Besides, the red and white plastic WE ARE NOT RESPONSIBLE FOR ITEMS LEFT IN CLOTHING! signs posted everywhere in the store pretty much cover it.

And one stupid quarter is small compensation for having to wait on Mr. Hanson twice a week, to maintain my professional smile and not gag every time he touches my fingers when he hands me his ticket, licks his purple, livery lips and stares at my boobs.

Ugh.

I think about it a moment longer. Take the quarter back out, retrieve two pennies from the bowl, drop it all in an envelope and staple it to his main ticket.

I don't want anything from him, especially not in my jeans pocket.

There are four more bundles of dirty clothes under the counter waiting to be pinned, so I shake off the specter of his disgusting-ness and get to work, letting the familiar rhythm of searching pock-ets take over and gazing absently out the plate-glass window into the nearly empty parking lot.

Weird.

It's almost rush hour and this place should be bustling. Besides us, the minimall has an ice cream depot, a laundry, a liquor store and a bagel shop, and when I started work at three there was a line at the ice-cream place but instead of getting busier as school let out, it's dead quiet.

Even the traffic on Main Street is lighter than usual.

I don't know. Maybe it's the weather.

I finish the first bundle—a silky Diane von Furstenberg dress, black skirt and jade silk blouse—and take them back to the Monday bin. Stop at the radio Eva left playing softly in the background—Terence, the presser, loves classic R & B and Eva will do almost anything to keep him happy as he presses clothes faster when he's in a good mood than when he's crabby, and Eva's country music sta-tion definitely makes him crabby—and spin the dial, trading Stevie Wonder's "Isn't She Lovely" (my father, in his wise-guy moods,

sings this to me when I wake up rumpled, cranky and bleary eyed)
for Evanescence's "My Last Breath."

Go back out front and start on Mrs. Malinowski's mother-of-
the-bride dress from her son's wedding, a daffodil-yellow chiffon-
and-sequin number that I have to be very careful pinning because
chiffon is not a fabric that forgives and forgets puncture wounds.

There's a lipstick smudge on the bodice so I put a little stain-
arrow sticker on it, carefully drape the dress and jacket over a hanger
and leave it on the line near the press. The ticket is marked for next
Friday but she probably won't pick it up then or even within the
month, because according to Eva, single-use event wear always gets
left here until we make our quarterly *Your dry cleaning has been here for
three months and we're just reminding you to pick it up* phone calls. Still, unless there's a last-minute rush today and we get loads of clothes due
for tomorrow, Terence will have everything in this place clean and
pressed by ten, and Helga, the surly, uninspired morning clerk, will
have it all bagged and filed, including the gown.

I hope it doesn't get so slow that Eva lays me off.

Not now.

Just . . . not now.

No more bad news allowed.

This whole week has been a mess.

If I hadn't cut school six long, miserable days ago to meet stupid Justin and get left at McDonald's, then my father would never
have left his patrol area to bring me home in the police car.

And if he hadn't done that, then he wouldn't have been anywhere near Victory Lane when Corey Mahoney decided to jump
off of the overpass and take his baby with him. No, someone else,
whoever was patrolling our area that day, would have caught the
call and been the one to try to stall Corey until the county crisis
negotiator arrived.

Someone else would have done all he could and still lost them,
right in front of his eyes.

Someone else would have been debriefed by the critical incident stress counselor, been left with no appetite and sleepless nights, gone to the funerals alone and come home pale, drawn and silent, looking almost as haunted as he did at Grammy and Pop-Pop's funerals two years ago and—

A police car turns into the mall and cruises slowly toward the dry cleaner's. Pulls up in the fire lane and a cop gets out. It's Vinnie, my father's partner and best friend.

I wave and pull out a cleaning ticket as he gathers an armload of uniform pants and shirts and comes striding in. "Hey, Row, how's your boat?" He's been greeting me with that same lame joke since I was what, fetal? And he still cracks himself up every time, still flashes that cheerful Vinnie grin, white teeth gleaming beneath a proud hawk nose and neatly trimmed, veteran-cop mustache.

"Sinking, how's yours?" I say, smiling as he dumps the pile of blues on the counter in front of me and sorts through it. "You might as well stop. I have to count them myself. Eva says."

"And what Eva wants, Eva gets," he warbles, turning to keep an eye on his patrol car. "Where is the queen of clean, anyway? I want to make sure she works you till you drop."

"Ha, too bad. She's gone for the day," I say absently, counting his stuff. "Three shirts, three pants, and I hope you left lots of change in your pockets because I'm saving for a car." I smirk to show I'm kidding. Sort of. "So when do you want them?"

"Hold on." His head snaps around. "She left you here by yourself? For how long?"

Crap, I should have known better. "I'm closing up at seven, like normal. It's fine. She gave me a key." I fish it out of my pocket and show it to him. "I've been here a month, Vinnie. I know what I'm doing."

"You're a sixteen-year-old girl here alone with a register full of cash," he says, looking at me like I'm an idiot. "Jesus, why not just put a sign out that says 'Rob Me Now'? What the hell was she thinking?" He steps back, rubbing his forehead. "Does your father know about this?"

"Nobody's going to rob me," I say, exasperated, scribbling his name and the item count on his ticket, ripping off the stub and thrusting it at him. "Here, they'll be ready tomorrow after three and no, he doesn't know and don't you *dare* tell him. He doesn't need anything else to worry about right now."

"Hmph." He scans the parking lot, mouth tight. "So does this place have a panic button under the counter for the silent alarm? No? How about a surveillance camera?"

"A surveillance cam?" My heart skips a beat. "Uh . . . I don't know." I glance around the front of the store and up at the recessed lights in the ceiling, thinking of the loose change I've pocketed in the last couple of weeks. Holy shit, what if that was all caught on camera? What if Eva *watched* me take that stupid money? What if leaving me alone here today is really a test to see if I'm trustworthy and if not . . . Oh my God, *stealing*? What am I, stupid? What if I get fired for taking three lousy dollars' worth of quarters, dimes and nickels? And then what if she calls my *parents* and tells them?

No. No. That absolutely cannot happen.

The humiliation would be nothing compared to the disappointment in my mother's eyes, not to mention my father's. Cutting school? Forget it. This would change the way he looked at me forever. He would never trust me again, and—

Wait.

Don't panic.

It's not over. Nothing has even happened yet.

I gaze around the cleaner's. Wood-paneled walls. A manual cash register. An AM/FM radio—no CD player, no Sirius—sitting on a shelf in the back by the press. This place is still as lost in the seventies as the day it opened. If Eva hasn't renovated by now then she'd never spring for an expensive, high-tech surveillance system.

God, I'm sweating.

I can still fix this.

Tomorrow I'll bring back the stupid pile of change and leave it under the counter somewhere like I was just being sloppy. Or better yet, I have three dollars on me. I'll just make change now, put it in the communal lunch money coffee can and casually mention to Eva that—

"Don't you have any friends who can come down and hang out with you until closing?" Vinnie says, giving me a funny look. "C'mon, Rowan. Help me out, here."

I take a deep breath, trying to get ahold of myself.

"What about your sidekick? Why can't you call her?"

"Who, Nadia?" Only Vinnie would consider Nadia *my* sidekick, rather than the other way around. "I can't, she's . . ." I see the stubborn set of his jaw and surrender. "Okay, okay." I move the stool aside, retrieve my phone from the shelf under the counter and, hands still trembling, punch out a text. "There, see?" I hold it so he can read the *I'm alone at work till 7. Want to come hang out?* and when he's done I hit send. "Happy now?"

"No." He frowns slightly, watching my hands. "Why are you shaking?"

Oh my God, doesn't *anything* in my life go unnoticed? "Because you're freaking me out." It's the first and only answer I can think of, and since I can't look at him or he'll know I'm hiding something, I shove his dry-cleaning ticket into the middle of his pile of clothes, bundle them all into a ball and stuff them under the counter for pinning.

"Hey, I'm just trying to keep you safe," he says, giving me a look from beneath his straight, black eyebrows. "Listen, I have to get going but I'll stop in again if we don't get busy." He falls back a step, holding my gaze. "And, Row . . . That thing you said before, about your father not needing anything else to worry about . . ."

"Yes?" I say ominously, thinking, *Here it comes, he's gonna go call my father*—

"You were right. Today in briefing they told us that somebody leaked the dashboard-cam video to the press . . ."

This is not what I was expecting and it takes a moment to

actually sink in. "What? From Daddy's patrol car? Wait . . . of the *suicide?*"

"Film at six and eleven," he says grimly, shifting and settling his hands on his gun belt. "Great, right?"

"But why?" I say, plopping down on the stool in bewilderment. "It's already done, solved, the funerals are over. Yes, it was tragic but Corey's *dead*. There's no one left to punish so why stir it up all over again?"

He starts to say something, then holds up a finger in a *wait* gesture. Cocks his head, listens to dispatch on his radio and says, "Eight oh two central, Victory and North Main." He heads for the door, keying his radio. "Ten-four." Glances at me. "Accident on Main Street with injuries. Later."

And then he's gone, peeling out of the parking lot with lights and sirens. I'm left sitting here with my stomach knotted and my thoughts in a dark, foreboding whirl.

Chapter 2

Nadia texts back, *Can't. Shopping with Danica.*

Yeah, I already knew that, but Vinnie's gone so it doesn't really matter anymore.

I wonder if my father knows about the video.

He must. He probably just watched it on the news.

Great, like he doesn't feel bad enough already.

Aggravated, I head into the back to my purse, grab three dollars, open the register and make change. My movements are big and exaggerated; I double-count the change and make sure the three singles I give in return are very visibly tucked neatly back into the cash drawer, because if there *is* surveillance and she saw me taking the pocket change then I want to make damn sure I'm seen putting it back, too.

I drop the change in the lunch can by the phone, make a note on the pad—*Eva, I've been putting found pocket change in here. Is that okay?*—and leave it where she can't miss it.

Whew.

Never again.

And just so I don't forget and piss Terence off in the morning, I switch the radio station from my music back to his, catching the end of something with a funky beat. Yeah, okay. I've grown up with this stuff, my parents love it and it's still light-years better than Eva's station.

I go up front and perch on the stool, absently watching the sky darken and the clouds boil closer as I pin Vinnie's uniforms, then carry them into the back and stuff them into the Friday bin.

My father didn't do anything wrong that day on the overpass.

I know, because when I stand at my desk, lean to the right and peer around the trees, I can see the overpass from my bedroom window.

My mother and I saw it that day, too.

Clearly, because it was bright and sunny and there weren't any leaves on the trees yet. We were all up in my bedroom and he was in the middle of yelling at me for cutting school when the urgent jumper call came through and he had to go.

Honestly? I was thrilled at the interruption, glad the attention had been diverted from me to someone else.

It wasn't often we got to see my father in action.

Now I know there's a good reason for that.

What we saw that day, even from a distance . . . well, my mother hasn't forgiven herself for not pulling me away from the window and closing the blind while there were still four people and a dog on that overpass. She had to shake me to stop me from screaming.

My father won't forgive himself, period.

I shake my head, grab the next bundle of clothes and start going through the pockets of Mr. Hill's elegant, gray Armani suit.

And bam, the first thing I find is a pen left in the inside jacket pocket.

"Nice," I mutter, removing the pen and dropping it in an envelope. "What're you trying to do, get me fired?" Pens are deadly in dry cleaning—they always leak and stain, and nothing pisses Eva off faster than finding a missed pen in the cleaning drum and ink spots on all our customers' freshly cleaned clothes.

I know, because I've made that mistake twice already.

I check his pants and find a business card, a toll booth receipt and his checkbook. Stick it all in the envelope with the pen, seal it and staple it to his ticket.

Thunder rumbles and I look up in time to see the first giant raindrop splat onto the sidewalk out front.

I glance over at the clock—almost six thirty—and pull the final bundle out from beneath the counter. It's a black dress, plain with long sleeves and a V neck, unremarkable except for the brooch up near the shoulder, a big, sterling silver safety pin with blue beads and three little dangling charms.

A teddy bear, an S, and a heart.

"I hope this thing comes off," I mutter, and nearly jump out of my skin as lightning flashes nuclear bright, thunder crashes and the rain comes down, hammering the roof and falling in great, torrential sheets.

The lights dim, then surge; Lauryn Hill's "Can't Take My Eyes Off of You" hiccups; and suddenly a big dog followed by a guy carrying a plastic bag runs into sight and stops under the overhang in front of my plate-glass window. Laughing, the guy runs a hand up over his forehead, pushing back the long, dark, wet strands that have come loose from his ponytail. He's tall and lean, arms sleek with rain. A brown leather watchband encircles one wrist and a leash the other. The leash is attached to a huge black and tan German shepherd that shakes itself off, splattering the window with spray, and then jumps up and puts its front paws on his stomach, leaving muddy prints on the bottom of the soaked black T-shirt plastered to his chest.

The guy takes the dog's furry face between his hands, says something and rumples its tawny fur. He steps away, forcing the dog back down, and glances at the wet fur clinging to his hands. He shakes his head, drops the bag and steps to the far edge of the overhang, holding them out in the rain, palms up, rinsing them clean.

"Whoa," I whisper, mesmerized.

As he's wiping them on his jeans he turns and looks into the dry cleaner's, right at me sitting spellbound on the stool, and his sudden, easy smile gets me square in the heart.

It's Eli Gage, from that day on the overpass.

Chapter 3

"Mind if I bring her in?" He pauses in the doorway, his words softened by a slight drawl, the dog wedged tight against his leg. "I wouldn't ask but she's afraid of thunder and—"

"No, sure, she can come in. It's okay." I wave them in, heart pounding, the dry cleaning spread across the counter in front of me forgotten. "Are you kidding? We're totally pet friendly here." The specter of Eva's scowling, gnomelike face rises in front of me. "Well, at least we are when *I'm* working." Why am I talking so loud? Why is it so hot in here? Does he know who I am? No, how could he? I only saw him briefly, from a distance that day from my bedroom window. He's never seen me.

Lightning flashes and thunder rumbles across the sky, deep and threatening.

The dog lets out a desperate, strangled yip and lunges, dragging Eli into the cleaner's. She barrels through the aisle between the counters and around back, frantic, winding her leash around my legs as she dives into the corner, runs past me and circles back again. "No, wait," I say, as she tries to belly beneath the counter. "It's okay. You're okay." I keep my voice as calm and soothing as I can because she's huge and terrified, and I really don't want to be bitten. She gazes up at me, ears back, the whites of her eyes showing in a silent plea, pressing her solid, trembling bulk against my leg, the salty smell of wet dog rising around me, and then Eli is there, too, joining us in this tight space between the counter and the wall, reaching his arms around me to unwind the leash, exasperated laughter in his voice as he mutters, "I'm really sorry," and "C'mon, Daisy, behave." His scent, cool rain mingled with a hint of warm, dark musk, makes my head spin. "Sorry." He steps back, cheeks pink, leash retracted, and leads a cowed Daisy back around the front of the counter. "It's okay, girl. It's just thunder." And to me, "She's not usually this bad. It's the PTSD."

"It's fine. Really." I have no idea what he's talking about and looking at him burns my eyes, so I busy myself tucking my hair back behind my ears and smoothing the damp spot on my jeans. "My cat doesn't like thunderstorms, either." Lame. Try again. "So, uh . . ." I fumble under the counter for a blank dry-cleaning ticket and give him what I hope is a bright smile but he isn't looking at me anymore, he's gazing at the black dress spread out on the counter, all traces of good humor gone. He touches the sterling silver safety pin, the letter S charm, and then his hand falls back to his side.

And then it hits me. I glance at the name on the ticket—Well, as in Payton Well, mother of the deceased baby Sammy—and I realize this is what she must have worn to the funeral, this dress and her mother-son pin. My stomach plummets. "Here, let me get this out of the way." Fumbling, I roll up the dress and put it under the counter, hugely aware that out of sight is not necessarily out of mind. "So . . ."

Lightning flashes and six Mississippi seconds pass before the thunder rumbles a response.

"Uh . . ." I clear my throat, glance at the clock—quarter to seven—and poise a pen over the blank ticket. "Are you dropping something off?"

He starts, blinks. "Oh, uh, yeah. Sorry." Runs a hand over his hair and hefts the plastic bag onto the counter. "A suit." He pulls a folded two-piece, navy blue pinstripe out of the bag. "There's a spot on the front."

"Okay," I say, pulling an arrow sticker off the roll and putting it above the stain. "Last name?"

"Gage. Eli." Pause. "You?"

"Rowan," I say, scribbling his name on the ticket. "Areno." I wait a heartbeat and glance up to find him staring at me. "Yes, that one."

"Wait . . . Nick, the cop?" he says in surprise.

I lift my chin. "He's my father." It comes out sounding like a challenge.

"Okay." He blinks and rubs his forehead. "I was *not* expecting that." He searches my face and nods. "Yeah, I can see it. You look like him."

"Right, especially around the big gray mustache," I say dryly, and am rewarded with a spontaneous snort of laughter. "Thanks a lot."

"That's not what I meant," he protests.

"Oh sure," I say, giving him a sparkling look from beneath my eyelashes.

"I *meant* you're both tall and have those brown eyes and that same . . . Give me a break, will you?" he says, laughing and going pink at my teasing. "Wiseass." He shakes his head, runs a hand over his damp hair. "So how's he doing, anyway?"

"Oh, fine," I say without thinking, still lost in the warmth of our shared laughter and the dazzling feeling that we're standing much closer to each other than we really are. Smiling, I flick my hair back à la Nadia, plant a hand on my hip and give him a flirtatious look, only then noticing that the lightness in his expression is gone, replaced by serious consternation. "Uh, well, I mean he's not *fine*, but . . . you know." Damn, so we're back to that. "Um, how're you?"

"The same, I guess. I don't know." He shrugs and glances out the window at the pounding rain. "I saw him at Sammy's funeral but he was at the back of the room and he left before I could catch up with him."

"So it was crowded?" I say, because my father hasn't said much, if anything, about either of the funerals, and I haven't asked.

"Packed. Lines of mourners to the casket. News crews, too. Payton said she knew maybe eight people. The rest either heard about it and wanted to pay their respects or were just gawkers." He toys with one of the dog's velvety ears. "It was pretty bad."

"I can imagine," I say, and then, "I don't know Payton."

"No, I didn't either, before this." He falls silent a moment, as if torn between caution and conversation. "I was at headquarters when they brought her in to take a statement and afterward, we just started talking. Her family's down in Florida and the only people she had up here were Corey and the baby, so . . . It's a rough time to be alone. Me and the Daze are gonna go pick up some BK and head over there now. Make sure she has something to eat and somebody to talk to if she needs it." He shrugs and shifts in place, as if uncomfortable. "It's no big deal."

I study his solemn profile, the sleek, shining swath of hair, the blank black T-shirt advertising nothing but him, the worn boot-cut Levi's and scuffed brown leather boots with the squared-off toe that are either cowboy or biker, I'm not sure which, and decide he's definitely not from around here. Not only looks-, conversation- and drawl-wise but because yes, what he's doing for Payton *is* a big deal. I can't see Justin putting himself out like that for anybody, much less a grief-stricken stranger.

Hell, I can't even see *me* doing it.

"I don't know how your father shows up for tragic shit like that every day without letting it get to him." He turns back to me, a shadow in his eyes. "I mean, how do you try like hell to save somebody and then watch him kill himself anyway?"

I gaze back at him, embarrassed to admit that I've never really thought about it, that the police stories my father and Vinnie tell are always funny ones of tragedies averted, narrow escapes and chaotic close calls, stories in which the bad guys get caught, the good guys live on and the punch lines always make us laugh . . .

Stories that are *nothing* like what I actually saw happen on the overpass.

Hmm.

Eli hesitates, and then, as if he can't help himself, says, "I tried to get Corey to come down before your father got there. He wouldn't give me the baby, either."

"I didn't know that," I say quietly.

"Yeah, nobody really does. I told your dad about it afterward so I guess it's in the police report but . . . I don't know. I feel like I should have done more." He rubs his chin, toys absently with the patch nestled beneath his lip. "Christ, I can still see it in my mind. One minute they were there, and the next . . . nothing."

"I know." His bleak tone makes me shiver.

"Your dad was cool, though. When we got back to headquarters he got me coffee and took the time to sit down and talk with me. I mean besides just taking my statement. I won't forget that. He reminded me of my—" And then he stops, face tight, and looks away. "Just tell him I said hey and, uh, thanks again for the coffee." He turns to leave.

"Wait," I say quickly, thrown by the abrupt change and holding up the dry-cleaning ticket. "I need your phone number."

"Oh right," he says distractedly, and rattles it off. "It's my cell."

"When do you want your suit back?" I say, glancing past him into the parking lot. I don't see my mother's car yet but it's almost seven and she should be here any minute, and now I'm wondering if he knows about the video or if I should tell him. I wish we had more time. "Tomorrow?"

"No rush," he says with a shrug. "I only wear it to funerals, so . . ."

"Then how about next Thursday?" I offer, giving it one last halfhearted shot and wondering if he'll make the connection: Picking up the suit means seeing me again, and a week is a long time to wait. Seven whole, chancy days. Drag your feet that long and anything could happen.

47

"Yeah, that's good," he says, and I feel like kicking something.

"Great," I say, ripping off the ticket stub a little more vigorously than necessary and handing it to him. "See you then."

"Okay, thanks," he says, stuffing it in his pocket and flashing me a small, crooked smile. "So uh, good talking to you, Rowan. Stay dry."

"You too," I say, and as soon as he and Daisy disappear into the rain around the side of the building I spring into action, cursing under my breath, oddly near tears while pinning his pieces, searching his pockets, finding a hair tie, a half roll of breath mints and a sad little funeral card decorated with Jesus, angels and lambs for Samuel "Sammy" Well, whose time on this earth totaled a depressing three months and thirteen days.

Terrible.

Thirteen days ago, none of us had ever even *heard* of Corey Mahoney and Sammy Well. They could have been anybody, random strangers on the street, and now it's like all roads lead straight back to them and we're entwined forever, their deaths and our lives tangled up in one big, wretched knot.

I don't know how my father does it, either.

Maybe it's time I asked him.

I stick Eli's things in an envelope and staple it to the ticket, run his stuff back to the bin and then, grabbing the black dress, pin a ticket stub on the label in the neck, unpin the silver baby pin, drop it into an envelope, seal it and staple it to her ticket.

I grab my purse and jacket, turn off the lights and the radio—good night, Smokey Robinson—slip out the door and lock it behind me.

Turn as headlights splash across the wet, gleaming pavement and see my father, not my mother, pull up in his pristine, rain-streaked black Blazer and stop in the fire zone in front of me.

One look at his face tells me all I need to know.

Chapter 4

"Hey, Dad," I say, opening the SUV door and climbing inside. The air-conditioning is chilling after the humid heat, and the radio is silent.

That's a bad sign.

"Hey, Row." His smile doesn't quite reach his eyes. "How was work?"

"Okay," I say, reaching for my seat belt because he won't drive away until it's buckled and I want to get out of here before he asks me about—

"So where's Eva?" he says, looking past me into the shadowy dry cleaner's.

Damn. "Oh, she had to take her car to the shop," I say casually, and then, to divert him, "Hey, Vinnie stopped in to drop off his uniforms." Evasive maneuvers are a long shot, because my father has seen it all, but still worth a try. "He had to leave though, because there was an accident on Main Street. With injuries. I don't know who it was or anything, or how bad." I shrug and buckle the belt. "Okay, ready. God, I'm starving. What're we having for supper?"

"Lasagna," he says absently, glancing in the rearview mirror to make sure there's no one coming, and then pulls up to the stop sign.

"Really?" I say, glancing over at him in surprise. Lasagna is my father's all-time favorite but it's still usually an occasion meal in my house, like for Christmas or Sunday dinner, and one my mother only makes when she has extra free time, never on the days she works down at the library. "Why?"

He meets my gaze for a long moment and then looks back at the road, his mustache twitching into a slight smile. "Well, between you and me, I think your mother's trying to fatten me up so I'm not so irresistible to women."

I snort a laugh. "Yeah, I'm sure that's it. No, c'mon, Dad, really: What's going on?"

"Nice. My own daughter throws me under the bus." He signals, pulls out onto North Main and makes the quick right onto Victory Lane, his hands steady on the wheel. "So anyway, what was wrong with Eva's car?"

"I don't know, and who cares?" I say, suddenly impatient with his stall tactics. "C'mon, I'm not a little kid anymore, okay? Stop trying to protect me. I already know about the dashboard video being on the news tonight." It comes out sharp, accusing even, and the lightness drains from his face, making me immediately feel bad. "Sorry, but seriously, why are they doing this? I mean, it's a week old. Corey's dead. There's no one to arrest. I thought it was done."

The windshield wipers squeak, sweeping drizzle from the glass.

"So did I, but I guess not," he says finally as we cruise past the woods. "Word is that the media's doing a story on the effects of budget cuts to emergency services and whether this whole thing could have been avoided if ERT and the county crisis negotiator had shown up sooner. Hey, hindsight is always twenty/twenty, right?" There's an edge to his voice. "But that's okay; let them go to the mayor, the city council and the controller. Interview whoever cuts our budget every year." He glances across the dark car at me. "The truth is that I don't think county crisis would have made a difference. Corey's mind was made up. He wasn't going to wait."

"You could tell that just by talking to him?" I ask, reaching out and lowering the air-conditioning. "That he'd definitely decided to kill himself, I mean?"

He sends me an inscrutable glance. "Not at first, no. You never assume anything. That's the fastest way to miss seeing the truth. You have to question, observe and assess the situation, then stabilize the scene, take control and calm things down so nobody gets hurt. You try to buy time and humanize the hostage."

"So then how did you know?" I ask, nudging him back on track.

"Instinct. Experience," he says, flicking on the high beams and slowing to a stop as an opossum waddles across the road in front of us. "I got a bad feeling when he said nobody knew what he was going to do and he didn't want to talk to any of his people. That's never good." He waits until the opossum's tail disappears into the weeds and then accelerates again.

I think about that a minute. "So he didn't tell because he didn't want to be stopped?"

"Right," my father says, nodding and smoothing his mustache. "When someone threatens suicide, when they tell somebody they're going to do it beforehand they're reaching out, hoping someone will stop them. The problem is that people who aren't depressed don't always understand that and have a hard time believing it. To them, the idea of killing yourself to end pain is inconceivable. They think it's nothing but drama or a bid for attention and if they ignore it or reason with them, they'll come to their senses and life will go back to normal," he says, slowing the car as our old farmhouse appears on the left and the deserted overpass comes into sight up ahead on the right. "Most times it doesn't happen that way. The ones who *don't* tell anyone beforehand . . ." He shrugs. "They've already made their decision and planned it all out to make sure they succeed. We find them after the fact, when it's too late." He glances over at me, his gaze hooded and assessing. "Why the sudden interest?"

"Don't worry, I'm not suicidal, if that's what you think," I say, because I *knew* he was going to ask, and then I go on to tell him about Payton's funeral dress, Eli stopping in to the cleaner's, what he said and how haunted he looked. "I felt bad for him, especially when he said he should have done more to try and save Sammy. But seriously, what could he really have done?"

"Nothing," my father says, shaking his head. "I know how he feels but second-guessing yourself is deadly. You can't beat yourself up afterward. Easier said, of course, than done, but . . ." His mouth tightens. "He's a good kid and that video airing isn't going to help matters any. He doesn't need this mess on top of everything else."

"Okay, but how do *you* deal with this kind of stuff over and over?" I say doggedly, because now I really do want to know. "Like when you caught that janitor who killed that first grader or Corey jumping or the time you hurt your back dragging that fat drunk guy out of the burning apartment and got your valor award . . ." My gaze falls to the wristwatch he wears every day, an engraved honorarium given at a commendation ceremony with the valor medal, and in that instant I understand that all those funny police stories he's told were born of calls more dangerous, sick and frightening than funny, that finding humor in even the scariest situations is just his way of coping and of sharing his day with us. "You've seen some really bad things, haven't you?"

"Yeah," he says with quiet, matter-of-fact resignation. "People don't call the cops to celebrate; they call us for trauma and disaster and chaos. I'm there at the crisis moments of their lives, trying to stop things from getting worse, and the only way to do my job is to separate myself, step back, and function." He flips on the signal light even though there's no one else on the road and turns the car into the driveway, pulling up beside my mother's white Sebring. "Something like losing Sammy . . . You take it to heart, even though you know you have to get past it and keep going." He shifts the car into park but doesn't turn off the engine, just sits staring out through the rain-speckled windshield. "Corey didn't hate his son. He loved him and he was convinced he was doing the right thing by not leaving him behind. That's what made him so dangerous." He shakes his head. "The look in his eyes . . . there was nothing there. No hope, no anything but emptiness. It was like he was done. Used up."

I sit very still, listening, because it's not that often my father talks to me like this. He's actually giving me what I asked for and treating me like an equal, not a naïve little kid anymore . . .

And for some reason, that makes me want to cry.

"Yeah, I had a bad feeling about him." He takes a deep breath, releases it slowly. "I wish I was wrong."

I sneak a peek at his profile, see the tears glistening in his eyes and feel mine filling, too.

"I see that kid every time I close my eyes." He looks at me now, the naked pain on his face like a knife in my heart, and I don't know what to do, what to say to erase it—

The sunporch light blinks and, startled, we both look over.

My mother is standing in the doorway, head cocked and hands raised in question.

My father nods, clears his throat and shuts off the engine. "So that's the story. I've been on the phone with headquarters and my PBA rep ever since the videotape aired, and I'm going in tomorrow for a sit-down with the brass."

Even *I* know that a sit-down with the brass is never a good thing. "But—"

"It's okay," he says, and the smile he gives me is tired but real. "That's tomorrow. Tonight your mother worked her butt off making lasagna so we're going to go in and enjoy it, right?"

I gaze back at him, wishing more than anything that I was little again and could just throw myself at him like I used to, certain he'd make the whole world right.

But I'm not anymore, and he can't.

"Okay," I murmur, giving him a weak smile. "And, Dad?" I say, laying my hand on his arm as he starts to open his car door.

"What?" he says, pausing to look back.

But the words that make my throat ache so badly still won't come and so I just gaze at him hoping he knows, and he must because he smiles in a soft, sweet way I haven't seen in a long time, and putting his hand over mine he says, "Come on, Rowie. Everything's going to be all right. I promise."

He's protecting me again and we both know it, but this time I don't mind because I want so badly to believe him.

Chapter 5

I arrive at the bus stop the next morning to find I'm a minor celebrity, and not in a good way.

"Hey, I saw the tape of your dad trying to talk that asshole down off the ledge," some chubby-cheeked freshman says, swiping a hand across his snub nose and trying to sniffle up all the snotty little bats hanging in the cave. "Guy was a loser, man. Should have just shot him and grabbed the kid. Bam! One down. Next?" He flashes a cocky grin at his creepy little clutch of cohorts, who spill forward to high-five each other. "That's what *I'm* talking about."

Oh my God. "No, you don't know *what* you're talking about."

"And that guy with the dog," a short, pimply kid says, overriding my words and snorting with laughter. "What a wuss. He was frigging useless."

"Yeah, try saying that to his face," the gangly one sneers, shoving the pimply kid. "He'd kick *your* ass."

"He's in my third-period gym class," snotty nose says, punching pimply kid in the arm. "I'll tell him you're looking for him."

Wait . . . what? Eli goes to East Mills?

"Don't waste your time, he already knows he blew it," pimply kid says with a sulky scowl, rubbing his arm and fast losing his bravado. "Ow, that hurt. You're a dick."

Gangly, snotty nose and a third twerpy freshman exchange laughing glances, drop their books, jump him and start pummeling.

The bus pulls up and I leave them there, tumbling and yelping like a pile of mangy puppies.

Our crackhead driver gives me a nasty sideways look as I get on and a wave of silence billows in my wake. I plop into an empty seat, pull out my phone and punch out a text to Nadia: *did you see the video?*

She answers almost immediately. *Yeah. Talk when you get here.*

But when I get off the bus she's leaning against the wall in the courtyard with Danica and Bree, our peripheral friends, and tucked under Brett's arm. I wave, hoping she'll detach herself and meet me halfway, but she doesn't. One senior, two sophomores and a junior try to stop me on my way through the crowd but I just blow them off and keep moving until I finally get there.

"Hey, guys," I say breathlessly into the sudden silence, smoothing my hair and giving Nadia an expectant look. "God, this place is mobbed. You'd think nobody ever saw a sunny day before."

Danica smirks. Brett lifts his chin in greeting and tightens his arm around Nadia's waist. Nadia snuggles closer and shoots me a cautioning *Just wait* look from under her lashes. Bree does nothing but close her eyes and hold her face up to the brilliant morning sun, apparently working on getting some early color.

And it feels wrong, all of it. Too quiet, too casual, too pregnant with the unspoken. I look at each one of them trying so hard not to look at me and say, "So what did you think of the video?"

Brett loosens his grip on Nadia, shrugs and looks away. "Whatever." He gives her a gentle shoulder-bump and murmurs something too low for me to hear. "Later," he says to the rest of us in general, and slips through the crowd to Justin, who is standing over by the steps flirting with some junior girls.

Nadia shoots me an exasperated look. "Thanks, Row. You couldn't wait five more minutes?"

"No, because this is important and in five minutes the bell's gonna ring and I'm not going to see you again till lunch and everybody'll be there and we won't talk about it then, either," I say, scowling right back.

"Well, maybe I don't *want* to talk about it," she says coolly, fluffing her hair and avoiding my gaze. "Did you ever think of that?"

No, I didn't, and all the things I was going to tell her about the serious talk with my father and this bizarre video fallout, meeting Eli and discovering that he actually goes to this school, stick in my throat.

"Hey." Danica nudges Bree and glances at her watch. "C'mon, we have to get that, er, thing out of your locker before the bell rings. See you guys later." She grabs Bree's arm and all but drags her away.

We stand in unhappy stalemate.

"It looked bad, okay?" Nadia says finally, staring out over the courtyard. "What do you want me to say? They showed what, maybe a minute of it, and it looked like your father and that guy with the dog just stood there while that psycho killed his kid." She catches the outrage in my gaze and heaves an impatient sigh. "I'm not saying that's what *happened*, Row. I'm saying that's what it *looked* like, okay? A lot of people hate the cops anyway. You know that. So yeah, they're pissed."

I can't believe this. "Nadia, he did everything he could."

"Brett says he should have just tased him," she says, checking her phone.

I open my mouth, shut it again and count to five, trying not to say that I don't really give one shit about what Brett thinks because that'll just make things worse. "Corey was holding the baby. If my father had tased him, Corey could have fallen forward right off the bridge and down onto the highway. *With* the baby."

"Yeah, well, he did anyway, right?" she says with a cool shrug.

Oh my *God*. "But nobody *knew* that at the time! He was trying to keep Corey calm, talking and alive until ERT got there." I don't get this. She's been at my house a million times, sat at our table for a thousand dinners and snorted milk out of her nose, laughing at my father's stories . . . I thought she'd be *mad* at what they were saying, not a part of it. "You've known my father for what, six years? Has he ever done *anything* half-assed, especially police work? I mean, c'mon." I gaze at her, bewildered and feeling more than a little betrayed. "Why are you being like this?"

"Why are *you*? God, just because I don't agree with you doesn't mean I'm wrong, you know," she says, sticking her phone in her jacket pocket. "I'm entitled to my opinion."

"Oh, right. Don't you mean *Brett's* opinion?" The words are out there before I can stop them.

She gives me a long, level look. "Think what you want," she says finally as the bell rings. "You asked and I told you, and now you're mad. I knew this was going to happen. Why do you think I didn't even want to talk about it?" She turns to leave, pauses and glances back. "You coming?"

I hesitate, then nod, mouth tight and hugging my books fall in behind her. She weaves through the stream of students without looking back, confident, I guess, that I'll follow, but my chest is hollow and my footsteps grow slower and slower. By the time I reach the lockers a solid wall of kids has filled the widening gap between us and I can't see her at all.

| | |

Thirteen snide comments, one flat-out hostile "Fucking East Mills PD are all assholes," endless curious looks and one intense, burning "They should *never* have aired video of a mentally ill man dying" from the psych teacher later, my stomach is knotted, I can't concentrate and all I want to do is go back to being invisible.

When lunchtime comes, instead of heading straight for the cafeteria to meet up with everyone like usual, I stop at the vending machines; grab bottled water, a granola bar and a bag of Doritos; and decide to disappear.

I find Eli sitting out in a sunny, deserted spot against the wall on the grass in the front corner of the school. He's leaning back against the brick, head down, hair loose and spilled forward, and is scrolling through his phone.

"Hey," I say, ambling up beside him. "You're sitting in my spot, you know." And when he looks up, startled but then shading his eyes against the sun and searching my face, I see the recognition dawn and smile.

"Hey, Rowan." He gives me a surprised but welcoming smile, then glances back down at his phone. "Good to see you. Have a seat."

I do, sitting next to him on the grass with my back against the wall and my legs stretched out. The sun warms my cheeks and the breeze, fresh and sweet with the new life of spring, ruffles my hair. "Nice." I set my stuff in my lap, tear open the granola bar, snap it in half and offer him a chunk. "Want some?"

"Thanks." He takes a bite and, chewing, tilts the phone so I can see the photo on the screen. It's a close-up of a man, a soldier with tired eyes and a wide smile, a weathered, sunburned man in rumpled, dusty fatigues cradling a shaggy, black and tan German shepherd pup in his arms. The dog is impossibly small, skinny and neglected looking, its fur dusty, matted . . . and it's licking his cheek, eyes bright and tail frozen in a blur of wagging. Eli swallows and says, "My dad and Daisy, right after he rescued her."

"Wow, where is this?" I say, opening the bottled water and handing it over.

He takes a swig, says thanks and hands it back. "Iraq," he says, scrolling to the next photo. "He found her and her sister Rosie lying in the road when they were only like six weeks old, starving, dehydrated and covered in fleas." He shows me a photo of his father and some other dusty, cheerful-looking men crouched in the dirt with the puppies between them. "He brought them back to base to try to save them." He's talking faster now, like the story's been bottled up inside of him and waiting too long to be told. "I never met Rosie, one of the other guys adopted her, but the first time I saw Daisy, me and my dad were Skyping and she was just sitting there on his lap. He was like, 'Surprise!'" He smiles slightly at the memory. "He always had her with him when he called after that, because he wanted her to get used to me and my mom. To recognize us as part of her pack. And she did. Shepherds are smart."

"Cool," I say, and break off a small piece of granola bar. "So your dad's in the military?" I pop it in my mouth.

"Was," he says after a moment. "He was killed in Iraq right before they pulled out. He was a marine. An IED got him."

Oh no. I take a hasty gulp of water, swallow hard and say, "I'm sorry. I didn't know." Which is kind of dumb because why *would* I know, but I've never met anyone my age whose dad has died before, and I have no idea how to handle it. The only family members I've ever lost are my grandparents on my father's side, who died when I was fourteen. That was sad and I miss them, but grandparents are not the same as parents. So should I keep talking about it, or ignore it and change the subject? I don't know, and for a panicked moment all I want to do is jump and run. "Uh . . . When did he die, if you don't mind me asking?"

"A little over a year ago." He scrolls to the next picture, an older one of a tanned, wiry, dark-haired boy of eleven or twelve wearing board shorts and caught in the headlock grip of his father. Both are laughing, the man grinning straight at the camera, the muscled arm hooked loose and loving around the boy's neck, the boy gazing up at him, face shining, eyes so bright they make my heart hurt. "They said he never knew what hit him, which is better than seeing it coming, I guess. I don't know. Either way sucks, if you ask me." He shakes his head and looks away. "Sorry. I don't usually talk about it. I mean, who wants to hear somebody else's sad story?"

I could agree with him, change the subject to something light and meaningless just to pass the time until lunch is over, but there's something in his voice, a thread of loneliness or yearning maybe, woven beneath his words, that gets me just like that photo did, and so instead I say, "No, it's fine. Really. So your dad found Daisy in

Iraq?" And I know the minute his expression clears that I've done the right thing.

"Yeah." He puts the last of the granola bar in his mouth, chews and swallows. "Jesus, that was stale." Catches my affronted look and grins. "Sorry. Next time I'll buy."

"Deal," I say, crumpling the wrapper and shoving it into my purse.

"So yeah, anyway, he worked hard trying to get Daisy out of there before his unit pulled out. He knew when they left she'd be killed, and he didn't want that to happen. By the time he died, she was already in Houston with me."

"Why would she have been killed?" I ask, ripping open the bag of Doritos and popping one in my mouth. I offer them to him but he shakes his head.

"The Iraqi army had squads that swept through after we left, shooting all the dogs—"

"Why?" I say, horrified.

"They think of them as vermin, like rats or something. My father said it was awful." He takes a sip of water and recaps the bottle. "Anyhow, he looked online for help and found one of those animal societies that help service people get the dogs and cats they adopted back home safe. The procedure was pretty complicated but he wouldn't give up. He got all the guys to chip in what they could and we raised some money back in Houston, too. Once she was approved he had her flown home. The last time we Skyped she was sitting there with me instead of him and she went nuts when she saw him on-screen. He got all choked up and was like, 'Take good care of her for me till I get back.'" He glances at me, his hair drifting into his eyes. "Best present he ever gave me. Last one, too."

"I'm really sorry," I murmur, and take my time selecting just the right Dorito from the bag to give him a chance to recover. "It's good that you have her, though. She's a sweetheart."

"Yeah, she is," he says gruffly, and scrolls through several more photos until he finds the one he wants. "She really misses him.

Here." He leans closer until his shoulder touches mine and shows me the screen.

It's a funeral scene both beautiful and terrible, a gleaming mahogany casket being borne into a church by solemn, ramrod-straight marines in crisp full-dress uniforms and Daisy, head down, tail tucked and body wilted, her forehead wrinkled with what could only be grief, padding slowly along behind.

I look up at him, tears in my eyes.

"Semper Fi," he says softly, and closes the screen. "'Always faithful.'" He tilts his head back against the wall and closes his eyes.

After a long moment, so do I.

We sit in silence until the bell rings and lunch is over.

| | |

I learn several things during afternoon classes, none of which are good.

Nadia isn't going to come looking for me, either.

The video's been posted pretty much everywhere and gone viral.

The kids I go to school with, most of whom have never done anything more heroic than wrestle a banana from the bunch, all believe they know *exactly* what my father should have done to save baby Sammy and insist on telling me, whether I want to hear it or not.

They suggest tackling. Tasing. Lassos. Giant blow-up stuntman cushions placed down on the highway. Nets. Snipers on rooftops. An aerial assault team from a hovering helicopter. A hypnotist. A dart gun.

And on and on, like the murder/suicide video wasn't real, only a scene from a high-budget action movie or a video game instead of two final, irreversible deaths.

And who knows, maybe I would think the same thing, be just as quick to judge, as arrogant and critical, if I didn't know anyone in the video, either.

It's a disturbing thought.

Somehow, I make it through the rest of the day without scream-ing, and when the final bell rings, I don't wait for Nadia at my locker or scan the crowd for a glimpse of Eli, only head straight for the bus idling at the curb. From here it's one quick ride to the stop near the dry cleaner's and—

"Hey, anybody catch East Mills's finest on the news last night?" the frizzy-haired driver says loudly as I pass. "There's your tax dol-lars at work. Thanks for nothing."

I stop right in the middle of the aisle. Turn, heart pounding, and meet her narrowed gaze in the mirror. "Are you done?" My knees are trembling but my voice comes out cool, controlled, polite.

For some reason this strikes me as important.

She grunts. "Not hardly. That whole thing was a friggin' dis-grace. He should hang his head in shame for letting that kid die. If that baby had been a *donut* you can bet your ass he would've jumped for it and not just stood there talk—"

Somebody laughs and the mocking sound shatters my polite paralysis, sends me charging past the others standing frozen and wide-eyed in line and right back up front, shaking and furious. "*No*, Sammy Wells died because his father killed him, and you know what? The day you quit smoking crack and get a *real* life, then you can talk about my father, but for now, why don't you just shut up and drive the fucking bus!"

She stares at me, mouth agape. "You little shit! Where the hell do you get off talking to me like that? Get off my bus. Let your old man haul your ass back and forth to school from now on, since that's all he's good for. I'm filing a complaint against you with the principal."

"Oh, please do!" I say wildly, caught in an adrenaline-fueled, full-body, trembling fury. "I can't *wait* till he asks me what hap-pened and I can show him and the school board all these videos, because look, everybody in here has their phone out. So." I turn away, wobble to the back of the bus and collapse into an empty seat. Hear the shuffle and clump as the other kids file on, feel the weight of their gazes, the sick flurry of hushed, excited whispers all around me, and I don't know what to do or how to make them stop. I pull out my phone to text Nadia and then remember, and don't. Stare blindly out the window, sweating, my heart racing and my thoughts in a scared and jumbled whirl.

The bus rumbles to life, pulling away from the curb with a jerk.

The snotty-nosed freshman from this morning's debacle dives across the aisle and into the seat in front of me. He swivels, eyes bright, cheeks pink, and with a look of absolute awe, says, "Dude, you *rock.*"

Oh my God.

Chapter 6

Work is slow and Eva, who looks grimmer than usual, is uncharacteristically quiet on the whole video subject. She leaves at four o'clock, giving me plenty of uninterrupted time to finish pinning the clothes, find Eli's Facebook page—friends-only, damn it—and then Google him.

Most of the links lead me right back to the Corey video.

I hesitate, finger poised. I really don't want to relive this, don't want to start questioning or blaming or letting all that general-public poison sink in too deep, but . . .

I just don't get how we could all watch the same tape and see it so differently.

So I search further and find one on YouTube.com that shows the whole fifteen-minute video, not just the sixty edited seconds the local news aired. Plant myself on the stool, take a deep breath and turn up the volume.

This time, for the first time, I hear it all. I listen to my father try to forge a bond with Corey, humanize little Sammy, defuse the situation and stall until county crisis arrives. See the growing stress on his face, the tension in his shoulders, the sweat darkening the cool blue of his police shirt, and suddenly I can feel what he feels and it's hard to breathe. I watch through blurred eyes as he steps in front of

Eli to shield him, Eli who is ghostly pale and has a white-knuckled grip on Daisy's collar. Watch as my father moves closer and closer to Corey, trying to get close enough, I guess, to grab him and pull them both back to safety. Close enough, though, to put *himself* in danger of being grabbed and dragged over the side with them . . .

Watch, heart pounding, as my father's and Eli's faces suddenly flood with shock and horror as Corey tips forward and disappears from sight.

Fifteen minutes later I'm fumbling around under the counter for a handful of Eva's tissues to wipe my face.

The psych teacher was right. Corey's last moments, the utter despair in his words and on his face . . . That was nobody's business and should never have been made public.

I scroll down the page to the comments section and feel like throwing up at what's written. The stuff about my father is sickening, and Corey was right when he said that if little Sammy lived he'd have been subjected to an ugly stream of forever Google-able insults and contempt for his father.

The commenting public plastered the walls with their blind, hateful fear, calling Corey a despicable coward, a selfish jerk, a loser. He was stupid, a waste of space, an insult to God; he should have just snapped out of it, changed his life; he'd go straight to hell and burn there forever—a never-ending flow of judgment with no thought or care as to who's reading it or being hurt by it.

It's horrifying.

I follow links and discover that Sammy's mom, Payton Well, didn't fare much better. A news clip of the baby's funeral is posted with an overdub about how she was planning to take Sammy and move back to Florida, and instead of empathizing with her pain they ripped her up in writing, calling her a bitch for taking the kid and trying to leave, saying she was spiteful, vicious and deserved to lose him, saying she belonged in hell beside Corey and that maybe next time she'd keep her slutty legs closed, calling her stupid for sleeping with somebody so messed up, as if she were an oracle instead of a twenty-two-year-old Applebee's hostess with an accounting degree and an overbite.

And last but not least, they went off on Eli, too. The comments are cruel and scathing, saying he's useless, he should've manned up and wrestled that baby away, that he should've put on his big-boy panties and sicced the dog on the guy or something, anything, rather than be caught by surprise and stand there in shock, a mere mortal instead of an instant action hero. One loser actually had a vicious hoot at Eli's pained, "Don't t-talk about my f-father," asking, *stutter much dickhead?* and earning himself a flood of LOL kudos from his audience.

The motion-sensor doorbell rings and I look up to find old Mr. Hanson coming straight at me, his purple lips stretched into a familiar leer.

And here I thought this day couldn't get any worse.

I close the screen and shove my phone and tissues under the counter, hoping I don't look like I've been crying. "Hi, Mr. Hanson."

"There she is, Miss America," he warbles, and holds out his cleaning ticket. "The only girl in the world besides Mrs. Hanson who's allowed to put her hands in my pants."

Oh God, not now.

I take his ticket, trying not to shudder as his hot fingers brush mine. Glance at the clock—ten to seven; he's usually not this late—and, pulling free, hit the conveyor-belt switch. "You just made it. We're getting ready to close." Stop the conveyor, retrieve the hanger with his pants and the envelope of loose change stapled to the plastic bag, and hang it out on the hook where he can reach it.

"Well, I certainly hope you don't have to walk home alone in the dark," he says, and with a fake look of surprise, like a lightbulb just happened to go off in his head, says, "I can give you a ride if you'd like." He pulls a wad of cash from his pocket and peels off five damp, limp dollar bills. "It wouldn't be any trouble." He hands me the money, his watery gaze dropping to my boobs. "Maybe we could stop for ice cream, too."

No, maybe we can't. Maybe I'll just take your pants and hurl them out into traffic, instead. How about that?

"Thanks anyway, but my father's picking me up," I say, and hand him his change. "I'll tell him you offered, though. You spell it H-A-N-S-O-N, right?" I meet his alarmed gaze with a tight, pointed smile. "Have a nice night."

He leaves huffy and without saying good-bye, and although I know Eva needs every customer she can get, I really hope he never comes back.

Seven o'clock. *Finally.*

I slip on my jacket, turn off the lights, lock the door and step out into the twilight, where, to my surprise, my mother and not my father is waiting.

Chapter 7

I can hear her music pulsing from here. I open the car door and get pummeled by the relentless, bouncing bass line.

It's the Gap Band's "Burn Rubber on Me."

Not a good sign.

"Hi," I say cautiously, sliding into the passenger seat, lowering the volume and becoming very busy buckling my seat belt because all I can think is that the bus driver filed a complaint against me with the principal and they called my mother into school. "I thought Daddy was picking me up. What, did you get off work early today?"

"Yes," she says, and gives me a slight, preoccupied smile, a strand of chestnut hair too long to be a bang but too short to be tucked behind her ear falling into her face. "Vinnie came by. He and your father are out in the wood shop working on your hope chest." She glances in the rearview mirror and pulls away from the cleaner's.

"No kidding," I say, trying to sound enthusiastic. "Great." My father's been building me a hope chest, not exactly something I'm dying to have —that would be a car, or at least the money to buy one—but back when I turned sixteen my mother got it into her head that we needed a tradition and so he's been working on it in his spare time, drilling, sanding and whatever else goes into it. I don't know; I'm not allowed to see it till it's done which is fine, as I don't have anything to put in it, anyway.

"Yes," she says absently, pausing at the stop sign. "It's an excellent distraction from all of this."

"All of what?" I say in a tone of doom as we pull out onto the road. "What else has happened?"

And then she tells me about the video going viral and the ongoing fallout, how even though my father's response time was stellar—thirty-eight seconds to arrive once the call was dispatched—and he did all he could in the twelve short minutes he was there, the media was focusing on why the local PD allowed a beat cop untrained in crisis negotiations to handle such a delicate situation.

There was no budget-cut angle at all.

"Liars," I mutter as we make the right onto Victory Lane.

Worse, they totally ignored the fact that if my father hadn't kept Corey talking he probably would have gone over the side much sooner, before the cops even had a chance to establish a perimeter and stop traffic down below on the highway, clearing space so that if he *did* jump, he wouldn't land on the windshield of some poor, oblivious soccer mom driving along in a minivan full of kids, causing a major pileup and taking even more innocent people with him.

No, they totally skipped that part.

And then, my mother says, besides my father writing a detailed report and briefing the brass, having to recall every single moment of that wretched call over and over again, basically defending himself for doing his job, thanks to the media and mounting public pressure, the department has decided to launch an internal investigation on whether he violated procedure in any way. Until it's complete and he's exonerated, they're taking him off of the road and assigning him to a desk.

"Are you serious?" I say in disbelief.

"Oh yes," my mother says bitterly, flicking on the signal light to turn into our driveway. "I mean, public relations are everything, right? So what if the murderer is already dead; people are still howling for someone to blame, so why not sacrifice a highly decorated officer with almost twenty years of experience behind him just to toss the mob their pound of flesh?" She turns up the driveway and parks next to the porch behind my father's Blazer. "Disgusting." Shuts off the engine and opens her door. Starts to slide out, pauses and looks back at me. "Do you know why I came home from work early today?"

I nod. "Because everybody's got something to say about Daddy all of a sudden, right?"

"Rowan, I never came so close to hitting an old lady in my life." She scrubs a hand across her forehead as if it's all too much. "Do you remember Grandma's friend Mrs. Thomas?"

"The short one with the chameleon eyes and glasses who sticks her nose into everybody else's business," I say, nodding. "Sure."

"Well, she stopped into the library today and just *had* to come up to me while I was busy checking out a stack of books for someone else and just as loud as she possibly could, said, 'You poor thing, it's such a disgrace. You must be so humiliated and embarrassed for your husband.'" She looks across the car at me, her face in shadows. "And in that instant I swear to you, my hand came up and I almost slapped her right across the face. Thank God I caught myself in time." She gathers her purse and keys but doesn't move to get out. "I don't know what happened. I dealt with rude comments all day about that video and didn't lose my temper, but at that moment . . . I'm not a violent person, you know that, but the way she said it, with this nasty kind of *glee*—"

"I know, I yelled at our crackhead bus driver today, too," I confess, and if I get grounded for it, well then I just do. "She insulted Daddy really bad and it was like, the last straw." I bite my lip and glance over at her, hating to ask but needing to know. "Mom, do you think he really did everything he—"

"Yes," she says firmly. "I do, Rowan. He's always gone above and beyond, especially for children, and I believe he did everything he possibly could to save them both."

71

"I do too, but . . ." I sit for a moment, fingers knotted in indecision. "Oh, crap." I pull out my phone and quickly go online to the local news site. "Can I show you something?" I find the page that's killing me and hand it to my mother. "Read the comments."

"Sweet Jesus," she murmurs as she sees the headline, then scrolls down to the comments section.

Infant Dies, Police Watch Powerless

stupid fuckn pig why didn he taze him tazers work I been tzed 2x it works

Tthat cop shud rezine n shame

How could he not save the baby? He should be fired and mad to pay for the funral.

the wrong guy went over the side!!!!!!!!!!!

He is just as guilty of murder as the father and should be hung they will both goto hellfor killing that baby jesus loves children god will judge them

east mills pd is a joke lame ass cops dont do dick

And on, and on.

She reads in silence and abruptly closes the screen. "Don't show this to your father."

"Like I would," I say, taking the phone back and shoving it in my purse. "God, it would kill him." I don't mean that literally, of course; my father's been cursed out by the general public a thousand times before and has always seemed to let it roll right off of him because it comes with the territory. What I *mean* is that it would just make him feel worse than he already does because no one is ever as hard on my father as he is on himself.

"What are people thinking when they post things like that? I mean, just because we *can* be cruel doesn't mean we *should*. Doesn't anyone think before they hit send anymore?"

"Nope. People are twisted, Mom. Daddy knows. He deals with them every day."

"It's a wonder he's not an alcoholic," my mother murmurs, shaking her head. "Well, let's just keep this to ourselves. He doesn't need any more grief right now." She stops. "And don't post anything back." She catches my mulish look. "Rowan, look at those comments. There's no use trying to explain anything. They don't want to understand. They just want to wave their pitchforks and feel superior. Don't engage them."

"But why should they be able to get away with saying stuff like that? It's not right. Somebody should defend him."

"We are," my mother says quietly. "And we're doing it in the way that'll help him the most. So just let it be, Rowan. Please."

I hesitate, frustrated but struck by the worry in her gaze. "All right, I won't say anything online."

"Thank you," she says, not seeming to notice my choice of words. "Now let's go warm up the rest of the lasagna so we can eat."

"Okay." And as I slide out of the car and follow her up the steps it hits me that despite all the bad stuff that just keeps happening, getting home still feels like a giant, welcome exhale after holding your breath all day.

The sunporch light is on, the windows open, and Stripe is sitting inside on the sill. The night is quiet, the lights are glowing in my father's wood shop out back and the breeze is soft, clean and carrying the spicy scent of fresh-cut pine. I pause on the step, holding open the screen as my mother unlocks the inside door and then follow her into the porch. I love this old house with its warm, comfy, unflappable personality, quirky room layout and funky little sunporch tacked onto the side of the kitchen like an indulgent afterthought.

I hang my jacket on the wall hook next to my father's crisp, blue police department windbreaker, pry off my shoes and nudge them between my mother's kicked-off sensible black work pumps and my father's worn brown slipper moccasins. "Hey, handsome."

I scoop Stripe off the sill and his rumbling purr vibrates deep into my bones. My father found this cat eight years ago, alone, abandoned and starving, a scrawny, terrified kitten dodging trucks and living under a Dumpster in the industrial area. Stripe was so weak that all my father had to do was walk over, pick him up and bring him home.

Not quite as dramatic as Daisy's rescue from Iraq, but not bad.

"Lucky cat," I whisper as he kneads my collarbone and nuzzles my temple.

And I have an odd, fleeting thought: *Lucky me, too.*

Chapter 8

I give in and text Nadia that night: *sorry. I miss you.*

Me too xoxo, she texts back. *Having pizza with Brett. Talk tomorrow?*

I gaze at that for a long moment, then sigh and text, *Sure.*

But we don't because I'm at work all day Saturday and she's out with Brett on Saturday night and Sunday. I don't see her again until Monday morning at school, where Brett lets go of her long enough so we can hug in the courtyard, have our happy, public reunion and be friends again. She laughs and chatters, I smile and nod, we snap a few BFF shots for our pages.

She never brings up the video or asks about my father, and I never mention anything that really matters to me, and it hurts my heart.

Chapter 9

What a difference two weeks make, and not in a good way.

It's the Thursday *after* the Thursday Eli was supposed to pick up his—

"Don't forget the inside pocket," Eva croaks from the next counter.

I look at her blankly, then down at the suit jacket I'm pinning.

"You didn't check the inside pocket," she says, and pauses to blow her nose for the hundredth time, leaving her nostrils damp, chapped and painfully red. "I was watching."

Of course she was. Even with her pollen allergies raging, her eyes swollen to bloodshot cracks and her being so dizzy she tilts sideways while waiting on customers, she just won't give in and go home and let me work the counter again alone.

Probably because of stuff like this.

"Sorry," I say, and, reopening the jacket, stick my hand in the inner pocket, my fingers searching and closing around—of course—a pen. I'm tempted to leave it there, both to deny her the satisfaction of being right and to finally get myself fired—third time's a charm, right?—but I need the money, and so some stubborn spark of pride makes me pull it out and hold it up. "Good call." I drop it in an envelope and staple it to his ticket.

"Every morning I tell Helga the same thing: You *have* to *check* the *pockets*," she announces hoarsely, pounding a gnarled fist on the counter for emphasis, and then sneezes into her cupped hands. Looks at them, scowls and says, "Oh, hell. I need another tissue."

"Bless you," I call after her retreating back, and give a mighty exhale when she's gone.

Sad to say, but this five-minute break is pretty much the one and only good thing that's happened lately.

I only got to have one more vending-machine lunch with Eli— cheese crackers, chocolate cupcakes and Gatorade, and he bought— because he found out he was a credit short and had to make up a whole semester's worth of senior health class in that one free period every day.

"I'll do it, I don't care, because I'm *not* going to summer school," he said. "I just want to graduate already. I mean, being new in senior year, for like, the last couple months of school? It sucks. I would have rather graduated with my class back in Houston but after my father died my mother got it into her head to move out here closer to my grandparents, so . . ." He ran an aggravated hand over his hair. "Whatever."

"So then this is our farewell feast," I said, hiding my disappointment and trying to lighten his dark mood. "We should have a toast." I lifted my Gatorade and waited until finally, lips twitching into a reluctant smile, he did the same. "What should we toast to?" I asked, hoping he'd say us.

"How about senior health?" he said dryly, tapping his plastic bottle against mine.

"Which, in case you didn't know, is 'Love and Sexuality,' so here's to you acing it." Blushing, I tapped bottles right back and hoped he wouldn't notice the heat in my cheeks.

"Is it really?" he said after a moment, giving me an owlish look.

"Yup," I said, becoming very busy reading the label on the bottle.

"Are you in that class, too?" he said after a long moment.

"I'm not a senior," I said, and that seemed to kill the subject, as we moved on to what was happening with my father—nothing good—and then the bell rang and lunch was over. I've seen him walking down the hall a few times since then, once with a senior girl who, if you listen to gossip, could supposedly *teach* sexuality, and he always looked happy to see me but we haven't really talked at all and—

A phone rings, startling me, and I'm halfway to the landline when I realize it's Eva's cell.

She really should get a ringtone.

I roll up the suit and stuff it into a Monday bin. Nod at Eva wiping her nose and grumbling into her phone, and head out front. Grab the next bundle and unroll it. Police uniforms. I glance at the name on the ticket.

Lieutenant Walters.

Ugh.

I count the pieces—two pants, two shirts and a tie—and search his pockets, grimly hoping to find something scandalous like a condom, weed or a receipt from the shabby little No-Tell Motel out on the highway, which advertises hourly rates.

Anything I can put in an envelope and staple to his ticket, watch his face when he picks up his uniforms and opens it. Something that will remind him of how bad it sucks when you try to do everything right and then one small, random act changes the way people look at you forever.

But my search turns up nothing. He did what he was supposed to do, was responsible, followed the correct procedure, and so his pockets are empty; there is nothing there to tarnish his reputation, nothing incriminating to discover.

And that's exactly how he trained my father twenty years ago, to be thorough, do right, follow procedure . . . So how can he *stand* being part of the internal investigation now, when he *knows* my father didn't do anything wrong?

"Asshole," I whisper, viciously balling up his uniforms and striding back to shove them into a bin.

A dog barks outside.

I look up to see Eli, Daisy and a short, sturdy, dark-haired girl with blond tips who looks vaguely familiar walking toward me across the parking lot.

Oh God, he has a *girlfriend?*

"Interesting," Eva rumbles from right behind me, making me jump. "Grief certainly does make strange bedfellows."

"What?" I glance back at her, puzzled.

"That's Eli Gage and Payton Well, together," Eva says, giving me a look. "Don't you watch the news?"

"Yeah, and I've already met Eli but . . ." I look back, trying not to be obvious, and she's right. That *is* Sammy's mother. I only saw her in the funeral clip and she looks really different in jeans and a tank.

"I'll wait on them," Eva says, nudging me toward the back.

Eli spots me and, smiling, lifts a hand in greeting.

I smile and return his wave.

"Go in the back," Eva says, tweezing her tissue from her sleeve and dabbing at her nose. "I don't want you involved in a scene."

What is she talking about? "Why would there be a scene?" I've been waiting to talk to Eli again, actually dreamed about him once and—

"Rowan," she says impatiently. "Please."

So I go, irritated, sending Eli a quick, regretful smile before I slip into the back and linger out of sight by the cleaning bins.

I hear the bell go off as the door opens, feel the rush of cool air and the sound of traffic—

"No dogs allowed," Eva says, and blows her nose. "Sorry."

I forgot about Daisy. I bite my lip, hoping Eli doesn't give me up.

"No problem," he says easily, and then, "Here's my ticket, Pay. We'll wait out here."

"Okay." Her voice is listless. "Uh, I'm picking these up." Pause. "Eli said I left a pin on my dress when I dropped it off."

"Let's take a look," Eva says noncommittally, and suddenly the line of clothes starts to move, whooshing past me to a sudden stop. "Here's one." The line flows again, plastic cleaning bags whispering as they pass, and then stops. "Yes, here you are."

I hear an envelope being torn open. Peek my head out from behind the bins and look straight at Eli, who is standing outside with Daisy at the edge of the plate-glass window and gazing right back in at me. He cocks his head and gives me a questioning smile.

Mortified, I shrug and grab a pair of pants from the closest bin, pretending to check the tag pinned on them, hoping he has no idea what I'm actually doing back here—lurking—and pretending to be very, very busy.

"Good," Payton says, her voice thick with tears. "I thought I lost it." Sniffle. "Shit. I don't have a tissue. Oh, thanks. What do I owe you?"

"Nothing for the dress," Eva says after a long, silent moment. "I'm sorry for your loss." Pause. "The suit is ten fifty."

I hear the register open and change being made. I risk another peek out at the front window but Eli is gone.

I scowl and fling the pants back into the bin.

"That boy out there with the dog," Eva says casually. "Isn't he, uh . . . ?"

My ears perk up.

"Oh right, I guess I should have known. Nothing's really free, is it? Yeah, that's Eli from the video and no, he's not my boyfriend," Payton says in a clipped and angry recitation, as if she's answered this question a hundred times already. "He's just a friend. And yeah, he *was* on the overpass that day. And no, I wasn't sleeping with him and cheating on Corey. I didn't even know him before this." Her voice rises. "And yeah, I *am* sick of people judging and asking me stupid fucking questions and then getting pissed when I don't answer because it's none of their business and I don't owe them a goddamn thing. So hey, thanks for the *free* cleaning. Have a great day."

I hear the rustle of bags, the motion bell go off, the door open and close again.

Eva comes into the back and sees me standing there with my mouth hanging open.

"Wow," I say, shocked. "What was that about?"

She shakes her head and stuffs her crumpled tissue back into the sleeve of her cardigan. "Do you see now why I didn't want you involved?"

I have no idea what she's talking about and it must show because she gives me an impatient look, her watery, bloodshot eyes squinty behind her glasses, and says, "You're Nicky's daughter and she's very angry. What if she blames your father for—"

"No," I say. "Eli wouldn't have brought her here if she did." I stop. Would he have? *Why* would he have? "No."

"You don't know what she's thinking, Rowan. Her son was murdered and the police didn't save him." She catches my hurt look and holds up a gnarled hand. "Listen, she's a grieving mother. Her life has been torn apart. The world isn't fair anymore and there's no making sense of it. She's probably out there right now raging about how wrong it is that an old misery like me is still breathing while her beautiful baby boy isn't. Trust me." The tissue reappears. "There's a lot more to grief than just crying and wearing black. You don't go to the funeral, pack up a few mementos and it's over." Motioning for me to follow her, she goes back out front and parks herself on the stool behind the counter. "Has anyone you loved ever passed away?"

"What?" How did we switch from Payton to me? What kind of conversation is this, anyway? "Uh, my grandparents on my father's side died about two years ago." I can't just stand here so I reach under the counter and pull out, yes, a pair of old Mr. Hanson's pants to finish pinning them. "Pop-Pop had a heart attack maybe three weeks after Grammy died in the hospital from pneumonia." I stop, wondering how much she wants to know. "He was taking the garbage cans out to the street. By the time somebody noticed him lying there and called my father it was too late to save him." I reach under the counter into the box of safety pins and pull one out. "It was sad. My father was . . ." I stare down at the pin and the ticket stub. "They were really close."

"I lost my son," Eva says softly. "Forty-two years ago, when he was four. And I can tell you now that not a day goes by when I don't think of him, and miss him."

"I'm sorry," I say awkwardly, gazing out at the parking lot and wishing desperately for a customer to come in and interrupt us.

"Thank you. After all of this time it still has the power to make me tear up." She wipes her eyes and stuffs the crumpled tissue into her pocket, plucking a fresh one from the box under the counter. "We grow up believing that bad things don't happen to good people . . . but sometimes they do. It's a hard truth to accept, that life is not fair."

"There's a cheery thought," I mutter, scowling down at my pinning.

"And grief is such a difficult maze of emotions," she says, continuing as if she doesn't hear me. "It's funny, I remember the stages as if it were yesterday: shock, denial, numbness, fear, anger, depression, and finally acceptance, understanding and moving on. Although I'm not sure *moving on* is the right phrase for it."

"Why not?" I like the sound of *moving on* best, of putting all the depressing stuff behind you and getting on with your life. I'd like to do that right now, as a matter of fact.

"Because it suggests leaving your loved one behind and I don't think you do that," she says, knotting her arthritic fingers together and gazing out the window. "You learn to live with the loss and when you're ready, you go on. You carry their memory with you forever." She glances at me, face grave. "That young woman, Payton, has a very difficult journey in front of her, and she'll never be the same. Grief . . ." She shakes her head. "You can't hide from it. There is no over, under or around it. No avoiding. It will stay until you make your way through it." She squares her thin shoulders. "It's the only way to heal and find happiness again. God bless her, I hope she can do it."

"Well sure, yeah, of course," I say, at a loss. Eva, sticking up for Payton after she got told off? Why, because she lost a kid, too? I don't know. Why is it so quiet in here? Where are all the customers?

I glance at the clock, sweating. Forty-five more minutes to go.

I'll never make it.

"I have a question," I hear myself say loudly, tweezing up the polyester pants and holding them out in front of me. "Not to change the subject or anything, but why are Mr. Hanson's pockets always damp?"

She blinks and her expression eases. "Isn't it horrendous? I'm one step from having Terence burn a big hole in them and giving the old lech twenty dollars to get a new pair."

"I'd donate to that," I say, pinning the ticket stub on his waistband and balling them up for the bin.

"Rowan," she says as I start toward the back.

I stop. "Yes?"

"Your father . . . He hasn't been in lately. How is he taking all of this?"

"Okay," I say automatically, but to my horror, my eyes fill with tears.

"I see," she says quietly, and nods as if confirming something to herself. "Well, please tell him that he has my support and not to be a stranger."

"I will," I mumble, and escape into the back.

And I mean to give him the message, I really do, but Nadia texts me on the walk home about a party she wants me to go to Friday night. Her excitement is as contagious as always and by the time we finish making plans I'm thinking about who's going to be there, what I'm going to wear and if I can sleep over her house, because that means we can stay out a lot later, since her parents never wait up for us to get in.

I run up the front lawn to the porch and into the house.

Finally, something *good* is happening.

Chapter 10

"He's *beautiful*," I say in a loud whisper, leaning against Nadia's shoulder and gazing up at her. "Oh my God, I'm so serious." I drain the rest of my beer, only spilling a little down the front of my V-neck top. "Crap." I blot it with the back of my hand. "Anyway, you didn't see him except in that video. *I* saw him in person, and trust me"—I slap my wet hand over my heart, give her a solemn, owl-eyed nod—"oh . . . my . . . God."

"Really," Nadia drawls, giving me an interested look and shifting away so that I suddenly list and have to regain my balance. "You never told me you met him."

I laugh and say in an airy voice, "Well, I don't tell you *every-thing*, you know." And then I clamp my mouth shut because I wasn't supposed to tell her that.

"Oh yeah, since when?" she says, raising an eyebrow in cool amusement like she thinks I'm only kidding. "So what else haven't you told me?"

"Well, um . . ." I blink, thinking hard, and slowly a smile dawns. "Oh, no you don't," I say, laughing and poking her in the shoulder. "That was a trap so I would tell my secrets. Why don't you tell me yours, instead?"

"Because I don't have any secrets from you," she says, tossing back her long blond hair and gazing with studied nonchalance around the room. "Anyway, whatever. Did you know Justin was here?"

"No, where?" I crane my neck and spot him over by the keg at the same moment he spots me. He lifts his chin in brief greeting and goes back to hitting on some girl.

"Good thing you don't like him anymore," Nadia says, giving me a sideways look.

"Hmm." I stare at him a moment, trying to decide, and finally shrug because I can't remember why I thought I liked him in the first place. "Eh."

Nadia snorts.

"What?" I ask, tilting my plastic cup up again to catch the last drop of beer and lowering it again, frowning. "I want another beer."

"That's what, your sixth?" she says.

"Fifth, and what are you, counting?" I say, and give her a friendly hip-bump. "This is the first fun I've had in like, a month. Seriously, you don't *know* how bad it's been at my house ever since Corey took that header." I know I'm not supposed to bring it up but it just comes out.

Nadia snickers.

"No, quit it, it's not funny," I say, but her laughing is making me laugh and I don't even know why. "My father's totally sinking into this black pit of despair and my mother's running crazy cooking all this stuff to tempt him to eat and trying to talk to him and all." I hiccup, laughter fading. "It not funny. I'm so mad." My voice gets gravelly. "Stupid Justin. I never should have cut school for him." I wipe my eyes and glare across the room at the back of his ugly head. "I just want things to go back the way they were. Happy. Everything was fine and everybody was happy."

"No offense, but this is starting to get old, Row," she says absently, smiling across the room at Brett, who's lounging by the pool table. "I mean it's not like that psycho guy and his kid were family or anything. You need to just put it behind you and move on."

"No kidding," I mutter, but it's easier said than done.

"So you're okay here, right?" she asks, smoothing her slinky black shirt down over her flat stomach. "Because Brett's——"

"Go," I drone, rolling my eyes and giving her a light shove in his direction. "I'm gonna get another beer."

"Last one?" she says, pausing and looking back at me. "Seriously, I'm not dragging you up to my room tonight. If you pass out, you're sleeping where you fall."

"I'll be fine, *Mom*." I laugh as she gives me the finger and saunters over to Brett, then look into my empty cup and sigh. "It's just you and me, kid."

I weave through the crowd toward the keg, only bumping into two people and ignoring Justin and the girl; fill my cup; and head back toward the stairs. This place, this *basement*, is better than my living room, with a pool table, fireplace, bar, enormous flat-screen TV, kickass sound system and dimmer lights.

Not to mention the hot tub outside on the deck.

"That's gonna be trouble," I mutter, cracking myself up, and ease down onto one of the carpeted steps to upstairs. I can see everyone coming or going from here and although I know Eli probably isn't going to show up, probably wasn't even invited, you never know.

I really want to see him again.

I pull out my phone, go on Facebook and send him a friend request.

At least I think it was him. I don't know, my eyes are bleary and all those Elis listed kind of got away from me.

I watch Nadia and Brett for a while—they really are good together—and when they finally head past me up the stairs holding hands, Nadia pauses and says, "Everything good?"

"Yes, Mom," I yes, rolling my eyes.

She snorts, says they'll be back and then they're gone.

I finish my beer and get another. Get stopped by a drunk junior dancing alone and sway along with him until he sticks his sweaty face in mine and with a sly smile says, "Your old man offed that baby, right?" like it's somehow our little secret.

Astonishment gives way to rage and my hand swings round to slap him, only I'm still holding a full cup of beer. The golden amber sails out in a wave that not only splashes an arc across the front of me but explodes over him when the plastic cup connects with the side of his stupid face, collapsing into shards against his jaw.

He staggers back, gaping, hits the debris-covered coffee table and goes over, knocking garbage everywhere and landing across the laps of two guys and a girl sitting on the couch, who immediately shove him off to the floor and give me really dirty looks.

I stare back at them through a blur of tears, heart pounding so loud I can't even hear the music, then turn, dropping my smashed cup, and reel blindly up the stairs.

My father didn't kill anyone.

I make it up to the main floor and look around. "Nadia?" The house is big, noisy and confusing. Or maybe it's me, because no matter which way I walk, everything is still out of focus and unfamiliar.

There are twenty people in the bathroom line but none of them are Nadia.

I squeeze past them and keep looking.

There's a crowd doing body shots in the dining room and some other stuff I don't want to know about in the den. When I finally get to the staircase leading up to the bedrooms it seems a mile high and all of a sudden I just don't have it in me.

"Waiting for me?" some guy says, sliding a chunky arm around me and pulling me close. His chin is bristly and his mouth sloppy wet, sliming my chin. I twist my head and dig an elbow into his ribs, prying myself free.

"Get off of me," I say, shoving my tangled hair from my eyes and glaring at him. "Asshole." I stagger away, bouncing off walls because the floors keep tilting and I can't walk straight. Once I make it to the living room there's nowhere left to go but out the front door, so I do. I pause on the porch, fumble out my phone and with trembling fingers call Nadia, listening as it goes straight to voice mail. "Nad, it's"—I squint at my watch—"a quarter to three. Where are you? I'm out front waiting. Come *on*."

Hang up, shivering in the cool night air, and wait.

And wait.

Text, *I'll meet you at your house. Call me.*

And wait.

"Fine," I say, and shoving my phone in my pocket, I lurch down the middle of the shadowy, deserted side street toward the center of town.

It's going to be a long walk.

Chapter 11

A lean, scruffy-looking cat darts across a driveway ahead of me.

A night bird trills, sleepy, disturbed.

The streetlights hum.

My stumbling footsteps are the only sound of human life.

Just getting to Main Street seems to take forever.

The cool air clears my head some but I know I'm not sober.

I never should have left the party.

I should have crawled up those stairs and banged on every door until I found her.

Or sat on Brett's car until they came out.

Walking is a stupid idea.

I lurch onto Main Street, which is eerily still and silent, feeling very exposed out here in the open like this. How far to her development? A mile? And then another half mile in to her house?

God, I won't get there till four in the morning.

I hug myself and shiver.

My father says that something like two-thirds of crimes like sexual assaults and rape happen at night. I glance behind me, heart pounding, see nothing but long, dark shadows and walk faster. What if somebody's watching me? No, what if that beer-drenched guy who called my father a murderer is really pissed and following me?

I pull my phone out of my pocket and hold on to it.

Maybe I should call home and ask my father to come pick me up, even though I'll be grounded for wandering Main Street in the wee hours of the morning reeking of alcohol when I'm supposed to be at Nadia's fast asleep. I can hear his lecture now, asking me how someone so smart could do something so stupid, telling me that this is how girls disappear without a trace and their nude, beaten and bloated bodies are found later by some poor homeless guy searching for empty cans along the weedy side of the road.

I glance behind me.

On the other hand, he always said I should call him if I needed a ride, no matter what.

But then I'd have to explain why I'm not at Nadia's, where I was and where I left her, which will get her in trouble, too.

Damn.

And of course there's no way to sneak into her house, not without banging on the door and waking everybody up. There isn't even anywhere to sit outside because her pool furniture doesn't come out until Memorial Day and she doesn't have any porch steps, just this flat, ground-level cement entrance that really sucks to sit on.

"So what the hell am I supposed to do?" I yell in frustration, and cringe at the broken silence. Well, if that guy is lurking anywhere out there, he definitely knows where I am now. Idiot.

Somewhere off in the distance a dog barks, and that spurs me on past the bakery, the hair salon and the Dunkin' Donuts, all closed up tight.

My phone rings, making me jump.

It's Nadia. "Rowan, where the hell *are* you?"

"Where the hell are *you*?" I shoot back, bristling.

"Oh, for . . . Leaving the party so we can come find *you*," she snaps. "Why didn't you wait for us? What happened?"

"Nothing, I just wanted to go and I couldn't find you," I say, putting a hand to my pounding forehead. "I'm at the bank down on Main Street. By Dunkin' Donuts."

"Christ, she's down by Dunkin' Donuts already," she says off to the side, and then to me, "Stay there, okay? Don't go anywhere. Just wait. We'll be there in ten minutes."

"Why is that dog still barking?" I say, distracted, and suddenly realize the shadows are shifting and I'm standing in a growing pool of light. I turn to see a patrol car pulling up alongside me.

"Rowan, don't—"

"Cops. I have to go." I hang up, hoping it's Vinnie and I can somehow talk him into dropping me at Nadia's house and not telling my father about any of this.

But the officer who steps out of the car isn't Vinnie.

It's Lieutenant Walters.

I panic, whirl and take off running.

Chapter 12

I tear down the alley alongside the bank. Hear him shouting, hear dispatch on his radio and the thunder of pounding feet growing louder and louder behind me.

"No, no, no," I pant, frantic, and without warning something slams into me from the back, knocking me straight into the wall, shoving my cheek up against the rough, cold bricks and yanking my arms behind my back. My chin scrapes the wall and my teeth clack together. The taste of blood makes me cry.

"Don't fight. Hold still," he says from behind me, breathing hard. "Why did you run?" He snaps the cuffs around my wrists and, taking me firmly by the upper arm, leads me stumbling out of the shadows and back out to the streetlights on Main Street. "Stand here and don't move." He puts me up against the side of the police car and radios for a female officer to pat me down. "What're you doing out here alone at three thirty in the morning? Have you been drinking?"

"I'm sorry," I blubber, lifting my head and peering at him through my hair. "Please let me go, Lieutenant Walters. Please. You don't understand, my father's going to kill me."

"Jesus, not again," he says, falling back a step in dismay. "Nick's daughter?"

"I'm sorry," I wail, still drunk, totally humiliated and unable to stop crying. "That guy said b-bad things about my father and I had to g-go. I swear I d-didn't d-do anything wrong, I just want to g-go home. Please take me home . . . puh—puh—please?"

He takes a deep breath and slowly releases it. "You've got really bad timing, Ms. Areno." He gazes at me with the most awful look on his face and then, as if he doesn't know any better, says, "Do your parents know you're out here like this?"

"*No*," I say, knees shaking so hard I can barely stand. "I was j-just t-trying to g-get h-home." And then the tears flow harder because my nose is running, there's blood in my mouth and I'm nauseous, gross and stupid, I can see it all in his eyes just like last time, and I can't take it. "Do you have a t-tissue?"

"In a minute." He sighs again and radios in to cancel the female officer. Opens the back door to the patrol car and, turning me around, says sternly, "If I take these off, are you going to behave?"

I nod, snuffling, and suddenly my hands are free again. "Thank you." I wipe my nose on my arm and it leaves a long, slimy smear of blood. "B-b-be c-c-careful," I say in a hitched voice. "I have b-body fluids everywhere."

"Just get in," he says tiredly, and when I do, he hands me a wad of tissues and shuts the door behind me.

Chapter 13

What the hell were you *thinking*?

You could have been killed, Rowan. You could have been snatched up off the street and we never would have known what happened to you!

Drunk, and walking the streets alone at almost four in the morning.

Why didn't you call us for a ride? My God, when I think of it . . .

Why did you run from him? You must have known who he was; what the *hell* were you thinking?

You're grounded. Just go to bed.

And on, and on.

I flop over in bed and wipe the tears from my cheeks, my mother's furious voice echoing through my pounding head, the bandaged scrape on my chin stinging, my heart sick at the expression on my father's face when he opened the door and saw me and Lieutenant Walters standing there.

He'd driven me home in silence, led me to the front door and knocked. Dying of nerves, I'd babbled that nobody ever knocks on our front door, they always go straight to the sunporch door but he just stood silent, waiting beside me until the lights inside came on and then the front light itself. When I heard the door open I peeked up from under my hair and saw my father standing there in his sweats, his expression dazed from sleep, slack with surprise and then, as he saw me and the lieutenant, tightening with a rush of embarrassment, anger and concern.

"I think this one's yours," Lieutenant Walters said with a smile that tried for camaraderie but couldn't get past awkward. "I found her down on Main Street."

"What?" my father said, eyebrows high. "Alone?"

The lieutenant nodded. "She's been drinking."

"Get in the house, Rowan," my mother said from somewhere in the foyer, and then, leaning out the door past my father, forced a smile at the lieutenant and said, "Thank you, Arnold, for bringing her home. She was supposed to be sleeping at her friend's tonight." She glanced at me, fire in her eyes. "She has a lot of explaining to do."

"Sorry about her chin," the lieutenant said, stepping back. "I didn't recognize her and when she took off—"

"She *ran* from you?" my father said in an ominous voice.

I slipped inside then, sidling past my parents, hoping to make it up to my room, but my mother was right behind me, grabbing my arm and stopping me dead in the living room.

"Sit down," she said in a voice I'd never heard before, and so I sat while she got a wet washcloth and silently cleaned the scrape on my chin, applied antibiotic ointment and a bandage.

"Mom," I said weakly, but she only she stepped back, mouth tight, and glanced over at my father standing in the doorway. "I swear I didn't mean to . . . I'm sorry, I . . ."

And then the fireworks began, but from my mother, not my father like I'd expected. He just stood there, face drawn, his gaze weary and filled with disappointment.

Nothing like he normally was, no hard questions, no interrogation, no demanding the details of how this whole debacle had transpired, and his lack of reaction scared me.

I yelled back once, trying to push him, maybe, into a response. My mother was ranting, incredulous over the fact that I'd done the dumbest thing possible, *run* from a policeman who we all not only *knew* but who was officially investigating my father, and looking at me like she didn't even know me.

"I hate him," I shouted. "He hurt my chin and he didn't even call EMS!"

"Lower your voice," my mother snapped.

"You brought it on yourself. He could have taken you to the ground or brought you into headquarters for processing but he was doing me a favor," my father said quietly, looking away. "He knows the last thing we need right now is an incident report on how my drunken underage daughter resisted arrest and ran from *the man*. Forget the internal investigation; you think the news wouldn't have jumped on that?"

I stared down at my hands, feeling even sicker at making my father beholden to someone who could hurt him. "I'm sorry."

"You're grounded," my mother said, sighing and turning away. "Just go to bed. We'll finish this in the morning." She looked at my father expectantly but he just shook his head and, avoiding her gaze, said, "You go ahead. I'm gonna watch TV for a while."

She hesitated. "Are you all right?"

He nodded. "I'm fine. Go ahead." And to me, "You'd better go get some sleep, Rowan. You're supposed to be at work at eight." And then he turned away and went into the kitchen, and my mother gave me a look that said, *Let's go*, and so we went.

"I'm really sorry," I whisper again into my pillow, into the darkness, and wait, listening hard, but there is no response and I fall asleep still hoping to hear my father's footsteps coming up the stairs.

Chapter 14

Saturdays at the cleaner's are an all-day mob scene, preventing Eva from doing any more than give me the occasional curious glance between customers, wondering, I guess, at the dark circles under my eyes, why I'm moving so slowly and why, when Lieutenant Walters arrives to pick up his uniforms, my face gets hot and I wait on him without ever once actually looking at him.

Eva doesn't ask though, and for that I'm grateful, as there's no way I can describe the grimness dragging me down. Part of it's the hangover but the rest, the heaviness and the dread . . .

I can't seem to shake it.

When the day's over Eva simply hands me my paycheck and I'm out of there, head pounding, calling Nadia on the sunny walk home to tell her what happened and that I'm grounded, and finding out that of course she made it inside without getting caught.

Great. Well, at least she won't feel bad ditching me to be with Brett, as I'm not going to be around for a while, anyway. I say that and hurt her feelings, and then feel bad and apologize but she has to go anyway because Brett is texting her and they're going out tonight.

And that makes me feel like slapping Eva for pissing off Payton Well and blowing the one chance I had to talk to Eli again, and then I get mad at Eli for even *bringing* her to the cleaner's anyway—what the hell was *that* about?—and my anger snakes all the way back to Corey for killing himself right in front of us and screwing up everybody's lives, and then to stupid Justin for ditching me in McDonald's that morning and kicking the whole thing off.

I walk the rest of the way home feeling like the marrow in my bones has gone bad, trudging past the woods and up the front lawn, past my father's car and into the house.

And know, instantly, that something is wrong.

Chapter 15

My father is sitting alone at the kitchen table, staring out the nook window. His hair is disheveled, he's still wearing his sleep sweats and Stripe is curled up on his lap. The house is a tomb, no radio, no TV echoing in from the living room, no food smell, nothing.

I stand in the kitchen doorway, afraid to break the silence and afraid not to. "Dad?"

He starts, blinking as if waking up from a deep sleep, and runs a hand over his hair. "Hey," he says, and clears his throat. "Is it five o'clock already?"

"Almost six," I say, walking cautiously into the room and slinging my purse across the back of my chair. "Where's Mom?"

"Oh, she had to run into work this morning," he says with a small, automatic smile at their long-standing "library emergency" joke. "It's just me and Stripe today." He settles a gentle hand on the cat and Stripe's purr revs up. "She's bringing home a couple of pizzas."

"Okay," I say, uneasy. Why is he still in his sweats? Has he actually been sitting here like this all day? No, that's impossible . . . unless he's sick. "Are you okay?"

"Sure," he says after a second, glancing back out the window.

"Okay, good," I say, and wait, but he doesn't add anything. "So uh, what's going on? Did you work out in the wood shop today?"

"No," he says after a long moment, gazing down at Stripe as if ashamed that I've caught him being idle. "I'm sorry. The hardware for the hope chest was back-ordered and it just came in a couple of days ago. I know you've been waiting but——"

"No, I wasn't pushing," I say quickly. "It's fine whenever. I'll be sixteen for a whole year and besides, I don't even have anything to put in it, yet." My lame joke passes unacknowledged. "I was just wondering, that's all." What is happening here? Why isn't he yelling at me for last night? "Um, I'm going to make coffee. Do you want a cup?" I head over to the counter, expecting a swift yes—my father *never* turns down coffee—and almost drop the carafe when he says slowly, "I don't think so. No. Maybe later."

"Oh," I say, putting the carafe down again. "Um, okay."

"You can still have some though," he says, sitting up and looking worried. "Don't not have it just because I don't want any."

"No, it's okay," I say.

"Rowan, please make it anyway," he says, leaning forward in his chair. "If you don't have a cup I'm going to feel guilty for stopping you. Please." The expression on his face is serious, upset even, as though he can't bear being responsible for my not having a cup of coffee. "Make it."

"Okay," I say faintly, wondering when *okay* became the only word in my vocabulary and setting up a small pot of coffee. "So uh, what's new? Anything?" My father's unnatural stillness unnerves me, makes me far too aware of my own movements, and that makes me clumsy; I spill coffee grinds on the counter and almost drop my mug as I pull it from the cabinet.

"Not really," he says, toying with Stripe's ear. "I got a call this morning from Captain Schwarz up at headquarters. I'm officially out of work on medical leave, starting today." He glances up, catches my stunned gaze and gives a self-conscious shrug. "It's all right. I think it'll help. I have an appointment with a shrink on Monday." He looks back down at the cat. "I wasn't going to say anything until your mother got home but—"

"Mommy doesn't know yet?" I blurt.

"Mommy doesn't know what?" she says from behind me, struggling in through the kitchen door with two pizza boxes, her purse, her tote bag and three books tucked under her arm. "Grab the books, Row. They're slipping."

I do and glance at the titles: *Surviving Critical Incident Stress* and *Beating the Blues.*

"So, what don't I know?" she says, smiling at me and then glancing at my father. "Hey, sweetheart, you look nice and relaxed." Her smile wavers as she drops a kiss in the middle of his rumpled hair. "Hungry? I got one with the works, your favorite."

My father has the same tortured expression on his face that he had during the coffee incident but he forces a smile and says, "I could probably eat a slice."

"Good," she says, casting me a glance. "Let's eat before they get cold. Rowan, will you set the table, please?"

So I do, working around my father, who seems to have somehow deflated even more, and giving my mother a burning look behind his back, a look that says, *What's going on? What's wrong with Daddy?*

But my mother doesn't act like anything's wrong through dinner and so I try not to, either, eating three slices of pizza to my father's one (and he didn't even eat the crust) and listening to her chatter about library doings and all the donations for the big book sale in June.

Is my father listening? I glance over, see him toying with the uneaten pizza crust on his plate, and the sight is so off, so wrong, that I hear myself say, "Hey, Dad, guess who came into the cleaner's the other day to pick up his suit?" This isn't the first time we've played this guess-who game, seeing as how he knows so many people in town, and so I hold my breath, hoping he starts with the twenty questions, trying to narrow it down.

"I don't know," he says after a moment with a helpless shrug. "Who?"

I sit back, disappointed. "You're not even going to try?"

"I . . ." He shakes his head, looking miserable. "I can't. I'm sorry."

And suddenly it's as if the entire world narrows to a terrifying pinpoint with this sad, deflated stranger huddled at the center, and the simmering fear inside of me flares into anger. "Oh my God, Dad, what're you *doing*?" I cry, pushing my chair back from the table. "Why are you *being* this way?"

"Rowan, stop it," my mother says, setting her slice of pizza back on her plate.

"It was Eli, okay?" I say, hating the way he just stares down into his plate and doesn't even stand up to me. "He came in with Payton. Did I ever tell you that Eli told me you talked to him after the whole Corey thing and it really helped him?" No response, and that only fuels my fire. "He thought you were really brave, he wanted to know how you were dealing with it and I said fine but I guess I was lying."

"Rowan!" My mother snaps, appalled. "Who do you think you're talking to?"

I turn to my father, silently daring him, begging him to get mad and yell, to ground me for last night or for now or even to smile his old warning smile and tell me I'm getting way out of line, something, anything normal, because the bleak sadness on his face is turning my bullying anger to a sick, stomach-twisting guilt and—

"I'm sorry," he says, planting an elbow on the table and dropping his head into his hand. "I know I'm not myself. Just try to be patient with me, all right?" He glances at my mother, gaze dull. "I'm out on a medical leave, Rachel. I requested it. I don't know what else to do. I can't eat or sleep . . . I can't function. I have an appointment Monday with . . . I . . . I need help." And then he covers his face and begins to weep. "I can't help it."

For a moment my mother and I sit stunned, caught in stricken paralysis, but then she says softly, "Oh, Nicky, honey, it's okay," and goes to him, arms open, while I panic and flee the room, telling myself it's to give them privacy, but in truth I should never have seen that.

I cannot bear the sight of my father breaking.

Chapter 16

May always gives my mother spring fever, and she stalls as long as she can so as not to stress my father but finally, almost halfway through the month on a Wednesday night, she can't take it anymore and decides the dining room needs a fresh coat of celery-green paint.

"I'll do it," my father says slowly, rousing from his spot in the recliner. He's wearing his reading glasses and has been staring blankly at the same page in Stephen King's latest novel for the last fifteen minutes.

I know, because I've been surreptitiously watching him from over the top of *my* book. Observation has pretty much become the routine we've settled into, seeing as how talking about how he feels, even to try to help him, has the exact opposite effect and only makes him feel worse for failing us.

His words, not ours.

"Really?" my mother says, sounding surprised, and then adds hastily, "Well, that would be great. I'll pick up the paint tomorrow after work. If we can get it done by Saturday I'll invite the grandparents over for Sunday dinner." She catches the sudden distress on my father's face and adds, "Or whenever. There's no rush. And we don't have to have company right now. We can always do it next week, or even the week after. Whenever you feel up to it."

He nods slowly, his expression easing, and goes back to staring at his book.

I glance at my mother, who gives me a slight shrug, a quick smile, and gazes down at her laptop.

Ten bucks says she's researching depression, because that's the way it is now here at home, with my quiet, slow-moving father seeing his psychiatrist once a week and my mother doing everything she can to keep life as calm as possible until his antidepressants kick in and hopefully get him back to normal again.

And I have to give her this: She's really trying. When the TV is on and we're talking and it's too much for him, kind of a sensory overload I guess, the TV goes off and we move to the kitchen. She makes his favorite foods and pretends she's not crushed when he can't bring himself to eat them. She gives him vitamins. Stays cheerful, thoughtful, supportive. She's taken over all the chores he used to do so he isn't struggling with the weight of impossible-to-fill expectations right now and I got home from work yesterday to find her near tears, wrestling to replace the stupid spool on the weed whacker so she could finish trimming the grass.

And him standing helpless in the living room, wringing his hands and watching her.

The problem is that he's depressed, not stupid, and he *knows* what she's doing, he can see it even though she's trying her best to make the added burdens no big deal. He is very much aware that he's letting her down—his words, never hers—and he keeps apologizing because it torments him . . . but it's like he's suddenly an invalid, paralyzed with no physical wound to justify it, like everything he was got sucked out of him and left this terrible, gray, empty shell sitting and suffering in a chair in the dark.

So I took the weed whacker from her, fitted the spool and finished the trimming, quick, sloppy but done, feeling his anguished gaze on me the whole time, and then all but threw the stupid thing back in the garage because really, it's *grass,* and if my father can angst over grass then he can get better and go out and do it himself.

I want the real him back, goddamn it.

I feel like I'm two completely different people forced to live in two different worlds, that I have to leave the cheerful, happy, hopeful me at school or work every day and shift into a quiet, tiptoeing, worried me just to get in the door at home.

I hate it, and I hate seeing us like this.

I don't understand why it's happening and why he just can't somehow be *himself* again. I want my father back, the smart, brave, reliable man who runs into burning buildings and drags people out, the man who once held a child's bleeding, chopped-to-the-bone leg together until EMS arrived, after she'd slipped and fallen under a riding lawn mower while the blade was engaged. I want the man who was given his wristwatch at a commendation ceremony for being a hero, the man who protects us, who locks the house up every single night without fail, who cuts the grass and changes the oil in the cars, the one who promised to teach me how to drive and is making me a hope chest.

And sometimes I want to yell, "Stop it, Dad! *Please* be yourself again!" to try to snap him out of it—but I don't because he's always on the verge of tears these days as it is, terrible, helpless tears, and it would kill me to make him feel even worse.

This is exactly what happens the afternoon I come in and see him sitting alone in the living room, eyes closed, laptop open on the coffee table, the screen glowing in the shadows.

I stand in the doorway gazing at him, thinking he's asleep and not bothering to mask the impatience on my face, the scared, angry wish of an immature, self-centered girl for him to just stop it, to get up and be all right again so life can go back to normal, when he opens his eyes and looks right at me. The torment in his gaze rocks me, knocks me speechless, and I stand there unable to move until he turns his face away as if ashamed and says in a dull voice, "Go, Rowan. I don't want you seeing me like this."

And one side of me whispers, *Get in there and hug him, say something nice, something filled with love and comfort, because he looks so sad,* but the other side is riveted, aghast, because the screen he has open is the website with all the terrible, hateful comments about him. Knowing he's read them leaves me helpless, furious at their malice, at his weakness and my own, embarrassed by the stranger he's become, and so I just mutter, "Sorry, Dad," step back, and leave him to battle his demons alone.

Chapter 17

"Finally," Eli says, catching up with me in the hall the next morning before homeroom. "You're a hard girl to track down. What're you, avoiding me or something?"

"Me?" I glance up in surprise, catch the mischief in his gaze and give him a friendly hip-bump. "Yeah, sure. I spend my whole day trying *not* to run into you."

"I thought so," he says, lips twitching. "So check it out: I caught up to the rest of the class in 'Love and Sexuality' so now I have Thursday lunch free again and I was thinking that if you're not doing anything and nobody stole our spot then . . . ?" He flicks back his hair and gives me a killer smile. "Cheetos, pretzels or potato chips. Your choice, my treat. What do you say?"

"Sounds like a celebration to me," I say, leaning back against my locker and returning his smile. "That's really great, Eli. And Cheetos will definitely work."

The bell rings.

"Damn," he says, glancing down the hall and giving me a regretful look. "I have to go. My homeroom's on the other side of the building." He falls back a step, head cocked and holding my gaze. "So I'll see you at lunch, then."

"Same time, same place," I say, wondering if my cheeks are as warm as they feel. "Bye."

"Bye," he says with a sudden grin, and takes off down the hall.

Yeah, two *very* different lives.

| | |

I check my phone between classes, find a text from Nadia and read it while walking down the hall. *"What?"* I say, astonished, and read it again.

Me and Brett, you and Shane, Sr prom Sat night. S has 2 tickets. Say yes!

"That's the day after *tomorrow*," I say, stopping dead in the flow of students. "What is she, insane? I don't have anything to wear to a prom! And who the hell is Shane?" I try to remember who Brett hangs out with besides Justin and can name all but the quiet soccer guy with the hair in his eyes and the big nose. Is that Shane? If it is, I had coed gym with him last year and he blocked a volleyball that was headed straight for my face. And blushed when I said thanks.

Nadia texts again. *Row? Are you there? PLEASE?*

I have nothing to wear, I text back.

You can wear my red dress, she texts back. *PLEASE?*

Oh. Her red dress is hot.

Meet me by the upstairs girls room, I text, and when I get there she's waiting, practically dancing with excitement, and all of a sudden I cannot *believe* how much I've missed this, how easy and how good it feels to slip right back into BFF mode the way we used to be.

"Oh my God, Rowan, please say yes," she burbles, seizing me by the arm. "You don't have to worry about anything, you can wear my red gown and—"

"I don't have any shoes—"

"You can wear mine."

"My feet are bigger than yours. I'm a nine."

"Shit," she mutters, chewing her bottom lip, and then brightens. "My mother's a nine. She'll have something hot we can borrow. Rowan, please say yes."

"Which one is Shane?" I ask.

"Oh, he's really nice," she says quickly. "You'd know him if you saw him: He plays soccer—"

"Big nose, hair in his eyes?" I finish to her enthusiastic nod. "Yeah, okay, but what's with the emergency date? Does he even know you're doing this?"

"Of *course* he knows," she says, laughing. "He's been going out with that girl Becca but she just had to have her tonsils out like, yesterday and—"

"Wait," I say, holding up a hand. "Becca with the ginormous boobs who got suspended for kicking in that girl's windshield?"

"Yeah, but that was last year and it was her cousin messing with her boyfriend. Put it out of your mind, Row. Her throat's a mess and she knows he's stuck with the tickets and the tux and the limo and all—"

"And you know this *how?*" I say, cocking an eyebrow.

"God, why are you always so suspicious? Don't you *want* to go?" She gazes up at me, pleading. "Please? You don't have to sleep with him; it would just be a friend thing. A good deed. Please? Then we could all sit together and have a blast."

Hmm, go to the senior prom in a killer dress with my best friend and a cute guy I hardly know instead of sitting in the house all night with my parents. Wow, what a dilemma. "Okay," I say, and am rewarded with a shriek of delight, a violent hug and the sight of her whirling and darting off as the first late bell rings, presumably to text Brett to text Shane and tell him that he *is* going to the prom with a complete stranger.

Right.

Now all I have to do is call my parents, ask if I can go, corner Eva and ask if I can get off work a little early Saturday afternoon, figure out what to do with my hair, somehow get to Nadia's for the dress and the phantom shoes, find jewelry . . .

And tell Eli.

| | |

I call my mother at the library between third and fourth period.

"You're supposed to be grounded," she says in a low, distracted voice when she comes to the phone. "And we don't even know this boy."

"Mom, c'mon, I've been home for like, weeks and I've been good, too," I say, pacing the hallway outside the history room. "You know I have. And this is the senior prom. Not very many sophomores get asked to go. It's kind of a big deal. And Shane's really nice." *I think.* "He plays soccer." *So what?* "Please?"

"You don't have anything to wear," she says, and then off to the side, "I need your library card, please." And to me, "Rowan, this is a really bad time. Let me——"

"Mom, please just say yes so I can tell them," I interrupt in a rush. "Time is running out. He bought the tickets and everything and he needs an answer because if not he's gonna be out like, five hundred dollars." Actually, I have no idea what it costs. Maybe I should have said a thousand. "And it's not gonna cost me anything, Mom. Please?"

"Thank you and have a nice day," she says, and then to me, "We don't even know this boy and——"

"Why are you so stuck on that? You wouldn't know anybody who asked me to go until tomorrow, anyway. And besides, he already has a girlfriend with her tonsils out and we're only going as friends," I say, giving it everything I've got. "Please? It's just this one time. I've never been to a prom . . ."

"You're not staying out all night," she says, and that's when I know I've got her. "I'm serious, Rowan. You're only sixteen and——"

"Oh, thank you!" I crow, and spotting Nadia coming down the hall, I give her a triumphant wave. "And no, I know, we won't. Thank you, Mom. Let me go so I can tell him. Yay!" I hear her laughing, rueful good-bye and, hanging up, grab Nadia, who's clutching my arm. "I can go!"

And as she's shrieking Shane and Brett saunter up and it's funny that it's so easy for me to say hi to Shane and talk and laugh with him. Maybe it's because I know we don't like each other that way—an image of Eli flashes through my mind—and so it takes all the pressure off and I can relax.

"Glad you can go," Shane says, and suddenly his nose looks fine in his long, thin face and when he shakes his hair back I notice his eyes are hazel. "You were in my gym class last year, right?"

"Volleyball," I say mournfully, and when he laughs I do, too, because something about the sound of it cracks me up.

Yes, I think, *this is going to be a blast.*

| | |

Eli is already sitting on the grass in our spot out front when I get there, which surprises me because I pretty much jogged the whole way.

"I'm impressed," I say breathlessly, sitting down beside him and eyeing the feast spread out before us. "Grape juice, too. I like that."

"Glad you approve," he says with a grin, and hands me a bag of Cheetos. "I was going for kind of a wine-and-cheese thing, so . . ."

"Oh, you're a funny guy," I say, laughing even though I'm starting to feel guilty about the prom, which is stupid, I know, because it's not like Eli and I are going out or anything. Hell, for all I know he still has a girlfriend back in Texas waiting for him.

That thought makes me queasy.

"A toast," he says, handing me a cold bottle of juice and waiting until I twist open the top. "To, uh, new beginnings."

"To new beginnings," I say, smiling and clinking my bottle to his. I take a sip of the cool, sweet juice, rip open the bag of Cheetos, and pop one in my mouth. "Excellent. You can treat me to vending-machine lunches anytime." And then, because I really can't take the suspense anymore, I say ever so craftily, "Unless, of course, your girlfriend back in Texas would have a problem with it."

"Who?" he says with a frown, tearing open his Cheetos. "I don't have a girlfriend in Texas. Where'd you get that?"

"No clue," I say, inwardly rejoicing. "Could have been anywhere. People gossip so bad here. So uh, you don't?"

"No, nobody serious since Crystal but that was a while ago. We were together for maybe six months when my father died and she dumped me a month later because—get this—I never wanted to do anything and I wasn't any fun anymore." He snorts and gives me a wry, sideways look. "Nice, huh?"

"That must have hurt."

He shrugs. "Yeah, I guess. I don't know. There was a lot more important stuff going on back then than her bailing." He chooses a crunchy orange puff and pops it into his mouth. "I mean when you lose your dad, everything else seems pretty insignificant." He studies the bag, sets it aside and takes a long swig of grape juice. "So anyhow . . ."

Right. I take a deep breath and say, "So are you going to the senior prom?"

"Who, me? With who?" he says, giving me an amused look. "I don't know anybody out here."

Hunh. "You know *me*," I say, giving him a mock-offended look.

"Yeah, *now*," he says with a teasing nudge. "Too bad I didn't know you while they were still selling tickets. They've been sold out for like, a month. I already checked."

Well, it's now or never. "I'm going."

He blinks in surprise. "To the *senior* prom?" he says after a long moment, and it might be my imagination but I swear he just shifted away from me a little.

"Yeah, with my friend Nadia, her boyfriend and his friend, because his girlfriend just had her tonsils out and can't go and he already bought the tickets, so . . ." I shrug, smiling like it's no big deal. "I just thought that if you were going then maybe I'd see you there and we could dance or something." *Dance? Where did that come from?*

"And this guy's girlfriend is okay with him taking another girl to the prom?" he says, leaning back and cocking a skeptical eyebrow. "Come on . . . Has she ever *seen* you?"

I stare at him, puzzled. "What? I don't know, why?"

"I bet she hasn't," he says in a satisfied voice, nodding like he's got it all figured out. "I'm telling you, if she saw how hot you are, she'd kick his ass for even suggesting it. That boy wouldn't make it three feet out the door on prom night."

His tone is teasing but the warmth in his dark gaze is real and a delicious, shimmering ribbon of happiness unfurls inside of me. "Well, thank you but . . ." I stop and shake my head, at a loss. Am I blushing? I think so. I glance down at my Cheetos, then back up to find him still watching me. "What?"

"Nothing," he says softly, mouth curving in a small smile. "So where's this thing happening, anyway?"

"Um, at the Hilton right in town," I say, resisting the urge to fan the heat from my cheeks. "I haven't told Nadia and them yet but I have to be home by like, midnight. No all-nighters for me." I shrug. "My parents are a little overprotective. Especially my father."

"Yeah, well, who could blame him," Eli says, raising the bag of Cheetos up to his mouth and tipping the rest in. "Oh shit," he says in a muffled voice, eyeing the cascade of orange crumbs tumbling down the front of his shirt in dismay.

"Nice," I say with a snort of laughter, and, reaching over, brush my hand once, twice, three times lightly across the contours of his chest, meaning to sweep the crumbs away but instead sending them all right down into his lap. "Okay . . . hmm. This is gonna be a problem." I glance up into his face, catch the silent laughter in his eyes and crack up. "Brat. Do it yourself."

The bell rings as he stands to brush himself off, so we quickly gather the garbage and then he reaches down, offering me a hand up. I take it, skin tingling as his fingers close around mine, and then I'm standing beside him so close I can smell the sun on his skin, so close the breeze nudges a strand of his sleek, silky hair across my cheek.

"Oh yeah," he murmurs, his gaze searching my face. "She is gonna beat his ass for a week once she gets a look at you." He releases my hand, fingers lingering, and ambles back a few steps. "So would you have gone? To the prom with me, I mean?"

"As a friend?" I tease, sauntering after him.

"Hell no," he says, flicking back his hair and giving me a slow, dangerous, pirate smile.

Oh God, my heart. "Well, what do *you* think?" It comes out husky, almost a whisper.

He studies my face a moment and his smile widens. "I think I should have asked."

The warning bell rings and the moment is over but the glow lasts all day.

| | |

Later at work, I tell Eva about the prom and ask if I can leave early Saturday afternoon.

"You're leaving me in the lurch, you know," she grumbles, looking pointedly at all the bundles of clothes stuffed under the counter waiting to be pinned. Her allergies are finally easing; her eyes are huge and bright again behind her glasses, and her drippy nose has thankfully dried up. Is it a coincidence that the less gross she gets, the more business comes in? "And on our busiest day."

"I know, I'm sorry," I say cheerfully, grabbing and unrolling the first bundle. Two suits, no vests. "It's only this one time and I really appreciate it." I search the pockets, every last one of them, and come up clean. "Oh, and guess what? My father said he would paint the dining room tomorrow."

"Really?" she says, and it's the way she says it, the way her voice lilts and her eyes light up, that tells me she understands exactly how big a move this is, and it makes me want to walk right over and hug her. "That's wonderful news, Rowan."

"I know, isn't it?" I say, beaming and pinning a tag on the waistband of the suit pants. "I guess the antidepressant is really making a difference."

"That is truly remarkable," Eva says, smiling back at me. "Which one is he taking, if you don't mind me asking?"

I tell her and am totally unprepared for the odd expression that crosses her face. "What?"

"Nothing," she says thoughtfully. "It's just that . . . well, I was on the same drug after my husband passed and I distinctly remember the doctor saying that it could take four to six weeks before the medication actually kicked in and I would feel a difference." She cocks her head. "How long has he been on it?"

"I don't know," I say, trying to think. "Maybe like, three weeks? Not more than that." My good mood fades slightly. "Why?"

"Hmm." She catches sight of my face and immediately rallies. "Well, no matter. They say it's different for everyone and whatever the reason, it's just wonderful that he's trying to pick himself up and go on. Give him my best regards. Oh, and you know what?" Smiling, she bustles over to my counter, opens the register and pulls out a ten-dollar bill. "I'm in the mood for ice cream. If I buy, will you run over and get it?"

"Sure," I say, surprised at the sudden switch. "What kind do you want?"

And it isn't until I'm trotting back from the ice cream depot with two cones, hers mint chocolate chip and mine coconut, that I wonder if this ice cream treat was just a diversion—and if so, from what?

And even stranger, why?

I think about that a minute, then snort at my own wild suspicions, decide I've been hanging around cops too long and take a hearty lick of my ice-cream cone.

To new beginnings.

Chapter 18

The weather's gorgeous so I walk home after work. My spirits are high and even though I try to tone them down some, I'm still in a pretty decent mood over dinner. I talk and laugh a little too much though, I guess, because halfway through my father mumbles, "I'm going into the living room," and leaves without taking his burrito with him.

"Sorry," I say, although there's no denying we can breathe a little easier without the grim weight of his depression hanging over us. It's a terrible thought, one I feel guilty for having and would rather die than ever admit aloud, but it's still true.

And we're right in the middle of splitting the last bit of black bean salsa between us when there's a knock on the sunporch door. My mother gives me a curious look and says, "Are you expecting somebody?"

"No," I say, rising and heading for the porch because it could be Nadia, or even better, it could be Eli, although I've never actually told him where I live. "Coming."

I open the door and peer through the screen to find Lieutenant Walters waiting outside and my smile dies. "Oh."

"Hello, Rowan," he says, shifting in place. "Is your father here?"

"Uh . . ." I glance over my shoulder, at a loss. What am I

supposed to do? He's here of course, and the lieutenant knows it because his Blazer is sitting there big as life in the driveway, but he's also slumped in the living room in the dark, wearing sweats, sporting three-day stubble and his grubby old house moccasins. "Well . . ."

"Rowan, who is it?" my mother says, coming up alongside of me. "Oh, hello, Arnold," she says, giving me a look and moving past me to open the screen door. "Come on in. What brings you here?"

"Thank you, Rachel," he says, stepping into the porch, which immediately shrinks down to the size of a shoe box and is suddenly way too uncomfortable. "Is Nick here?"

"Yes, he is, but . . ." She hesitates. "Can I ask what it's about? I'm not trying to interfere, Arnold, honestly, but I don't know if he can take any more bad news right now."

And then it hits me. Of course, the internal investigation.

"And I won't give him any," he says, and answers her questioning look with a reassuring smile. "May I speak with him?"

My mother searches his face, takes a deep breath and says, "Certainly, follow me. I'll put on some coffee."

"Excuse me," he says because I'm standing right in the way.

"Oh, sorry." I step to the left at the exact same time he does, then step to the right as he does again and am so embarrassed I can't even see.

"Stop," he says, holding out a hand so I don't move and stepping around me. It might be my imagination but I swear there was a momentary flash of humor in his eyes that totally belied the stern expression on his face.

"Impossible," I mutter, and, scooping Stripe up off the windowsill, cuddle him close and go back into the kitchen, where my mother is making a fresh pot of coffee. Her expression is fixedly calm but her hands are trembling slightly and I sidle up next to her at the counter. I can hear the low murmur of voices from the living room but not what they're saying and suddenly I'm really, really scared. "He better not hurt Daddy," I whisper fiercely, hugging

Stripe so tight he squirms free and jumps to the floor. "I'm serious, Mom. We should be in there with him."

"Arnold isn't going to hurt him," she whispers back, but she doesn't sound as sure as I want her to be and, biting her lip, glances over at the entrance to the shadowy living room.

"You don't know him like I do," I whisper darkly, and then shut up fast as he appears in the doorway.

"Almost ready," my mother says in a high, bright voice that betrays the extent of her nerves. "Do you take cream and sugar, Arnold?"

"Thank you anyway, Rachel, but I'm afraid I can't stay," he says, and smiles, although his gaze is grave. "I have to get back to head-quarters. I just wanted to deliver the good news in person." He looks shell-shocked though and more than a little distressed, and for some reason that scares me more than anything.

"What is it?" I say, knees quivering.

He meets my anxious gaze, clears his throat and says, "Well, I'm sure your father will want to tell you the details but he's been cleared of any misconduct. The investigation is closed and—"

"Oh, thank God," my mother breathes, tears in her eyes. "His record?"

"There are no charges being brought, so there's nothing to tar-nish his record. The department will be issuing a formal press re-lease tomorrow announcing the result of the investigation. It will also go out to all the local media outlets."

It's all I can do not to cry.

"So, like I told him"—the lieutenant exhales and shifts toward the door—"whenever he's up to it we're ready to have him back. The place isn't the same without him." He glances toward the silent liv-ing room and then back at us, the concern in his gaze plain to see. "Well, if you have any questions or I can help in any way, feel free to give me a call." He raises his voice. "Bye, Nick."

"Bye," my father says dully from the next room after a long mo-ment. "Thanks, Arnie."

"I'll walk you to the door," my mother says, and together she and the lieutenant move into the porch and then outside.

Relief hits me like a wave and I break for the living room. "Dad, it's done! You're clear! Oh thank you, God. It's over." I drop to my knees beside his recliner and beam up into his face. "It's finally over."

"Is it?" he says, passing a trembling hand over his damp eyes.

"Well yeah," I say, and draw back, puzzled. "Tomorrow they're announcing that you've been cleared and he said you've been totally reinstated and can go back to work whenever you're ready. Dad"—I lean in close and touch his arm—"this is *good news*. Come on."

He shakes his head, avoiding my gaze, and a tear slips down his cheek.

"What?" I say, tightening my grip on his arm. "Dad, please. What is it? I mean, I thought you'd be happy, I thought that this was why you got depressed in the first place but now it's over so why . . ." I stop, at a loss. "What *is* it?"

Another tear slides down his cheek and disappears into the salt-and-pepper stubble along his jaw. "Too much pain," he finally whispers, turning his face away. "Please, Row, just let me sit here alone for a while. Please."

I kneel there gazing at him, bitter disappointment clogging my throat, and then in a voice almost as hopeless as his, say, "God, Dad, what's happening to us?" and he says, "I don't know, Rowie. I don't know." He starts crying in earnest and so do I, and I reach up for him right as he's reaching out for me and this is how my mother finds us.

Clinging, crying and together.

Chapter 19

I tiptoe past the bedroom and then barrel down the stairs the next morning to find my father up, dressed in jeans and an old work shirt and spreading a drop cloth over half of the dining room floor. All the furniture has been moved to the other side of the room—when did he do that?—and the drapes taken down, flooding the room with light. "Whoa," I say, wide-eyed. "Hey, Dad." My heart lifts with hope. "You're really painting today?"

"Well, I'm going to try," he says, and although his gaze is still hollow there's a new air of calm about him, of purpose even, like last night *did* make a difference, like he's made up his mind to do it and so he will, just like normal. "First, I have to find a way to keep Stripe out of here or there'll be little green cat footprints all over the house."

I nod, smiling, willing to agree with anything he says right about now.

"Oh, and do me a favor: I left a bag with uniform pants and a shirt on the kitchen table. Could you drop them off at the cleaner's on the way to the bus stop?" He kneels in front of the paint can and starts gently prying the lid up with a screwdriver. "I'd appreciate it."

"Okay, then I'd better get moving." I glance at my watch and hesitate, almost afraid to say the words. "Are you going back to work already?"

"No, not yet, so I don't need them back any time soon. Make them for next week," he says in a muffled voice, lifting the paint can lid and carefully setting it down on the drop cloth. "I'll find the rest of them later and send them in with you tomorrow." He glances back at me. "Thanks, Row."

"No problem," I say, and the words are so easy, so casual and exquisitely normal, that they feel almost too good to be true.

I run the bag of uniforms into the cleaner's and leave them with Helga, the morning clerk, who looks like she'd rather be anywhere but there, telling her no rush and to put them for next week, and then jog the last block to the bus stop. The bus lumbers up less than five minutes later; the driver and I studiously ignore each other, the only term in our unspoken truce, and I get a seat in the middle to myself.

Smooth.

Nadia meets me in the courtyard with a huge, bulging Nordstrom's shopping bag. "I put everything you're going to need in there for tomorrow." She burbles out the rest of the plans as the bell rings and we make our way down the hall toward the lockers. "And, Rowie, Brett got us a room in the hotel so—"

I make a face. "I have to be home by midnight."

"What?" she screeches. "Rowan, it's the *senior prom!* Oh my God, the party doesn't even really *start* until then!"

"Yeah, well, that's probably the point," I say dryly. "But it was the only way they'd say yes, so . . ." I shrug, resigned. "The limo can drop me off or I can call my mother or something."

She bites her lip, thinking fast. "Okay, well, don't tell Shane. Hopefully he'll be so drunk by then that he won't even notice you're gone."

"Why should he care, if we're just going as friends?" I say as a sneaking suspicion unfurls itself in my mind, and when she flushes and looks away, it's confirmed. "Oh my God, you told me it was *just friends* and—"

"It is but he thinks you're hot, okay?" she says quickly. "He told Brett that he got his own room for uh, you guys afterward." She catches the look on my face, holds up her hand and grins. "I know, I know, I told Brett to tell him that it wasn't going to happen but . . ." She shrugs. "You know guys: Where there's life, there's hope."

And that cracks me up. "Yeah, well, thanks for the warning."

We spend the final moments before the bell rings laughing, joking and trying to stuff the shopping bag full of prom clothes into my locker. It isn't easy but somehow we make it fit just long enough for me to slam and lock the door.

"Done," she says, satisfied.

| | | |

When I get to work, Eva makes me take the balled-up red prom dress out of the bag so Terence can press it for me.

"You don't want to look like a ragamuffin," she says, giving the vivid scarlet material a narrow look. "Hmm, not much to it. Are you sure—"

"It stretches," I say quickly, hoping it does.

Terence takes it from her, gives me a twinkling look and hangs it carefully by his press. He starts singing Marvin Gaye's "After the Dance" under his breath.

"I can hear you, you know," I say, lips twitching. "And you've got it all wrong. He's just a friend." *I like someone else,* I add silently. *A lot.*

"Mmm-hmm," Terence says, and goes on singing.

Ten minutes later my mother calls, sounding harried, says they're in the middle of painting and asks if I'd mind walking home after work.

And I don't mind at all because it's a gorgeous day and Eva, in a fit of uncharacteristic generosity, lets me go a half hour early so I can get home while it's still light. I hook my finger in the hanger loop, drape the red dress, beautifully pressed and glowing beneath the plastic dry-cleaning bag, over my shoulder, hoist the shopping bag, and head out.

| | |

I all but skip up the front lawn, excited about tomorrow, excited about the dining room and the simple fact that life is looking up again. Not that I expect miracles, I tell myself, opening the porch door and slipping inside. But every step forward is a good one.

I can hear music playing softly inside and smell the fresh paint. Feeling very merry, I hang the dress, pry off my shoes, set down the Nordstrom bag and pad in, wanting to surprise them.

I peek into the dining room. Two walls are painted, two are not, and the can, paint tray and brushes are still set on newspaper.

He must be taking a break.

I hear murmuring coming from the living room and peek around the doorway. See my father curled up on his side on the couch, his head on my mother's lap. She's stroking his forehead, his hair, his temple; her iPod is docked and their wedding song—Aaron Neville's "You Send Me"—is playing softly from the speakers.

My first thought is an embarrassed *Oh God, what did I walk in on?* because they've always been affectionate and I've come around corners and found them kissing before but then the scene registers and—

"It's going to be all right, Nicky," my mother says softly, gazing down at him. "You're *not* a failure. Don't even think like that. I'll finish painting after supper. It'll be fine." She leans over and kisses his temple. "I know you feel like the medication's taking forever to work but you *did* have energy this morning and that's a great first step. It'll happen, I promise. We'll make it through. This isn't going to last forever. It's just for now."

"How do you know?" my father says dully. "What if it *does* last, Rachel? What if the medication never works and I'm like this forever, and you have to do everything because I'm useless?"

A chill ripples through me.

"Honey, it's only two walls," my mother says helplessly. "I don't mind finishing."

"You weren't supposed to have to do *any* of it. You're carrying a big enough load as it is," my father says, turning his face away from her. "But now I just put another burden on you." He covers his eyes, voice cracking. "I'm dragging you down. I'm no good anymore. You can't count on me. You should leave me and go find somebody who can—"

Divorce? *My* parents? I put a hand against the wall, woozy.

"No," my mother says sharply, pulling back and glaring down at him in astonished outrage. "Stop it, Nicky! Oh my God, don't you *dare* talk like that to me!" She grabs his forehead, leans over and kisses it again, hard this time, like she's trying to push the kiss right into his mind. "I love *you*. My God, you and Rowie are my life, we're a *family* and I am *not* walking away from that!" She jiggles his arm. "Do you hear me? I'm not, Nicky. I *love* you."

He nods, tears slipping out from beneath the hand covering his eyes. "I'm so sorry. I really am."

"Honey . . ." She gazes down at him, helpless, and for the first time I see the frustration I know so well and feel so guilty about on *her* face, and a cold wash of fear floods my veins because I really thought she had it all under control, that she knew something more than I did about helping him, maybe even that he was different in private with her, better and not worse, but now . . .

"Come on, sit up," my mother says gently, petting his forehead. "Rowan's gonna be home soon and she's so excited about this prom. Come on."

I fall back a step before they see me, knees wobbling, and then another until I hit the sun porch door, my heart thundering in my ears. Fumble it open and slam it again, call out a strangled, "I'm home," and seizing the Nordstrom bag, go right up to my room, unable to look at either one of them for fear of giving myself away.

But I needn't have worried as by the time I get ahold of myself and come back downstairs my father is out in the wood shop and my mother painting the dining room, and nobody but me seems to notice that we're all home tonight but none of us are really here.

Never deprive someone of hope; it may be all they have.
—H. Jackson Brown Jr.

Chapter 20

My father is up again on Saturday morning, sitting at the table drinking coffee and gazing out the window.

"Hey, Dad," I say, pouring myself a quick cup because I got up late and really have to run to make it to work by eight.

"Hey, Row," he says, looking over. "So I hear you have a prom tonight."

"Yeah," I say, searching his face, noting the effort behind his simple question.

He nods. "When your mother told me, my first thought was that you were going with Eli but then she said no, his name was Sean."

"Shane," I say. "And we're just friends."

He sets his cup on the placemat. "Is Eli going?"

"No," I say, pouring half-and-half in my cup and stirring it. "He didn't get a ticket in time."

"Oh. That's too bad." He mulls a moment. "You know, I called him once, right after the video aired, just to see how he was doing. Caught him at a really low moment, poor guy." He sighs. "He's got a lot of weight on his shoulders for someone so young. He could have used a nice night out with a pretty girl."

"What kind of weight?" I say, and take a sip of coffee, watching him over the rim.

My father runs a hand over his stubbly chin. "His mother. The dog. His future. Graduating. Moving to a strange place. Catching flak because of that video. Feeling like he should be there for Sammy's mother because she's falling apart. Losing his dad . . ."

"But that was over a year ago." And then I think of Eva still teary about her son after forty years and of my own grandparents, my father's parents gone for two years, and—

"It's too much pain," my father says, shaking his head.

Great. Somehow I've knocked whatever good mood he had right out of him and that leaves me both irritated that it's still so easy, that good moods have somehow become rare and fragile things easily crushed by normal life, and mad at myself for being such a jerk. "I'm sorry."

"I worry about him," my father says quietly, looking back out the window. "I hope he's all right."

"He is. We had lunch together Thursday and he was fine, so don't worry anymore, okay?" I dump the rest of the coffee, set the cup in the sink and force a bright smile. "I'm getting off of work early to get ready for tonight. You have to take a picture with me when I'm dressed. It'll be a new tradition."

"We'll see," he says without looking at me.

"Okay, well, I really have to go or I'm gonna be late." I hesitate, then lean over and give him a hug and a quick kiss on the temple. "You good?"

He nods again, head bent, and a tear splashes down onto his hand.

And there it is, that flash of impatience mixed with helplessness creating the dilemma that twists me up inside: Stay or go? If I stay I embarrass him, will be late for work, feel like I'm coddling and encouraging him, but if I go I'm disregarding his pain, ignoring it, saying, *Look, I know you're sad but life goes on,* and it makes me feel cold and uncaring and guilty. "Okay, well," I say, backing up a step, and as I turn to leave I spot another bag of uniforms. "You want me to take these in and get them cleaned, too?"

He clears his throat. "Yes, and there's a tie in there, too. Make them for today."

"Okay," I say, and, relieved, grab the purse and the bag. "Oh, but I made the other one for next week."

"That's all right. I just want some clean uniforms hanging in my closet again." This time he does glance up at me, his eyes dark and wet. "I want them there waiting for me when I'm ready." He looks away, toys with the place mat. "You have a good day."

"I will, you too," I say, and hope it doesn't sound as hollow as it feels.

Chapter 21

The best part about a crazy day like this is that it keeps me running and doesn't leave me time to think about anything but dry cleaning.

I leave work at four, exhausted, excited, with Eva's good wishes ringing in my ears, and am halfway across the parking lot before I realize that I forgot my father's uniforms and have to run all the way back to get them. Think briefly about checking on the ones due for next week but decide this batch is heavy and awkward enough, slippery in its plastic bag and a real pain in the ass to jog all the way home with since I have to keep stopping and making sure I haven't lost his tie.

I burst into the house to find my mother putting new batteries in the camera and my father sitting at the kitchen table drinking coffee. He's wearing jeans and a sport shirt, and he's shaved.

"What time is the limo coming?" my mother calls as I zoom through and up the stairs.

"Wait, I'll be back after I take a shower," I yell, hanging the uniforms on my parents' bedroom door and ripping my clothes off as I head for the bathroom.

By the time I'm done my skin is glowing from the heat and my fingers are pruny but I'm soft, shaved and smooth. I bundle my hair in a towel, throw on my bathrobe and barrel back down the stairs.

"Whew," I say, fanning myself and grabbing a bottled water. "The cleaner's was nuts today." I take a sip and lean back against the counter, surveying my parents. "You guys look nice." My father looks almost normal, and my mother's wearing one of her work outfits, navy blue slacks with a fitted fuchsia pullover.

"Thank you," she says with a smile. "I didn't have time to touch up my roots, though." She runs a self-conscious hand over her shiny brown hair. "I was hoping they wouldn't show in the pictures but now I don't know." She sighs. "I usually have some dye in stock but the last time I stopped at the drugstore all the chestnut brown was gone! I thought about using another color but . . ." She glances at my father, waiting for his automatic protest, because he's always loved her hair that color, says it's exactly the same shade as when they first met and makes her eyes look just as pretty as a fawn's.

He shifts in the chair but doesn't say anything and only I see the disappointment cross her face.

"No one's gonna notice, Mom," I say, and, reaching out, play-fully fluff her hair. "It looks great. I don't know what I'm gonna do with mine yet." I shrug. "Probably just curl it or something. I'll save the updo for my own prom, if I even go."

My mother takes the bait, never guessing it was a deliberate diversion, and gives me the rules while I nod and drink my water—yes, I'll be home when it's over; no, no drinking; yes, I'll have my phone with me if something goes wrong and I need a ride; no, no staying out all night, and on and on.

My father doesn't say anything, just sits and listens, eyes down-cast.

And then it's time to run and do my makeup, my hair—long, tousled curls sprayed to within an inch of their lives—and put on a strapless bra and stockings. I slither into Nadia's red gown, some-how manage to zip it up and look in the mirror.

I gaze wide-eyed at my reflection for a moment and burst out laughing. "Oh my God, they're never going to let me out of the house in this!"

It's a bombshell dress, hot, sleek and fitted, with a strapless sweetheart bodice, shirred waist and mermaid bottom. I turn and look over my shoulder to check out my butt.

"Oh boy," I say weakly, eyeing the curves. "Who knew?"

I reach back into the Nordstrom bag and pull out a clutch purse and Nadia's mother's shoes, which are gorgeous, scarlet, thin-strapped stilettos that shoot me up another four inches. Next, a black and red embroidered silk wrap in case it gets chilly, and underneath all of that is a pair of huge, thin gold hoop earrings and matching bangle bracelets.

The only thing missing is a necklace, but as I stand there ogling myself, knowing I'll probably never look this hot again, I decide I don't even need one.

"Rowan? The limo just pulled up out front and there's a boy in a tux coming to the door," my mother calls excitedly. "Are you almost ready?"

"Yes," I say, spraying on a sultry, floral musk cologne and tossing my makeup, brush, phone and money into the clutch. "Coming." I take one last look at myself, tweeze a small rogue clump of black mascara from the edge of an eyelash, smooth on lip gloss—God, if only I was going with Eli tonight—and, taking a deep breath, square my shoulders and walk slowly out of my room and down the stairs to the foyer.

"—home right after it's over," my mother is telling Shane when she turns and sees me. Her eyes widen, her jaw drops, and she looks like she doesn't know whether to laugh or cry. Shane reaches around her to give me an enthusiastic high five. "Hot."

"Thank you," I say, trying not to laugh.

"You look beautiful, Rowie," my father says gruffly, his gaze soft with a mixture of love, sorrow and pride, with a look that says, *I know you have to grow up but God, I don't want you to,* and brings an answering rush of tears to my eyes.

"Thank you, Daddy," I say, and, blinking hard, turn to my mother, who gives me a *We'll talk about that dress later* look and then hugs me and arranges us all for pictures.

It takes effort but my father rallies and participates, and in an off moment while my mother is talking to Shane, he slides his arm around me almost tentatively, as if he's afraid I'll slap it away or something, and murmurs, "Remember when you were little and you'd come out to the wood shop and sing me that song over and over so I could learn it, too?"

And I laugh and say, "Wow, I haven't thought about that in ages. What song? I don't remember."

"I do," he says, and sings me a soft verse of "Butterfly Fly Away."

It knocks the wind out of me because yes, now I *do* remember, but I never thought he would.

"Those were good days," he says quietly, looking down at me.

"Yes, they were," I whisper, and smile not for the camera but for him, for me and for us, because at this moment I truly believe we are fine, that everything is going to be all right and we really are going to make it.

Chapter 22

Shane gives me a bracelet corsage—gold wire, red ribbon and a fabulous white orchid—but I forget all about his boutonniere until we pick up Nadia, gorgeous in sapphire blue, and Brett, and Nadia hands me a small florist box.

"Shane's boutonniere," she says with a grin. "Never say I don't have your back, girl."

"I won't." I take the flower from the box and try to pin it on his lapel, jabbing him when the limo driver makes a turn. "Sorry," I say, grimacing, and make sure it works the second time.

"No problem," he says, glancing down at it and nodding. "You do nice work."

And it hits me as funny and a little sad, too, that this is my first formal dance, that I look better than I ever have before and that I'm here with someone I only like as a friend.

"Woo-hoo," Nadia calls, bouncing in the cushy seat and beaming as the limo pulls up to the Hilton. "Check it out, people. We have *arrived!*"

Her enthusiasm is catching and suddenly it doesn't matter that this isn't going to be the most romantic night of my life, because the driver is opening our door and I can hear the Black Eyed Peas' "I Gotta Feeling" echoing out of the speakers.

The driver treats us like royalty, helping us out of the car, and even though there's no red carpet there are velvet ropes holding back a decent-sized crowd of parents and underclassmen who smile and stare, take pictures and video. The fading light is tinged golden, the dusky sky smudged pink, and the breeze teases our hair, ruffles our gowns.

It's amazing.

Shane flicks the hair from his eyes and, smiling, offers me his arm. "Ready?"

"Absolutely," I say, sliding my hand through the crook of his elbow and turning toward the doors.

We've taken maybe two steps when Shane stops dead and says, "Oh shit, wait—" and suddenly there's a short girl in a pink gown planted in front of me, a girl with cold fury in her narrowed eyes and an astonishing eight inches of naked cleavage bulging out of her neckline.

"Get the fuck away from him, bitch!" she croaks, and body-checks me so hard my hand is ripped from Shane's arm and I fly backward into the limo driver.

All hell breaks loose. The driver catches me and I hang there stunned. The sounds of *Tonight's gonna be a good night,* gasps from the crowd and Nadia's shrill *"Oh my God, Rowan!"* blend with the strange roaring in my ears. The principal and one of the teachers run toward us from the edge of the crowd. The driver carefully sets me back on my feet. Nadia gazes at me with huge, stricken eyes. My chest aches where Becca's shoulder hit, because of *course* it's her, and of course it was *never* all right that Shane went to prom without her. And as the teacher picks up my clutch bag and hands it back, asking if I'm all right, and some idiot in the crowd chants, *"Fight, fight!"* I take a deep, shaky breath and, burning with embarrassment, turn and look straight into Eli's dark, astonished gaze.

Chapter 23

The sight of him standing there behind the velvet rope in jeans and a T-shirt, Daisy sitting by his side, wrenches something open deep inside of me and to my horror, tears fill my eyes.

"Rowan," Nadia calls from behind me.

"Rowan?" the teacher says.

"Yo, bitch," Becca croaks furiously. "Get your skanky ass away from my boyfriend and—"

"Easy," the principal says, warning her.

"You okay?" Eli says, searching my face.

I nod, not trusting myself to speak.

Daisy rises, ears up and tail wagging, and gives me an expectant look.

"Rowan, we'd like to try to figure this out," the teacher says from behind me.

"Rowan, come *on*," Nadia calls.

Eli's gaze flickers past me to Shane, who now has Becca clinging to his arm and is looking very uncomfortable, and then back to me. "This doesn't look good."

"No, I know," I say in a husky voice, feeling like a fool.

"I thought she'd be kicking *his* ass, not yours."

"Major miscalculation," I say, because even though my heart is still pounding and my adrenaline high, my sense of the absurd has also kicked in.

"Yeah, hmm." Eli nods, thoughtful, and strokes the little black soul patch under his bottom lip. "So if there's no real reason to stick around, unless you plan on fighting her for him——"

I snort. "Not hardly."

"——then how about I buy you a cup of coffee instead?"

"Rowan, come *on*," Nadia yells. "What're you doing?"

"Rowan?" the teacher says, and all around us people are babbling, recording this whole mess with their iPhones, gossiping, staring, and in the background is the pulsing reminder that tonight is gonna be a good night.

"That'll work," I say, and, putting a hand on his arm for balance, lean over and pry off Nadia's mother's stilettos. "Okay, I'm ready."

Funny how nothing can turn into something when you least expect it.

Chapter 24

"So I guess we're not going to Dunkin' Donuts," I say as he leads me off down a ramshackle side street and pauses in front of a cloudy glass door with an old, faded cup of coffee painted on it. "What is this place?"

"You've never been here?" he says in amazement, and then goes on to tell me that not only do they have the best coffee in town but the atmosphere kicks ass, too. "Come on, you'll see." He opens the door and ushers me through. "After you."

The place is dark, cozy, delicious with the scent of ground beans and, from what I can see, empty except for the trio set up and playing a song in the corner of the room.

The barista blinks when he sees me, exchanges a casual *hey* with Eli and tells us to sit anywhere we want.

"I can't believe he let Daisy in," I say, sliding into the booth across from him and feeling the dog brush against my legs under the table and settle down with a sigh on my feet. "That's really cool."

"Yeah, they're usually pretty good about it. I never bring her when they're crowded but it's still early tonight and there's really nobody here yet, so . . ." He shrugs, smiling, and glances over at the corner of the shadowy room where the trio, two middle-aged guys with guitars and a woman with lap bongos and a bunch of rhythm instruments, is softly playing and singing Maroon 5's "Out of Goodbyes." "I've seen these guys before. They play a lot of older stuff but they're good."

The barista arrives and after a quick scan of the menu, we order an espresso macchiato and a mocha latte, almond macaroons and a very decadent-sounding chocolate dessert for two.

"Hold up," he says before the barista leaves, and looks across the table at me. "I never asked if you had dinner."

"Oh, I had a late lunch," I say with a dismissive shrug. "I'm fine."

He gazes at me a moment as if deliberating. "Well if you get hungry they have some great wraps here, so . . ." He glances at the barista. "We're good. Thanks, Jed." And when he leaves, Eli sits back and cocks his head, smiling slightly and gazing at me.

"What?" I say, getting a little nervous. Is there something on my nose? My eyes? My teeth? Do I need to hit the ladies' room right now?

"Nothing, I'm just thinking about your prom buddy and how his loss is definitely my gain," he says. "Nothing like being in the right place at the right time."

"I know." I smile back, cheeks warm. "And why *were* you there, anyway?"

"Because I wanted to see you." He looks at me like no other guy ever has, like he likes me and wants me to know it, like he's having a blast and is real enough not to hide it. "So, prom queen." There's mischief in his eyes. "Want to dance?"

"Here? Now? Are you serious?" I say with a surge of excitement as the band goes right into Lifehouse's "You and Me." "What about Daisy?"

"She'll stay." His smile widens. "Come on, we've got the place to ourselves." He slides out of the booth and stands there with his hand out, waiting for me.

I take it, heart pounding, feel his fingers close around mine, warm and strong, and feeling very self-conscious, follow him to the dance floor. He slides an arm around my waist and, still holding my hand, tucks our hands up between us, my knuckles resting against his chest, his brushing my bare collarbone.

Nothing in the world could have ever prepared me for this.

"Okay?" he says, smiling into my eyes as we slowly sway together. I nod, hoping he can't feel my knees quivering.

"Good." He pulls me closer, fitting me to him, and rests his cheek against my hair. "You look beautiful, you know."

"Thank you," I whisper, pierced by happiness so sweet it's almost unbearable.

The band never lets us off the dance floor, going straight into song after song, from "Wild Horses" to "Fade into You" to others I don't recognize and barely register. I am lost, melted into a dreamy, shimmering haze of sensation. Eli releases my hand, sliding both his arms around my waist as mine slip up around his neck. My cheek nestles on his shoulder and my nose against his neck, breathing him in. His lips brush my cheek, his breath warm and uneven, and his arms tighten—

"Get a room," someone calls in a voice heavy with ribald laughter.

"You dick," a girl snaps. "He was finally gonna kiss her and you ruined it."

I blink, rudely wrenched from the dream, and step back, embarrassed.

"Guess we have an audience." Eli gazes at me, eyes smoky, cheeks about as pink as mine must be, and gives me a small, wry smile. "Nice, huh?" He takes my hand, sends the bulky, big-mouthed guy at the far table a good-natured *You're killing me, dude* look, and leads me back to our booth.

Our coffees are lukewarm but we drink them anyway, mostly, I think, so that we don't have to talk. I sneak peeks at him from beneath my eyelashes, wondering if he's as shaken as I am, and once, when he glances up and our gazes meet, I think he is.

And when the silence stretches too long I somehow manage to clear my throat and say, "Daisy's being really good."

"Yeah, she is," he says, leaning back and looking under the table. "Hey, you." He reaches under and pets her. "Doing okay?"

Her wagging tail swishes against my knees.

"So how old is she?" I ask, breaking off a tiny chunk of macaroon and popping it into my mouth.

"About a year and a half," he says, sitting back up and tucking his hair behind his ear. "I was supposed to take her to the vet's for a checkup because she's drinking more than usual but that was back when Corey, uh, did his thing and I keep forgetting to make a new appointment."

"So call now while you're thinking of it and leave a message on their voice mail to call you back," I say, pouring some water into my cupped palm and leaning over in the booth, then carefully sticking my hand under the table and offering it to Daisy, who laps it up. "Then it'll be done."

"Nice," he says, giving me a look of admiration, and does, reciting a quick list of symptoms—drinking more, peeing a lot, losing some weight—that one by one steal the shine from his eyes, and by the time he hangs up, his face is solemn.

I take my time drying my palm with my napkin to give him a chance to recover.

"I'll be right back," he says after a long moment, and slides out of the booth. "Do you want anything?"

"No, I'm good," I say, watching as he heads for the men's room, wondering why every single conversation has to lead back to that terrible day and hoping it hasn't ruined his good mood, the night, my chances forever.

I sit for a minute, trying to figure it out, then give up and rummage through the clutch bag for my phone.

Nadia's probably sent me a hundred texts by now and I should call my parents and tell them I'm not at the prom, I'm at a coffeehouse, but if I do and they tell me to come home then the night is over and I really don't want it to be.

I mean, it's only quarter to ten.

But when I find my phone I see it doesn't matter anyway because it's broken.

Great. It must have happened when Becca shoved me and my purse hit the sidewalk.

"Crap," I mutter, and glance up to find Eli standing there looking apologetic. "What?"

"Jed says it's gonna start getting busy, so we should get moving," he says, bending and picking up Daisy's leash. "Come on, girl. Time to go." He rises, flicks back his hair and says, "Feel like taking a walk to the little park?"

The little park has huge old weeping willow trees and a flower garden with a gazebo where they take a lot of wedding pictures. It's on the outskirts of the town near the minimall and will bring me a lot closer to home, which is good, considering I'm supposed to be in by midnight.

"Sure," I say, gathering my things.

Eli holds the door for me and, smiling, I step out into the night.

Chapter 25

It takes us a good half hour to stroll out to the little park, with Daisy taking full advantage of being outside again and stopping to sniff every single blade of grass that she considers even mildly interesting.

"C'mon, Daze, you're really pushing it," Eli says dryly as the dog pauses over a crushed and ancient cigarette butt. "I know what you're doing. Let's go." He's got the leash wrapped around his wrist and my shoes dangling from the same hand, and the other holding mine.

I like it.

Daisy gives him a merry look, stops so I can scratch her head and, tail wagging, picks up the pace and leads us straight down the cobblestone path into the little park, where the huge branches of the graceful willows create living curtains around soft, deep pockets of darkness and the air is sweet with the mingled scents of lilacs, lily of the valley and the ever-present autumn olive.

"Wow," I say in a hushed voice as we round a bend and come to the fountain. The air is cooler here, alive with the sound of swirling, rippling, dancing water.

Daisy goes right over, sticks her head in and drinks.

"Want to sit down?" Eli says, waiting until Daisy's finished and motioning toward one of the benches placed far enough from the fountain to be dry.

"Sure," I say as he sits next to me and knots Daisy's leash around the leg of the bench.

"Is this okay?" he says, sitting back up and settling his arm around me.

"Perfect." Wild, fluttery tendrils of possibility spread through my veins as I breathe him in—the stirring scents of clean cotton, sun on skin, and a darker, woodsy musk, maybe sandalwood—and feel his calloused hand run gently up and down my arm.

"Yeah, it is," he says softly, resting his head against mine.

A strand of his hair slips forward and down across my collarbone. It's sleek, black silk in the moonlight and I wind it gently around my finger, then ease it free again.

"Cold?" he murmurs, and I sigh, nestle closer. He shifts, stretching his legs out in front of him, and I am very much aware of the heat coming off of his lean, muscled forearms, the way his faded jeans fit over his thighs, the tingle as the patch under his bottom lip brushes my forehead. His breath sweeps softly across my skin; his heart, quick and strong, beats under the palm I've settled against his chest. I don't remember putting it there, don't remember when his hand first slipped up beneath my hair to caress my neck.

The night slows, blurs. Awareness rises, skin smolders. His fingertips graze my cheek, soft, questioning, and I lift my chin, hold his smoky, half-lidded gaze until his mouth finds mine and then we are both seeking, finding, staying.

Chapter 26

We kiss forever, hot and hotter, straining, tangled, delirious, until Daisy sticks her cold nose right into our joined faces and snuffles, forcing us to fall back and away, laughing, gasping, stunned, hair disheveled, lips soft and tingling, the top of my strapless gown and the bottom of his T-shirt in disarray from our hungry, eager hands touching, stroking, exploring the thrilling and mysterious unseen.

"Holy shit," Eli says, and shakes his head, dazed. "Rowan." His sleepy gaze drops to the front of me. "You have to fix that or . . ."

I blink and glance down at myself. "Oh." I tug the fallen side back up to a respectable height. "Better?"

"No," he murmurs, and leans forward to kiss me.

"Do you know what time it is?" I ask dreamily when we finally come up again for air.

"Sure," he says, holding up his watch and hitting the glow-light button. "Eleven thirty-seven." He kisses my nose. "Time to get you home." Laughs huskily. "Hell, where *is* home? I don't even know where you live."

"We'll probably make it," I say, easing out of his arms and sitting up.

"Then let's get moving," he says, leaning over and untying Daisy's leash. "I don't want to get you in trouble. I don't want anything to mess this up." He rises, his voice soft now, his gaze wondering, and draws me to him in a hug, enfolding me in an embrace that says far more than any words he could ever speak.

And when we finally start walking up Victory Lane our hands are clasped tight and our steps swift with purpose because I don't want to be late either, don't want to be grounded, don't want my parents to associate anything negative with him, or with me with him.

"It's right up here," I say as we're halfway past the woods.

"You live across from the overpass," he says in a peculiar voice.

"I do," I say, and tighten my fingers around his. "That's why my father got the call and was there so fast. Because he was home, and close." I hesitate. "He caught me cutting school and brought me home." I glance up at him, see his set jaw and feel my stomach sink. God, I don't want to end the night like this. "So I guess if I hadn't cut school he would never have been here, and then we never would have met."

"The ripple effect," he says after a long moment, and gives me a small, sideways smile. "Corey jumps and the ripples just keep spreading." He sighs and shakes his head quickly, impatiently, like he's trying to dislodge the thought. "Anyway."

Oh, hell.

"This is it," I say, trying to sound cheerful after we walk past the rest of the woods in silence and reach the foot of my driveway. My mother's car, my father's Blazer. Stripe in the porch window, the TV light glowing in the living room.

"Eleven fifty-two," Eli says, checking his watch.

"We made it," I say, and take a reluctant step backward, our hands still joined but slipping now. "So thank you for tonight. Best prom I ever had."

"Hey," he says softly, and steps closer, pulling me into his arms. "Don't mind me. It's not you, Row." His voice is muffled against my hair. "The whole overpass thing . . . I'll tell you about it sometime, okay? But not now." He draws back, searches my face, and his mouth curves into a smile. "Now's for me taking your phone number and username and e-mail and—"

"Okay, but Becca broke my phone," I say, and for some reason that strikes us as hilarious and the shimmering night rings with our laughter until I say, "Shh, shh! Come on, shh," and whisper out my info, leaning against him as he punches it in and saves it in his phone. "I really have to go now."

"Yeah, you do." He kisses me one last, head-spinning time and lets me go. "Good night, beautiful girl."

"Good night," I say, backing slowly up my driveway so I can still see him.

"You're gonna hear from me," he says, ambling backward up the lane toward the overpass. "Count on it."

"I will," I say, and then, frowning, "Why are you going that way?"

"Because I live up there," he says, giving me an owlish look. "In the town houses past the shopping center. I've been walking Daisy down this road ever since we got here." His smile turns teasing. "Don't pretend you never saw me go by."

"I *didn't*," I say, laughing and thinking, *Wow, more ripple effect.*

"Yeah, well, you'd better go before I get you in trouble," he says with a smile that stops my heart, and then follows Daisy across the street and up onto the overpass, where they grow smaller and smaller until they disappear from sight.

I turn and find my mother at the door. Her face is lit bright by the sunporch light and my father is standing behind her, Stripe in his arms, his face lost in shadows.

"Rowan?" she says, holding open the screen door. "How was it?" There is excitement in her voice, anticipation, love and worry too, the worry that someone might have hurt her daughter, been cruel to her, laughed at her, ruined her first special evening.

And even though it's too new to share, too magical to scrutinize, there is still no way to keep this feeling to myself, and so, beaming, I say, "Absolutely amazing," and the relief in my mother's smile, the delight, draws me to her like a magnet and as she's enveloped in my fierce hug and laughing in surprise, my father reaches out and gently touches my cheek as if to say he's glad I'm home safe and then turns, shoulders slumped, drowning in sorrow, and trudges back into the house.

"So, tell me everything," my mother burbles, drawing back in excitement. "Are you hungry?"

"Starving," I say absently, watching him go, and then follow her into the kitchen, where we eat oatmeal cookies and I tell her a lot but not everything, and by the time we're done I'm exhausted.

"You go ahead, I just want to clear the table," she says. "Good night, honey. I'm so glad you had a good time."

"Good night," I mumble, and lurch away up the stairs.

My parents' bedroom door is shut so my father must already be in bed. I hesitate for a moment, tempted to knock, to tell him about Eli and say good night, but if he's somehow finally managed to fall asleep it'll wake him up and that would be terrible, so I just stagger to my room, peel off my clothes, drag on my pajamas and fall into bed.

Best night of my life, I think dreamily, and that's the last thing I remember before sleep envelops me.

Chapter 27

In my dream Eli and I are trying to dance but the music is wrong, the beat too fast, drumming, pounding—

Bam! Bam! Bam!

I open my eyes and shoot bolt upright, dazed, disoriented, blinded by the sharp early-morning sun, and hear it again.

Bam! Bam! Bam!

"What the hell?" I croak, throwing back the covers and scrambling out of bed. "Mom? Dad?" I stagger over and open the door in time to see my mother, hair disheveled and barely awake, coming out of her bedroom. "What is that?"

"I think someone's at the front door," she says as the pounding starts again. "Jesus, it's six o'clock on a Sunday morning. Honey? Nicky, can you get that?" She starts down the stairs, me hot on her heels. "Nicky? God, what did he do, lock himself out? Nick?"

"Dad?" I call, growing uneasy because the pounding is urgent, intense, and he isn't answering and there's something wrong, I can feel it because why would he knock on the front door when I know he has a spare porch door key hidden outside somewhere; why isn't he using it?

"I'm coming," my mother yells, but she's moving too slowly, taking too long, and the pounding won't stop, so I slip past her down the stairs to the door, fumble with the dead bolt and yank it open.

Vinnie is standing there in uniform, his police car parked in the driveway behind my mother's car.

The spot where my father parks his Blazer is empty.

I don't understand that, it doesn't make sense, and I look back at Vinnie for the answer, Vinnie whose face is a miserable, ravaged, sickly gray-green, Vinnie who is crying, his eyes sunk into tragic, wounded black holes brimming with the end of the world, and in that split second before the earth gives way I grab on to his arm and in a high, tight voice that doesn't sound anything like me say, "What happened? Where's Daddy?" and when he says those terrible words that he can never take back, my mother makes a hoarse wounded-animal sound and, reaching for him, begging, cries, "Are you sure? Are you *sure?*"

"Yes," he chokes out, weeping. "I'm the one who found him."

My legs buckle and I go down.

Chapter 28

No.

Vinnie's wrong.

He *has* to be wrong.

Oh God, I can't breathe.

My father wouldn't do that.

I can't stop crying.

Mommy, no, don't believe him. Please, *please* don't believe him.

It's a mistake. He doesn't understand that Daddy wouldn't do that to us.

He would never leave us.

Never.

Oh God, *please*.

Please.

Chapter 29

Time stops.

The house fills with people.

Every time the door opens I know it's going to be my father, and it isn't.

But it will be. I know it.

Because this isn't real. It *can't* be real.

It can't.

My grandparents are here.

I don't know who called them.

Auntie Kate who is my mother's sister and Auntie Brooke, who is my father's, hugging my mother and sobbing.

I don't know who told them.

Hugging me and sobbing.

Saying they can't believe it, over and over again.

Neither can I.

Chapter 30

My grandfather takes my stunned and weeping mother to police headquarters to be questioned for the report. Then they will identify my father's body. There is going to be an autopsy to establish the method of death, and then there will be a funeral.

My phone is broken and I don't care. My laptop is upstairs and I can't summon the energy to go get it. It doesn't matter. There's only one person in the world I want to see right now.

I sit and gaze at my father's chair, willing him to appear.

He will.

He has to, he hasn't finished his new Stephen King book yet and he never stops reading midbook. I stare at that, too, left open to mark his place, spine up and lying on the end table with his reading glasses. See, there is proof. He never goes anywhere without his reading glasses.

My grandmother makes coffee and breakfast, and cries. My damp-eyed uncles arrive and can't eat it. My aunts make phone calls in hitched and quavering voices. Pace the room, crying, and pause to hug me. Bring me coffee. Bottled water. Stop and gaze tearfully at our family portrait hanging over the mantel. Tell me he loved me so much, more than anything on earth, and I should never doubt that. Should never forget it. Wash the dishes. Answer the phone and the door.

My mother's best friend, Kelly, arrives from out of state and the crying begins anew.

They are everywhere and they have taken over our house.

I want to hide under the couch with Stripe, watching but not involved, waiting for my father to walk in and put an end to this nightmare.

This day has to start over because I just don't understand it.

I don't understand why I didn't wake up earlier, hear my father stirring downstairs, and instead of turning over and sinking back into a dream, get up, go down there and stop him from taking his off-duty .38 and driving one last time to headquarters, parking in the back lot, putting that pistol to his head and pulling the trigger.

Because that's what they're saying he did, and I swear to *God* I don't understand how I could be sleeping while he was dying.

While he was killing himself.

So all I need is a chance to do it over, just one chance, and this time, *this time* I won't go to the prom. I won't go anywhere, I'll just stay home and sit here with him all night, won't leave even if he tells me to, will stay up all night waiting and be there at dawn.

I didn't know my chances were limited.

I didn't know they could run out but now I do, I really do, and so all I need is one more chance to change it. In a world where anything can be bought, sold, stolen, begged or bartered, reversed or advanced, it's not a lot to ask. It really isn't.

It's just one chance to save one man.

"Please," I whisper as the tears well and overflow.

Just one.

Chapter 31

My grandfather returns alone, his face haggard, walking like each step exhausts him. He goes straight to the kitchen table and sinks into a chair.

"Did they find a note?" my grandmother says, setting a steaming cup of coffee in front of him and resting a gnarled hand on his shoulder.

"No," my grandfather says, and begins to weep. "Jesus, Edie, I can't. Not now." He waves her away but she doesn't go, just wraps her arm around him and rests her cheek against the top of his head.

"Where's Mommy?" I say.

"Outside," he says without looking up.

It's slow going. My knees are weak and heavy. I plod through the porch, push open the screen door and spot her standing in the driveway smoking a cigarette, her arm wrapped around her waist like she's been gutted and her own grip is the only thing keeping everything inside of her from spilling out. "Mom?"

She lifts her head and finds me. "Rowie." Her eyes are swollen and desolate, her nose red and her shoulders bowed just like Grandpa's, just like the aunts', just like mine. "Oh, honey." She holds open her arm and I wobble over, tucking myself close and burying my face in her shoulder for a long, agonizing moment.

"Did you see Daddy?" I ask finally, stepping back and wiping my eyes. Not that it matters; the tears pulse like a heartbeat now, starting and stopping on their own. There's no controlling them. I don't even try.

She shakes her head, mouth trembling. "I couldn't. I just couldn't. They said he shot himself here"—she touches her temple—"and there was impact trauma to his face . . ." She takes a hitched, steadying breath. "Grandpa saw him." She drops the smoldering cigarette butt, steps on it and lights another one.

"And it was really him?"

"Yes," she whispers, taking a drag off the cigarette and huddling into herself. "Did you call Nadia?"

"No," I say. "My phone's broken."

"Use mine." She reaches into her jacket pocket and pulls it out.

Her screen saver is an old photo of me, Daddy and Stripe as a kitten, snuggled together on the couch. I shake my head, the photo blurring, and look away.

I can't call Nadia, or Eli or even Eva.

Cannot imagine saying the words aloud, putting them out there as if they're true.

Not yet.

"You know, your father and I quit smoking when we found out we were pregnant with you," she says after a moment, staring absently at the smoke curling up around us. "We were determined to do everything we could to make sure you were a strong, healthy baby." She takes a drag off the cigarette and, turning her head, blows the smoke away from me. "Isn't it funny; add a person to the family and smoking stops. Lose one, and it starts right back up again." And then she crumples, her body wracked with great, shattering sobs, and she drops the cigarette and takes me in her arms, holding me like she'll never let me go.

| | |

This day is a hundred years long and there is nothing to do but wait for it to end.

Only it won't.

I can't make myself say the words, so after lunch, which no one eats, I drag myself up the stairs for my laptop.

Typing them is worse.

My father is dead.

I erase it. Type it again. Erase it.

Over and over and over.

Finally send it to Nadia.

Remember that my father said he'd called Eli once, so he must have his phone number. Get up and plod back downstairs to the kitchen. "Mom, where's Daddy's cell phone? I need to find a number."

"On the windowsill with his wallet," she says.

And that's when I know something really is wrong, because my father never goes anywhere without those two things, ever, anywhere, and yet there they are.

I reach for the phone, hands shaking, and hold it to my cheek. It smells faintly of fresh-cut wood, aftershave and his dear, familiar person scent, and the pain crashes over me with a force so strong that it steals my breath and it's only because my parents quit smoking to make sure I was healthy that I know I'm not dying.

| | |

I find the number but don't call from my father's phone. That doesn't seem right, to have his name show up on caller ID when it's not really him.

I use the portable landline instead.

Eli's phone goes right to voice mail.

"Hi," I say, and clear my throat, but it's no use, this girl's hoarse and terrible voice isn't mine. "It's Rowan. Eli . . . my f-f-father is d-d-dead. I'm sorry. I have t-t-to g-g-go."

I look up to see Nadia in the kitchen, crying and hugging my mother. Her parents are right behind her, and like a slap I realize that I will never have both of my parents right behind me ever again.

| | |

She hugs me, crying. Can't stop saying, *Oh my God, what happened? Rowan, I thought he was doing okay, you never said anything, oh my God why? I can't believe it, it just doesn't make sense! Row, there's no way. Oh my God, why?*

"I don't know," I say helplessly, pulling free and sitting back down on the couch. "I . . . I don't know. The depression, I guess."

"Well, what happened last night when you got home? Did you guys have a fight or something?" She sinks down beside me, gaze locked onto my face. "I mean did he *say* anything?"

"No," I say, rubbing my forehead and trying to think.

"Well, something must have happened," she says, sitting back and giving me a frustrated look. "People just don't kill themselves for no reason!"

I stare at her, at a loss. "I don't know. I swear to God, I don't. Nothing happened."

"And he never said a word?" she says, giving me a penetrating look. "People always drop hints, Row."

The ones who don't tell anyone beforehand . . . They've already made their decision and planned it all out to make sure they succeed. We find them after the fact, when it's too late.

The words, my father's, flow unbidden into my mind but I can't speak them, only stare back at her, stricken.

"What did his note say? Can I see it?"

I gaze down at my hands, barely able to speak the words. "He didn't leave one."

"What?" she says, pulling back in shock. "That's *impossible*. Out of all the people in the world who would leave a note, Row, your dad is like number *one*."

I start to cry.

"I'm sorry," she says, hugging me again. "I just can't even believe it! Do you want me to tell Danica and Bree and all? I can, don't worry. It's okay. What about Eli? That was him last night, right? Did you tell him yet? What're you guys going to do now?"

"I don't know," I say numbly, huddling smaller and smaller, and then Nadia's parents come in, hug me and tell me they're sorry. And in some odd, twisted corner of my mind I notice that they're all dressed up, that her mom is in full jewelry and makeup and so is Nadia, that they took the time to do all of this before coming over, not like my grandparents and the aunts who dropped everything to get here, and that their gazes move constantly around the room, taking everything in.

I step in front of my father's chair and shield it, block the sight of his Dollar Store magnifying reading glasses and the remainder mark on his book because he's ours, not theirs, and it's none of their business.

They linger a moment, say that if we need anything all we have to do is call and that they'll see us at the funeral.

I say, *Yes, thank you, okay.*

Nadia hugs me and says, *Call me, Row.*

I say, *Yes, thank you, okay,* and finally, they're gone.

| | |

Eli calls.

I gaze at the number for a long moment and answer it. "Hello."

"I just got your message." His voice is low, subdued. "Rowan, I'm so sorry."

I nod even though he can't see me. Take a short, hitched breath. "Thank you."

"Do you have people with you? Your mom? Family?"

Everyone but my father. "Yes," I whisper, covering my mouth so I don't burst into tears. "They're all here."

"Yeah," he says softly, as if he remembers, and exhales. "Row . . .

I can be there in five minutes but I have to ask . . . Do you want me to come now or is today better for you with just your family?"

"I don't know," I cry, closing my eyes as the tears slip out from beneath my lids. "Nothing is better. I j-j-just w-want him to c-come h-home." The pain in my chest cracks wide open. "That's all I w-want, Eli. I j-just want him to come h-home now and then I w-want to go t-to sleep and w-wake up all over again."

"Oh, baby girl," he says with a sigh. "I am so, so sorry."

And for some reason the knowing in his voice makes it worse, the empathy is too awful and I can't bear it, can't handle the fact that he isn't shocked and denying it, that he can just accept this obscene and inconceivable thing as true instead of rejecting it in violent disbelief, and so I choke out, "No, don't come. Not now. I'm sorry but—"

"It's all right," he says quietly. "I understand. That's why I asked."

No, he doesn't understand. No one can. "Okay."

"I'll call you later and if you're up to it, I can come by tomorrow," he says, and it sounds like he's near tears himself. "Or if you change your mind, or you need me, call. I'll be there, Row. It doesn't matter what time it is. Just call and I'll come, okay?"

"Okay," I whisper, reeling. "Bye."

He hesitates and then says softly, "Bye."

Chapter 32

Later that night, after my grandparents and my uncles have given in to their exhaustion and gone home, after a three-minute phone call with Eli where the few, sad words we exchange vanish as soon as they're spoken, after fielding three calls from Nadia—I can't, I just can't—and endless discussions about where my father might have left us a note if he wrote one, the aunts, my mother and I gather in the living room to write my father's obituary and his eulogy.

My auntie Kate builds a small fire in the fireplace to cut the chill in the air.

My auntie Brooke pours us each, even me, a glass of wine.

My honorary aunt Kelly brings a pad, a pen and her laptop, my mother her worn, well-loved copy of *Bartlett's Familiar Quotations*.

We settle in on the floor around the coffee table, my mother and I in spots close enough to lean back against my father's recliner. None of us knows how to start so Aunt Kelly goes online and finds the newspaper's questionnaire, which makes it easier and lets us condense a beloved man's whole life into several medium-sized paragraphs.

"You have to put Stripe in it, too," I say when they get to the *Survived by* blank. "You can't leave him out, Mom." I cuddle Stripe close, his fur damp with my tears. "He wouldn't even be alive if it wasn't for Daddy."

"I know," my mother says with a small smile, and adds Stripe to my father's survivors.

The eulogy, it turns out, is much harder to write than the obituary, and it doesn't fall into place until my mother, paging feverishly through her *Bartlett's*, stumbles across an epitaph for someone named Sir Philip Sidney, a quote that makes her catch her breath, pries a small, pained whimper from her lips, and when she reads it to us, we know it's perfect.

Death slew not him, but he made death his ladder to the skies.

The rest of the eulogy, all those proud, beautiful, heartbroken words we weave together to pay tribute to my father, come easily after that.

Chapter 33

Every day that passes is worse than the one before it.

I wake up each morning with a jolt of hope so huge that I'm certain it's all been a nightmare, a mistake, that none of this is real and if I lie there very still and listen very hard, I'll hear my father whistling downstairs, hear my mother laughing again, and it will all be over.

And every single morning I'm wrong.

The funeral home calls. The autopsy has been completed and the body—my *father*—is being released to them. Would my mother come down please to discuss the cremation, discuss a viewing casket and the funeral service?

Auntie Kate, her sister, goes with her.

Auntie Brooke and Aunt Kelly have been left in charge of finding a place for the small, post-funeral luncheon, so they make a short list of restaurants near the church, ones with private rooms, and head out to book one.

My grandmother cleans our house; my grandfather cuts the grass.

My father's Blazer isn't home yet because Vinnie, with his dear, devastated lion's heart, is going to clean it for us before he brings it back, wash away all of my father's blood and pain and whatever else remains of the last few moments of his life.

My mind can barely touch this thought before it swerves away again, seeking refuge in the numbing, growing fog.

We need black clothes for the funeral.

I stare into my closet for far too long, because everything looks jumbled and foreign and I'm unable to decide.

Eli calls and dully I say yes, sure, come over.

He does, face soft with compassion, eyes red with sorrow, and holds me in his arms for a long time. He brings me coffee from the coffeehouse and I stare at it blankly for a moment, as if it all happened in another world and to someone else.

And so slowly, in words that scrape my throat raw, I tell him what happened.

He gathers me close and strokes my terrible, stringy hair. When was the last time I took a shower? I don't know. I brushed my teeth this morning, I know that, but my eyes are too swollen for mascara, my cheeks too raw for blush, and I don't care about them, anyway. I'm still wearing the clothes I slept in, the T-shirt wrinkled and the black leggings dusted with Stripe's fine gray and black hairs.

And still, Eli holds me.

He doesn't say much, which is good because there is nothing to say.

"I'm here for you, Row," he says when I walk him to the door. "Anything I can do, I will. Okay?" He touches my cheek, gentle, fleeting. "I'll be there tomorrow at the funeral home but if you need me before then just call."

"Okay," I say, and then he hugs me again and is gone.

I should care more, I know, but there's nothing left inside of me.

Only pain.

| | |

For the second time this month, I'm riding in a limo.

This time with leaden limbs and boxes of tissues.

My father is going to be cremated but the viewing is an open casket.

My mother says people won't believe he's really dead unless they see him.

Maybe she means *we* won't believe it.

I do, when I see him.

He's wearing his police uniform, complete with badge, tie clip, ribbons, medals, his valor watch and his wedding ring, which my mother says will all be removed before they cremate him. The funeral home worked hard to patch up his shattered temple, put plenty of makeup over the trauma marks and tried to comb his hair down over the cave-in on the side in a way that would make him laugh if he ever saw it.

But he won't and so it isn't funny, it's sad, it makes me want to block the casket and not let anyone see him so vulnerable, but I can't because the place is mobbed and the line to say a prayer over him endless.

And besides, he has police to watch over him. The place is full of solemn-faced cops sporting black mourning armbands. Vinnie and Lieutenant Walters, both in full dress blues, faces solemn, eyes red and chins high, stand guard at the head and the foot of the casket. They don't smile or speak, only stand and bear witness, keep watch, pay final tribute and honor one of their own.

They are beautiful and looking at them makes my heart hurt.

Nadia comes with Danica and Bree, all dressed in black minis and stilettos, and drape themselves over me, whimpering. Eva comes, looking like she's a thousand years old, and hugs me without speaking. Terence comes, takes my hand, looks deep into my eyes and says in a low, gravelly voice, "He was a good man," which nearly kills me.

Why did he do it? What happened? I can't believe it. Why, why, why?

The room swirls with questions, with person after person asking my mother, my grandparents, even me the exact same thing: why?

We don't know. There is no answer we can give them.

It's exhausting.

I'm standing up front with my mother, holding on to her arm, accepting the condolences of a vast, weeping blur of people, when an old, vaguely familiar-looking woman comes up, sticks her face right into my mother's and, with her chameleon eyes bright as a squirrel's behind her glasses, says, "I'm a friend of your mother's, dear, and I'm sorry for your terrible, tragic loss." She starts to move on and then, as if she just can't resist, pauses, lays a hand on my mother's arm and adds, "And I just have to tell you that I'm *shocked* at the Catholic Church for agreeing to provide his funeral mass. My goodness, he committed suicide and that's a mortal sin, you know."

My mother's eyes widen and she falls back a step, speechless, as if the woman has slapped her right across the face.

I stand there mute, too stunned to speak, and suddenly the aunts are there edging the old lady out, helping us to our seats and bringing us paper cups full of water. My head is pounding, spinning from the unrelenting scent of the flowers, cool and sweet, the thick, choking heat of milling bodies and the salt humidity of tears.

The line of mourners shifts as Payton Well walks up. Her handshake is limp and her gaze disconnected. "Sorry for your loss." She moves on, leaving a trail of whispers behind her.

"Nicky went to her son's funeral," my mother murmurs, mopping her eyes.

"I know," I say, and when I look back Eli is waiting in front of me, head lowered in respect, a small gold cross in his earlobe, his dark, bruised gaze holding mine. He's wearing his navy blue suit, his sleek, black hair pulled tight in a ponytail, a small shaving cut on the side of his jaw, low under the curve where you can't see it unless you're looking up at him. I reach for him, our hands fumble and meet, the slight tremor in his anchoring the violent one in mine, and in that joining is recognition of all the wishes that will never come true, the questions that will never be answered and the prayers that will continue unheard.

He makes this all too real.

Chapter 34

The house is empty.

The funeral is over and everyone has gone back to their lives.

Except us.

This is what we have to go back to.

There is no right direction so we go in no direction at all.

Sometimes the most we can do in a day is feed Stripe.

Eva tells me not to rush, to come back to work when I'm ready.

I don't think I'll ever be ready.

My grandparents call every day. So do the aunts.

So do Nadia and Eli.

Sometimes I answer and sometimes I don't.

I just can't seem to care.

The only thing I want is my father.

I say that to Eli and after a long, unbroken silence he says quietly, "Do you want me to stop calling for a while and give you some breathing room? I'm not trying to put pressure on you, Row. Whatever you need me to do. Just tell me. I won't take offense, I swear." His voice drops so low I can barely hear him. "It's bringing a lot of past stuff up for me, too, and now with the dog and all . . . I don't want to make it worse by putting all that on you."

"No, you're not. I . . ." I what? What do I want? I rub my

forehead, trying to clear the fog in my brain and sort his words, but my thoughts are scattered and I don't know what's happening. "Wait."

"It's okay," he says, sounding miserable. "I won't come by, either. Not till you tell me to. I don't want to make you feel like you *have* to see me because—"

"Wait," I say again, even more confused. "Are you saying we're done?"

"No," he says vehemently. "But I know what it's like, having all these people around expecting things and wanting pieces of you when you don't have anything left to give them, putting pressure on you just by *being* there waiting. I don't want to do that to you. I care about you, Row, a lot. I don't want to lose you."

"Like Crystal," I say numbly.

"No, she was . . . That wouldn't have lasted, anyway." He stops and when he starts again, his voice is slow and heavy. "Rowan, I didn't know what to do when my dad died. I mean, I was *lost.* Mad. So pissed off that I ran Daisy all over Houston just to wear myself out so I wouldn't put my fist through the wall. Like I was punishing myself for taking the dog or my dad for sending her home, because there was this 24/7 loop in my head going, *What if she'd sniffed out the IED before it blew? What if the only reason he died was because he sent her back to me instead of keeping her there with him?*"

"No," I whisper, because I've been what-iffing, too.

"Yeah," he says with a ragged snort. "She was sick with grief and I was running her because I was sick, too. Christ, I'll never forgive myself for that. It was so fucking hot and now . . ."

I don't know what to say, can barely follow his words.

"Anyhow . . ." He clears his throat. "I stopped running and started partying. Way too much. I just couldn't take it. My friends had no idea how to deal with any of it. They tried taking me out like two weeks later to 'cheer me up'—I mean, come on—and when that didn't work they just ignored it, like if they brought it up I would all of a sudden remember that my dad was dead. Like I was really ever going to forget. And when that didn't fly, one by one they all just kind of fell away . . ."

I shake my head and wipe my wet cheeks. It's all too much.

"You know how they say never make any major decisions while you're grieving because you're not thinking straight?" His voice is tired now. "Well, my mom did. She was crazed. She started packing and donating and handing my dad's stuff out to all the relatives and I was like, *Wait, would you? I don't even know what you're getting rid of!* but I swear she never even stopped to sleep. It was like she had to keep busy so she wouldn't think about it or something. And then the next thing I know the town house is up for sale and I'm like, *What're you doing?* and she says we're moving and leaving everything behind . . . I wasn't ready for that."

"No," I whisper, wishing he would stop because his words pile on me like bricks, one after another, heavy, crushing, and there's not enough left of me for this. I'm already buried alive in my own misery and I can't stand the weight of his pain, too. "Eli . . ."

"Oh my God," he says suddenly, sounding stricken. "Rowan, I'm so sorry. Christ, I just did exactly what I said I wasn't gonna do."

"It's okay," I say automatically.

"No, it's not," he says. "It's really not. I'm sorry. I am. I'm gonna go now."

"Okay." I just want to go lie down and be small and quiet.

"I won't call you. I'll wait till you call me. You have to think about yourself now. Nobody else. Do what's right for you, okay?"

"Okay," I say because I cannot wrap my mind around any of this.

"I'll be thinking of you though and if you need me . . ."

"I'll call," I say, closing my eyes.

"Christ, I can't believe I'm doing this," he mutters as if to himself, and then to me says, "Okay, well then . . . good night, Row."

"Good night," I say, reeling.

I hang up, curl into a ball and cry myself to sleep.

Chapter 35

Nadia doesn't give me that kind of space.

She and Brett have broken up and now she wants movement, improvement, answers, action and girl time, and so two weeks later I find myself sitting in her house drinking and smoking weed while her parents attend a weekend college reunion out of state.

Big mistake.

I don't remember much past throwing a bottle of beer at her when she suggests I slow down but when I come to I'm curled up on her bathroom floor with puke in my hair, my shorts soaked with pee and my eyes swollen to burning slits from crying. The door is shut and when I crawl over and fumble it open, Nadia's sitting out in the hallway on the floor. She looks like she's been crying too and has a long, fresh, nasty-looking scratch down her nose.

"Stop," she blurts, scrambling to her feet. "Stay there."

"What happened to you?" I say thickly, squinting up at her.

"You did," she says, and stares at me like she doesn't even know me.

It turns out I got hysterical, cursing Corey, blubbering about how he started it all by jumping and killing Sammy, and then my father killed *himself* because he couldn't save him, and now it was a cycle that was never going to stop and *I* didn't save my father so why should I still be alive when he's dead . . .

"And then you ran to the door screaming and I tried to stop you but you were fighting really hard," she says, and, pausing, turns her bare leg sideways so I can see the huge, ugly purple bruise forming on her thigh near the bottom of her shorts. "You were really out of it, Row. You scared me bad." Her big blue eyes are wounded, pissed, shining with tears. "I didn't know what to do so I just held on, and that's when you *really* kicked my ass." She wipes her eyes on the back of her hand. "You grabbed my hair and scratched me and dragged me down to the ground and said you hated me because my father's still alive. You *punched* me."

"I'm sorry," I mumble, stomach churning. "I don't hate you." But even as I say it, I know it isn't true. I *do* hate her now—hate her normalness, her happiness, the fact that she can still say good night to both of her parents, that she's still so sure of her life. I want to tell her it isn't personal, that I hate *everyone* who has two parents now, that I'm so jealous it makes me physically ill, but the words won't come.

"Yeah, well, it sure looked like it." She touches her fingers to the bridge of her nose and, wincing, gingerly traces the vivid, scarlet furrow. "I mean, look what you did to my *face*. What if it leaves, like, this big gross scar and I have to get plastic surgery? It's almost summer, Row. How am I supposed to go down the shore looking like this?"

"I'm sorry," I say again, peering blearily up at her. "You can't really see it."

"Oh my *God*," she says, falling back against the wall with a thump and gaping at me in disbelief.

"What?" I say, bewildered, and let out a deep, sour, rumbling burp. "Ugh." I wave a sloppy hand in front of my face to disperse the fumes. Catch her look of disgust and feel something deep inside of me twist. "No, listen. Don't be mad. Look." I gesture at myself, feel deep sorrow at the sight of my puke-clotted hair, my peed-in shorts. "Please?"

"Okay, all right, I'm not mad, but look, Row, you can't do this again. I'm serious. I mean I know life sucks right now and I want to be there for you but honestly?" She pauses, biting her lip, and then says in a rush, "I wish your father hadn't done it, okay? I'm *so mad* at him for hurting you guys. And I wish he'd left you a note or something, so you knew *why*. You were asking why a lot," she adds, searching my face. "It really bothers you."

"Yeah." My head is spinning, pounding. I grab the countertop, pull myself up to my knees, and wobble to my feet. "Oh God," I groan, and, turning, heave a smelly, stinking mess into the bathroom sink. Slide back down and kneel there with my head against the vanity door, blubbering. "I'm sorry."

Her phone calls lessen after that, and the one and only time we go out in public together is to some senior's graduation party at the end of June.

I go with the vague, hazy notion of seeing if Eli is there. I saw his name in the newspaper's list of graduates, so I know he made it. I have no idea what I'll say to him if I do see him though, besides congratulations. The night of the prom is distant, blurred, like it happened a million years ago, and to two completely different people.

The party is a fiasco.

I know the minute I walk into the backyard and see all the happy people eating, drinking, laughing and splashing in the pool that I don't belong here. Nadia re-dressed me before we left her house, horrified at my thrown-on jeans and T-shirt, and now the black halter straps dig at the back of my neck, and the white shorts, *her* shorts, too short and too tight, ride right up my butt. The music makes my stomach jitter, the mingled scents of beer, chlorine, sizzling beef and weed nauseate me, and the raucous noise fractures my thoughts. The whole scene spins in my mind like a kaleidoscope, throwing me way off balance.

"Oh my God, this is going to rock," Nadia says excitedly in my ear. "How does my nose look?"

She means the scratch, of course, scabbed over and buried beneath a hearty layer of concealer that almost but not quite matches her tan. "Good."

"Good," she says, beaming. "Want to get something to drink?"

"I guess," I say, stomach sinking, and follow her toward the keg and the coolers. There's bottled water and I take one, wait as she gets a beer, then follow her through the crowd and around the pool, stopping and waiting, numb, as she laughs and flirts and talks and shoots me increasingly anxious looks.

"Are you okay?" she says finally, pulling me aside.

"I'm fine," I say automatically.

"You don't look it," she says, searching my face.

"Nadia," I say, my jaw aching from being clenched so tight, "my father just died and I don't give a shit about any of these people. I'd trade them all in a heartbeat just to get him back. All I'm doing is trying not to lose it." I see the hurt cross her face, know I caused it and don't care. Can't feel it. It's small, so small compared to the finality of death. *Everything* is small compared to that, so what does any of it matter, really? "I'm doing the best I can, okay? I don't know what else you want from me."

"Nothing," she says, straightening and taking a step back. "God, I'm sorry I even brought you here. I just thought it'd be good for you to get back out for a while, you know? I mean it's been a month already, Row, and it's *summer*. I was hoping you'd have some fun, maybe think about something other than . . . you know. But you're not even trying." She says it like it's a personal slight, like I'm insulting her by rejecting some fabulous gift she's given me, like I'm purposely refusing to be a good sport and just buck up, pin on a smile and dance the night away.

She doesn't even get that one month is nothing compared to forever, *nothing,* and that it's taken a monumental effort just to get up, get dressed and come here with her.

An effort that's been a huge mistake.

"So, what do you want to do?" she says coolly, lifting her chin, tossing back her hair and crossing her arms in front of her. She stares past me, mouth tight and the beer in her hand vibrating with anger. "Do you want to leave?"

More than anything, but I know she wants to stay. "Not yet, I guess."

"Well then you're going to have to try a little," she says, still not quite forgiving me. "Open up. Talk to people. God, at least smile. You look like a zombie." She stops, bites her lip and looks around. "Hey, there's Danica and Bree. Come on. And *smile*." She grabs my arm and leads me through the crowd to the pool house, where Danica and Bree are doing shots and flirting with some senior guys.

Our arrival—*my* arrival—casts an immediate pall over their high spirits, and I hear one of the guys mutter, *"Isn't that the chick whose old man just offed himself?"*

I stand there looking at him until he glances my way, meets my stony gaze, realizes I heard, flushes, mutters something to his buddy and wanders away.

Danica whispers something to Bree and they both shoot me dirty looks.

"What are you *doing?*" Nadia asks me, scowling.

I shake my head, heartsick, unable to speak.

"Do you want to go?"

I nod. "You stay. It's okay." I turn and head blindly back through the crowd, around the house and out to the street.

She doesn't follow me.

I walk home by myself, past the deserted minimall and the dark woods, past cars whose headlights flare over me and either steer wide or, once, slow alongside. The middle-aged man driving rolls down his passenger window, leans across the seat and leers at my legs, saying a pretty girl like me shouldn't be out walking all alone at night, and do I want a ride?

"No, but my father's on duty so I'm going to get your plate number and report you for being a pervert," I snap, stepping back and pulling my phone from my pocket like I'm going to take a picture of his car.

"Bitch," he says, and speeds off, which is exactly what I was hoping he'd do.

I'm done with partying.

My father would be happy about that.

Chapter 36

July

Home is the loneliest place in the world, with the exception of my heart.

And yet it's the only place I belong.

Chapter 37

August

Aunt Kelly sends us a huge basket of chocolate chip cookies and says she hopes they help.

I hope they do too, because the numbness is starting to wear off and the protective fog dissipating. What's left of us is growing clearer and I really don't like what I see.

Chapter 38

I wander out of the bagel shop empty-handed and in a daze, letting the door close behind me. Pause, squinting as my eyes get accustomed to the sunlight, as the shimmering heat burns the AC chill right off of my pale, indoor skin and fills each breath with the thick, mingled scents of onions, scorched grass and baking pavement.

I can't believe Justin just asked for my phone number.

I start across the parking lot. Stop and shake a pebble from my sandal.

And I can't believe I gave it to him. Five months ago he was just a guy who flirted and moved on; now he's someone I smiled at and said could call me because . . .

I swipe the hair from my eyes.

Because it's Sunday, the longest, emptiest day of my long, empty week, and every Sunday for the past month I've plodded down to the minimall, bought a dozen bagels for my mother, trying to cheer her up, and come home again, but this time, today, Justin was in there buying a bagel too, saying hi and smiling like his McDonald's bail never happened, like running into me was a good thing, a normal thing, without any of that awkward, uncomfortable fake sympathy or trying to edge away as soon as he got the chance.

Smiling like I wasn't *Poor Rowan* but just Rowan again.

And that casual pardon, that chance to forget everything, even if only for a little while, was enough for me to make a truly pathetic decision, a mistake so embarrassing that I can't even stand being alone with myself right now.

And suddenly I want to talk to Nadia, am seized with the overwhelming urge to see her again and put everything behind us, to start my confession with the old, ever-familiar *Oh my God, you're not going to believe what just happened to me!* and talk, laugh, hang out again just like we used to.

I pull my cell out of my shorts pocket.

One bar left but that should be enough. I can talk fast, spill it all before the phone goes dead . . .

No.

It's been too long. I should do it in person.

I stick the phone back in my pocket and follow the sidewalk to the heart of town.

Pause, take a deep, steadying breath and turn onto Main Street.

I can do this.

I've walked this town my whole life, just not recently, so I make myself keep going, heart thundering, my gaze on the ground, moving as fast as I can without making it look like I'm running, trying to make it through without seeing the double takes as I pass, without hearing the murmurs that kick up and rustle behind me like brittle leaves swirling in the wind.

. . . that Rowan Areno?

. . . such a tragedy.

. . . the hell happened to them?

My sandal catches the edge of the sidewalk and I stumble. I right myself before I fall, face burning, and only the thought of seeing Nadia again after all of this time keeps me from turning and going straight home, the thought of showing up on her doorstep just like I used to, the resurrection of the long-lost me, of seeing the shock and excitement on her face and hearing her *Oh my God, Rowan!* shriek of happiness.

Of hanging out again with my best friend.

And hopefully her mother can drive me home afterward.

That keeps me moving.

But when I finally turn onto her street it looks different from the last time I was here. I don't know if the trip through town rattled me and my perception is still skewed or if the pristine, white sidewalk really *is* tilted and endless, stretching on and on in an unnerving gauntlet of perfect suburban normalcy. Don't know if I'm just hypersensitive or if the neighborhood really *is* disturbingly chaotic, with kids darting and shrieking and playing everywhere, if it really is as smug as it feels with all these happy, two-by-two parents standing out in their driveways socializing without a care in the world, if the houses really are as neat, the lawns as lush and tidy, the flowers so brilliant they don't look real . . .

My footsteps slow to a stop.

I don't belong here. I'm not that girl anymore, the one who ambles confidently down the street with her chin up and her shoulders back, sure of her place in the world and the welcome waiting for her at the end of the cul-de-sac.

I'm not sure of anything anymore, and it paralyzes me.

A car creeps by, and the old lady in the passenger seat gives me a curious look.

But I just can't stand here forever.

I force myself to take a step, then another, passing house after house, feeling the weight of the neighbors' startled gazes, hearing the animated chatter die and the wave of silence that billows in my wake.

It's worse than I thought it would be.

I fasten my gaze on her mailbox, reach her walk. Pavers, set in an intricate box pattern. Nadia hates them because her stilettos get caught in the gaps.

I ring the bell, heart pounding.

The door opens and I step forward, knees shaking, and say, "Hey, guess what? I'm—"

But it isn't her.

"Whoa," her father says, eyes widening and falling back a step at the sight of me. "Uh, wow." He's wearing swim trunks and the blue print pool shirt that Nadia's mom always says matches his eyes, and carrying a mug of coffee. "Uh, hey, Rowan."

"Surprise," I say, forcing a smile and pushing my sweaty, tangled hair back from my face. "Hi, Mr. Kovalcyzk. It's been a while, huh?" I reach for the handle of the screen door, push the thumb button and start to pull it open but he fumbles for it and grabs it too, pulls it right out of my hand and shut again.

"Uh, sorry," he says, flushing and grimacing down at the coffee splashed across the front of his shirt. "We uh, can't let the cat out. Heh heh."

"Oh." I didn't know they had a cat and so I wait, still expecting him to invite me in, but he doesn't. "Is Nadia here?"

"I . . . uh . . . well . . ." He brushes at his shirt, his gaze flickers over me and suddenly I'm all too aware of my baggy shorts and tank, bought back when I was ten pounds heavier, my bedhead hair and my eyelids still puffy from months of crying. "You know, I uh, don't actually know. If she's here, I mean. Heh heh. You know Nadia, miss social butterfly, always running in and out with her friends . . ." His voice fades into a brief, uncomfortable silence. "Hey, let me go check for you." He steps away, then sticks his head back around the door, his gaze focused somewhere past my ear. "And uh, nice seeing you again. Give our best to your mom."

"I will," I say, but he's already disappeared back into the house.

Okay, so that was weird, even for him.

I wait on the porch, stomach quivering, trying not to think, listening for the happy shriek of surprise, the thunder of Nadia barreling down the stairs to greet me, but something's wrong, it's taking too long, and I'm just about to try the door again when she appears at the screen, head cocked, chin high and arms folded across her chest.

"Hi," I say faintly, thrown by her silence. "You look great." And different. Distant. Glossy. Her skin is flawless, her nose smooth and unscarred, her makeup perfect. Her tan is deep, rich, and makes the new blond streaks in her hair look even lighter. She's wearing tiny pink shorts and a white bandeau bikini top, a style she always said she hated. "You got a new bathing suit. It looks good."

"What are you doing here?" she says, like she didn't even hear me. I blink, at a loss.

"You can't just show up like this. I have stuff going on." She meets my stricken gaze and grows instantly defensive. "No. Don't even give me that look. I tried to help you, Row. You *know* I did. What was I supposed to do, just sit around all summer and wait until you decided you were ready to like, live again? Oh my God, it's been *three months*. You're the one who blew *me* off, remember? So don't stand there acting like this is *my* fault."

"No, I . . ." I don't know what to say. "I'm sorry. That's not what . . ." I wish she would open the door. "I didn't do it on purpose." My voice wobbles. "I couldn't *help* it. You don't understand—"

"You're right, Row, I *don't* understand, and you know what? It's fine. I don't want to. Here." She thrusts open the door and shoves a plastic Macy's bag at me. "That's all your stuff. I don't even remember what I left at your house but I don't care. I don't want it back. Just pitch it, or whatever."

I stare at her, speechless.

She hesitates, glances over her shoulder and then back at me. "Just go, Row," she says in a softer, pleading voice. "I'm serious. My mother thinks something really bad was going on in your house and she doesn't want me anywhere near you guys. I'm not even supposed to be talking to you right now." Her voice drops another notch. "She wanted to sue you for what you did to my nose, but me and my father talked her out of it and I had to swear to her that I wouldn't . . ." She shakes her head and for a moment I see the old Nadia in her face. "I just didn't want to do that to you. Your life sucks bad enough now as it is. So I'm not mad or anything, okay? I'm really not. You just did what you had to do, and so did I. I don't hate you. Shit happens. People change. It's okay. I've moved on." She has one hand on the door and pity in her eyes. "You should, too."

"I'm trying," I say in a thick, rusty voice, but even as I say it I realize we're talking about two completely different things. "I really am, and I thought maybe—"

"I have to go." She steps back, won't look at me again.

"—we could talk," I say, knotting my hands together.

"I can't. I have to go." The door shuts softly but with a firm click of finality.

Chapter 39

Tears fill my eyes but I don't wipe them away, will not give anyone the satisfaction of saying they saw me crying right out here in broad daylight.

I'm not numb enough for that anymore.

The neighbors automatically part for me now, and as I plod past a high, piping, little-kid voice says, "Is that lady hurt, Mommy?"

"Shh. No, honey." Hushed and low, tinged with embarrassment. "She's a friend of Nadia's."

Was, I want to say. She *was* a friend of Nadia's.

"But she looks sad," the kid says insistently.

"Yes, she probably is. Something sad happened. We'll talk about it later. Now shh!"

Something sad happened. It sounds so simple and falls so far short of even *beginning* to explain that I almost laugh out loud, but I don't, I can't, because if I start I'm not going to be able to stop, and that's the definition of hysteria.

I trudge back down Main Street, around an empty trash can lying in the middle of the sidewalk, right through the middle of a swarm of yellow jackets buzzing around the dirty red juice stain running down the side, and keep going.

Walk past the florist, the sub shop, the side street where the coffee shop is (don't look, don't think) and on toward the end of town.

Something sad happened.

. . . such a tragedy.

I will not cry here.

I pass the bank and feel like putting my foot through their shiny glass doors.

I've moved on. You should, too.

Should I? Should I, Nadia? Gee, why didn't *I* think of that instead of spending the last ninety fucking days of my life in pure and total agony? Why, I'll just do what you say and *move on*. Wow, who knew?

It's so easy to talk when it isn't happening to you.

And her mother sure as hell didn't think there was anything bad going on in my house all those times she let Nadia eat or sleep over, do homework or spend half her life up in my room talking, laughing, sharing clothes and makeup, dreams and secrets . . .

Only now.

There's an empty Frosty cup rolling in the gutter. I step off and give it a savage kick. It lands in the road and a car flattens it.

Good.

I pass the senior citizen center, hesitate, and take the shortcut across the police department's pristine front lawn, through the long, sharp shadow cast by the late-afternoon sun, around the marigold bed and the flagpole, the snap hooks on the flag clanging against the metal pole in the quiet. Catch a choking whiff of fresh, hot blacktop hanging heavy on the breeze and, glancing around the side of headquarters, see the unused patrol cars parked up on the grass along the driveway, the orange cones guarding the empty, newly paved parking lot, the old potholes, stains and painted lines buried beneath the smooth, flat, glistening new expanse.

They've moved on.

Paved right over the past, like it never even happened.

I walk faster, heart pounding. Pass the last house in town and then the little park, the minimall with the bagel store that closed at noon and the dry cleaner's I haven't been back to yet, and finally reach Victory Lane.

I've moved on. You should, too.

I hate that phrase, hate it more than any other, but . . . at least she told me.

I have to give her that.

At least she didn't look right into my eyes and lie, making me think there was still a reason to hope. It's better to just say it, to get it over with no matter how much it hurts.

I trudge past the woods.

I've moved on. You should, too.

Brutal but honest. It lets you know where you stand instead of leaving you all naïve and happy, and holding on to a dream that will never come true.

Shit happens. People change.

Yes they do, and not always for the better.

Chapter 40

Our lawn needs mowing.

I go up the driveway past my mother's car, and then, parked half on the grass near the side of the house under the apple tree, my father's. The Chevy Blazer, once an immaculate, shiny black, is now dusted with a layer of grainy, greenish-yellow pollen. Three months' worth of bird crap has dried on the windshield from the robins nesting on the branch above and the tires have gone soft, sunk in the cushiony clover springing up all around them.

The sight of it still surprises me sometimes, usually when I'm lost in thought and come around the corner. I catch sight of it and for one breathless, heart-stopping moment I forget he's dead and think he's home, and all I have to do is tear into the porch and yell, "Dad?" and he'll be there, sitting at the kitchen table, drinking his coffee and talking with my mother just like he used to.

I drop the Macy's bag, pause at the driver's window, close my burning eyes and rest my forehead against the glass. It's warm from the slant of the late-afternoon sun. My prayer is the same simple *Please, God* I've said a thousand times before, leaning against the driver's door and pleading, apologizing, praying, because this was the last place on earth my father was alive, the last place he ever drew a breath, and if his spirit or his soul or his love is lingering anywhere, I figure it would be here.

I've haven't climbed into the Blazer though.

His car keys are still hanging on the hook in the kitchen but I've never taken them, unlocked the door and gotten in.

I'm afraid to.

Even though it's spotless now, scrubbed and rinsed, I'm still afraid that if I do get in, instead of finding comfort I'll end up freaked by the sight of a faint, lingering bloodstain or stray bone fragment, nauseated by a hint of that thick, metallic smell. I'm afraid that the dent in the door frame behind the driver's seat, the place where the bullet struck after it passed through him, will not just be proof of his end but will somehow push me even farther away, horrified and sickened, and I couldn't bear if that happened.

So here it sits, and here I stand.

Death knows exactly how to break your heart, over and over again.

I gaze at my reflection in the smudged and dusty glass.

Dark, wet eyes; long, tangled brown hair. Nose red, runny.

What a mess.

I heave a shaky sigh and step back. One of the robins swoops past and its fledglings cheep like crazy in the branches above me. I don't want to go inside yet and tell my mother I got distracted and didn't bring the bagels, which was something my father used to do for her every Sunday brunch when he wasn't on duty, so I wander across the side lawn bordering the highway below and plop down on the bench under the enormous old copper beech tree. Glance back at the house and then out at the overpass.

No cars, no joggers, nothing.

Good.

I pull out the cigarette I stole from my mother, smooth the wrinkles and light it.

Exhale a stream of smoke and stare at the overpass.

I flick my ashes and take another drag. The smoke curls up and burns my nose, brings tears to my eyes.

What a stupid day.

You're right, Row, I don't *understand, and you know what? It's fine. I don't want to.*

She never did, either. Lucky her.

I'm stuck in the middle of it and I *still* don't understand it, hate the endless speculation, the fact that I'll never know anything again for sure. Hate the random memories that come back to me bit by bit, as if shock has given me some kind of temporary amnesia, making me forget, letting me remember.

I hate knowing that from now until forever my life will be divided into Before Daddy Died and After.

So far, the After really sucks.

I've tried hard to figure out exactly why he did it—it was the big question everyone asked at the wake, studying our faces as if my mother and I knew why or, worse, had done something to cause it—searching back through the weeks leading up to his death to find the single, definitive moment that shouted, *Here it is! This is it! This is the reason your father killed himself!*

But it isn't that easy.

I can try to guess why, trace a path of events that I *think* are right, but I still can't find one absolute cause, nothing big and glaring, only a steady, unrelenting and growing pile of misery being heaped on his shoulders, burdens that, taken one by one, were difficult but not deadly, stuff he could have easily handled . . .

Had it not been for the depression.

But nobody wants to believe it could be as quiet, as simple and as complicated as that.

They want a *reason*, an event, something they can pinpoint and steer clear of. One solid, understandable betrayal that pushed him over the edge, one horrible, unbearable secret found out, one *something* that was huge, ugly and intolerable, concrete and seeable, touchable and ultimately avoidable.

And I have nothing to offer them but the sad, slow drain of a chemical imbalance.

I shift and take a drag off of my cigarette.

Tilt my head back and exhale, dispersing a cloud of gnats.

Take another drag, pull it deep enough to make my chest ache.

When my father was alive I could have stood up with absolute, unshakable belief in his good, strong, reliable heart and told the world he was a man who cared, a man who always went above and beyond to protect and serve, a man you could trust with your life.

A dog barks, out near the road.

But I don't know what's true anymore, don't know what to believe, don't even know if he kissed me good-bye one last time while I was sleeping that morning, if he stood over me in the soft, pre-dawn light, heartbroken, needing to go, wanting to stay, or if he did nothing, never came back upstairs at all, just picked up his .38 and slipped out the door to die.

I don't even know that, and it's all I want.

I just want to know if I was worth saying good-bye to because . . .

He didn't even leave us a note.

I wipe my eyes. Look down at the cigarette smoldering between my fingers for a long moment. Lean over, stub it out in the dirt and, rising, wander over to flick it in the road.

The dog barks again.

I look up, following the sound to see a chubby woman with a Rottweiler power-walking by on the overpass.

It isn't Eli.

I knew it wouldn't be and yet . . .

I'm starting to wish it was.

Chapter 41

I fumble my key from my pocket, unlock the door and step into the porch. The windows are shut and the air is close, stagnant, smelling faintly of dirt, smoke and litter boxes. The room is crowded with bags of potting soil, gardening tools and flowerpots that weren't used this year, unopened bags of birdseed stacked against the wall and a brand-new feeder that never got hung.

Three of my father's jackets still hang on the pegs, his gloves still sit on the shelf, his worn slipper mocs are still lined up beneath them.

A spider's built a web in one of them.

I slip off my sandals, nudge them into the corner.

Cleaning out the porch was next on his old to-do list, still posted on the fridge. His last project was painting the dining room, but nobody's eaten in there since my mother finished it.

It's hard to have a family dinner without a family.

"I'm home," I mutter, and ten anxious, milling cats race to greet me, tails high, eyes bright, twining and rubbing against my ankles. "Hey, guys. I guess you haven't eaten yet." I bend and give each of them a quick, reassuring pet, then plow gently through the herd and into the kitchen.

laura wiess

Stripe is sitting and waiting amidst the huge stacks of unopened mail scattered across the kitchen table.

"Come on, Stripey. You know you're not supposed to be up here," I say, picking him up and setting him on the floor. He gazes up at me, questioning, solemn, and when I still don't miraculously turn into the one person he's been waiting so patiently to see, he turns and, tail twitching, stalks off to sit by the empty food dishes.

I disappoint him every day by not being my father.

It's been three months but he still looks up, eager and alert, whenever the door opens, and still has his hopes dashed every time. It's awful. I wish I could find a way to make him understand that his best friend is gone and never coming back so it's all right to stop waiting, stop hoping . . .

But how can I, when a corner of my own heart is still waiting and hoping, too, even in the face of all evidence against it?

Somewhere in these piles of unopened mail littering the kitchen table is a big manila envelope from the county medical examiner's office, and in it is an autopsy report. Evidence of death. Of suicide.

I noticed it when it came in, told myself that knowing is always better than not knowing, that this was about my father lying defenseless and alone on that cold steel table and that for all the times he protected us, in the one moment when *he* needed protecting, we were not there for him.

Facing it felt like the least I could do, so I opened the report. Read his name, his vital statistics, and thought, hands shaking, papers rattling, that I could do this. I could read what they discovered because he was my father and I loved him, but when my gaze slid to lower lines and other pages, absorbing the words *rigor mortis, lividity, slice, vitreous, basilar skull, charring, fragments, stomach contents, brain, incision* . . .

I'd gone dizzy, couldn't breathe, frantically stuffed the report back into the envelope, but it was too late.

I couldn't erase the terrible new images swirling through my mind.

They had cut him apart.

Evidence of death.

There is more.

There is always more.

We still have the clothes my father wore that last morning.

My mother wanted them back and the funeral parlor gave them to her, everything. She brought them home, her face as white as the plastic bag they were bundled in, the handles tightly tied, and then she . . . what?

What did she do with them?

I put a trembling hand to my forehead. It comes away wet with sweat.

I don't know. I never saw them again.

His wallet is here, soft, worn-looking brown leather curved from his back pocket, still sitting on the windowsill by the sink, where it's been ever since the police returned it to my mother that morning.

Breathe.

Was it in his pocket when he died, or did he take it out, put it in plain view on the dashboard to make identification easy for whoever found him?

Probably. He was always thoughtful that way.

I grope my way to the table and drop into the closest empty chair.

My father's chair.

"Oh *God*, Daddy," I whisper, covering my face as a wave of pain envelops me. I don't want this, don't want any more freak death thoughts, can't wrap my mind around the idea of that bag sitting somewhere in this house with his jeans and shirt, socks and shoes and underwear folded up inside, can't stand wondering if they were washed before we got them back or if his blood is still on them, if all of the pain he felt as he lifted the pistol and placed it to his temple is somehow still bound up and lingering in that cloth.

"Stop," I whisper, pressing my fingers to my forehead, but it doesn't prevent the rest of the memory from rising, doesn't stop me from remembering how my mother looked that day when she returned from the funeral home, how she stood in the doorway, shattered, and how what she said seemed to make such perfect sense at the time.

"These are his things, and they belong here at home with us."

And that was it. She turned and left the room, taking the bag with her, and I've never seen it again, never even thought of it until now . . .

And never want to think of it again.

Chapter 42

"Rowan? Is that you?"

"Yeah," I say, sticking my head around the door and into the living room, where my mother is still curled up on the couch exactly where I left her; under an afghan, a cup of coffee and stack of books on the end table within reach. The ashtray is full of cigarette butts. "I'll feed the cats."

"Oh, thank you," she says, but her smile is only a ghost of her real one. "I guess the day kind of got away from me again." She yawns and sits up, smoothing the limp brown hair from her forehead and exposing an inch of gray roots. "Grandma and Grandpa were here earlier. Grandpa cleaned out the gutters and Grandma left noodles and cabbage, if you're hungry. You know Grandma."

"Food is love," I say automatically, and even though I don't feel hungry, my well-trained stomach growls in anticipation. "Do you want a bowl?"

"If you're having one," she says, studying my face. "Rough day?"

"Eh." I shrug because really, what am I going to say? "I forgot the bagels, though."

"That's all right. I'm not in the mood for them, anyway. But you know what?" she says, voice brightening, and stretches out a hand to Peach, one of the three small, fuzzy kittens she brought in to live with us a couple of weeks ago. "Come in here for a minute, Rowan. Sit down."

"Now?" I say, but still trudge in and perch on the edge of the love seat. The cats have been sharpening their claws on the arm and the burgundy damask is pebbled with pulls. I smooth them down, tug at a long, loose thread but it doesn't give.

"Yes, now," she says, sorting through the pile of books. "I want to show you something."

Oh God, no, please. I've looked through that stack and every book in it is about coping with grief, loss, the death of a spouse, a parent, and worst of all, the psychological impact of suicide on the surviving family.

I opened that last one on a very dark day about a month ago, desperate for some kind of comfort, for reassurance that I wasn't going crazy feeling this bad, that it was normal and would someday end, paged through it despite my rising dread at the cold, clinical language and landed on a sentence that made my head spin: *It has been established that individuals who have had a suicide in their family are at greater risk for suicide than those who have not.*

I don't know how long I sat there chilled, shivering and staring at that sentence, but when I finally looked up dusk had fallen and it was time to turn the lights on.

I never told my mother about that, either.

She's probably read it herself by now, anyway. Almost all she's done these last months besides sleep, cry and collect cats is read constantly, as if examining her pain, tracking, exploring and confirming it, will somehow help her through it.

But I'm not her. I don't want to dissect it. It's hard enough just living it. Sometimes I wish I could just go into a coma and not wake up until I'm better.

"Here we are," she says, sliding two thin books with paisley covers from the pile and holding one out to me. "It's a grief journal. I got myself one, too. It has places to write your feelings, inspirational sayings and a month-by-month suggestion list that's supposed to help heal." She shrugs, suddenly self-conscious, and opens her journal. "I don't know. Maybe it's stupid."

"No, it sounds great." I reach out and take it. "Thanks, Mom." I set it on my lap but don't open it because even one cutesy, inspirational saying or suggestion to *Smile!* will make me scream right now. "I appreciate it."

The counselor at school, back in June, when I was delusional enough to try to go again, told me that grief is not my enemy; it's my body's natural response to a trauma too intense to handle all at once. Grief numbs me, protects me; shields go up and come down again inch by inch, only allowing me to see as much of my wretched new reality as I can handle at the time.

I guess she was trying to help but the idea that it was going to get worse, that this pain would intensify as my protection faded, was too much to hear that soon, and so I stopped going to school and finished the work from home.

I don't know what I'm going to do when junior year starts in September.

Maybe the grief journal will solve that for me, too.

"Well anyway, I just thought maybe it would help," she says quickly, paging through it. "Here, like this one for the first stages of grief: shock, denial and numbness." My mother tucks her hair behind her ear and glances over at me, as if to make sure I'm still listening. *"Be gentle with yourself, for you have suffered a great blow and you will heal at your own pace.* Or this one: *Don't be afraid to feel."*

"Right," I say dully, wrapping my arms around myself and gazing down at my feet.

There's a blade of grass stuck to my big toe.

"There are some good ones in the second stage. Let me find them." She ducks, scanning the pages as if she's afraid I'm going to leave before she gets there. "Okay, here, we're three months in and I think this is where we are, at least some of the time. *Take a first step. Do something different. Surround yourself with life."* She glances pointedly across the couch at Peach, who is stalking her bare feet. *"Do your mourning now; don't avoid it.* Or this"—she gives a little laugh—"which is good because I've been doing it all along: *Don't be afraid to talk or write to your loved one about unresolved issues. It can lessen the burden and help you heal."*

I shake my head and look away.

"Supposedly every emotion we have during this journey is necessary, even if we don't understand it." She pages further. "Trying to avoid the pain, blocking it out, self-medicating with drinking or drugs—"

Okay, enough.

"—only stalls the healing. The unresolved pain is still there, trapped inside and—"

"So is that what you were going to show me?" I interrupt, reaching down and flicking the grass off of my toe and onto the rug, where Plum immediately pounces on it. "Come on, I want to go eat." I glance up, see the hurt on her face and immediately feel like crap for shutting her down. "Sorry. Go on."

She pauses a moment longer and when she resumes reading the animation in her voice is gone. *"The next stages are fear, anger and depression—"*

"Great," I say, unable to stop myself. "More depression." I stand up. "Want some noodles?"

"Rowan, wait," she calls as I go into the kitchen. "It's all right. This is a *good* thing. They're saying we won't feel this bad forever. The final stages are understanding, acceptance and recovery."

"Are they, Mom?" I mutter, and, grabbing a spoon, dig a big hunk of noodles and cabbage out of the bowl and dump it onto my plate. "Even for the survivors of suicide?" Stick the plate in the microwave and punch in two minutes. "'Cause that's not what the other book says."

"What?" she calls, and now there's an odd note in her voice.

It has been established that individuals who have had a suicide in their families are at greater risk for suicide than those who have not.

"Rowan?"

"I said do you want some noodles?" I yell back.

I wish I'd never read that stupid sentence.

Grief Journal

Daddy, please.

I can't take this silence anymore.

So if you won't talk to me, then I guess I'm finally going to talk to you.

It's what you always wanted me to do, right?

Talk, especially when I was in trouble and couldn't figure things out on my own?

Well, here I am.

God, I don't even know how to begin.

All I know is that my heart is broken, I miss you so bad.

You've never left before, not even for a week, and now it's been ninety-two terrible, empty days and that's long enough for me to finally start getting it through my head that you're really not coming back, that you're gone forever and it's not a sick prank or a nightmare or anything I can change, no matter how desperately I want to.

The numbness is wearing off too, leaving all the other emotions exposed like live wires, raw, tangled and dangerous.

Totally out of control.

You always thought I was so smart but I don't feel that way now. I don't know why I tried so hard to ruin that pride you had in me. Maybe I was testing it, testing you to see if you would still love me if I made choices of my own.

Stupid, hurtful choices.

So do you? Still love me, I mean?

Because I'd give a lot to take at least one of those choices back.

Shoulda, woulda, coulda.

They're like curses now.

You left me cursed by my own stupid, irreversible actions and by yours.

How am I supposed to live with that?

I should be mad at you but I can't be because before, when we got mad at each other, we were in the same place at the same time and talked, questioned, explained, and somehow we always got past it.

But we're not anymore, so the side of me that was left ripped open and bleeding when you went can never be healed now, can it? We will *never* resolve this the way I need to, you will *never answer me* and knowing that makes me want to scream.

And that's not drama. That's the truth.

So how do I keep going when you're not here to listen, understand, and forgive me? How can I be mad at you for leaving when it won't change anything, when I'll never know if you're sorry that you hurt me, so then I can say I'm sorry that I hurt you too, and we can both forgive each other like we used to?

How can I make it through if we never talk again?

I've waited and waited for you to say something, do something . . .

Are you sorry?

Because let me tell you, an apology would be a good start.

Or an explanation.

Or an *I will always love you, Rowan.*

Something, anything other than this empty silence that is everywhere, all the time now, inside of me and out.

I don't know how to live the rest of my life without you.
I don't think I can.
Can a person actually die of sadness?
How about of a broken heart?
I've thought about it a lot and yes, I think so.
You did.
So maybe I will, too.

P.S.: It's really hard to say this but I *know* that if I hadn't cut school and you hadn't caught me and had to bring me home, you would have never been anywhere *near* the overpass that day and someone else would have responded to that jumper call. Someone else would have lost Corey and the baby, not you, and if that had happened . . .

Oh God, if only that had happened.

Chapter 43

When my father was alive, we used to eat together at the kitchen table.

Now we eat on trays in front of the TV in the family room.

It's not the same.

I finish before my mother, who's settled in behind a wall of cats and has her nose stuck in another book, set my bowl on the others piled in the sink, call, "I'm going outside," and before she can answer, head back across the side lawn to the bench under the tree to smoke the cigarette I just stole from her pack.

I could have stolen the *whole* pack, with how much attention she's paying these days. Next time I will.

I glance back at the house to make sure she hasn't had a sudden fit of conscience and followed me out to talk some more and when the door stays shut I shrug, light up, inhale and blow a few big, fat smoke rings.

My father would hate this.

Of course if he was alive, I probably wouldn't be doing it.

"Oh well," I say rudely, and take another drag off the cigarette. Hide it as a car goes by, just in case it's someone we know, but it isn't.

It never is, anymore. Not like when he first died and everyone showed up at the house to talk, comfort and console.

Everyone was here for us back then, arms open.

I take a hitched drag off my cigarette and let it out, slowly.

But time never stops ticking, and people have to go back to their normal lives.

No, they *get* to go back to their normal lives and pick up where they left off, relieved, guilty and on some private level desperately thankful that they're not us.

The smoke drifts up and disappears into the tree branches.

I lean forward and glance at the overpass.

Nothing, of course.

He doesn't walk this way anymore.

I flick my ashes.

I glance back at the house. Still clear. Take another drag off the cigarette.

I don't know what I'm so worried about. My mother isn't going to come out here. She hasn't really been out of the house since the funeral, except into the backyard to feed the stray cats that live in the woods. She became kind of obsessed with them after my father died, standing at the window watching as, skinny, starved and frightened, they crept out to the food plate and ate like it was their last meal.

"I can't stand this," she said, turning to me with a look of agonized urgency in her eyes. "They're going to die if we don't intervene and then I'll never be able to live with myself." And so she ordered a Havahart trap online and started catching them, handing them over to my grandfather, who dutifully took them to the vet's for shots and fixing, and then brought them back to her for food, shelter and gentling.

It was weird at first, coming into a house that started with Stripe and now held eleven cats in various stages of domestication, but somehow it ended up being no big deal.

Maybe because when every single thing in your life has already drastically changed, adding a few new cats isn't even a blip on the radar.

And I don't mind them. I really don't.

What I mind is when she crawls into her nest of blankets on the couch, pictures of my father on the tables around her, cats in her lap, and shuts the rest of the world out, reading until she goes to bed and then starting up again over coffee in the morning.

I hate eating meals with her when she's on the couch.

It makes me feel alone, abandoned, and that makes being lonely even lonelier.

My cigarette's gone out, so I push myself up off the bench to go ditch it in the road.

The overpass is empty.

Everything is empty.

I drop the butt in the thin layer of grit on the shoulder, with all of the others.

Step on it, pressing down hard until it's completely flattened.

Look both ways, and walk out to the center yellow line.

Pause.

Step slowly over it into the other lane and then up onto the sidewalk on the overpass.

They all stood here—my father, Eli, Corey and the baby—and now I'm here, too.

I can hear the traffic speeding by on the highway below and slowly, as if drawn against my will, I put my hands on the cement wall where Corey and his son sat, where they went over, and peer down.

The highway's crowded with cars weaving in and out of lanes, commuter buses, trucks . . .

I watch them, mesmerized, until my vision blurs and then, with growing trepidation, blink away the haze and search the pavement for the spot Corey and Sammy hit. I don't know what I'm expecting—a stain, a mark, chalk outlines—but there's nothing there, only the remnants of a makeshift memorial off to the side of the road.

A white plastic cross stuck in the weeds and tied with sagging, faded blue ribbons. A weather-beaten teddy bear propped crooked at its base.

The full horror of it hits me.

I snatch my hands from the wall and step back, shuddering. Wipe them on my shorts once and then again, and that's when I hear my mother calling my name.

Chapter 44

"What the hell were you doing out there?" she yells the minute I walk in the door, sending a panicked wave of cats bolting for cover.

"Nothing," I say, taken aback.

"Nothing?" Her face is flushed and furious, her gaze wild. "You're standing out on that goddamn overpass staring down over the side and you call that *nothing*?" She crosses the kitchen and grabs my arm, stares hard into my face. "What were you doing over there, Rowan? Tell me!"

"Mom, you're scaring me," I say in a small voice, and try to pull free, but her fingers are digging into my skin. "Ow." Her breath is hot and stale, the scent of her sweat sharp with fear. "You're *hurting* me."

"*I'm* hurting *you*?" my mother says, but she releases me and steps back, breathing hard. "You could have fallen, Rowan, you could have lost your balance and gone over and been *killed*, do you realize that? You could have *died* and I couldn't have done anything about it!" She stares are me, chin trembling, her terror too huge for the room. "When I saw you, I thought . . . oh my God." Shaking, she puts a hand to her face and, groping behind her, sinks into a chair. "I couldn't live if anything happened to you, Rowie." She gazes up at me, tearful, beseeching. "Please, *please* swear to me that if you ever feel that bad you'll tell me and let me help you, *please*—"

"I will," I say, crying now, too. "I wasn't going to do anything, Mom. I swear. I was just——" I stop, confused. I was just what, looking? Spellbound? What? What was I doing?

I don't know.

"Rowie, listen." She reaches out, catches hold of my hand. "I know it's hard without your father. I do. And I know it's up to me now and I don't know how that's going to go, I honestly don't, but I do love you so please——"

"I'm sorry." I drop to my knees and hug her back, feel the pain and desperation in her sobs, the fear that makes her cling so tight. "We're going to be okay, Mom, we are," I say, and through the tears realize this is the first time those words have come out of my mouth since my father died, and so I say them again, hear them again, but no, in my heart I still don't believe them.

But my mother nods, dries her tears, accepts the reassurance, and it scares me, how much easier it is to comfort someone with a lie than it is to tell them the truth.

Chapter 45

Surprisingly, my mother doesn't retreat and disappear right back into her books but instead, shyly, as if not wanting the closeness to end, suggests we make popcorn and watch a movie, and so, wrung out, exhausted but strangely gentle with each other, we curl up on the couch, content to be close and watch mindless TV together until bedtime, just me, my mother, eleven purring cats and my father's urn on the mantel.

She sees me looking at it, shakes her head and with a wry smile says, "Puts a whole new spin on family night, doesn't it?"

The comment catches me by surprise and my laugh shoots out before I can stop it. "Oh my *God*, Mom." I glance at her, torn between the incredible wonder of us feeling, even for a moment, light enough to laugh and the worry caused by such flip and blatant disrespect. "I can't believe you just said that."

"Why not? Your father would have said it if that was me up there in a jar," she says, lips twitching at my scandalized look. "Sometimes we need to laugh, or we'll go crazy. A little irreverence takes the edge off. He would have been the first to tell you that."

Yes, he would have, but the thought still leaves me uneasy. "What if he heard you, though?"

"What if he did?" my mother says, shrugging. "What's he

going to do, haunt me?" She glances at his picture on the end table and then back at me, trying to smile, but the humor in her gaze has faded and the loss sends a hollow spear of pain through my heart.

"Yeah, like that'd be something new, right?" I say quickly, wishing I just laughed and let it go, wishing I let that light in her eyes last a little longer. "I'm sorry," I say, knotting my fingers together and staring down at my hands. "I didn't mean to ruin it."

"What? You didn't ruin anything," she says, reaching over, tugging one of my clenched hands free and cradling it between hers. "You said what you felt, and there's nothing wrong with that. It's what you're supposed to do."

"But it made you sad again," I mumble.

"Oh, Rowie, it wasn't you," she says, squeezing my hand. "I'm sad all the time now and that's okay, it's a natural part of grieving. I never *forget* that he's gone but sometimes it's like the clouds part for a minute and a ray of sunshine shoots through, and then it's done and the clouds close over again, that's all. Hey." She jiggles my hand until I look at her. "It wasn't you. I promise, okay?"

"Okay," I say grudgingly, and, easing my hand free, offer her the rest of my popcorn.

And it seems like we're fine, or as fine as we can be, but later that night when I get up to go to the bathroom, I hear her crying.

I pause outside her door. "Mom?" Step closer and the nightlight in the hall lifts the darkness enough for me to see into the room.

She's standing on my father's side of the room, at his armoire, where all of his clothes still wait inside, where his navy blue, terry-cloth bathrobe still hangs on an outside hook. She's leaning against the bathrobe, nestled against the soft cloth, and weeping.

"Mom?" My voice cracks.

She lifts her head and says helplessly, "I don't know how to stop waiting for him." She presses the sleeve of the robe to her cheek. "Oh God, I miss him so bad."

"I know," I whisper, wrapping my arms around my waist.

"Do you remember how sad he looked at the end, so gray and hopeless? All I want to do now is take his poor, tired face in my hands and tell him not to worry, we'll make it as long as we're together. All that other stuff will pass, as long as he stays." Her voice catches on a sob. "That's what I should have told him, Row."

"You *did*, Mom, like a hundred times," I say, voice wobbling.

She shakes her head, refusing to be consoled. "I was impatient because of the stupid dining room and I thought maybe it would help if we tried to talk about it. God knows I'd tried everything else but now . . . if I could take it back, I would. I never should have done it. Talking only made him feel worse. I should have realized he was doing all he could just to hang on until the medication finally started working. I thought I knew how to help him, Rowan, but I didn't, and I'll never forgive myself for that. I won't."

"Don't, Mom." The guilt in her voice rattles me. "Please?"

"I can't even tell him I'm sorry," my mother says.

I go to her and for the second time today, she puts her arms around me. I lay my head against the bathrobe too, breathing in the last lingering traces of my father's person smell, and we huddle there lost in yearning, still wanting, needing, wishing for one last chance to hold the hands, kiss the cheek, feel the embrace of a man we will never see again.

This is what the survivors of suicide—the aftermath, the wreckage, the walking wounded—look like in the hours between dusk and dawn.

Grief Journal

Who am I now, Dad, without you?

Really. I need to know.

Because I'm not who I used to be, that's for sure.

Not even close.

Want to know some of the things I've learned since you left?

They're not good and you're not going to like hearing them but I can't help that. They're real and true, and I can't get them out of my head.

And you're the only one I can tell.

Okay, well, did you know that the American Psychiatric Association ranks the emotional trauma of losing a loved one to suicide as *catastrophic*?

That your decision forever changed the course of my life and who I am?

Did you know that most of the people who kill themselves have a diagnosable and *treatable* psychiatric disorder like depression at the time of their death?

That your depression wasn't something you did wrong but a chemical imbalance in your brain, not a choice, and could have happened to anyone at any time, regardless of sex, age, race or religion?

Did you know that it's pretty common for the first pre-scribed antidepressant not to work, and that there are others you could have tried?

A whole *slew* of others, and ones that might have helped? God, Dad.

Did you know that individuals who have had a suicide in their families are at greater risk for suicide in the future than those who have not?

That now, thanks to you, that means me and Mom?

We are at risk now, Dad. You, who always protected us in life, risked us in death.

I hate knowing that, and to be honest, I'm afraid to think too much about it.

I'm screwed up enough these days as it is.

And you can't save me.

Just kidding . . . but it's true.

That's one of the side effects of killing yourself. You get no say in anything anymore.

Actually, that's wrong. Every single thing we've done these past three months has been because of you.

And it only took me ninety-two days to figure that out.

Wow. I guess I'm not as smart as you thought I was, am I?

It's okay. You're not who I thought you were, either.

I hate knowing that, too.

So, this is the beginning of the fourth month.

I thought maybe it would be some kind of turning point.

Turning to what, I don't know, but anything's got to be better than this.

Have I ever told you what it's really been like for me?

What *grief* has been like so far, all up close and personal? No? Then let me try.

It's the perfect storm, Dad, and it hits like a wrecking ball, coming out of nowhere and slamming into your brain. It de-stroys everything. Your emotions are in shambles: One minute you're crying, the next you're laughing, the next you can barely lift your head for the agony. Life narrows: You don't care about stuff that used to matter and you overreact to the stuff that matters now. You need to be held but you want to be left alone. Your short-term memory is shot. Every step is like slogging through a mud pit. Exhaustion hits at random and all you can do is sleep. You second-guess yourself constantly. You can't meet anyone's gaze for fear you'll see blame there, or suspicion or judgment. You feel small, weak, guilty. You think weird thoughts, do strange things. Every nerve in your body is raw but your brain is a foggy, unreliable mess. You can't see from crying and food has no taste but all of a sudden you can smell a dirty sock three rooms away. Your moods are up, down, down, up, like a crazed, speeding, out-of-control roller coaster you can't get off of, no matter how long or how awful the ride.

And that's just the first three months.

Catastrophic.

Yeah, I'd say that's about right.

Chapter 46

I no sooner get downstairs the next morning, a parade of playful, tumbling cats following behind me, than my mother comes in and, like all the closeness of last night is forgotten, tells me that I have to go grocery shopping with my grandparents.

"What? Are you kidding?" I say as she hands me the list and the money. "I'm not going out. I'm not even dressed." I gesture at my baggy, wrinkled shorts and my father's faded old PBA T-shirt. "Why do I have to go again? Why can't you go this time?"

"Rowan. Look at me." Her shorts are stained, and her sleeveless blouse missing a button. Her whole face is swollen from last night's crying jag, her eyes bloodshot and her nose red and chafed from blowing. "Isn't it obvious?"

"But—"

"I put hair dye on the list," she says, and, with a self-conscious gesture, tucks a lank strand behind her ear. "I know it looks awful. I shouldn't have waited so long." She summons a crooked smile. "I got a good look at myself in the mirror this morning and realized that if I don't do something soon I'm going to look more like your grandmother than your mother."

She's not hearing me. I try again. "But, Mom—"

"So if you want to change your clothes you'd better hurry,

because Grandma and Grandpa will be here soon. You know they like to get their shopping done before noon, when the store gets crowded."

"I said I don't want to—"

"Rowan, please," she says, putting a hand to her forehead as if I'm giving her a giant headache. "Stop arguing and just do it, will you? I'm really not up to this today."

"Oh, but *I'm* supposed to be?" I snap, and, whirling, take off up the stairs to my room. "*God.*" I slam the door, rip off my shorts, yank on a better pair, then grab my mascara and the makeup mirror. "You're gonna have to go back out in public sometime, you know!" I yell, and, hand shaking, attack my eyelashes. "It's hard for me, too! If I wanted to see people I'd just go back to work!" Swipe, swipe, swipe with the wand. There. Next eye. "This is the last time I'm doing it!"

Silence.

"Great," I mutter, finishing and jamming the wand back into the mascara.

I hate going grocery shopping with my grandparents, the two kindest, nicest, slowest-moving people on earth. They stroll around the store like it's a day in the park and they *always* run into people they know and have to stop and talk—

"They're here," my mother calls up the stairs. "Rowan?"

"I heard you," I yell, and stomp back down the stairs, grab the list, the money and my cell phone, and without even saying good-bye, slam the porch door behind me and barrel down the steps to my grandparents' car. "Okay, let's go," I say abruptly, slipping into the backseat and folding my arms across my chest.

"Isn't your mother coming out?" my grandfather asks, eyeing me in the rearview mirror. "Ben and Jerry's ice cream is on sale and I wanted to ask her if—"

"Don't worry about it, Grandpa," I say, staring out my window and avoiding his concerned gaze. "She's in a mood again, so I guess we just have to do what she wants and deal with it. Like always."

The harsh words ring in the surprised silence and I immediately wish I hadn't involved my grandparents. "Whatever," I add with an irritated, end-it-now wave. "Let's just go."

"Drive, honey," my grandmother murmurs to my grandfather, and as he puts the car in reverse and creeps back down the driveway, she says chidingly, "Now, Rowan."

"Well, come on, you know it's true," I mutter, but am starting to lose steam because there's something very little-kid comforting about sitting in the back of my grandparents' pristine old boat of a Buick station wagon with the corded blue seat covers protecting the seats, the windows up and the air-conditioning on, shutting out the rush of the world. Even their music is from the past and one of my grandmother's favorites—Louis Armstrong's "What a Wonderful World"—is playing softly on the CD player. It's the same today as it was a year ago and the year before that, except that my grandpa's hair is thinner and grayer, and my grandma's slower, sweeter, and has new glasses.

"We don't mind helping out," my grandfather says, pulling out onto the road and heading toward the grocery store on the other side of the overpass. "Gives us old-timers something to do." He smiles at me in the rearview mirror and for a moment I could almost believe that nothing has changed and everything is fine, if it wasn't for the sadness in his eyes. "And besides, that's what family is for, Rowan. You need us and we'll be there." His voice roughens, and my grandmother glances at him and pats his arm.

"I was thinking about making chicken *paprikás* with *nokedli* for tomorrow," she says, and then, over the embarrassing sound of my stomach growling in eager response, says, "So, tell me, Rowan. Is your mother planning on going back to work soon?"

I know what she's doing, changing the subject to smooth over any lingering friction, and I'm willing to let it happen. "Not that I know of," I say, gazing out the window as the field gives way to scrubby woods and, finally, the grocery store.

Eli lives somewhere farther up this road.

I wonder how he is.

Probably going out with somebody else by now.

Somebody normal. Happy.

Whole.

"She *has* to go back to work soon," my grandfather says, signaling to turn into the grocery store parking lot. "Her leave of absence won't last forever. They've been good, giving her this long. She can't lose her job."

"I know," I say absently, scanning the half-empty parking lot for anyone I recognize. Nobody. I shrug, telling myself I'm not disappointed, grab the grocery list, and wedge my phone in my pocket. "You should ask her. We don't really talk about it."

"It's such a shame. She's worked so hard to get this far and now . . ." My grandmother points to an empty parking space up near the front of the store and my grandfather heads in that direction. "Nicky, Nicky, what were you thinking? One decision changes everything, doesn't it? Nothing is left untouched." She sighs, pulls a small bottle of lotion from her purse and commences rubbing it over her hands. "Hmm. Maybe I should make *kolaches* too. Your mother likes them."

She goes on to debate the poppy seed–versus–walnut roll dilemma and I fade out for a moment, caught in the question my grandmother asked my father. "Hey, Gran, do you talk to Daddy a lot?" I ask, leaning forward as my grandfather maneuvers the station wagon into the parking spot.

"Of course," she says matter-of-factly, putting the lotion back in her purse.

"What do you say?" I ask, unbuckling my seat belt.

"Well"—she takes her coupon wallet from her purse and tugs the zipper closed—"mostly I tell him that we love him and miss him, that he shouldn't worry about you and your mother because we're watching out for you both—"

"Okay, that's enough," I say, leaning back and fumbling for the door handle.

"—and that it's all right, he should rest in peace now because we forgive him."

"Wait," I say, pausing with my fingers wrapped tight around the door handle. "Who's *we*?"

"Well, all of us," she says as if surprised.

A surge of heat rips through me. I thrust open the car door and scramble out. Slam it too hard and stand in the baking parking lot, caught in a flood of anger. "You can forgive him if you want to but don't speak for me, okay?" I say without looking at her when she climbs out of the car. "I can do it myself."

"Hey, watch your tone!" my grandfather says, giving me a sharp, astonished look from over the roof of the car. "You're not talking to one of your friends, you know. That's your grandmother." He steps back, carefully shuts and locks the car door. "Have a little respect."

The anger dies and I stare at him, dumbstruck. My grandfather *never* yells at me and for a moment it's like the bottom has fallen out of the world all over again.

"Shh, it's all right. I understand. She won't do it again," my grandmother says, and lays a soft, wrinkled hand on my arm. "Come on, let's go shopping. The *paprikás* is going to take a while to cook."

My grandmother takes my grandfather's arm and together, leaning on each other, they start toward the store. I hesitate, wishing I was anyone but me, anywhere but here, wishing I could tell them there's an emptiness in me that food will never fill . . . but instead I just surrender and trail after them.

Chapter 47

I grab a cart and follow them through the store, trying to find the stuff on my mother's list, but my concentration sucks and all I can think about is the fact that they forgive my father.

Produce. Get lettuce.

Not that I want them to hate him or anything . . . but just forgiving him, like it's nothing? How did that happen? What did she say? *Well, we know you did a terrible thing, Nicky, and left a trail of shattered lives behind you that'll never be healed . . . but we love you anyway, so let's let bygones be bygones and we won't hold it against you?*

Deli. Get Swiss cheese, rolls and barrel pickles.

God, that makes it sound like they're just giving in and *accepting* it. Like it isn't something to mourn about or rage against anymore. Like saying *I forgive you* solves everything and now we can all move on. Do they really feel that way? Do they really think it's that simple?

Get coffee. Filters. Sugar.

I don't know but I'm not asking, especially now. Thinking about it has me teetering on the edge of some terrible, dark abyss and makes me feel wrong for not forgiving him, too.

Get Cup Noodles.

But how can I just forgive him? How can I——

"Rowan? Sweetheart, do you remember my friend Mrs. Thomas?"

I blink, startled, and return to find my grandmother and an elderly, chameleon-eyed woman stopped in the aisle and gazing expectantly at me.

"You met her at the wake," my grandmother says, and there's a warning in her eyes, in her careful, overly polite tone that at first I don't understand.

And then I look at the woman, really *see* her, and I do understand . . .

I didn't say anything to her at the wake, too floored to speak back then, but not now.

No, not now.

"I remember you," I say in a flat voice, completely disregarding my grandmother's warning and letting all the rage I feel fill my gaze. "You're the one who told my mother that my father was going to rot in hell for all eternity because he shot himself and God would never forgive him."

My grandmother gasps.

"Why, I . . . you don't . . . I'm . . . ," Mrs. Thomas babbles, turning red. "I'm sure you misunderstood—"

"No, I didn't," I say, holding her gaze, dimly aware that my grandfather has returned to his cart and my grandmother is talking to him in a low, urgent voice, but they're peripheral. Only Mrs. Thomas is front and center. "You said the Catholic church shouldn't have buried him, and you know what? Sooner or later somebody *you* love is going to die and—"

"Rowan!" My grandfather grabs my arm, and it's only then I realize that I'm in Mrs. Thomas's face now, and she's backed up against the frozen-food case, staring in alarm.

"You'll see," I say coldly, letting him pull me away, and when we turn the corner I stumble to a stop, shaking, dizzy and sweating. My knees are weak, my heart racing, and I don't know what to say, can't even bear to look into my grandfather's eyes.

"Give me your shopping list," he says in a voice I've never heard before. "And the money." He releases me and holds out his hand. "We'll finish. You go wait in the car."

"Wait, Grandpa, I . . . she . . ." But the words to explain won't come and I give up, hand him the list and fumble the money from my pocket. He gives me the car keys and I turn, choking on the unspoken, walk straight out of the store to the car, unlock it and slide into a wall of heat, leaving the door open and slumping in the backseat. Rub my face, press my fingers to my pounding temples, stretching the skin so tight it aches . . .

Lash out and kick the back of the seat.

"It isn't fair," I say, and hang my head, letting my hair swing forward to shield my face, and close my burning eyes.

Nothing is fair anymore.

Nothing is left untouched.

The ripple effect.

"God, I *hate* that," I mutter raggedly as my heart squeezes in my chest.

I hate it because it's true, and I don't want it to be.

I don't want everything changed. I liked life the way it was.

I was *happy* the way it was.

A bead of sweat trickles down my forehead and plunks off the end of my nose onto my hand. Another follows.

It's really hot in here.

I open my eyes and shove the damp hair back off of my face.

Gaze at the scuff mark on the front seat for a long moment, then lean forward and rub it off.

Shit.

I didn't avenge us by going off on stupid Mrs. Thomas. Instead of just ignoring her and denying her the satisfaction of knowing she'd hurt us, I did the exact wrong thing: got up in her face, mortified my grandparents and gave the old bat something to *really* gossip about.

The old bat.

That was one of my father's phrases.

My mouth tugs into a reluctant smile. "That's just wrong, Dad."

How many times did my mother snicker and tell him that nobody calls crabby senior ladies old bats anymore, and how many times did he just grin, glance pointedly at me and then say to her, "Hey, if it was good enough for my father then it's good enough for me. Besides, it's better than saying what I'm *really* thinking. Little pitchers have big ears, hon."

And he was right again, because I *was* always listening, soaking up everything just like a big fat sponge, absorbing the rhythm and flow, the rights and wrongs of our lives without even consciously knowing it, watching how he and my mother treated each other, how they disagreed, laughed and loved. I absorbed it all, would wrap myself in the comforting feeling of being rooted in a life I understood and a place I belonged . . .

I made it the gospel of the Arenos, the way a happy life should be, and now I'm starving for that feeling every second of every day. I have no safe boundaries without it, no anchor to keep me from swamping, sinking or bobbing off, out of control. The strong, protective walls have fallen and there's nothing to stop me from self-destructing now except me, and I don't know if I can do it.

I don't even know if I want to.

I wish I had a cigarette.

Sweating, I push myself back up in the seat and look around. "God, come on already," I say, climbing out of the car and scowling at the front of the grocery store. No sign of my grandparents. I sigh, impatient, and glance around the rest of the mall, at the pizza place, Agway, the drugstore . . .

"Hey." I shade my eyes, watching the short, sturdy girl with the brown hair tipped blond and the dark sunglasses come out of the pizza place, lean against the wall and light a cigarette. I can't be positive but I'm almost sure it's her.

Payton Well.

I bite my lip and glance back at the grocery store, then lock the car, pocket the key and take off across the parking lot.

Chapter 48

I jog halfway, sandals slapping against the steamy pavement, and then give up and slow to a walk, shade my eyes and squint in Payton's direction.

She hasn't moved, is still standing there against the wall smoking, her eyes hidden behind those sunglasses and her movements studiedly casual.

I cross the lane and step up onto the curb in front of her. "Um, Payton?"

She arches an eyebrow and takes a drag off her cigarette.

"You probably don't remember me," I say, feeling pretty stupid now. "I'm, uh, Rowan Areno. My father was—"

"Okay, yeah, you're that cop's daughter," she says brusquely, and exhales a stream of sour, alcohol-scented smoke. "What's up?"

"Well, I, uh . . ." What's wrong with me? "You came to my father's wake with Eli"—God, it feels so good to say his name again, and it must be obvious because she lifts her sunglasses and gives me a hard, assessing look—"and I just wanted to, uh, thank you."

"Hey, no problem." Her sunglasses go back down and her brittle laugh holds no humor. "That was all him, anyway. I was totally out of it. That whole time was nothing but a blur." She shrugs and takes a drag off her cigarette. "Still is."

"Oh." This is not going the way I'd hoped. I wipe away the sweat trickling down the side of my face. "Well, uh, I'm really sorry about Sammy, and Corey, too." I don't know how she's going to take that but Corey was more than just a murderer, he was her old boyfriend and her baby's father, and I feel kind of sorry for him. Even my father said it was the worst depression he'd ever seen. "I wish . . ." I catch her stony expression, shake my head and look away. "I don't know. I just wanted to tell you. I'm sorry to bother you." I turn to leave.

"Hey," she says grudgingly, and when I stop and look back she adds, "If you're not doing anything, stop by tonight around seven. I'm on Bedford Street. It's a brown cape with a big front porch." She lowers her shades this time and gives me a speaking look. "You'll know it when you see it."

"Okay," I say, taken by surprise. "Yeah, if I can I definitely will. Thanks."

"Whatever," she says as if she already knows I won't show up, and, shrugging, drops her cigarette, steps on it, yanks open the door, and disappears into the pizza place.

And as I walk back across the parking lot, bemused, trying to figure out what just happened, where the hell Bedford Street is, what kind of story I can come up with to get out there tonight and why I even want to, I realize that for the first time in a long time my shoulders are back, my head is up and I'm thinking of something other than what's happened.

I'm thinking I need a pair of dark sunglasses.

I veer off into the drugstore.

Chapter 49

I find a cheap but decent pair of shades and am at the counter paying for them when I hear a familiar burst of radio chatter. I go still for the instant it takes to remember that this is not my father in uniform, it's Vinnie coming toward me.

"Eight oh two central, be advised the subject is in CVS," he says, stopping in front of me. "Ten-four."

"Vinnie!" I hand the cashier money and turn to him, beaming. "How have you been?"

"What're you doing, Rowan?" Vinnie says, and he isn't smiling.

"What do you mean?" I take the change she hands me, and my glasses.

"I mean your grandparents called headquarters bawling their brains out, saying you'd run away—"

My jaw drops. "What?" Without even thinking I step aside, letting the line progress. "Why would they think *that*?"

"Maybe because they got out to the car expecting to find you and it was all locked up and you weren't there," Vinnie says, giving me a stern look and herding me toward the door. "So they called your mom, thinking that maybe you were mad at them, and had walked home—"

"Oh my *God*, are you kidding?" I stop walking and stare up

at him, aghast. "Why did they *do* that? I'm not running away!" I
gesture wildly at the sunglasses. "I'm shopping!" I can't believe this.
"Why didn't they just call me?" I fumble my phone from my pocket.
"God, I would have . . ." I stare down at it. "Great. It's dead."

"Well, when you charge it you're going to find some pretty
hysterical voice mails," Vinnie says, his gaze grave and his manner
nothing at all like that of the funny, easygoing guy I'm so used to.
"I don't know what you were thinking going off like that without
giving them a heads-up, but it wasn't your smartest move. Especially
now."

I look away, embarrassed by the lecture but also strangely com-
forted because it's almost what my father would have said. "I'm
really sorry. I just didn't think." I see how tired he looks, the strands
of gray at his temples, the bags under his eyes, and I realize, not
for the first time but almost like I have to keep being reminded to
notice, that my father's dying hurt him, too.

"Nicky would've given you hell for this, and he'd be giving *me*
hell for not giving you hell, but I think we've all had enough of it
lately, so . . ." He steps back. "Come on. I'm handing you over to the
firing squad. You can explain it to them."

He opens the door and I see my grandfather's stony face, my
grandmother's teary eyes and my mother's outrage all staring at me
from the back of his patrol car.

This is going to be bad.

Chapter 50

"What were you *thinking*?" my mother demands on the ride home, glancing in the rearview mirror at my grandparents, who are following us back with their trunk full of groceries. "How could you do that? My God, Rowan, Grandma was *crying* when she called me—"

"Talk about an overreaction," I mutter before I can stop myself.

My mother goes quiet a moment like she's counting to ten. "Do you have any idea how scared they were, not being able to find you? Girls go missing every single day—"

"I wasn't missing," I say.

"They didn't *know* that," my mother snaps, throwing on the signal light and careening into the driveway. She slams the car into park, fumbles off her seat belt and swivels to face me. "We didn't know *anything*. One minute you're shouting at Mrs. Thomas in the store, the next you're gone. What were they supposed to think? There was no note, no explanation. You were just *gone!*" Her voice cracks. "All you had to do was tell them where you were going or leave a note, just have the courtesy to let them know, but—"

"I'm sorry, okay?" I interrupt, unbuckling my seat belt so she can't see the tears in my eyes. "I just didn't think."

"Well, you'd better start," my mother says raggedly. "You can't keep being sorry *after* the fact. You need to think beforehand from now on. You can't just do whatever you want and disappear with-out—"

"Okay, Mom, I get it!" I say, shoving open the car door with a force that rocks it on its hinges. "I *said* I was sorry. God, why do you keep yelling at me? You never did before."

"I never *had* to before," she says.

I stop halfway out of the car and turn, scowling. "Well, you don't have to now, either, okay? I'm not a little kid anymore."

"Then stop acting like one," she says, slipping off her sun-glasses and rubbing her eyes. "I'm sorry but I don't know what else to say, Rowan. I really don't." She pulls the keys from the ignition and glances in the rearview as my grandparents' Buick creeps slowly up into the driveway. "You know, it's not just you I worry about. It's them, too. They haven't been the same since your father died. For the first time ever, they actually look old to me."

That deflates me, and we sit silent for a moment as a monarch butterfly flits past the car, its brilliant orange and black wings glow-ing in the sun.

"Well, I'll apologize but I still think they totally overreacted," I say gruffly, and then, because it seems to need saying, "Nobody would have freaked if Daddy was still alive. You would *never* have called the cops because I was gone in a *mall* for ten minutes, you would have just waited till I got back and been mad or something."

"I know," she says, sighing and passing a weary hand across her forehead. "We're all a little sensitive right now. I think it's because we missed seeing the first one and we'll be damned if we're going to get caught like that again." She reaches across the seat, touches my arm. "I'm sorry I yelled and I will try very hard not to do it again, but you have to try too, Rowan. We have to figure out how to be a family with-out your father and it isn't easy, so just bear with me, okay?"

"I know, Mom." I glance at her and then say impulsively, "You should ask Auntie Kate to come out for like, the weekend or some-thing."

"Oh, I don't want to bother her," my mother says, waving a hand. "She has so much going on right now that—"

"Mom, she's your little sister," I say, giving her a look. "She's used to you bossing her around."

"She is, isn't she," my mother says after a moment, a small smile playing about her lips.

"Well, I don't know what you're waiting for," I say, and slide out of the car, shut the door and start up the sidewalk to the house.

"Hey, don't disappear," she calls after me, and there's a sudden lilt in her voice that I haven't heard in a long time. "We have groceries to bring in."

Chapter 51

I hug my grandparents and tell them I'm sorry, and they say they accept my apology but they don't talk much while we're lugging in the groceries, don't accept my mother's offer of iced tea when we're done, and mumbling something about getting home so their frozen food doesn't spoil, they get right back into the Buick and leave.

"That was odd," my mother says, shading her eyes and watching them go.

"Yeah," I say, swishing my bare foot across the long, cool grass. "Grandpa didn't even notice that the lawn needs cutting. Weird."

"Did you apologize like we discussed?"

"Yes," I say, slapping at the hungry mosquitoes I just stirred up. "Ow! Gotcha. They didn't really want to talk about it."

"That doesn't sound right," she says, frowning and absently waving the bugs away. "Do you think I should call them and make sure they're okay?"

I shrug, still slapping, and back toward the driveway. "Grandma said she's making chicken *paprikás* for tomorrow. Why don't you just wait and see how they are then?"

"Hmm," she says, giving me a speculative look. "And you're *sure* you've apologized?"

"*Yes,*" I say with a touch of irritation, and head inside, leaving my mother standing out in the driveway alone, her hands on her hips and staring worriedly down the empty road.

The sunporch smell, hot, musty, more like an old attic than a main entrance, hits me the moment I open the door, and seized with sudden impatience, I crash my way through the bags of bird-seed and litter, past the bundles of newspapers my father tied for recycling and the cases of cat food to the lone window on the back wall. It's high off the ground and shaded outside, the one window my father always said was in the perfect position to let the cool breeze in, and I'm in the middle of fighting with the latch when I realize the screen isn't in, my father must have taken it out last fall and put the storm window down, and so I can't open it anyway.

And I know exactly where he put it, too: way out in the spider-filled back shed, stacked flat and neat and high up out of the way in the rafters.

I stand there sweating, stuck amidst piles of yesterday, frustrated, pissed off at the window, my life, my father, at his obsession with doing things right and his attention to every stupid detail. Rake the leaves, paint the eaves, clean the gutters, tune up the snow thrower, store the stupid screens . . . Why couldn't he have just slacked off for once and left them in the windows? Why did taking care of *everything* have to be so important to him? Why couldn't he have just cut himself a break and gone fishing or woodworking or *something* all of those Sundays, instead of spending them working? God, maybe if he didn't always try so hard to do the right thing . . .

I close my eyes, rest my forehead against the dusty glass.

If he didn't try so hard, he wouldn't have been him.

And for better or for worse, I wouldn't be me.

The ripple effect.

A fly buzzes up near the ceiling, searching for a way out.

"Good luck," I tell it as my fists slowly uncurl. Straightening, I shove my damp hair from my eyes and wend my way back out of the piles, leaving the kitchen door open so the cats can go into the porch and do a little fly catching.

The grocery bags, still full, cover the kitchen counters and balance precariously on top of the stuff on the table.

Okay, *this* I can do. By the time my mother comes back in I've sorted through most of the bags and put away all of the perishables, a move so shocking that instead of going back to the couch to lie down, she automatically opens a bag and starts emptying it.

The third thing she pulls out is her box of hair dye.

"This isn't my normal color," she says, gazing down in dismay at the pert, smiling, swingy-haired model on the front. "This is *ash brown*, not chestnut brown. Why did you—"

"I didn't," I say, standing next to her and peering at the box. "Grandma must have." I look from the model to my mother and back. "It's not bad. Why don't you just try it and see how it comes out?"

She sets the box down with a thump. "Because I don't want to just try it, all right? I like *chestnut brown*. I've been using *chestnut brown* for twenty-five years, Rowan. It's your father's favorite." She goes silent, staring at the box as the words hang in the air. "*Damn.*" Sags and runs a hand through her hair. "What am I doing?"

"You could go red," I offer, deliberately misunderstanding her. "That'd be pretty."

"Pretty." She gives a weak snort. "Who am I trying to be pretty for?"

"You," I say, throat tight. "Me." It's as far as I can think, as far as I can go right now.

"Maybe I should just shave my head and forget the whole thing," she says with a small, forlorn laugh. "Or bleach it blond—"

"And get a tattoo," I add, hoping to coax a real smile. I pull back and look at her. Nothing yet. "A big old tramp stamp right here." I touch the small of her back. "What do you want it to say?"

"Absurd," she says, lips twitching. "I'm not getting a tattoo, Rowan."

"But if you did, what would it be? And not a rose or a butterfly or a fairy, okay? Everybody's got those."

"A *fairy*?" she echoes, and there it is, the smile I've been waiting for. "Really, do I look like the fairy type to you?" She shakes her head, actually lets out a snicker. "A fairy. No, I'm sorry to disappoint you but I'm not getting a tattoo. This is about as wild as I get." Still smiling, she picks up the box of hair dye and starts for the stairs, cats trotting at her heels. "Wish me luck."

"Mom, it's going to look great."

"Decent will do." Her voice echoes back down to me, still amused. "A *fairy*."

I stand there for a moment, tears of surprise prickling my eyes because I didn't know it before, but I do now: I would do just about anything to see my mother smile like that again.

Chapter 52

My mother dyes her hair and it does look great, makes her look younger, prettier, makes the new grief lines in her face seem softer and her eyes more striking.

And she hates it.

"But why?" I say, standing in the bathroom doorway and watching in distress as she rakes all that clean, shiny hair back with her fingers and struggles to trap it in a coated rubber band. "Mom, it looks good, it really does. You look totally different."

"Come *on*," she tells her reflection, frustrated as the silky strands slip through her fingers. "Just cooperate, will you?" Savagely, she drags it all back, pulling the hair so tight the roots go white at her scalp and snapping the band around it. "There. That solves that. Next time maybe you people will understand that when I *say* chestnut brown, I *mean* chestnut brown." Her voice is ragged, the fear in her eyes mixed with something deeper, something that makes her turn away from the mirror as if unable to bear the sight of herself, push past me and thunder back down the stairs.

I stand there dazed, staring at the mess lying in the sink, the stained gloves, the empty applicator bottle, the box with the young, sexy, flowing-haired model on the front, and it looks like a war zone, like some kind of terrible battle took place, a fearsome tug-of-war between yesterday and tomorrow . . . and suddenly I get it, how choosing something new and different is like leaving the past and everyone in it behind.

But she isn't, right? I mean, it's only hair color . . .

Isn't it?

I don't know.

It's too complicated.

There are too many layers.

Too many traps, everywhere.

We take one small step forward and get knocked back a mile.

If there's a finish line out there, it isn't in sight.

And what's the point of it, anyway? Are we really going to be stronger, getting the emotional shit kicked out of us every single day and then struggling to stand up again? Is this what happens *every* time you love and then lose someone? Is this supposed to be some profound journey, some kind of warped and psychotic learning experience that will expand our brains and teach us—what, that it's better to not have your father kill himself?

"I already *know* that," I grind out, snatching up the remnants of the dye disaster and jamming them all in the trash can. It's full though, packed to the brim with damp, tearstained tissues, and the dye box teeters and falls out again. The hair model lies there smiling up at me, no longer perky and carefree but sly and challenging now, and with a surge of rage I grab the empty box, crush and rip and tear it into pieces. Hurl them at the can. They hit the wall, scatter all over the floor, and the sight of that smile, torn from her face but still landing in one piece, is too much.

I step back, breathing hard.

"Fuck you," I tell it, and, feeling stronger than I have in months, walk out, leaving the trail of destruction behind me.

Why not?

It seems to run in the family.

Grief Journal

Hey, Dad, I need to ask you something.

Do you think a turning point is an outside event or an inside one, or both?

I mean, what is it, actually, and what was yours?

What was bad enough to send you over the edge?

I don't really know why I'm asking that except . . .

I'm kind of worried about Mom.

I mean I know everybody mourns their own way on their own schedule, but . . .

You wouldn't even recognize her.

She sleeps a lot, doesn't get dressed or go out, and she hasn't gone back to work yet. There's like, three months' worth of unopened mail sitting on the kitchen table and twice so far the electricity's gone off and she's had to call and make a payment to have it turned back on. Same with the phones, Internet and cable, too. She's not cooking anymore, either, and sometimes she wears the same clothes for like, three days in a row.

Oh, and she yelled at me for "disappearing" without leaving a note when all I did was go into the drugstore to buy a pair of sunglasses.

You know what?

I think she was really yelling at you and just didn't realize it.

Or maybe she doesn't want to.

It's so weird. Neither one of us can stand being mad at you right now.

But I think we are, Dad. I do, even if we just can't admit it yet.

I don't know.

All I know is that Mom really misses you. I *know* she misses talking with you and let's face it: I'm no substitute, and neither are the cats, or Grandma and Grandpa.

Oh yeah, we have eleven rescued cats now, just in case I forgot to mention it.

Mom is really into saving things now.

Anyhow, she keeps reading about the stages of grief like she's charting herself a path through it but in all honesty . . .

I'm not sure she's getting anywhere.

I mean, remember the time it rained for like a week straight and you took me for a ride on your quad, and we went down the side hill and it shouldn't have been any big deal but when we tried to get up it again we only got maybe halfway, and then we just sat there spinning our wheels, digging ruts deeper and deeper into the mud? I had to stay on and steer while you got off and pushed just to get us unstuck and back up to the top . . .

But you're not here to push anymore, and I don't think I can get us unstuck alone.

I wouldn't even know where to start.

Chapter 53

I shut my bedroom door. Open my laptop, pull up Google Maps and chart myself a path. Change into a pair of black shorts and a plum-colored tank. Brush my hair and actually put on some makeup.

Stand back and stare at my reflection.

What good is a glossy outside, anyway, if your insides are nothing but a shredded-up mess? Sooner or later whatever's inside comes out, right?

Right.

Great.

I look over at the paisley grief journal sitting on my night table. Perch on the bed, reach over and pick it up.

Trust the process. You will see and feel what you need to when you are ready.

Trust. There's a word we're struggling with right now.

Grief Journal

Where are you? Can you hear me?

Can you see us?

If you can, then why don't you send us a sign?

Send proof that you still love us. Gather up your energy and blink the lights, rap three times, send a gentle breeze through the house, hold our hands, manifest a scent . . .

Do something.

It would go a long way toward saving us. Trust me.

This is the borderline.

The fourth month.

Time to step up and either say hello, goddamn it, or goodbye.

No. I take that back.

Don't say good-bye. Never say good-bye.

But say *something*.

God, Dad. You didn't even leave a *note*.

I'm sorry. I am. I didn't mean to yell at you. I just . . .

You put us in a really hard place.

Can I tell you something else, and promise you won't be mad?

I'm afraid to say it because once I do, I can never take it back, but . . .

I hate the way you died.

I'm ashamed that you *chose* to leave us, like all we had as a family wasn't enough to keep you here.

Like *I* wasn't enough to keep you here.

I'm ashamed of what it supposedly says to the world, hate the way people look at me now, like I'm so pitiful that I couldn't even keep my own father alive, or so awful that you killed yourself just to get away.

And I don't want to feel that way.

Don't want to spend the rest of my life hiding out here alone because I'm *less than* now, because even if people don't say it you can still see it in their eyes and it makes me feel small, really small and sick inside.

I don't want the terrible way you died to become more important than the wonderful way you lived but I don't know how to stop it.

You kissed me good-bye a thousand times before, Dad, but did you do it that morning?

Did you?

Because until I know that, I feel like I won't know anything at all.

Chapter 54

My mother calls Auntie Kate and spends almost two hours holed up in the bedroom talking with her, door shut, her muffled voice rising and falling, then comes downstairs looking exhausted and climbs right back onto the couch.

She doesn't eat anything, only takes the two Advil I bring for her headache and lies down under the afghan to sleep. I stand there gazing at her, at the psych-impact book now sitting on the top of the pile, and feel like burning it.

Instead, I bend down and kiss her cheek. "I love you. Hang in there, okay?"

She opens her eyes and looks at me, then closes them again. "I love you too, Rowie. I'm sorry for all of this."

"It's okay. I get it," I say softly, stroking the wisps of ash-brown hair back from her forehead, her temple. "Up, down, down, up. We're in the same club, here."

"Then I say we rescind our memberships," she mumbles with the ghost of a smile. "The perks suck and the dues are way too high."

"Yes, they are," I say, and stay there petting her hair until her breathing evens and I know she's asleep.

And then I rise, tiptoe into the kitchen, scrawl a quick note—
I'm going out for a while. I've got my phone. xoxo, Row—and, grabbing
some cigarettes from her open pack, slip out the door and head for
Bedford Street.

Chapter 55

I get to Bedford Street early, by twenty to seven.

It's on the south side of town, back in the World War II section of houses built around an old deserted, dilapidated tire factory. They're small and close to the sidewalk with maybe three feet of lawn. Some are neat, bright and proud, others shabby with chipped paint, scrubby-looking grass and sagging roofs. There are no driveways and so the narrow street is lined with parked cars and the occasional giant maple tree, the great, gnarled roots heaving the sidewalks.

I walk slowly, looking at each house, wondering what I'm even doing here and how I'm supposed to recognize Payton's. Brown with a porch. Right. This brown house has twin dragon planters brimming with pink begonias. That one is littered with kid's toys. This one has a dog chained to the railing that cracks an eye and watches me go by.

That's three brown houses so far, and none of them seem right.

Somewhere up ahead there's music playing, and even though it's faint I recognize the song: Evanescence's "Bring Me to Life."

"Save me," I murmur, and walk faster, following the music.

And when I finally get to the end of the street, to the brown house with the wide porch where the music is pounding and a motorcycle is parked up on the grass, I see Payton and another guy sitting on the steps, and another girl and guy hanging out on the railing.

My footsteps falter.

I wasn't expecting a party.

I don't know *what* I was expecting, and in that split second if I could turn around and sneak away I would, but—

Payton spots me and rises in surprise. "Hey, no shit, I didn't think you'd show." She picks up the wrist of the guy sitting next to her, looks at his watch, and her eyebrows go up. "Early, too. You must have really wanted to see me again."

She laughs and everybody else turns to look at me.

"Hi." I'm blushing, I know it. They're all older than me, wearing jeans and kind of biker-looking clothes, while here I am in my cute little black shorts and plum tank feeling really young, lame and stupid. "Sorry."

"No problem," she says as I walk up, and motions me after her. "Come on."

I send the others a vague, self-conscious smile and, feeling like a fool, follow her up the wide wooden steps worn smooth in the center, across the porch and in through the screen door, where an older CD player with the speakers facing the open windows is playing "Bring Me to Life" over and over.

"Good song," I yell, right as she lowers the volume to half of what it was.

"It'll work," she says, and motions toward the couch. "Have a seat. Want something to drink? A beer? A shot?"

Oh hell. "Uh . . . a beer, I guess."

"I also have Smirnoff Ice," she calls over her shoulder, heading into the kitchen.

"Um, okay," I say with a sinking feeling, and gaze around the living room. The furniture is random, worn and beaten, a rickety-looking bookcase, the brown and orange plaid colonial couch I'm sitting on, a faded blue oriental rug on the floor and an old, scarred oak coffee table.

But what grabs my attention is the lone eight-by-ten framed photo hanging in the middle of the blank, beige wall behind the TV.

I rise and edge around the coffee table to take a closer look.

"Oh," I say softly, because I've never seen them before, not close up.

So this is Corey, this husky, teddy-bearish guy with the round face, chubby cheeks and light brownish-red beard, with the gentle smile and the blue eyes fringed with ginger lashes gazing down in wonder at the bald, pink-cheeked, blue-eyed infant in his arms . . .

And that is Sammy gazing solemnly back, Corey's finger clutched firmly in his tiny hand.

My father was right.

Corey did love his son.

I can see it, too.

"Oh no," I whisper, and draw back, put a hand over my mouth as the sad obscenity of it rushes back, as the strangers I saw that day from a distance turn into real people with faces and a home and history. "Oh God." And as I start to turn my gaze falls on a sock, a tiny little blue-edged, inside-out baby sock lying on the floor back between the TV stand and the wall. I stare at it a long moment, then turn to find Payton standing behind me holding a bottle of beer and a Smirnoff.

"I'm sorry, I just . . . I wasn't . . ." I stop, flustered, like she caught me doing something wrong. "There's a sock down there on the floor."

"Yeah, I know," she says coolly, setting my drink on the coffee table near where I was sitting and sinking down into the chair. "Leave it." She cocks her head, studying me. "So, why did you come, anyway?"

I stare back at her, bewildered. "What?"

"Why are you here?"

Is this a trick question? "Uh . . . you invited me?"

"So? You could have said no," she says, quirking an eyebrow and taking a swig of beer.

"Wait. Am I missing something?" I say with an awkward laugh.

The screen door opens and the other girl sticks her head in. "Hey, Pay, we're out of here."

"Shit, already?" Payton says, rising and padding over. "We haven't even gotten to the whole bon voyage thing yet."

"Yeah, well, Clay wants to make Delaware tonight, so . . ." She shrugs and enfolds Payton in a hug. "You need to get away from here, girl, and come back down to Pensacola. Your mother would be happy to see you again."

"My mother," Payton says with a snort, and pulls back, her face hard. "If she wanted to see me she would have come up for the funerals. Christ, a stranger off the street's been better to me since Sammy died than she's been my whole life." She shakes her head. "No, she's just looking for a new drinking buddy now that my aunt finally got sober."

"So then come down for me," the girl says as the Harley roars to life outside. "Trust me, you could use some fun in the sun again."

"Yeah, we'll see," Payton says, and follows her out as if I've ceased to exist.

I sit there a moment listening to them all saying good-bye over the Harley's rumble and trying to figure out what Payton meant, asking why I came tonight.

What kind of question is that, and what kind of answer does she really expect?

Because I'm lonely and don't have any friends left or anything better to do?

I can't say that.

Because I feel like we're connected in a terrible, domino-effect sort of way and that maybe we should stick together?

I reach over, pick up the Smirnoff and twist off the jagged cap.

Take a sip and then another, longer one.

Suffer the brain freeze and then drain the bottle.

Because Payton is my only link to Eli?

Yes.

Those other sad, pathetic reasons are true too, but Eli is the only reason I came tonight.

There is so much I want to know.

Chapter 56

But I guess tonight's not the night I'm going to find out.

I take a swig of my third Smirnoff Ice.

Bring me to life.

I've been here for forty minutes now and that song is still on repeat, Payton is still ignoring my feeble attempts to talk about Eli, the four-pack of Smirnoff Ice is frosty cold and free and the twilight hot and steamy, thick with dead air.

Tilt the bottle and gaze into it.

There are only three of us left here now, and two of us are getting very friendly over on the faded old plaid love seat that someone must have dragged from Payton's living room out here onto the porch, while the other one of us sits alone on the wooden step pretending she doesn't see what's going on and wondering if she should just leave.

Too bad I have nowhere else to go.

I glance over at Payton, her hair woven carelessly back in a stubby braid, her bare feet propped against one of the love seat's overstuffed arms, her head resting on her boyfriend Richie's meaty thigh. My being here hasn't exactly held them back any, as so far they've smoked some weed, killed two four-packs of Smirnoff and are working on a third, and have been talking and laughing in slurred voices too low for me to hear.

At first I said, "What?" and "Excuse me, I couldn't hear what you said," thinking maybe she didn't get how rude she was being, but when she just smirked and said, "That's okay, I wasn't talking to you," and went back to murmuring, I decided that grieving mother or not, I really didn't like her.

Not that I think she cares.

Actually, I don't think she cares about too much of anything right now.

But I don't know for sure because she's so flip about it, because the one thing she did say while we were in the kitchen getting the rest of the Smirnoffs out of an otherwise empty refrigerator was that partying's what happens when life kicks your ass and leaves you for dead, if not on the outside then definitely on the in.

A fat, bristly horsefly lands on the edge of my bottle.

I wave it away.

The couch creaks.

"C'mon, babe," Richie says, hoisting himself to his feet and drawing Payton up along with him. He's short and stocky, just graduated chef school and works for UPS. "Let's go." He pulls her tight against him, mumbles something that makes her snicker and together they weave into the house without a backward look.

The old wooden screen door bounces shut behind them.

Great.

I swish what's left of my Smirnoff Green Apple Bite around in the bottle.

Stay or go.

I don't know.

I'm not drunk but I'm not exactly sober, either.

I smile wryly, tilt my head back and drain the bottle.

Set it down with a quiet thump on the step beside me and reach for the last one in the four-pack. I'm sweating, the bottle is sweating and my hands are too slick to get a decent grip. I frown down at it, my hair falling into my eyes, fighting to twist it open when someone says, "Uh, hi. Is Payton around?"

"She's inside with Richie," I say without looking up, still wrestling with the bottle.

And then, in quiet disbelief, "Rowan?"

"What?" I glance up, impatient, flick my hair from my eyes and go still.

Time hiccups and for a dizzying moment we're back in the park on prom night, laughing, happy, the sweet scent of autumn olive on the breeze, and then I blink and it's gone, all of it except for Eli, who is standing on the cracked and crumbling sidewalk, a leaner, raggedy, panting Daisy at his side, a bulging, grease-stained Burger King bag in his hand, and staring at me like he's just seen a ghost.

"Hi," I say, voice trembling, and hold out the bottle. "Can you open this for me, please?"

Be kinder than necessary, for everyone you meet is fighting some kind of battle.

—T. H. THOMPSON AND JOHN WATSON

Chapter 57

Eli does, taking the bottle from me, loosening the top and handing it back as if in a daze.

Bring me to life.

"Thank you." I set it down on the step next to me without drinking. "Hey, Daisy." I lean forward, holding out a hand for her to sniff because if I don't I'm going to stare at him until I cry. "You're skinny. Is this heat getting to you?"

Daisy wags her tail and licks my fingers.

"No, she's . . ." Eli stops and rubs his forehead. His hair is pulled back in a ponytail, revealing the sharp curve of his cheekbones and the shadowed smudges under his eyes. "So, wait. How are you?"

"Getting there," I say, wishing he looked happier to see me. "You?"

He shrugs, avoiding my gaze. "How long have you known Payton?"

"Since today. I met her this morning. She invited me over tonight, so . . ." I reach for the Smirnoff and take a healthy slug.

"Did she," he says in an odd voice, and glances up at the house.

"I didn't know you were going to be here, if that's what's bothering you," I hear myself say defensively, and stare down at my feet, miserable.

"No, but *she* did," he says.

My head jerks up and I meet his gaze, see a light in his eyes that wasn't there before.

"It's okay," he says with a quick shrug, and sits down on the step next to me. "Don't worry about it." He sets the BK bag down between us and opens it up, releasing the mouthwatering scent of hot, salty French fries. "Hungry?"

"Okay," I say helplessly, and take the large fries and wrapped sandwich he hands me. "Thanks."

"No problem," he says, setting one on the step beside him. "I brought extra. Payton had this whole bon voyage party idea but I guess we're it."

"What do you mean, bon voyage?" I say, stuffing French fries in my mouth because suddenly I'm starving. "Who's leaving?"

He's quiet for a long moment and when he looks at me his gaze is dark and unreadable. "I am, tomorrow. I'm going back to Houston." And then he takes an unenthusiastic bite of his sandwich and gazes out at the street, completely missing the moment the last of the numbness fades and I can feel again.

Chapter 58

"Oh," I say, staying very still. "Why?"

He swallows with effort and sets the Whopper down on its wrapper. "I have some stuff I need to take care of."

"But you're coming back, right? I mean, you're not going forever . . ." I set my food aside and stand, dizzy, wishing I didn't drink all of those stupid Smirnoffs. "Are you?"

"Hey," he says with concern, pushing himself up off the step and touching my arm. "Are you okay?"

I gaze up at him, searching his face. "Why are you leaving?" And it's none of my business, I know, because it's been too long and—

"I have to," he says, falling back a step and running a hand over his hair. "It's important."

I hear the truth in his words. He's leaving no matter what I say or what I want, and once again I'm going to be left behind to miss someone and there is nothing I can do about it.

Except this.

"Bye," I say, and, wheeling, take off down the street.

Chapter 59

I hear Daisy give a sharp yip of excitement behind me, hear Eli mutter, "Shit," Daisy's tags jingling and his hurried footsteps coming up behind me.

"Rowan, slow down," he says.

I shake my head and keep walking.

"Row, come on," he says as, panting, Daisy gallops up alongside of me. "She can't run in this heat."

"Wasn't it hot in Iraq?" I say, walking faster.

"She's in kidney failure," he says.

I stop and swivel. "What?"

"Yeah." His matter-of-fact expression cracks for an instant, revealing the despair underneath, and then is carefully smooth again, under control. "That's why I'm going back to Houston. Well, part of it." He glances at Daisy. "I want to visit my dad's grave, too. It's been too long."

Kidney failure. Daisy. His father.

Shame washes over me, hot and sobering. "I'm sorry, Eli. I didn't know." And that's on me too, for letting the months stretch and not realizing that while time stopped for me it didn't for everyone, that life is still happening all around me and I'm not the only one struggling, not the only one who could use a friend.

"So is Houston the only place they can cure kidney failure or something?"

He looks at me funny, like he's trying to figure out if I'm being wise. "No. There's no cure for it."

I frown. "What do you mean? She's just gonna have to live with it?" And then I see the dark truth in his gaze and something shifts deep inside of me. "Oh no." I look down at Daisy, who grins up at me, panting. "No, that's no good at *all*." I run my hand over her head, her velvety ears, and down her neck into her coarse, thick hair. "There has to be *something* they can do. I mean, come *on*."

"Well, there is but it's kind of a long shot." The look he gives me is wary, assessing, and I want to say, *Don't worry, I'm not going to run away again,* but instead I only say, "Tell me."

He shakes his head. "You're gonna think I'm crazy or like, stupid for throwing away my money. Believe me, I've heard it all."

"Eli," I say, laying a hand on his arm without thinking, like I just saw him yesterday, not months ago, like we were in it together before and we are again now. "Please?"

He looks at my hand and then, with slow-growing wonder, into my face. "God, where have you been?" he says so softly that I almost miss it, and then, with a quick shake of his head, says in a normal voice, "Okay, well, I'm thinking about a kidney transplant."

I nod. "Okay."

"Okay," he repeats, looking more than a little surprised at my lack of reaction, and then it all comes out. "Daisy has a sister, Rosie. Another guy in my father's unit adopted her when we brought Daisy home. She lives with him and his family back in Houston. I tracked him down and we talked a few times but he still hasn't committed to the whole idea. Not that I blame him, because it *is* a big deal," he adds, "but Daze can't wait forever on this, you know? She has to be strong enough to survive the operation, there's criteria she has to meet and there's only like, two or three veterinary hospitals in the whole country that will even *do* the transplant because it's really risky. So even if it happens tomorrow, there's still a chance that she won't . . ." His voice falters. "I have to try though, you know? I mean I promised my dad I'd take good care of her."

"You do," I say, and when I put my arms around him he goes still a moment and then his arms come around me too, and it feels like I can finally exhale again.

Chapter 60

We walk over to Main Street, where I run into the convenience store, buy bottled water, beg a plastic bowl from the clerk and linger outside while Daisy eagerly drinks.

She *is* much thinner and her face is stressed somehow, her furry forehead wrinkled, and it makes me want to pet her and tell her not to worry, to have faith because Eli loves her and is going to move heaven and earth to try to make her all right.

But I can tell by the way she looks up at him that she already knows that, and so I just gently scratch her rump and am rewarded with an acknowledging tail wag.

"We're going to have to start walking again so she can find a place to pee," he says, glancing at me. "You don't want to go back to Payton's, do you?"

I hesitate. "Not really . . . but if you want to, I will."

"No," he says, shaking his head and smiling slightly. "I'm pretty sure that party already served its purpose." He picks up the plastic bowl. "Want to head up to the little park?" And then he goes still as if suddenly remembering the last time we were there, and when he straightens his gaze is dark with an unspoken question and a pull so strong that it's all I can do to say, "Okay," without swaying toward him.

"Come on, Daze," he says gruffly, and falls into step beside me, watching her walk. "I should have gotten her to the vet sooner."

"You did what you could at the time," I say gently, because I know all about second-guessing and blaming myself these days. "How did they know what was wrong?"

"I gave them her history. Nobody knows what she was exposed to in Iraq, what kind of chemicals or whatever, so they did blood tests and a urinalysis and yeah, chronic renal failure," he says. "They're doing what they can; they put her on a low-protein diet, and I've been giving her sub-q fluids—"

"Wait, what's that?" I say.

"Bags of IV fluids with electrolytes that hang and drip into her. You stick the needle in under the skin and the fluids keep her hydrated," he says with a casual shrug. "It's not hard. I do it every other day and it seems to make her feel better, so . . ."

"Wow," I say in awe.

"It's not a cure though," he says, watching her amble along in front of us. "It's maintenance. Supposedly by the time you see the symptoms it's almost too late. Big dogs wear out faster and usually start getting it around seven years old. She's young." He glances at me. "That's why I had to find Rosie. Hopefully they'll let me set up the transplant at Penn Vet. Uh, the University of Pennsylvania's veterinary medicine school," he adds, catching my puzzled look. "It's the closest, and one of the few places that'll do canine kidney transplants. The survival rate isn't that great."

I step around Daisy as she pauses to sniff a telephone pole. "So you're saying she could . . . die."

"Oh yeah, but she can't live without at least one good kidney either, so what choice is there? I can't just sit around watching her get sicker and weaker, you know? Especially not after everything else." He gives a hopeless laugh. "Try telling that to my family, though."

"They don't . . . ?" I can't bring myself to say *think it's worth it?*

"I mean, don't get me wrong, my mom loves Daisy and all, but she thinks this whole transplant thing is a waste of time and money, like I'm obsessed with keeping her alive because of Dad."

I frown. "So what's wrong with that?"

"Thank you," he says with a quick, satisfied nod. "I mean to her a dog is a dog and there's always another one where that one came from, you know? Only there isn't."

"No, there isn't," I say, because I know exactly what he means. "But what does Daisy's sister have to do with it?"

"Less chance of organ rejection," he says promptly. "Compatible donors are hard to find for dogs so it's really important to get the kidney from Rosie. Without her, there's a good chance they won't even do the operation and then . . ."

"I see," I murmur, and want to add *I think your father would be proud* but I'm not sure I have the right, so I don't. "I think you're doing an amazing thing, Eli. I really do."

"Yeah, well, you're probably the only one," he says with a weary smile. "Rosie's owners haven't agreed to it yet and my family swears that if I spend this money on Daisy instead of putting it toward college that I'll end up living under a bridge somewhere."

"But with a happy, healthy dog," I say, and give him a friendly shoulder-bump.

"It's so screwed up," he says as we pause at the corner and get ready to cross over to the little park. "I only got this money because my father made the ultimate sacrifice, and you know what? I'd rather have him than the money any day." His voice is strong and sure now, like he's had a lot of time to think about it. "Now what, I'm just supposed to let Daisy die because saving her is too expensive? Are you kidding?" He reins her in and the three of us cross the street. "My father did his part and now I'm gonna do mine. Not because I have to. Because I *want* to. That's *my* tribute to a fallen warrior." He goes silent, then sighs and glances over at me. "Sorry."

"Don't be. It's how you feel, right? I like that you say it." And I do, because I get to learn about him as a person now and I like discovering that how I feel about him is more than just the magical memory of a hot, romantic prom-save.

I actually admire what he's doing.

And it inspires me, it makes me want to do something to honor my father too, like make a special photo album of just him and me or cut the long grass around the wood shop so it looks neat again and cared for, not abandoned, or maybe wash his Blazer and finally get up the nerve to open the driver's door and climb inside.

I wish I was braver.

And then I glance down at Daisy padding faithfully along beside Eli, graceful, trusting, loving, alive, the last gift his father ever gave him except maybe the guts to do what he believed was right even when everyone else thought he was wrong, and the wave of emotion that washes over me is so powerful that it stops me in my tracks.

"What?" Eli says, turning.

And I grope for words but none come, so I kiss him instead.

Chapter 61

"What are you doing?" he says huskily as I draw back dazzled, flustered and more than a little shocked at myself.

But I still can't answer because we're standing at the edge of the park and I can hear the water dancing in the fountain and the roses are blooming, filling the sultry dusk with their sweet, heady scent, and all I want is for *him* to kiss *me* now, to pull me back into his arms so we can pick up right where we left off three months ago . . .

But he doesn't.

"Wait," he says, and, falling back a step, runs a hand over his hair. "Rowan, I . . . Damn, I should have . . . I have to tell you something."

I blink and then it hits me. "Oh my *God*, you have a *girlfriend?*"

"What? No," he says, frowning. "Where do you get this stuff?"

"Then what?" I say, heart drumming.

He hesitates. "I don't want to do this here. Let's sit down somewhere." He looks around the little park but all the benches are occupied and a look of pure frustration crosses his face.

"I know where we can go," I say, because now I'm really worried and just want to hear whatever he's going to tell me. "Come on." I start walking backward down the sidewalk toward Victory Lane, motioning him and Daisy after me.

My hand brushes against his as we walk but instead of taking it he mutters an awkward, "Sorry," and widens the gap between us by a couple of steps. Embarrassed, I quickly wedge my hand in my shorts pocket and as we pass the minimall he finally says, "So uh, how's your boss doing?"

"Eva? I don't know," I say, glancing at the cleaner's as we pass. It's closed now; the lights are low, the front is empty and I feel a tug of something nostalgic stirring inside of me. "I haven't gone back to work yet."

"She's holding your job for you?" he says, surprised. "That's great."

"She's known my father forever." I don't tell him that I have no idea if she's held my job all these months, that all I remember her saying at the wake was that I should take my time and come see her when I was ready. "I might stop down there this week," I add, and glance back over my shoulder at the place.

Yes, I think I will.

I take my hand out of my pocket again.

But as the silence stretches the anticipation inside of me turns back to worry about what he wants to tell me, that if he's not gay and there's no other girlfriend then he's just going to flat-out say that he doesn't like me like he used to and that means we'll be done, so I start talking, saying all the stuff I've stored up before I lose the chance forever.

"You were really good to me when my father died," I say, glancing over at him. "I'm sorry for the way I acted. I just . . ." I make a helpless gesture. "I just couldn't."

"Hey," he says. "Don't apologize. Really, I get it."

"There's no second date when your dad dies," I say softly as we turn down Victory Lane. "It wasn't you. I couldn't even get my mind around the thought. I was just . . . wrecked."

"I understand." He's silent a moment. "It brought a lot of stuff back for me, too, and I couldn't be there for you the way I wanted to." He clears his throat. "I felt pretty bad about that. Still do."

"Well don't, okay? You were there when it mattered and that meant a lot," I say, wondering if that's what he wanted to tell me. "It still does."

He nods once in acknowledgment but doesn't say anything.

A dove lands on the edge of the road up ahead and pecks at the grit speckling the pavement. Another lands beside it, smaller and younger looking, and starts pecking, too. They stay until we're about ten feet away and then, with a flutter of feathers, take off.

"Do you know what someone actually said to me at the wake?" I say, watching them go. "That God never gives us more than we can handle. That wasn't true for my father, though." I shake my head. "I know she was trying to make me feel better but I felt like slapping her."

His mouth curves into a brief, wry smile. "I got a lot of that at my father's wake, too. People don't know what to say."

"Yeah, you're not kidding," I say, kicking at a pebble and sending it bouncing down the road. "That and the whole grieving process. They just don't get it. I mean my best friend wanted me to speed-grieve. Get it done, get it over with and get back to the party." I stop, feeling guilty. "Actually, that's not totally true. I was a mess and she tried but she just didn't understand that there's no quick fix."

"Been there, done that," he says, nodding and rolling his eyes.

"I know, right?" I laugh, and he does, too, and suddenly I can't *believe* how good it feels to be with someone who understands. "I mean it's *always* there, whether people bring it up or not." I glance at him. "You know what I really hate? When they say—"

"'You need to get over it and move on,'" he finishes, and grins as I clutch my throat and stagger a few steps. "Yeah, I heard that, too. You just learn to ignore it. The ones who say stuff like that? They don't know." His smile fades. "My mom bought into it, though. She packed up all of my dad's stuff like, maybe two weeks after the funeral."

"Wow, that soon?" It's the exact opposite of the way we've been mourning, clinging to every single thing my father ever owned as if it's unbearable to lose any more of him than we already have, and for the first time I really get what *Everybody grieves differently* means. I say as much, only it comes out sounding critical and quickly I add, "Everybody has to do it their own way, and that's okay, you know?"

"Yeah, but to just like, get rid of everything and move?" he says with a tinge of bitterness. "Come on."

"Well," I say lamely, and suddenly remember something, a flash of conversation we had back when my father first died. "Eli, don't take this the wrong way, but maybe she did it because she was *afraid* for you. You told me you were having a really bad time and partying and all . . . Maybe she was scared she was going to lose you, too, and all she could think of to do was go home."

He gives Daisy's leash a gentle tug and we start walking again, him in silence and me in worry that I've overstepped my bounds.

It's not enough to stop me, though.

"Have you ever asked her about it?" I say, and at his narrowed glance, I add, "Okay, so I could be totally wrong. You know better than I do about your family. It's just that sometimes what we think is true can turn out to be something totally different."

"You done?" he says after a moment, giving me a sideways look.

"Probably," I say glumly, plodding along beside him.

He snorts and I turn quickly, catching the flash of amusement in his gaze. "I'm not saying you're right," he says, lips twitching as I get all excited.

"But you never thought of it that way though, did you?" I say, beaming.

"It's worth asking her about," he says with a nod. "Maybe when I get back."

"Good," I say as we exit the woods and my house comes into sight. "Is Daisy going with you?"

"No, I don't want to put her through all of that stress," he says. "She's staying here. I'm paying one of the vet techs to come by and do the sub-q fluids and walk her and all. Just to keep an eye on her and make sure she's okay until I get back."

"When is that?" I ask, and head for the bench under the copper beech tree, motioning them after me.

"Shouldn't be more than a week," he says, following me. "Where are we going?"

"Right here," I say, and part the low-hanging branches. "See? A bench."

"Hey, check it out," he says, ducking and stepping under into the little cove. "All the times I walked this way and I never even knew this was here." He ties Daisy's leash around the arm and double-knots it, tugging to make sure it won't come loose. "Really cool, Rowan." He sits, uncaps the bottled water, fills Daisy's bowl and sets it down on the grass, and she pads right over to drink.

I sit beside him. "So."

He tucks his hair behind his ear and glances over, catching the burning question in my gaze. "Oh yeah." His smile fades. "Christ, I can't believe I'm doing this."

I knot my hands together in my lap and sit very still.

"Okay, well . . ." He gazes out into the twilight. "I should have told you sooner but . . ." He rubs his chin, toys with the patch beneath his lip. Sighs and says, "Okay, remember that when your father died, I said it brought up a lot of old stuff for me and I just couldn't handle it?"

I nod.

"Well, it wasn't just that. I mean I could've toughed it out if . . ." He takes a deep breath and turns to me. "When I stopped on the overpass that day and asked Corey what he was doing climbing up on the wall with his kid he told me to just keep walking, that it was none of my business, and he was right. I *should* have just kept walking because—"

"No," I protest, laying a hand on his arm. "You did the right thing."

"—he was going to jump anyway, no matter what, and if I hadn't—"

"But you didn't know that," I say. "You had to try to save them."

"—if I hadn't called 911 on him," he continues doggedly, his eyes dark with anguish, "if I had *just kept walking,* Rowan, then your father would never have been there that day, and Jesus Christ, he'd probably still be alive."

"Oh," I say in a very small, faraway voice as his words sink in, and then the world pulls away.

Chapter 62

I don't faint or go hysterical, nothing like that, but for a second my senses shut down and everything disappears, recedes, and there is nothing but white noise inside me, surrounding me, and I can't even see—

"Rowan?"

"No," I say, coming back fast and pushing it away, far away, because it's too terrible a thought. "No, Eli." I'm sweating; every single cell in my body is on fire because I cannot believe for one second that something as simple as a phone call could have been the beginning of the end for my father. A phone call that didn't save anyone, anyway. "Don't say it again."

"I won't," he says, resting his elbows back on his knees and staring at the ground.

I don't know what to do, what to say. The sun is almost down, the overpass shrouded in shadows, but I stare at it anyway, willing myself to see it, to look until my eyes burn. I've spent months hurting, pining, lost in an emotional maelstrom I couldn't control, months hating myself for cutting school that day, Corey for jumping, the news for making a big deal out of it, the brass for persecuting my father, the haters for their vicious comments, Nadia for her whole happy family, Mrs. Thomas for her ignorance, the pain, the loss, my life, just hating, hating, hating . . .

All because one sad, desperate man chose *this* overpass while Eli was walking his dog and my father was bringing me home.

It just can't be that simple and that random.

Can it, God? *Can* it?

"Do you want me to leave?" Eli says in a husky voice. "I'll understand if you do."

I turn my head, slowly, and meet his miserable gaze. Do I want him to leave? Do I want to send away the one guy who actually understands what I'm going through, the first one who's ever gone out of his way to tell me the truth even though I might hate him for it? Do I want to throw away *all* that could possibly be for us in the future simply because the universe tilted and a strange and terrible assortment of random pieces clicked into place?

I cut school in my father's patrol area and got caught.

Payton chose that weekend to leave Sammy with his father.

Corey picked that first beautiful, sunny day to end his misery and his son's life.

Eli, new to town, walked his dog straight into the hornet's nest and, trying to save lives, called the police.

My father responded, and the rest . . .

Is done, and cannot ever be changed.

"No," I say, and look back at Eli. "Stay."

Grief Journal

Did you hear that, Dad?

Eli blames himself for your dying.

I blame myself.

I bet that if I asked, Mom, Grandma, Grandpa, Vinnie and even the aunts would find reasons to blame themselves, too.

So are we *all* really guilty of failing you, or is this claiming responsibility just a part of punishing ourselves for surviving when you didn't? Is it real? Did we *all* miss chances to help you, or did we do the best we could at the time, and it's only stupid, cruel hindsight that insists on showing us the choices we didn't think to make?

And what about you? What's your responsibility in all of this?

Isn't it funny that if you had lived, there'd be no guilt, wondering or punishment?

If you had lived what we did to try to get you through would have been right, and we wouldn't even be having this conversation.

Well, this monologue.

I really wish it was a dialogue.

Chapter 63

"So." Eli pulls a pack of cigarettes from his T-shirt pocket, wedges one in his mouth and lights it. "Do you hate me?" He offers me one, but I still have the two I took from my mother, so he lights one of those for me.

I blow a smoke ring and watch as it expands, thinning, fading, wavering, until it breaks and floats away. "No. I don't hate you."

"Good." He doesn't ask for more, only blows a series of mini rings that drift around us like widening bubbles, blurring and finally merging into one great cloud that drifts off into the night.

"And it wasn't your fault," I add, watching it go. "You did the right thing." All those stars up there, shining so bright, and so many already dead. "I mean that."

The warm breeze sweeps across my skin and rustles the leaves. Lightning bugs flash and somewhere nearby, a bird warbles a soft, sleepy-sounding whisper song.

Daisy heaves a giant sigh and flops over onto her side.

"I smoke too many of these things," Eli says finally, glancing down at the smoldering cigarette and then at me. "Want to quit?"

"I have another one left," I say, rubbing my thumb across a patch of rough paint on the bench seat. My father planned on painting it again this year, a deep, striking blue instead of the old barn-red that clashes with the copper beech leaves, but—

"Hold on." He tweezes his pack from his T-shirt pocket, flips the top and glances inside. "I have three. How about when this pack's done we are, too?"

I glance over to see if he's joking. "Are you serious?"

"Yeah, why not? How long have you been smoking?"

I shrug and flick my ashes. "Not that long."

"Did you start after your dad died?" he says.

"Is it obvious?" I say dryly.

"Yeah, that's when I started, too," he says, leaning back and stretching his legs out in front of him. "Smoking and a mess of other stuff. You know, trying to make it all disappear. I just couldn't deal, so why not self-destruct?" He snorts. "He would have been so pissed if he knew. Disappointed in me, too. That one's the worst."

Yes, it is. "Do you think they *do* know?" I ask, watching him. "I mean, do you think they can still see us?"

He tips his head back, staring up into the dark tree branches. "I guess it depends on what you believe."

"What do *you* believe?" I say, tucking my leg up beneath me and shifting to face him.

"What do I believe." He flicks his hair back and searches my face. "Honestly?"

"Yeah," I say. "Honestly."

He takes a drag off his cigarette and exhales, long and slow. "I think my dad's still looking out for me."

"Do you?" I say wistfully. "I wish I did. I mean I wish I knew for *sure* he was." I flick my ashes. "He didn't leave a note, Eli. I mean he planned his own death and he *still* didn't leave one. They gave my mother all his personal possessions from inside the Blazer afterward and we looked on his phone, all the laptops and in his desk, and nothing." I gaze out at the overpass, throat tight. "I don't get that at all. Didn't he care? Wasn't he sad about leaving us? How could he just go forever without saying good-bye?"

"I don't know." Eli slides an arm around me and when my tears finally slow he says, "He had to be hurting bad by then, being in a constant, twenty-four/seven battle with himself or with the depression, however you want to think of it. He fought the good fight though, didn't he?"

"But he lost," I say brokenly.

"But *before* he lost, he protected and served, and fought for his life with honor and valor for as long as he could, don't you think?" The question is solemn, powerful and different than anything anyone's ever asked me.

Protect. Serve. Honor. Valor.

My father.

"Yes," I say, and the sweeping pain is fierce, welcome. "He was like that my whole life, and oh my God, Eli, he tried *so hard* to stay." The hot tears well and flow again, rising from somewhere deep and untapped. "He was hanging on for dear life and I didn't even know it."

"Maybe he didn't want you to." His voice is gentle, careful, as if he knows from experience what a delicate minefield talking about dead fathers can be. "Maybe he was trying to protect you from getting hurt."

"Well it didn't work, did it?" I say, wiping the tears from my cheeks. "This is nothing *but* hurt." And then I shake my head and sit up, suddenly impatient with myself. "Sorry. Sometimes it's like, two steps forward, three steps back. There are just so many pieces left that I don't understand and who knows, maybe that's the point. Maybe I never will. Maybe I'm just supposed to accept it and *move on.*"

"Maybe," he says after a long, silent moment. "You know what my father used to say when I was having a really hard time with something?" His mouth curves into a small, reminiscent smile. "He said it exactly the same way every time, too. Used to kill me. *You don't have to have all the answers right now. Don't worry, they'll come. All you have to do* is just keep breathing and everything will work itself out. *Just keep breathing."* His smile widens. "So there you go. I'm passing it on to you."

"Well, thank you." I can't help smiling back. "So that's the answer to making it through, huh? Just keep breathing?"

"Yeah," he says. "And it's working, isn't it?"

Amazingly, it is.

Chapter 64

"Hey, Daisy never showed you her trick," Eli says suddenly, as if he just remembered, as if it's important that she does it right now, before he leaves, before she goes in for her transplant and possibly never comes out again. "Want to see it?"

"Sure."

"Hey, Daze." He leans over and taps the dog. "Semper Fi."

Tongue lolling, Daisy sticks her paw into his hand.

"Yay," I say, clapping, and for a second we're so normal I want to cry.

"Good girl," he says, releasing her.

Daisy thumps her tail.

"So what does that mean again?" I say, leaning over and scratching the top of her head.

"Semper Fidelis." His expression turns serious. "Always faithful. It's the Marine Corps motto."

"It's beautiful," I say softly.

"They mean it," he says, glancing at his watch and grimacing. "Ten o'clock. I'm gonna have to get going soon. I still have to finish packing, make sure all my paperwork is in order and get Daisy's stuff set up for the vet tech."

"What time is your flight?" I say, rising along with him.

"Eight thirty," he says. "I have to be at the airport by what, six in the morning?"

"That's early." I gaze up at him, wanting to wish him luck, to tell him I'm so glad to see him again even if it *is* thanks to Payton and that I'll be thinking of him, Rosie and Daisy, to call or text me if he wants to talk, if things go wrong or right, something, anything to forge some kind of solid connection again before he goes. "Eli . . . I really, really hope everything goes okay."

"This is the easy part," he says, sighing and gazing down at Daisy.

"Well, if the vet tech can't come and you need somebody to walk her, just let me know, okay? I'm serious."

"I will." He says he still has my contact info but I don't have his, so I pull out my phone, and punch it in. "Good deal," he says when I finish. "Thanks, Row." His dark gaze searches my face, softens into a sweet look I recognize and a smile that goes straight to my heart. "Don't let me forget to thank Payton for this." He reaches out and smoothes a strand of hair back from my eyes, his fingers lingering a moment on my cheek. "You're sure you don't hate me?"

It takes me a second to figure out what he means and when I do I feel a brief pang, a lightning-quick wish that he didn't remind me. He must see it on my face because his smile turns questioning, and, mad at myself for not being able to just let it go already, I say, "No, I could never hate you. God, just the opposite. It's just . . ."

"You have a boyfriend?" he asks abruptly, his hand falling back to his side.

"No," I say, and stifle the crazy desire to laugh. "But . . . you've had over a year since your father died to figure things out, Eli. I've only had three months and I'm still dealing with it."

He doesn't say anything, just watches me.

"I mean sometimes I just start crying," I say earnestly, spreading my hands. "I can't help it. And my thoughts are all over the place and I already told you how bad I feel about the whole no-suicide-note thing. And look what I did to you before at Payton's. You said you were going to Houston and I ran away because in *my* mind it translated to being left behind again, do you see? I know it doesn't make sense but there it is. I couldn't deal with it so I just shut down and walked away. That's not normal, Eli. Not for me. I'm a very stable person, or at least I was." I gaze up at him, imploring. "The person I am right now? It's not the whole, real me. I'm *way* better than this."

"It's okay," he says, crouching and untying Daisy's leash. "You don't have to explain. I understand."

"Yeah, but . . ." I stop, frustrated, and rub my forehead, because no, I don't think he does. "I'm afraid I'm going to mess this up again, Eli, and I really don't want to."

"Row," he says, straightening and taking a step toward me.

"I mean we had the best night *ever* back in May and then *bam,* the next morning he's dead and what was that, some kind of punishment for being too happy?" I spread my hands even wider, frantic and near tears. "Do you see what I'm saying? Do you hear what's coming out of my mouth, Eli? These are the thoughts I have now and they're not normal. *I'm* not normal."

"Yeah, okay," he says, nodding. "Warning taken. But you *do* realize that tomorrow I'm flying to Houston to meet with my dog's sister's owner to try to convince him to let her donate a kidney in a dangerous operation that may tank and kill both of them, and either way, pass or fail, this whole thing's costing me upwards of fifteen grand but I don't care because *I* think it's worth it." He meets my boggled gaze with a shrug and crooked grin. "Come on, does that sound normal to you?"

"No," I say after a long moment, lips twitching.

"Right. But that's me since my dad died. I'm not who I was before and you're probably not gonna be either. How can we? Everything's changed. We know too much now."

"Okay," I say uncertainly, not sure if I'm disturbed or relieved.

"All I'm saying is there are no guarantees. All we can do is try. You're doing exactly what you're supposed to. You're where you need to be." He parts the copper beech's leafy branches and motions me out ahead of him. "I'm okay with it if you are. You want to talk, I'll listen, and if you need a shoulder to cry on, I've got two good ones. I'm serious. And who knows, *I* might be the one taking those three steps backward sometime." He ducks and follows Daisy out into the moonlight. "So think about what you want and when I get back we'll work it out. How's that?"

"Well, what do *you* want?" I say, and when he looks at me, yes, there it is again, that soft, fragile little flutter of hope against my heart that grows stronger when he opens his arms like all the pain and trouble and worry surrounding us have fallen away, and pulling me to him, he murmurs, "You."

Chapter 65

I sleep late the next morning and when I wake up, something is off.

I lie there for a moment, puzzled.

The light in the room is rich, golden and slanted differently, but that's not it.

It's me.

I feel . . . not as bad.

I wait, cautious, but no.

The crush of sorrow that usually greets me the moment I hit consciousness, when I remember my father's gone and realize it wasn't only a bad dream, is still there, but . . .

I don't know.

I stretch, feeling suddenly luxurious, and then remember something else. Roll over onto my side, fumble my phone off the nightstand and yes, there's a text from Eli.

Good morning sunshine. Made it to Houston. Miss me yet? :)

Smiling, I snuggle down and pull the quilt up under my chin, dislodging Peach, Plum and their brother Willow, all curled round my feet. They rise, arch, stretch and, when I don't get up, lie back down and tuck themselves in along the curve of my legs.

It felt good, being with Eli last night. Really good.

I shift onto my side, earning dirty looks from the cats, and curl up, watching scattered dust motes floating in a shaft of rich, golden sunlight.

I will never understand how life can rip your heart out with one hand and then give you a small, warm piece of it back with the other?

How can something so good come from something so terrible?

I don't know, and thinking about it tarnishes my bright mood, so I snake an arm out from under the covers and look at my watch.

It's noon.

"Oh my God," I blurt, throwing back the covers and sending the cats scrambling.

I never sleep this late. Why didn't my mother wake me up?

"Mom?" I call, padding into the bathroom, peeing and brushing my teeth.

No answer.

Where the heck is she?

"Mom?" I call, thumping down the stairs, the cats romping along beside me. "It's after twelve. Why didn't you wake me up?" I stick my head into the living room but the afghan is lying in a rumpled heap and the couch is empty.

Pause in the hallway. "Mom?"

Nothing.

"What the hell?" I say, and, nervous now, walk into the deserted kitchen. "Where are you?" Yesterday's bags full of nonperishable items still wait on the table and the counters. "Mom?" Too loud in the stillness.

And a sharp, fearful voice inside my head, an immediate echo of past shock and dread, whispers a silent, *Oh no, oh God please, not again, please . . .*

Because now, in my world, when parents disappear without warning, they don't come back.

I put a trembling hand on the coffeepot.

Cold.

It's too quiet.

I look at the chair.

The only purse hanging on the back of it is mine.

"Mom?" Knees shaking, I turn to the sunporch door.

There's a square of white paper taped on it, right in the center of the glass, and for a moment it doesn't register. A flood of adrenaline sweeps through me, and I wobble toward it, staring at the one word in that note that stands out.

Hospital.

"Oh my God," I say, and, clutching the door frame to steady myself, read the rest.

Grandma called. Grandpa hurt himself. Took them to the hospital. Be back soon. Love, Mom P.S. Leave me a note if you go out.

I blink, sweating, read it again, feel like dropping with relief and am about to call her when I hear car doors slam in the driveway and voices sounding way too loud and cheerful heading toward the porch.

It's them.

"You scared the crap out of me," I say, propping open the door and squinting into the eye-piercing sunlight. "What happened? How's Grandpa?"

My grandmother reaches the steps first. "Oh, he's fine," she says with a smile. "Hello, sleepyhead." She hands me a big, bulging grocery bag and kisses my cheek. "I hope I didn't wake you when I called this morning but you-know-who just *had* to go out into the garage to sharpen his lawn mower blade at what time, Albert?"

"Six thirty," my grandfather grumbles, coming up the steps behind her. "Why not? I'm not sleeping good these days anyway and it's better to cut the lawn early when the sun isn't as strong. Otherwise the grass will burn."

"That's *watering* the garden, Albert, not cutting the grass," my grandmother says, giving me a look and bustling past into the kitchen. "He hasn't had his coffee yet."

"I'll make some right now," I say, more than a little boggled.

"Wouldn't have mattered," he says, and, stopping in front of me, holds up a finger wrapped in an enormous swath of blinding-white gauze. "Just missed the tendon. You should have seen that sucker bleed."

"Come on, Dad," my mother says, stepping into the porch and steering him past me. "Go in and sit down." Her hair is loose, out of the freakish, punishing ponytail and tucked hastily behind her ears, and she's wearing a blouse with all its buttons. "The doctor said you should take it easy today."

"Humph. What does he know? I've got undershorts older than that doctor," he says, but weaves his way through the cats and over to a chair anyway. "I can still drive." His face is pale, the circles under his eyes dark, and twin spots of color burn in his cheeks.

"Now, maybe," my mother says. "Not while you were bleeding." She notices me standing there with the bag in my arms and shoves our grocery bags aside to clear a space for me to put it. "You found my note?"

"Yes," I say, dumping the bag on the counter and heading for the coffeepot. "But it was really weird, waking up with you not here. *Really* weird. Like, scary."

Our gazes meet.

"I'm sorry. It was just so early . . ." A wide yawn interrupts her. "Oh, excuse me. You were sleeping so peacefully that I didn't have the heart to wake you up."

Wait . . . what? "You came into my room? I didn't hear you."

"That's because you were *sleeping*," my mother says, giving me an amused look.

"Yeah, but my door was shut," I say, frowning.

"And I opened it," she says, lips twitching. "Believe it or not, I do have that power."

"Yeah, but . . ." This bothers me. Not that she came in but that I never heard her do it. Has it happened before? Has anyone else done it? Did Daddy ever do it? I want to ask, but . . . Not now. I shake my head. "Forget it."

"Don't worry, I didn't touch any of your stuff," she says, and yawns again. "Sorry."

"Albert, why don't you and Rachel go sit in the living room and relax for a while?" my grandmother says, reaching past us and prodding my grandfather's shoulder. "You both look all worn out."

"Good idea. C'mon, Dad," my mother says, waiting until he pushes himself up and then gently taking his arm and helping him out of the room.

"I'll call you when the coffee's ready," I say, and as I'm measuring out the grounds and filling the carafe with water, my grandmother comes over and begins rummaging through the big bag.

"Ah! Here it is." She plops one of those giant, family-sized packages of cut-up chicken on the counter, glances over at me and says, "We stopped back home after the hospital because your grandfather insisted he could drive and so I could get my ingredients. I've decided to make the chicken *paprikás* here instead of cooking it there and then bringing it all the way back."

"Oh." This is a first. "Uh, cool." I move some of our grocery bags to the crowded kitchen table, catching one as it starts to slide off of a pile of unread newspapers.

"Well, I thought it was high time we all sat down for a meal as a family again," she says briskly, washing her hands in the sink. "Structure is important and—"

One of the cats jumps up on the counter, lured by the scent of the chicken.

"No!" She shoos it down again. "Bad kitty." She wags a stern finger at it and then turns to me. "How does your mother cook with all of these cats in here?"

"I don't know," I say, shrugging and opening the first of yesterday's grocery bags. "She hasn't really cooked since we got them, I guess." I gather the boxes of mac 'n' cheese and carry them to the pantry.

When I come out, my grandmother is waiting. "Well if no one's cooking, what have you been eating?"

"Pizza, Chinese food, the stuff you bring over," I say, opening the next bag and pulling out the Cup Noodles. "This." I hold one up. "Why?"

She looks at the foam cup full of dehydrated noodles and powdered broth, then past me at the kitchen table piled with newspapers, mail, books, pens, an open carton of cigarettes and Petal curled up sleeping among it. "You can't possible eat *there*."

"No, we eat on trays in the living room," I say, and shake the Cup Noodles so that the hard, wizened little green peas and carrots inside rattle. "These things only take a couple of minutes, anyway." I tote them to the pantry, and when I return another cat is poised to leap up onto the counter. "Come here, you," I say, scooping him up and moving him. "That's not allowed."

Sage, the cat, blows me off and trots back to twine around my grandmother's ankles instead.

"Move him, please, Rowan," she says, shifting. "I don't want to step on him."

I retrieve the cat and set him over on one of the chairs next to Stripe. "Now stay there."

Sage gives me a look, leaps down and trots right back to my grandmother.

I pick him up again and take him into the living room. "Keep him here, okay? He's being a brat," I say, setting him on my mother's lap and heading back to the kitchen.

"I don't know how anyone can get anything done around here with all of these interruptions," my grandmother grumbles when I return, opening one of the bottom cabinet doors and peering inside. "Where does your mother keep the big pots?"

"Not in there," I say as three more cats run in from the living room, tails high and gazes expectant. "That's where we keep the cat food." And to them, "No, sorry. It's not time yet. Go back to sleep. Go." I herd them back out into the hall. "Good."

"The coffee's done," my grandmother says, and there's a slight edge in her voice now that wasn't there before. She plants her hands on her hips and, frowning, gazes around the room. "How in the world can you people find anything in this mess?"

I hope my mother didn't hear that. "Coffee," I call quickly, and, grabbing a mug, pour myself a cup because I haven't had any yet either. "Do you want me to bring it in, Mom?"

"No, we're here," my mother says as she and my grandfather reappear and settle into kitchen chairs. "But you could still pour it, and get the cream and sugar. Oh, and the Splenda. You don't take sugar anymore, do you, Dad?"

"No, I'm sweet enough," he says, and flashes a cheesy grin.

I gaze at my mother a moment, tempted to point out that I'm busy herding cats *and* putting away groceries, but instead say, "Sure," and do as she asks. "Here you go." I hand a mug to my grandfather and one to my mother and set Gran's on the countertop, as she's apparently given up the search for a pot and is busy rinsing the chicken parts and trying not to step on the cats winding around her ankles. They're getting to her though; I can tell because her lips are pursed and there's a sharp little V frown between her eyebrows. "Want some help?"

"Not now," she says, turning off the faucet. "Maybe later, with the *nokedli*."

"Okay," I say, because the dumplings are my favorite part of the dish. "Just yell when you need me." I glance at my watch. "Um, this is going be ready for supper, right? Around what, five o'clock?"

"Why?" my mother says before my grandmother can answer. "I hope you don't think you're going anywhere tonight, Rowan, because you're grounded thanks to that little disappearing act you pulled yesterday."

And there it is, my first punishment since my father died, announced right in front of my grandparents, and the sneaky looks they exchange make it obvious that they're all in on it together. I'm tempted to balk, challenge her, to throw the tantrum my grandparents are apparently expecting . . . but I'm not really feeling it and I'm *definitely* not into becoming a community project, discussed and dissected over dinner, watched during free time for signs of another freak explosion . . .

It's just not worth it.

"Yeah, okay," I say with a shrug, and root through another bag. "And besides, where am I going to go, anyway? I'm not exactly popular these days, in case you haven't noticed." Where I *was* intending to go today—and still am—is down to the cleaner's to see if I can get my job back, but I'll bring that up later. I grab the jars of peanut butter and jelly from the bag and head for the pantry.

"What about Nadia?" my mother says, losing the attitude. "Where's she been?"

"I don't know," I say, fussing with the stuff on the shelves and sorry I even brought it up. "Busy, I guess, or maybe on vacation. We haven't hung out in a while."

"Well, you must have other friends," my mother says, tucking her hair behind her ear and giving me a funny look. "What about Danica or—"

"Oh no! No! Give me that, damn you!"

I turn and see my furious grandmother caught in a tug-of-war with Sage, who is crouched up on the counter growling, a raw chicken leg clamped between his teeth.

"Stop it! Let go!" my grandmother cries, raising a hand as if to swat him.

"Sage, no! Mom, don't let him get it, he'll choke on the bones," my mother says, jumping up and grabbing the cat. "No. That's not yours." Ignoring his threatening rumble, she wedges his bulk under her arm and, using one finger, pushes his bottom lip over his tooth and into the side of his mouth. He opens his jaws and she pulls the leg free. "Here." She tries to hand it back to my grandmother, who looks at it like it's suddenly crawling with maggots and turns away. "Oh, for God's sake." My mother tosses it into the sink and sets the cat on the floor. "No," she tells Sage sternly. "That's *bad.*"

He goes into a quick fit of belly-washing and then rises, tail twitching, and stalks away.

"That was close," my mother says, reaching past my grand-mother to the faucet and washing her hands in the sink. "We're going to have to make sure all the bones are bagged up and put out in the garbage after dinner. Chicken bones are bad for cats. They get brittle after they're cooked and could splinter and perforate their intestines." She grabs a dish towel and dries her hands, then turns and meets my grandmother's ominous gaze. "What?"

"Is that all you have to say?"

My mother looks at her, puzzled. "What else do you want me to say? Thank you for holding on to that chicken leg?"

"No!" my grandmother says, cheeks flushed and mouth pulled tight. "Mother of mercy, Rachel, how can you *live* like this?"

"Like what?" my mother says, and the question seems to infuri-ate my grandmother even more.

"Like *this*! My God, look around you. It looks like a bomb went off in here! Groceries everywhere, shoes thrown around, dishes in the sink . . . And look at your kitchen table! Haven't you even opened any mail since Nicky died?"

Shocked, my mother tries to reply but my grandmother barrels on.

"You can't go on like this. I have tried to be patient and under-standing, Rachel, I have, but you have responsibilities and you need to start taking care of them again." She yanks a glass from the dish drainer, fills it with water and dumps it into the dying houseplant sitting on the windowsill. "There! Was that so hard?" Her gaze falls on my father's wallet. "And this, still here after all these months!" She reaches for it—

"Don't," my mother says, finding her voice.

My grandmother hesitates and drops her hand, leaving the wallet where it is, but she isn't done yet. "Well, then what about Rowan? She needs structure and guidance; she needs to know she can count on you to be a parent. Instead, she comes home to what? Clutter and neglect and irresponsibility! What kind of life is that? She says you haven't even made a meal in months."

Oh great. Thanks, Gran. "Hey, don't get me involved in this," I say, holding up my hands and shaking my head as my mother flashes me a betrayed look. "She *asked,* Mom. What was I going to say?"

"Don't you dare blame her for being honest. You're the one who is supposed to be in charge of your household. No wonder she's acting out. What kind of stability does she have anymore?"

"Now, wait a minute," my mother says, straightening her shoulders.

"No! I've waited too long already." My grandmother snatches up the dish towel my mother has left on the counter and folds it, her motions quick and jerky. "Your father and I haven't wanted to say anything because we know you're doing the best you can but—" A cat leaps up onto the counter, and she slaps at it with the dish towel, making it panic and leap off again. "These cats! How many *are* there?"

"Eleven," my mother says, lifting her chin.

"Eleven," my grandmother repeats flatly. "What are you going to do with eleven cats, Rachel?"

"What am I going to *do* with them?" my mother says coolly, and frowns. "Gee, I don't know, Mom. What do you normally do with a pet? You bring it inside, you have it fixed, you feed it and you love it. That's about it, I guess."

"That's not what I meant and you know it," my grandmother says, grabbing a paper towel from the roll. Wetting it, she scrubs the counter where the cat stood. "You're letting everything go and—"

"Wait, Edie," my grandfather interrupts. "Maybe this isn't the right time."

She turns on him. "Then when, Albert? If not now, when? We've talked about this over and over again, and you saw what that awful animal just did. We didn't spend good money on all of this food just to waste it on cats!"

"Enough," my mother says with a tight, brittle smile and, reaching into her purse, digs out a handful of change. "How about I just pay you for the chicken leg and we drop the subject?"

Chapter 66

My jaw drops.

"Hey!" My grandfather shifts in his seat and glares at her. "Don't insult me."

"Well she's insulting *me*," my mother says, pointing at my grandmother.

"She's your mother," he says. "She's just trying to help."

"How, by accusing me of turning into some kind of lunatic cat hoarder?" my mother says, and, catching the guilty surprise on my grandmother's face, barks a laugh. "Oh, come on, Mom. I mean, really." She reaches over, picks a sleepy Petal up off of the table and cradles her in her arms.

"I'm not accusing you of anything," my grandmother says, pushing her glasses up higher on her nose and giving my mother a look. "I'm just saying that animals do not belong on the kitchen table. It's unsanitary. Nicky never let Stripe up there."

"Well, I'm not Nicky, and besides, we don't eat at the table anymore," my mother says as Petal yawns and nuzzles her chin. "Look. This is Petal. Her mother was a stray, run over on the road. She left three hungry, orphaned kittens in my backyard. Petal was one of them. What did you want me to do, ignore them? Let them starve? Forget it. I saw a need, and I reached out to help, okay?"

"You have *eleven cats*," my grandmother says doggedly, opening a random cabinet, peering in and wrenching out a pot. The lid clatters to the floor and she scoops it up and sets them both on the stove with a bang. "Ten more than you had when Nicky died. You don't see a problem here? No one has eleven cats."

"Well, then I guess I'm unique," my mother says, and now there's a quaver in her voice that wasn't there before. "It's not about the number, Mom, it's about the need. What, is my compassion supposed to run out when I hit three? Five? Seven? Or just the socially acceptable numero uno?"

"Nicky thought one was enough," my grandmother says.

"Don't turn him into a saint just because he's dead."

"Don't talk like that," my grandmother says, turning on the stove burner, uncapping the oil and pouring some into the pot.

"Then stop wielding Nicky like a sword and bashing me over the head with what he would have wanted, okay?" my mother cries. "What am I, supposed to live the rest of my life trying to please a man who isn't even alive anymore? He's *gone*. The joint decisions are *over*. What I do from now on is *my* business."

"How can you say that?" my grandmother says, recapping the oil and slamming the bottle down on the countertop. "He's your husband—"

"Was," my mother says, and the pain in her voice fills the room. "He *was* my husband and I would have loved him forever but now he's *gone*. That was *his* decision, I had no say in the matter and the only stupid consolation prize left is that I get to make *my* own decisions now."

"Fine! Make them! But do they have to be so . . . opposite? So outlandish? He would hate this . . . this *disorder*," my grandmother says, waving an arm as if to take in the entire room. "He was so neat and organized, Rachel, and this is pure chaos." She snatches an onion from her grocery bag, a knife from the drawer and, jaw set, starts peeling. "Completely out of control."

"Well, maybe that's the way my life is now," my mother says, turning away.

"But it doesn't *have* to be," my grandmother says, and now it sounds like she's pleading. "My God, look at the table, Rachel. Can't you just clear it off? Can't you even *try* to straighten up a little, maybe put the house back in some kind of order, the way it was before? It was all right then. Not perfect, but livable."

"Why?" my mother says. "It's not going to change anything."

"Well, couldn't you even *try?*" my grandmother says, setting down the knife and gazing at her beseechingly. "If not for you or your daughter, then for Nicky? Couldn't you do it for Nicky?"

I stop breathing.

My mother pales. "You know what, Mom? You're right. Let me do for Nicky *exactly* what he did for me." She wheels and with one savage sweep of her arm, she clears the table and sends everything crashing to the floor.

Chapter 67

Oh.
   My.
   God.

Chapter 68

"There," she says into the stunned and ringing silence. "Happy now?"

My grandmother lays the onion and the knife down on the counter and turns to my grandfather. "Come on, Albert. We're not needed here."

"No," my mother says angrily, pointing at my grandfather, who has risen halfway, as if commanding him to stay seated, and turns to my grandmother. "You started this, now don't you dare walk away just because you don't like what I have to say."

"Well, I'm sorry, Rachel. Then I guess I can't do anything right," my grandmother says, and now there are tears in her eyes. "You're not the only one Nicky hurt, you know. We loved him, too. Do you think this has been easy, watching you go through this terrible pain when all we want is for you to be happy again?"

"And I *will be*, Mom, but you can't *push* me into it. I have to go through it myself, my own way, when I'm ready." My mother runs a hand through her hair and sighs. "I've been Nicky's wife for twenty-two years, and I never wanted to give that up but now I *have to* because I have no choice. I have to find a new way to live because it's really hard being married to a man who no longer exists. You ask him something, he doesn't answer. You reach for him, he doesn't reach back. You want him, there's nothing there."

"But at least you have beautiful memories," my grandmother offers, eyes watering as she picks up the knife and resumes chopping the onion.

You have me, I want to say, but can't speak the words.

"Memories. Yes, to remind me of exactly what I'm missing," my mother says, reaching past my grandmother and taking my father's wallet from the windowsill. She gazes down at it, rubs her thumb along the worn edges and cups it, the curve fitting her palm. "It's a lonely way to live." She puts the wallet back in its place. "Those vows we took? *Till death do us part? I* kept them, Mom. He didn't. It's done. I'm a widow now."

"I know," my grandmother says softly, sniffling and dumping the chopped onions into the pot.

"No, you don't," my mother says, stopping behind her. "Trust me. You don't know how lucky you are that you and Daddy got to grow old together. Do you know that I'm the *only one* in the world who knows the whole story of me and Nicky now? If I forget *any* of it, there's no one to ask. You know where that leaves me?" She holds out her hands, palms up and empty. "Standing here with all these emotions and nowhere to put them!"

I open my mouth to say *I know how you feel* but my grandmother isn't finished yet.

"Then maybe you should talk to someone, Rachel," my grandmother says, sprinkling sweet paprika into the pot. "And I don't mean your daughter or me or your sister, either. I mean a professional who can help, because . . ." She bites her lip and then says in a rush, "You sound very angry."

"Me? Angry?" my mother says after a long moment, staring at her in total and honest surprise. "No, Mom. I'm not angry."

The three of us gape at her in silence.

"What?" she says, scowling and falling back a step. "I'm not. I mean I'm sad and I miss him but I'm not mad at him. How could I be? I know why he left. I *saw* how miserable he was . . ."

"That doesn't mean you can't be angry at him too, Rachel," my grandmother says quietly. "Angry that he left you, that he isn't here now—"

There's a weird, hurtful grating inside of me, the scrape of stone against my heart, and I want to tell her to stop, to leave my mother and me alone, to stay out of it because she doesn't know, doesn't understand that we are not mad at my father, we *can't* be, it isn't fair, and even if we are it's not her business, it's *our* business, and yes, anger is one of the stages of grieving but we don't need that one, we're skipping it, and nothing she does or says can make us be mad at him because we love him and yes, he chose to leave us but—

"Stop it! What are you trying to do?" my mother says, and the look of fear, alarm, on her face scares me even more. "What do you want me to say? That yes, I *am* angry with him? Furious? That I feel deserted? Is that what you want?" She's shouting again, but this time it's not at me or even at them, it's at my father, who isn't here to defend himself, to say he's sorry he hurt her and that he'll never do it again. She's shouting into the void, filling it, and the echo is a blade slicing through me.

"Rachel, no, I—" my grandmother says, distressed.

"Then what? Do you want me to say that I forgive him? I can't. Not yet. Do you want me to say I hate him? Because I don't. I hate what he did to us but I love him, okay? And yeah, I'm mad. Oh God, I didn't want to be but I *am*." She's crying now, the tears streaming down her face. "I *know* he loved me, I *know* it was the depression, but I'm really mad that he just *left* me here, that he made a decision that changed *my* life and Rowan's and everybody's without even asking us!"

I look down at the table, stomach churning, glad now that I didn't say anything. It's one thing to have these thoughts myself, in private, another to hear them thrown right out into the air, big and harsh and accusatory. She's never admitted to being angry before and I don't like that she's mad at my father, that she's so fierce about his being gone now, like she's trying to drive home the point once and for all, make us accept it.

Make herself accept it.

My mother is a widow.

No longer married.

Single. A single mom.

I am the daughter of a dead dad and a single mom.

Chapter 69

"So wait, you're collecting cats to get back at Nicky for dying?" my grandfather says, leaning forward in his chair and frowning.

My mother takes a hitched breath. Wipes her eyes and stares at him for a long moment. "Oh my God," she says weakly. "You still don't get it."

"Well then, *tell* me so that I do," he says angrily, thumping his good fist down onto the table. "What, Nicky saved people and now that he's gone you have to save cats? You're the one who's big on all those words, so explain it. How many cats is it going to take until you stop feeling guilty? Twenty? Thirty? A hundred?"

My mother goes still.

"It wasn't your fault Nicky died," my grandmother says, exchanging a quick, speaking look with my grandfather and putting the chopping block and paring knife in the sink. "None of us thought he would ever do something like that. Your father and I believe he hid his intentions on purpose so we *couldn't* stop him, Rachel." She sets the lid on the pot and lowers the heat. "You couldn't have saved him, and saving all of these cats to atone for it isn't going to bring him back."

"No, I know, but . . ." She lifts her head, her face naked with pain. "I have to do *something* because I didn't do the *one thing* I could have done to save him: taken his off-duty pistol out of the house. I forgot all about it. I never even thought—"

"Listen, Rachel, if Nicky was determined to die he would have found a way, gun or no gun," my grandfather says gruffly, leaning over, picking up Stripe and settling him on his lap. "He'd handled plenty of suicide calls before. He'd found the bodies, investigated the methods; he knew all the ways to do it. If you'd taken his pistol he would have hanged himself or overdosed on his pills or cut his wrists . . ." He stops, throat working. "Mother of God, when I think about it . . ." He shakes his head quickly, as if to dispel the thought, and goes on. "All I'm saying is that if somebody really wants to die, they're going to find a way to do it. Look at that overpass."

"I don't know how you can stand to see it every day," my grandmother puts in. "If I were you I would think about selling the house and moving to a nice little condo somewhere in town."

I look at my mother in alarm but she doesn't notice.

"And what about Nicky's counselor?" my grandfather continues doggedly, and strokes Stripe, his calloused hand trembling. "She didn't think he was a suicide risk either and she was the one trained to spot it! She asked him if he was suicidal. He said no. She believed him and prescribed those goddamn drugs. Who knows what they did to his mind?" His jaw tightens. "Son of a bitch, that still makes me mad. What good is counseling if they don't know any more than I do?" He sets Stripe down, hoists himself up, walks across the room and, keeping his back to us, stares out the porch door. "You're not the only one who feels guilty, you know. I lie in bed at night thinking about how alone he must have felt and I swear to you, it rips me up inside." His voice cracks. "Why didn't he come to me? I would have listened. I would have done anything to help him. *Anything.*"

"Daddy, he knew that," my mother says, face crumpling as she goes to him. "He loved you guys. I don't think he *could* have asked, don't you see? I think the depression made him believe he'd be weak for asking. Or maybe he thought we wouldn't respect him anymore. You know how he was. He didn't ask for help; people called *him* to help *them*." She releases him, wipes her eyes. "I think the depression convinced him that if he wasn't big, strong, capable Nicky then we wouldn't love him anymore, and he just couldn't bear it."

"Of *course* we would have loved him," my grandmother says, taking the lid off the pot and stirring the onions. "How could he think that?"

"It was the depression talking, Mom," my mother says, picking up the colander full of chicken and bringing it to my grandmother.

"Terrible," Gran says, sighing and gently dumping the chicken into the pot. "I wish I could ask him." She pokes around inside it with the wooden spoon a moment and replaces the lid. "I wish I could sit him down and talk to him one more time."

"Yeah, me too," my mother says tiredly, slinging an arm around her mother's shoulders and giving her a quick, hard hug. "What a conversation that would be."

"He should have left a note," my grandfather says, running a shaky hand over his eyes. "It's not right, him going without saying good-bye."

"I know," my mother says, releasing my grandmother and sitting back down in her chair. "But that just shows me how bad he was hurting." She looks at her wedding ring and flexes her fingers, watching as the afternoon sunlight streaming in through the window makes the diamond sparkle. "I'm guessing, of course. We'll never know for sure." My mother glances over at me standing wide-eyed and silent among the scattered mail and groceries strewn across the floor. "Oh, Rowie." A myriad of emotions crosses her face and she pushes herself up out of her chair. "I'm so sorry. Are you okay?"

Am I? No, and I may never be again, but I nod anyway.

"My God, look at this mess." Bending, she picks up a handful of envelopes and one of the grocery bags. "That's the bad part about throwing a fit. You always have to pick up again afterward."

"I can do it." My mind is reeling and there's so much I want to ask her—but the only thing I seem to be able to do is start gathering the newspapers and mail spread out in front of me.

"All right." She meets my gaze and there's something clear and steady in her eyes that wasn't there before. "I'll keep the cats away from Grandma while she's cooking."

"Okay." We exchange strained, crooked smiles, and as the cats slowly venture back in, wary but curious, and my grandmother cooks, my mother shoos them out again while she puts away groceries and I gather the mail back into a pile, and my grandfather cradles Stripe on his lap and lets him bat at his bound-up finger, I am left with a hundred frightening questions about our future and at the same time, a heart that expands with an almost unbearable tide of love for the crazy courage, strength and beauty of my family.

Grief Journal

Something happened today, Dad.

Everybody fell apart and then, somehow, fell back together again.

But the stuff they said . . .

Scary.

I don't know whether they just forgot I was there or they figured that since I'm a part of it I'd understand, but it was really intense. I never heard Grandma go off, especially on Mom, or Mom go off on her like that.

Maybe the beginning of this fourth month is a turning point for them, too.

We're still so raw inside.

And Mommy feels really bad, Dad. I'm starting to think that it's not me you need to get in touch with but her, instead.

I never even knew you *had* an off-duty pistol.

Or maybe I did, way back a thousand years ago, and forgot too, because you never used it. Just kept it tucked away somewhere, I guess.

You knew Mommy forgot about it, didn't you?

You knew and you counted on it, and I'm sorry but that makes me mad.

Didn't you realize how much this would haunt her, or did you just not care because all you wanted was a way to exit and by that point you would have said or done anything to get it?

So, was Grandpa right? If she *did* remember the pistol, or if I did, and we somehow found it and took it away, would you have just found another way to do it?

I think you would have if you wanted to go badly enough, which apparently you did.

Or the depression did. I think Mom's right about that.

It wasn't you talking.

And isn't it weird that knowing it was the depression making you so miserable and not us or your life actually makes me feel a little better?

I guess that's what I'm reduced to now: Weighing what *could* have happened versus what actually did, and trying to understand it, accept it, take comfort in the fact that you didn't make your death as bad for us as it could have been.

Because I'm just now realizing, piece by piece, that it actually could have been worse.

Bleak, I know, but for some reason, it matters.

And what I've discovered so far is that suicide is better than murder/suicide, one quick, clean shot is better than hanging or slitting your wrists, doing it away from home is better than at home . . .

A note would have been better than no note at all, but I guess I can't have everything.

Only . . . you took such good care with all the other details in your life, so why not that, at the end of it?

I will never understand why not that.

Chapter 70

I make it to the dry cleaner's by three thirty, after promising to be home again by five so I don't miss my grandmother's early-bird-special *paprikás*.

It's funny; when I left the house my mother was making the *nokedli* and Gran the chicken, and Grandpa had coaxed the unrepentant Sage up onto his lap and, in between admiring the cat's clean, black-and-white tuxedo coat, was making a case for bringing him home, saying if anybody could teach him proper cat manners it was my grandmother.

And my grandmother snorted and gave my grandfather a knowing look . . .

But she didn't say no, and even more astonishing, neither did my mother.

The parking lot is sweltering, shimmering with heat waves, and stepping into the air-conditioned cleaner's is like stepping under an ice-cold waterfall.

The motion-sensor bell over the door announces my presence and from the back I hear Eva yell, "I'll be right there," in a voice filled with frustration.

"Take your time," I call back with a smile, and step in between the counters so she can see me. "Hi, Eva."

Her eyes widen and her jaw drops, and then she hurries toward me, arms out, her face creasing into the widest smile I have ever seen her wear. "Rowan! Oh, my dear, it's so good to see you." She enfolds me in a surprisingly fierce old-lady hug and that's when I tear up, because I didn't even know how much I've missed her.

"Oh no, now, we don't want to do that," she says, releasing me and rummaging in her cardigan pocket. "Here, I think this one's clean."

"Thank you," I blubber, laughing at the crumpled wad of tissue she thrusts into my hand. "So how are you? How's everything been? Is it busy? You got a new doormat, I see. It looks good. I'm sorry it's taken me so long to come by but—"

"You've gotten skinny," she says, hooking a gnarled finger into the too-big waistband of my shorts and giving it a tug. "What're you going to be now, a model?"

"Ha, right. And you've changed your hair," I say, knuckling away the tears and nodding in approval. "I like it. New haircut?"

"Cut, color, the works!" She makes a face like it's foolishness but her gaze dances behind her glasses. "You know why?" She motions me closer. "I have a man friend now and he likes that sexy Betty White look, so . . ." She shrugs, eyes twinkling. "I told him you pay, I'll do it, and he did. So now I look so good I can't keep him off of me!"

"Oh my God," I say, shocked and struggling not to laugh.

"I know," she says, nodding. "I told him no funny stuff until the ring is on the finger, but he's a musician, you know, and they're terribly hot to trot."

"Really?" I choke out. "Um, what does he play?"

"Mostly Johnny Mercer, but he does some Barry Manilow, too, for the youngsters," she says, patting her hair back into place and completely missing my gurgle. "He plays piano at the Hilton lounge on Tuesday and Thursday nights. That's how we met. I was at the regional dry cleaner's convention and we stopped in afterward for a nightcap." She gives me a preening look. "He invited me up to stand by the piano as he played 'Satin Doll.' Ah! Dreamy. I said to him, 'Oh, what a line you have, mister,' when it was over but it was too late. I was hooked."

"Wow, I miss everything," I say as she does a creaky little two-step. "I'm really happy for you."

"Ah no, enough me, me, me. What a stupid-head I am." She immediately stops dancing and solemnly peers up into my face. "How are you doing? How is your mother?"

"We're okay, I guess. We're getting there. It's hard. We miss him." I take a deep breath, ignoring the ache, and say casually, "I have a boyfriend now, too."

"Eli, the tall, skinny boy with the dog?" she says, and at my dumbfounded look, adds, "What? I saw the way he watched and stayed by you at the wake and the funeral. I'm not blind yet, you know." She smiles and pats my arm. "Love is a wonderful, healing thing. It helps you look toward tomorrow instead of always wishing for yesterday. He's good to you?"

"So far," I say faintly.

"He's not a bum," she says with a satisfied nod. "I didn't think so but God knows I've been wrong before. So"—she cocks her head and studies my face—"this is not a social call. Are you coming back to work now?"

Something about the simplicity of her question, as if my not coming back was never even an option, as if she always knew that at some point I would lift my head, take a deep breath and stand up again, makes me want to cry.

"I would really like to," I manage to say. "Eva, thank you so—"

"Good," she says briskly, snapping me right out of my weepy gratitude. "Then you can start tomorrow at two o'clock until closing at seven. Or is that too much all at once? Do you want to try less hours at first?"

"No, that's fine," I say.

"Good, because look at this mess," she says, and thrusts her scarred and crisscrossed thumbs up into my face. "Look at what pinning those stupid clothes has done to them. Rake, rake, rake, every day pins rake the thumbs. I have no fingerprints left!"

"Good time to become a criminal," I say, examining my own, and yes, even though the scratches have long since healed they've still altered the whorls of my prints. "Look, mine too."

"Partners in crime," Eva says, and then, giving the customer bill card rack a spin, says, "Tomorrow if you finish the pinning early you can start pulling cards and making the quarterly reminder calls, okay? Too much money sitting here waiting to be collected."

"Okay," I say, and glance under the counters at the shelves, expecting to see tons of clothes waiting to be pinned, but instead there's nothing. "Eva." I look back at her, suddenly suspicious. "Is it really slow right now? Because if it is and you *don't* really need me, I—"

"Rowan." She gazes at me for a long moment, then lifts her chin and says with much dignity, "Your father was my dear friend and you are, too." And then she gives me a mischievous grin. "Besides, I have a man and a social life now. Who wants to be stuck here?" She shoos me away. "Now go, and I'll see you tomorrow at two sharp."

"Okay," I say, and head for the door. I stop, turn and say, "Thank you, Eva," but she's already gone.

And it's only then in the quiet that I realize the song on the radio isn't Terence's R & B or even country, Eva's normal choice, but a guy singing "One for My Baby (and One More for the Road)," smooth, bluesy, jazzy, and so I tiptoe over and peer into the back and there it is, sitting on the counter right by the press.

A brand-new CD player.

And sitting next to it, a Johnny Mercer CD case.

I listen a moment longer and, smiling, pad back out.

Chapter 71

Funny how everything continues to evolve while you just keep breathing.

I make it back in time for dinner and am surprised when my grandmother asks me to set the dining room table. I glance at my mother, who hesitates, looks at the cluttered kitchen table and, sighing, nods.

And while I'm doing it, setting four places and leaving my father's chair empty, I realize that the newly painted dining room doesn't mean anything to my grandparents. They don't know about what happened, and for some reason that makes me feel better about having dinner in here, like for all the sad and terrible parts of my father's death that were made public, the three of us still had moments that no one else knew about.

I like that.

The *paprikás* is delicious and I eat too much, which makes my grandmother happy enough to give in to my grandfather's not-so-subtle hints about bringing Sage home with them.

"But not tonight," she says, giving him a look as he reaches down and pets Sage, who is purring really loud and twining around his ankles, hoping my grandfather will "accidentally" drop another piece of chicken. "Tomorrow morning we'll go to PetSmart and get him a litter box and whatever else he's going to need." She looks at my mother and with a small, reluctant smile says, "I suppose I should be glad you didn't decide to rescue snakes, instead."

"He's a good boy," my mother says, gazing down at the cat. "He's been with us for what, a little over a month now? And it's funny, Dad, that out of all the cats here you chose him, because he's always wanted to be an only cat. He's great with people but not that fond of being one of a crowd. Right, Sage?"

Sage walks right past my mother, jumps up on my grandmother's lap and gazes solemnly into her face.

"No, kitty, we're at the dinner table," she protests, and makes a motion to push him down.

"Wait, blink two or three times while he's looking at you, Mom, really slow," my mother says softly. "It tells him that you're not a threat and you mean no harm."

My grandmother does, looking self-conscious, and Sage, gazing up into her face, immediately starts purring and kneading her lap. "Ouch. Oh my."

"Sometimes they just need a little reassurance that the world is not a cruel and hateful place," my mother says, sitting back in her chair and smiling. "I think you have a fan."

"Oh my," my grandmother says again as Sage, overcome with his newfound love, stands up on his back legs, sniffs her eyeballs and then rubs his chin against the side of her jaw.

"I see I'm going to have to get another cat of my own," my grandfather says, winking at my mother and helping himself to more *nokedli*.

By the time we finish eating, cleaning up and waving good-bye to my grandparents, it's after eight o'clock. The sun hangs low in the sky, the breeze is soft and the shimmering light casts a rich golden sheen across everything, which would be even more beautiful if Eli was here to share it with me. I haven't heard anything from him since I responded to his *Miss me yet?* text with, *Yes, do you miss me?* and then because it sounded so needy added, *Crazy day here,* and then because my day was nowhere near as crazy as flying to Houston for a dog, added, *But not as crazy as yours I'm sure.*

And an hour ago, with still no response, I texted, *Hope it's going good with Rosie,* and am trying hard not to picture him out with an old girlfriend.

"Whew, what a day," my mother says, plopping down onto the couch and smiling as Stripe jumps up onto her lap. "Thank God it's almost over."

"Yeah, huh?" I say, fidgeting as she starts sorting through the books on the end table. I pull my phone from my pocket and give it a surreptitious glance. Nothing. I wish I'd thought to take a picture of us before he left. Damn. I glance up, catch her watching me and shove my phone back in my pocket. I haven't told her about seeing Eli again and I'm not sure why. Maybe it's because he's gone and it won't feel real until he's back. Or maybe it's just because I'm supposed to be grounded, and that usually means no company. I don't know, I—

The phone rings.

"I've got it," my mother says, reaching for the portable. "Hello?" Her face softens into a smile. "Oh, hello, Arnold. What a pleasant surprise."

I scowl and shake my head. *No it's not.* Even though I stopped hating Lieutenant Walters when he stood on casket watch at the wake, that still doesn't make us best friends. *What does he want?* I mouth.

"Oh, we're muddling along," my mother says, giving me an absent frown. "No, it hasn't been easy. Quite the opposite." She listens a moment and chuckles. "Well, that's because we haven't *been* out in public lately. It's been a very quiet summer. Exactly what we needed."

Hmm. I'm starting not to like this.

"Oh really? That's right, I forgot all about it," she says, and bites her lip. "That's very nice but I don't know. Can I think about it and let you know tomorrow?"

What's very nice? I mouth.

"All right, I'll give you a call back tomorrow," she says with a smile. "And thank you, Arnold. I really appreciate you thinking of us. Bye now."

"That was Lieutenant Walters, wasn't it?" I demand the second she hangs up. "What did he want?"

"Yes, it was," she says, giving me a curious look. "He called to remind us that the annual PBA picnic is this weekend and he hasn't gotten our RSVP form back. I couldn't tell him that it's probably buried somewhere on the kitchen table." She tucks back her hair and sighs. "I don't know, Rowan; what do you think? He said we would go as honored guests—"

"Whose, his?" I hear myself say snidely, and stop. "Sorry."

"No," my mother says in the overly patient, careful tone that means she's starting to get annoyed, "as honored guests of the PBA and the department, which, despite your rudeness, *I* think is a very thoughtful and generous gesture."

"It is," I say after a moment, feeling kind of stupid. "Are we gonna do it?"

"I don't know," she says, picking up a book and opening it to the dog-eared page where she's left off. "It'll be strange to go without your father. They were his friends and colleagues, not mine." She glances at me, her gaze thoughtful. "I haven't seen any of them except for Vinnie since the funeral. Our being there might make people uncomfortable." She shrugs. "It might make *us* uncomfortable, too."

"Why?" I don't like where this conversation is going.

She hesitates.

"Why?" I say, because her silence is even more unsettling than her words.

"Because I'm not sure we fit in there anymore," she says quietly. "Nicky's gone. He belonged there. He *was* an officer; he isn't anymore. It's over. They've moved on, continued to live their lives, and then here comes yesterday's bereft widow and her sad, fatherless child still holding on, walking reminders of what can go wrong for every single one of them. Talk about putting a damper on the festivities." She sets the book aside. "I don't know, Rowan. I think maybe it's time we started cleaning this place up. We could sort through your father's things and pack some of it. Not all," she adds hastily at my shocked look. "Just some, to start."

"Why?" I croak, clutching the arm of the couch. "What's the rush?"

"No rush," she says, taken aback. "I just thought . . . it's been months. Don't you think it's time to——"

"What, move on?" The words burst out unbidden. "Get on with your life?"

"Not just *my* life," she says, giving me a funny look. "*Our* lives. Rowan, Grandma was right. It *is* like a time warp in here." She glances around the room, her gaze landing on my father's jacket still hanging on the coatrack, the Stephen King book he was reading still lying open at his place on the table near his chair, the reading glasses on top of them. "Nothing has changed since the day he died, and that was all right; I know why we did it. We needed something to hold on to and it made sense back then but——"

"But not *now*?" I say, pushing myself to my feet.

"No." She stares at me, bewildered. "It's been too long. It makes me feel like every day is yesterday, and for the rest of my life I'll be nothing but the curator of the Nicky museum. And I don't mean that in a bad way, but keeping all of his things out like this, the way he left them, like he's only away and going to come back . . . it's not comforting anymore. It's paralyzing. Do you understand?"

"Sure," I say coldly, blowing off her words. "I get it. You want to *move on* and start your new life and Daddy's stuff is just in the way." I take a step backward, away from her. "Well, you can do what you want but I'm not going to *move on* and forget him, Mom, no matter how much——"

"I don't want you to forget him," my mother says, staring at me in disbelief. "Why would you think something like that? He was your father—"

"He *is* my father!" I yell, stamping my foot and making the cats run for cover. "He'll *always* be my father, my *only* father, and I don't care who you bring here but I'm never calling anyone else Dad, do you hear me? Never!"

My mother gapes at me, astonished.

"I *heard* what you said," I shout, infuriated. "You're a widow, that means you're single now, okay, and I get it. I do." I'm shaking all over, caught in the grip of some bone-deep, fear-fueled rage. "But you didn't ask *me* what *I* want and I don't *want* another father, I love *my* father and—"

"Stop," my mother says, and her voice is so quiet, so strong, that I fall silent. She gets up and comes to me, her face solemn. "Shh," she murmurs, wrapping her arms around me and pulling my stiff body close. "Shh." She strokes my hair until the trembling subsides. "Rowie, I love your father, too. No one could ever replace him. I feel sorry for any man who would try. He'll always be a hard act to follow."

"So then why did you say what you said about being mad at him?" I say, pulling away and wiping my face. My head is pounding and my heart feels like somebody took a knife to it. "Why did you have to say it out loud like that?"

"Because I had to," she says with a helpless gesture. "Maybe it was time. I don't know. These feelings come and go in waves, the anger, sadness, trying to find something to hope for or try to be happy about . . ."

"You still have me," I say in a small voice, wrapping my arms around myself and staring at the floor because I know that's not what she means but it's all I have to offer.

"I know, and you'll always be the best part of my life," she says, touching my damp cheek. "So don't worry about this now, all right? Forget I said anything."

"No, wait," I say as my phone signals an incoming text. "Mom, I'm sorry. I—"

"The packing was just an idea. Maybe a bad one. I felt pretty good for a minute and I maybe thought it was time but—"

"No, it's okay," I say, horrified at how completely her smile has died.

She shakes her head, puts a weary hand to her temple. "I'm going to lie down for a while. I have a splitting headache." She plods to the couch, wraps the afghan around her and eases down, huddling into a ball. "Turn off the lamp for me, will you?"

"Okay," I say, but don't move, only stare at her forlorn figure. I did this to her, *I* did, not my father or my grandparents, and suddenly it occurs to me that *we* mourn differently too, my mother and I. We may be in it together but our grief is different, and although sometimes our stages seem to be the same, they can't possibly be, because he was my father but he was her *husband,* and those are two totally different roles. We miss the same person but we each miss him in our own way and I don't know how I never saw that before. "Mom?"

She opens her eyes.

"I'm really sorry," I say, taking a step toward her. "We can start tomorrow morning before I go to work. I'll help. We don't have to do it all, we could just do some and see how it goes, okay? Please?"

She cracks an eye and gazes at me for a long moment, then heaves a sigh, sits back up and looks at her watch. "You know what? I'm sick of this stupid couch. It's a beautiful night for a walk. I wonder if the ice cream depot is still open." She catches my surprise and gives me a rallying smile. "When was the last time you and I went for ice cream together?"

I shake my head, throat tight, because I can't remember, because my father was usually the one with the urge for ice cream. "But what about your headache?"

"That's what fresh air is for," she says, rising and smoothing her blouse. "Let me grab some money and my keys, and then it's two scoops for everyone!"

"Mom?" I say without moving.

She stops in front of me. Searches my face and pulls me to her in a fierce hug. "I know these are baby steps, Row, but we'll get there. I promise."

"I promise, too," I whisper, and this time I actually believe it.

Grief Journal

Dad, I messed up again, and I don't know why.

Mom was actually feeling good, maybe even at a turning point of her own, and I don't know what happened but I just lost it, freaked, and knocked her backward again.

I made her feel bad. Really bad.

I don't know why I did that.

I mean I *knew* she wasn't trying to forget you, I *knew* that, but I just panicked . . .

She was only talking about packing away some of your stuff.

That's all.

Why did that scare me so much?

And why does it still?

Just because I can't see you doesn't mean I don't think about you.

I do, all the time.

But if we move your stuff . . .

If we get rid of the things you cared about, pack away the pieces of your life . . .

Then there'll be nothing but more empty space.

Without your stuff around there'll be no proof of your existence.

Like this isn't your home, like you don't live here anymore.

There will be nothing left of you to see or hold or touch, nothing left to give even the smallest comfort.

Without your stuff, you will really be gone.

Chapter 72

Eli texts, *Sorry this took* so long. *Met Rosie, she's great!! Carleton and Cheryl are good people and we're meeting for dinner to talk more. Send good thoughts, Row. They're worried that if something goes wrong for Rosie in the future she'll only have one kidney left. I get that but without the kidney Daisy dies. Can't wait to see you. Have to go. Love, Eli*

Love, Eli.

I smile to myself all the way to the depot and on the way back, eating ice-cream cones and ambling down Victory Lane in the dark with the lightning bugs flashing and the sweet scent of wild clover on the breeze, my mother and I talk about her going back to work, my going back to work, Eva's new boyfriend and finally, Eli.

"I'd like to meet him when he gets back," she says after a moment.

"You will," I say, trying to gauge her mood because she's gotten kind of quiet. "What is it, Mom?"

"Oh, I was just thinking about what your father said when he got home that night," she says, taking a lick of her butter-pecan cone. "After the whole overpass incident, I mean." She glances at me. "He had to take Eli's statement, you know, and he said he could have finished it in twenty minutes but Eli was so shaken up that he spent, like, two and a half hours with him just letting him talk. You know what really seemed to stick in his mind, Rowan?"

"What?" I say, curious but nervous, too.

"Well, let me see if I can remember how he said it," she says, frowning slightly and gazing off into the darkness. "He said something like 'He's a good kid trying to make the best out of being dealt a rough hand. He'd make his father proud.' He said he didn't tell Eli that, though, because he didn't want to overstep his bounds, but later he wished he had." She looks at me with a small smile. "So now you can tell him that your father thought he was a stand-up guy, and that he was always an excellent judge of character."

"No, you tell him when you meet him," I say as a strange and wonderful warmth floods my heart. "It'll mean more coming from you." I glance over and see an odd look on her face. "What?"

She bites her lip and then says, "I probably shouldn't tell you the rest—"

"What?" I say in alarm.

"Well"—she clears her throat, her voice husky—"he said, 'That's the kind of boy I'd like to see Rowan with someday. He'd always do right by her. I know it.'" She looks at me, eyes shining with tears, and laughs. "And look, now you are. Whoever said there was no such thing as miracles?"

We walk along in thoughtful, companionable silence, my mother and I, eating our ice cream and gazing at the stars. My mother brings her hand up under a lightning bug and lets it flash in her cupped palm, then gently nudges it off to me. We watch as it crawls to my fingertip, spreads its wings and flies away.

And when we get past the woods our house is there waiting— no, our *home*, with Stripe in the window and the porch light glowing a welcome. And for the first time since he left us, I get the distinct feeling that my father is smiling.

There is a land of the living and a land of the dead
and the bridge is love,
the only survival, the only meaning.
—THORNTON WILDER

Grief Journal

So is this how it happens, Dad?

The beginning of the healing, I mean, because me and Mom are starting to reach for each other across the empty space you left between us and every new moment we share that's just us changes something, makes the wound seem just a little bit smaller and just a little less hurtful.

I don't know exactly how I feel about that yet.

I never thought life would keep going but it has, and sometimes I hate it but sometimes . . . I don't.

This fourth month is so different.

We're going to start packing away some of your things now.

Not everything.

Never everything.

Just some of your clothes and stuff, I guess.

We're going to close the book you were trying to read and put it back on the shelf.

Fold up your reading glasses and maybe set them on the mantel next to your urn.

It drains me just thinking about it . . . but we're gonna do it.

Mommy was joking and said she's going to give Vinnie that awful talking-bass plaque you have hanging in front of the wood shop door, the one Grandpa gave you for your birthday that starts wiggling and singing "Don't Worry, Be Happy" whenever someone comes near.

Come to think of it, maybe she wasn't joking.

Poor Vinnie.

He'll never get a girlfriend with that thing hanging in his apartment.

Maybe I'll do him a favor and go get rid of it before Mom gets to it.

I'll do it soon, if I can get through the weeds back there.

Time to weed-whack again, I guess.

And, Dad?

I'm so glad you liked Eli.

I like him, too. A lot.

He's really worried about his dog, Daisy, right now, so if you run into his dad up there maybe ask him to send a little something Eli's way, okay?

Luck or love or whatever he can.

I know it's a weird request but I don't know what you guys are capable of anymore. What kind of powers you have, if any.

In life you had it all.

You were my hero, you know.

Still are.

Maybe now you could be my guardian angel.

God, I wish you could answer me.

Chapter 73

I wake up to texts from Eli that he sent me at two in the morning.

Hey, Row, are you around? No? You must be sleeping. Wish I was there, ha ha. Okay, well, there's good and bad news.

Oh no, now what? I rub the sleep from my eyes and keep reading.

Good is that Carleton and Cheryl said yes to the kidney for Daisy.

"Oh wow," I breathe, propping myself up on an elbow and jiggling my feet so that Peach and Plum wake up to share the good news. "Daisy's getting a kidney!" Peach yawns. Plum stretches. "Fine, be that way," I say, and go back to Eli's texts. "So then what's the bad news?"

Bad news is that now I don't know if I should do it.

What?

Rosie is a happy, healthy dog. She survived Iraq and her people love her. How can I risk her life after all she's been thru?

I read on, at a loss.

If I do this for Daze she might live another couple of years but she'll have to be on antirejection drugs for the rest of her life and they have side effects, not to mention the pain of soft-tissue surgery. Trust me, I had my appendix out and it hurt like a bitch. Do I really want to make her even more miserable for a 50%

chance of even surviving the operation? Quality versus quantity. A short, good life or a long, miserable one?

"Oh God," I murmur, scrolling further.

I went to my father's grave and told him everything, hoping I'd get some kind of answer or big revelation, but nothing. So I guess I have to make this decision on my own.

Hmm.

Maybe that WAS the answer.

Anyway, there are a couple of vets down here I want to talk to and see if they have any other ideas. I'll be home in a couple of days. Miss you. Bye. Xoxo

"Damn," I mutter, and fall back on my pillow.

"Row?" My mother raps on my bedroom door. "Are you awake?"

"Yeah," I call, putting my phone back on the night table.

"There's coffee downstairs and we can start any time you're ready," she says.

"Okay," I say uncertainly, thinking, *Start what?*

Oh, that's right.

Today we start packing up my father's life.

| | |

We begin with his bureau and immediately hit a snag.

We don't know what to do with his underwear.

"Some of it's almost brand-new and I hate to throw it out, but what am I going to do with it?" my mother says, standing in front of the open bureau drawer and gazing at me in dismay. "I can't give them to anyone. I don't even think the Salvation Army would want them."

"Probably not," I say, and busy myself opening a second garbage bag. "I guess we can make this the *get rid of* bag." Because it's just too wrong to say *throw away*.

She stares at the underwear for a long moment. "Why is this so difficult? It's just underwear."

Yes, but it's my father's underwear and throwing it out is so final, an absolute acknowledgment that he really isn't coming back.

"So, save a pair and pack it away and get rid of the rest," I offer. "It doesn't have to be all or nothing, Mom. We can do it any way we want."

And that seems to break her paralysis, because she chooses one of the newer pairs and drops it in the pack-away bag, and then drops pair after pair into my garbage bag, finding stray buttons, his extra police tie clip, a small wad of singles, his rookie number twenty-nine badge, his pin-on commendation ribbons and an old photo of the ceremony with us and his parents all gathered around him beaming with pride.

"He missed them so much," my mother murmurs.

"Well, I bet they're really happy to see him again." We gaze at it together a long time and then, wiping her eyes, my mother sets it gently aside.

We move steadily through the rest of his bureau, dividing his new sweat socks between us, tossing the rest, keeping his favorite T-shirts and jeans and donating the rest.

And in every drawer we find bittersweet surprises: the Father's Day card I gave him last year with a brief, scrawled *Love you, Dad!!! You rock!!!* that makes me wish I had taken a little more time and thought of something better to write, an old love note that my mother gave him way back when they were first going out that she tucks away for later, a big, smiling butterfly I drew him once, scribbled in crayon, a bunch of wood screws, ChapStick, a pen, and his father's old, engraved Zippo lighter from the war.

"You know, for a man who dealt with tragedy for a living he certainly was sentimental," my mother says, closing the last drawer and rising. She hesitates, staring at his limp, terry-cloth bathrobe still hanging on the hook, says, "Not yet," and moves to the closet. Takes a deep breath, says, "This is going to be hard," and opens the doors.

The faint scent of his cologne and the sight of his uniform hanging there freshly cleaned and still in plastic hits me like a spear through the heart.

"Oh my God," my mother whispers, voice wobbling, and lifts it from the rod. "Oh, Nicky." She hugs it to her, lays it across the bed and gazes down at it. "I knew this would be hard, I *knew* it would, but I never thought . . ." And then her voice changes. "There's only one uniform here."

I wipe my eyes. "What?"

"We buried him in one, and here's one. He had three pair of uniforms, Row. We're missing one," my mother says, turning back to the closet and rummaging through the sport shirts and dress slacks hanging inside. "Where is it?"

"I don't know," I say with a shrug, and then a vague memory stirs to life. "Oh, I bet it's still down at the cleaner's. Daddy asked me to take it in right before he died and I totally forgot to pick it up. Wow." I lie back on the bed. "What do I have, amnesia?"

"Temporary amnesia, I think, and join the club," she says with a sideways smile, and turns back to the closet. "Bring it home with you tonight, all right? I want to keep everything together. I don't want pieces of his life getting lost or left anywhere."

"Okay," I say, and, sitting up, glance at my watch. "Whoa, I have to get ready to go. Do you want to wait on doing the rest of the closet until tonight when I get home?"

"No, you go ahead," she says, pulling a navy blue dress shirt off the hanger and holding it to her cheek. "He looked so handsome in this." She carefully folds it and puts it in the pack-away bag. "I'll just do what I can. I won't throw anything away until you look through it later. And who knows, maybe he *did* leave something tucked away for us somewhere, Row. Maybe it's here and we just haven't found it yet."

"Maybe," I say softly, because I didn't know she was still hoping for it, too, and hearing it makes me realize how futile that hope really is.

"I should go through all that mail next," my mother says. "God only knows what's in there."

"Good idea," I say, and bolt for the shower, vowing to hide the autopsy envelope before I leave for work.

My father isn't the only one who knows how to protect our family.

Chapter 74

When I get to work Terence is still there pressing and the day's lot of clothes is all lined up on hangers and waiting for me on the rack. "What's this?" I say in surprise, as bagging the clean clothes is usually the morning clerk's job and is done by the time I get there. "What happened to Helga?" I stop, frowning. "That was her name, right?"

"She's gone," Terence says, bopping along to Smokey Robinson and the Miracles' "I Second That Emotion" as he works. "Has been for months, thanks to three pens, an iPhone and a ruby necklace all wrecking my machine. The queen said go, and she's gone. Good to have you back, little sister." He grins. "You want a raise, you'd better ask for it now. The queen is flying high with this new man and you being back. She's out there getting us all ice cream to celebrate. Take advantage of it."

"No, I'm good, but thanks for the heads-up," I say, laughing and grabbing the first ticket and batch of clothes to bag. "I'm just glad to be employed again." And I am, but I'm working the back *and* the front of the cleaner's today at the same time, and trying to concentrate and remember all the steps of the job is easier said than done. Twice I have to sneak back up front while Eva isn't looking and check the pockets of the clothes that I was pinning and forgot to search.

In one of them I find a pen.

"Damn it," I mutter, rubbing my forehead. "Come on, you can do better than that." Sweating, I pin the suit and shove it back in a bin. Hear the bell go off and trot up front, only to discover gross old Mr. Hanson standing there with his nasty, damp-pocketed pants. "Hi," I say with a forced smile, and grab a blank ticket from under the counter. "One pair of pants?"

"Oh, you're here," he says happily, his creepy gaze immediately fastening on my boobs. "That's nice. This place wasn't the same without you." He licks his thin, livery lips with his terrible darting, lizardlike tongue. "The air-conditioning is very cold in here today, isn't it?"

And suddenly, I have had it. "No," I snap, slamming a hand down on the counter and sending him back a step in shock. "What is wrong with you, anyway? I'm sixteen, you're a thousand and it's disgusting, so *stop* it." I flex my stinging hand, willing myself not to wince and pick up a pen. "Now, when do you want these pants?"

"Right now," he gasps, blinking, and snaking out a hand, he grabs them from the counter. "You don't talk to customers like that. I'm taking my business elsewhere."

"Good riddance, you old perv," Eva says, coming up behind me.

"It was a *compliment!*" he cries in a querulous voice.

"Well, go compliment Dave over at One-Hour Martinizing and see how he likes it," Eva says, licking her ice-cream cone and waving him away.

"Dave will deck him," I say conversationally.

"Oh, I'm counting on it," she says with a bright smile.

Mr. Hanson stomps out, swearing and shaking his fist.

"One down," she says with a shrug, and toddles off into the back to call her boyfriend.

A police car pulls up in the fire zone out front.

My heart skips.

Vinnie climbs out, his arms full of uniforms.

"Hey, look who's back!" he cries when he sees me, and, dropping his clothes on the counter, comes right around and grabs me up in a giant bear hug. "How long have you been here?"

"Just today," I say, laughing and prying myself loose. "C'mon, Vinnie, you can't do that. You're in uniform! Someone will see and complain."

"Let 'em," he says with a huge smile, but steps back to the front of the counter. "I don't care. This is a red-letter day." He starts sorting through his uniforms, counting pieces and giving me searching looks at the same time. "So, how're you doing? How's your mom? I was thinking about coming by one night and taking you both out to eat. What do you think?"

"We're getting there and yeah, that'd be nice," I say, watching him with fond exasperation. "You might as well stop. I have to count them myself. You know that." I pull out a fresh ticket, write his name on it and count his pieces. "Two pants, two shirts. When do you want them?"

"Tomorrow," he says absently, listening to dispatch on his radio. "Gotta go. Can't anybody drive without crashing anymore?" He flashes me a quick smile and with uncharacteristic gentleness, says, "If you need me, Row, call. I'll always be around."

And then he turns and is gone.

"He's a good friend to us, Dad," I murmur, sticking his ticket in among his uniforms, rolling them all up together and wedging them under the counter for pinning later.

And the sight of them touches off a memory, something I'm supposed to do . . .

"Oh, right," I say, going to the ticket rack and spinning it around to the A's. "Allen, Alonzo, Appleby . . . here we go. Areno." I pluck the ticket, wrinkle my nose at Helga's barely legible handwriting, check the date—more than three months old, so we would have been part of the quarterly reminder phone calls—and with a terrible, draining sadness at knowing this is the last time I will ever bring my father's uniform home from the cleaner's, I go over to the conveyor and hit the power button. The plastic bags rustle and whisper as they whoosh by and when my father's ticket arrives, I stop the conveyor, reach out to pull the clothes from their slot and stop.

There is an envelope stapled to the ticket.

An envelope.

He left something in his pockets.

"Probably a pen." But my heart is pounding and I'm caught in a flood of memories, of his face when he asked me to bring these in and how he didn't send them all together with the others, that he said he didn't need these for a week but in a week he was already dead and he planned *that*, so did he plan this too, did he know I would find them or am I . . .

Hand shaking, I reach out and touch the envelope.

Smooth. Some bulk.

No pen.

"It's paper," I whisper, and clap a hand to my mouth, but the sob barrels out.

It's paper.

"Oh God, please," I say in a hoarse voice, rip the stapled envelope from the plastic and stare down at it, terrified to hope, terrified not to. I turn it over, wedge a finger under the sealed flap and tear a jagged length across the top. My breath is hitched, my hand palsied. "Please, Daddy. Please let it be from you. Please."

There are two small, sealed envelopes inside the bigger envelope.

I pull them out.

To Rowan.

In my father's handwriting.

I stare at it, caught in a wracking, full-body tremble, unable to move as tears well and flow, and then, as if in a dream, I look at the other one.

To Rachel.

"Rowan?" Eva says from behind me, and her voice breaks the spell.

"He left a note," I cry, holding them out, clutching them to me. "Eva, he *did*! Oh my God, I have to go!" And whirling, sobbing, I tear out of there, across the parking lot and all the way down Victory Lane to home.

Because he did.

He left a note.

May 18th

Rowie,

    I've loved you from the minute I first heard your heartbeat in the doctor's office and that will never, ever stop. You're the best thing that ever happened to me.
    I'm so proud of you.
    I have to say good-bye. I can't stay here anymore.
    Please forgive me if you can.
    I'm so sorry.

                                   Love forever,
                                       Dad

How lucky I am to have known someone so hard to
say good-bye to.

—ANONYMOUS

Chapter 75

Sweating, I shut off the weed whacker and push my father's safety goggles up on the top of my head, stepping back to survey my work.

"Not bad," I say, and my voice sounds funny after the gas trimmer's roar. I lay it on the ground and, digging the key out of my pocket, follow the path I just cut through the tall grass and goldenrod to my father's wood shop.

A big, intricate spider's web hangs in a triangular veil from the post to the overhang, and I duck under it so as not to ruin such hard work—or rain dozens of dead, mummified fly carcasses down on my head.

"Don't worry," the big, fake bass hanging on the door sings, twitching and writhing on its plaque, when I step into range. "Be happy."

"That's the plan," I tell it, but my hand is unsteady and it takes me three tries to fit the key in the lock.

It's September third, Labor Day, my father's birthday, the first one without him, and while the aunts are gathered in the kitchen with my mother and my grandparents are due any time now, while Vinnie is outside firing up the grill and Eva is standing beside her smooth, silver-haired boyfriend's keyboard clapping her hands off time to a very bouncy "Copacabana," I am back here alone, finally ready to claim the gift that has been waiting for me all of this time.

The key clicks in the lock and I turn the knob.

I push the door open and am greeted with a hot, woodsy smell so intense that I clutch the door frame, swaying.

The sharp, clean scent of cut pine, stain and glue, the cool metallic tang of screws and nails, all mingle to form the familiar scent of my father after a day of woodworking.

I take a deep breath and step inside, my hand going automatically to the light switch.

The fluorescents flicker and hum to life.

And there it is, sitting by his workbench on a pair of dollies.

My hope chest.

It's been made to last, strong, solid, its sturdy, block feet planted firm and level on the dollies, the smooth wood stained a deep, rich mahogany and blanketed with a thin, undisturbed layer of dust.

"Oh Dad," I say, and, crouching, realize that he *did* finish it, that the back-ordered hardware has been installed, that adding this shining brass plate in the shape of an exquisite filigree butterfly must have been the last thing he ever did in this little wood shop that was his joy and his solace, his place to work and have something good and solid and real to show for it. "It's so beautiful. Thank you."

And because I know my father, I turn the key, lift the lid and read the inscription he painstakingly carved on a matching wooden plaque fastened inside:

For our daughter Rowan on her 16th birthday
Love Always,
Mom and Dad

I gaze at it for a long moment, reach into my pocket, pull out my father's good-bye note and place it inside. Slowly shut the lid, turn the key and rise.

Walk out, gently closing the door behind me.

Grief Journal

Happy birthday.

Today you would have been forty-four.

It always seemed so old to me before—wow, forties—but now it doesn't.

Now it just seems too soon.

It's also on Labor Day this year, so we had kind of a little picnic.

The aunts and uncles came, and it felt really good to be with them again. Grandma and Grandpa came, too. I don't know if I told you but they adopted Sage, one of our rescue cats, and apparently they're getting along just fine. Sage loves being king of the house and despite Grandma's blustering about his manners, I've been over there twice so far and both times Sage sat right next to her on the kitchen table, fat, sassy and triumphant, while we drank our tea.

Things are definitely changing around here.

It's not all bad news anymore.

Vinnie came over and the first thing he said when he saw me was, "Hey, Row, how's your boat?" just like normal, but then he hugged me in that strong, emotional way of love and sorrow that reveals so much without speaking a word. He's your friend, Dad, and by inheritance ours too, but I don't know if he'll stay without you.

I hope so, but I'll understand if he doesn't.

He was your rookie and he always said you taught him everything he knew but this end, *your* end, is one thing he can't afford to learn, it can't even be an option, and let's face it, seeing us without you is a constant reminder.

Because I look a lot like you, you know.

Especially around the big, gray mustache.

Kidding, kidding.

Anyway, Eva is turning into quite the socialite with Antonio, her new rock-star man friend. They came and didn't stay long, just about seven songs' worth of time, enough to turn Aunt Kelly into a groupie and make Auntie Kate beg to borrow my iPod. Seeing Eva glowing with happiness was really good but bittersweet too, because you and Mom used to look like that.

So I was kind of kicking myself for even inviting them, worriedly watching Mom watch them with this naked look on her face, and I was just about to drop my plate or jump up screaming like there was a hornet biting me or something, anything to distract her, when all of a sudden she started, blinked, put a hand to her cheek and smiled, Dad, a *real* smile, and I think you know *exactly* what I'm talking about.

And okay, yes, maybe she imagined it, maybe it was a stray strand of hair wisping across her cheek or one of those awful dangly-legged mayflies flitting by . . . or maybe her yearning was so strong that she felt the physical memory of a kiss from long ago.

But maybe it was something else, something more.

I don't know and I'm leaving it at that because whatever it was, it made her smile the way she used to, and that alone was worth listening to a bunch of old-people songs.

Oh, and Barry Manilow, of course, for us youngsters.

That just cracks me up.

Eli came over today, too.

He said he'd stopped by Payton's on the way just to check in and that he'd found her packing. She said she's going back to Pensacola where she belongs.

And all I could think was that it's a good thing little Sammy is buried next to his father because otherwise he'd be here all alone.

Eli said she was drinking when he got there, and it was only ten in the morning.

Scary.

He brought Daisy over with him, too. She's stabilized now, and he's working hard to keep her that way even though he knows it can't last. After much agonizing he decided not to go through with the transplant—taking one of Rosie's kidneys, even for the best of reasons, and maybe ruining her health really haunted his conscience—and so instead he's chosen to make whatever time Daisy has left (months, years?) as happy, healthy and full of love as possible.

It's a sad plan but not a bad one.

Not defeat, Dad. Understanding and acceptance.

And in the end, isn't that all any of us can try for, anyway?

He hasn't given up on saving her; he just doesn't want to do it at Rosie's expense. He's taking Daisy down there to visit her in a couple of weeks, and is researching chronic renal failure, new diets and natural supplements, too.

Will he find the answer he's searching for?

Honestly? I think in his heart he already has.

It's just not the one he was hoping for.

He takes Semper Fi seriously, though, and if there is a way to save Daisy, he'll find it.

If there isn't, he says that at least he'll know he did all he could to save her and that sometimes that's just the best you can do.

It's a part of his healing, this monumental effort, and I get it.

He also bought a used Jeep. They ride around now to save her the physical stress, and she loves it.

I do, too.

We are a strange and sometimes happy threesome, Dad.

And you were right.

He *is* good to me.

And *for* me, because he understands.

He and Vinnie carried the hope chest out of your wood shop today and upstairs into my room.

Mom started crying when she saw it and that set the rest of us off, which was actually okay because it wouldn't have happened unless it needed to and somehow, in a strange and beautiful way, it cleared the air, let us admire your work and remember you again.

Your life, Dad. Not just your death.

Oh, and Auntie Kate, with her dear, good heart, showed up early yesterday and took Mom out shopping when she got home from work.

Yes, Mom is finally back to work at the library and yes, she went clothes shopping.

And she actually bought something.

It's a pretty, navy blue top and she looks damn good in it.

You would think so, I know it.

Even with her new, shiny, ash-brown hair.

Two steps forward and maybe this time, just for a little while, no steps back.

Tomorrow they're taking me school clothes shopping because I've decided to give East Mills High another try. Why not? I figure if I can survive losing you, I can survive anything.

And speaking of Mom, she's thinking about selling your Blazer and putting some of the money toward helping me with a car. She washed it this morning, unlocked and opened the doors to let it air out for a while, but she didn't get in and neither did I.

We don't need to, Dad, and it's okay.

She's also giving Vinnie the police tie pin she found in your drawer instead of the bass plaque. Grandpa is taking the bass back and hanging it in the garage, where it will drive Grandma nuts every time she goes out to start the car. Knowing Grandma, I wouldn't be surprised if it just *happens* to fall off the wall one day and she runs it over by, er, mistake.

I got your commendation watch, the one inscribed with the words *Valor Award* and your name, *Nicholas Areno*, on the back. It's a strong, sturdy watch, the links solid and comforting around my wrist, the back worn smooth from you wearing it every day.

It's too big, but I plan on growing into it.

Mom was right. There will never be another you.

And I have to go now, Dad.

Everyone is down in the kitchen cleaning up and the sound of their voices, their laughter, is echoing through the windows and out into the night.

It's the sound of life, and I feel like I need to be in it.

I *want* to be in it.

You've probably waited a long time to hear those words come out of me.

So don't be sad or worried anymore, okay?

Be at peace. Rest. Relax.

Stripe says go fishing.

He just wandered in and leaped up on my hope chest. Sniffed it like crazy and now he's rolling around all over it, kneading, purring and rubbing his chin against it.

He looks like he finally found you.

I feel that way, too.

Like we're really gonna be okay.

I wouldn't say it if I wasn't truly starting to believe it.

Oh, and guess what?

Mom just told me that you used to sneak into my room every morning and kiss me good-bye without my knowing it.

Thank you for that, and for loving me so much.

I'll always love you, too.

And, Dad?

Don't go yet. There's one more thing.

I'll be right back . . .

Chapter 76

I slip out into the clear, starry night. Pad barefoot across the lawn, following the path I forged this morning.

Duck under the spiderweb, endure the bass.

Unlock the door, take a deep breath, and flick on the lights.

Step inside, the smooth cement cool beneath my feet.

Shut the door behind me and lean against it until my knees are steady again.

Gaze around the wood shop.

All my father's tools are put away. The floor is swept. The wood is stacked, the cans of stain shelved.

The workbench is empty.

I look at his tool belt hanging on the hook, at his calendar hanging on the wall. The top is a photo of a trout, the bottom the month.

It is still May.

I move closer. Stand and stare at the terrible, blank white square for Sunday the twentieth until the date blurs, then close my burning eyes and slowly, gently rest my forehead against it for a long, still moment.

Exhale.

Step back, pick up a pen from the cup on the edge of the workbench and, flipping the calendar forward to today, write, *I forgive you, Daddy.*

Me Since You

laura wiess

Introduction

Rowan Areno is a normal sixteen-year-old trying to walk the difficult line between rebellion and responsibility, finding her own path and trying to do right by her loving and slightly strict parents. But when her father, Nick, a decorated police officer, tries and fails to stop a tortured young man from leaping from an overpass to his death, everything in Rowan's life begins to fall apart. As the media seizes on Nick's failure to stop the suicide, he slides deeper and deeper into an irreversible depression, until finally, the unthinkable happens, and he commits suicide as well. Rowan can't understand how her father could choose to leave her, and acts out, pushing away friends and taking risks with her safety. Rowan's mother, wracked with her own guilt and sorrow over failing to save her husband, stops going to work and collects stray cats for comfort. Grief, fractured and unpredictable, rules their lives now. But when Eli Gage, a witness to the original suicide, comes to Officer Areno's funeral, his own father killed in action in Iraq, he and Rowan find a connection to each other they hadn't had before. Together they must find a way to survive a tragedy with no comforting, set answers.

Topics and Questions
for Discussion

I. *Me Since You* opens with a quotation from Søren
   Kierkegaard, the first of its many epigraphs. What do
   you think this quotation means in the context of the
   novel? What special meaning do you think it has for
   Rowan? Do you agree or disagree with the sentiment the
   quotation expresses?

2. Although everyone close to the event of Corey's suicide believes that the video of his death should never
   have been aired, the media broadcasts it anyway. Why
   do you think the media decided to air the video? Why
   do the Arenos, as well as Eli, disagree with the decision to broadcast the video? Do you think people have
   a right to see such things, or should they be kept private?

3. Once the video is aired, many people criticize the decisions Nick and Eli made in trying to save Corey, or
   think they would have done better themselves. Do you
   think Nick and Eli acted appropriately? What would
   you have done in their place? Why do you think so

many people were convinced they could have done a better job, or saved Corey and/or his son?

4. In addition to dealing with people's comments in person, Rowan also struggles with the online commentary about Corey's suicide. What is the difference between the two? Why do you think people are so comfortable saying things online that they wouldn't say in real life?

5. Before the suicide, Rowan's closest friend is Nadia. But after, Rowan and Nadia drift apart. Why do you think Nadia behaves the way she does as Rowan deals with the aftermath of Corey's suicide, and her father's? Do you think she acted appropriately toward Rowan? What would you have done in Nadia's place? Do you think Nadia is a true friend?

6. On page 82, Rowan's boss, Eva, reflects, "We grow up believing that bad things don't happen to good people . . . but sometimes they do. It's a hard truth to accept, that life is not fair." Do you think this is true? Why or why not? Why would it be hard to accept? What are some examples from your own life that either prove or disprove this sentiment?

7. As Rowan's father sinks deeper into his depression, Rowan struggles with the frustration and pain of watching him struggle, finally admitting that, "I cannot bear the sight of my father breaking" (p. 103). Why do you think this is so difficult for Rowan? Why is it so difficult for children to see their parents' vulnerability? Do you think that there was anything Rowan could have, or should have done for her father?

8. Throughout the book, Rowan reflects on the meaning of depression as a "burden," both on the sufferer, and the people around them. Why do you think depression feels like a "burden" to be carried, and why does it affect everyone around it so deeply? What is the difference between suffering from depression, and suffering through a loved one's?

9. After the suicide of Rowan's father, both Nadia and Eli reach out to Rowan, in an attempt to comfort her. What is the difference between their two approaches? What do you think this says about the difference in their friendships, and experiences? Which do you think is better for Rowan? Why?

10. When Eli attends Nick's funeral, Rowan says that his presence "makes this all too real" (p. 166). What do you think this means? Why is Eli the one who brings the full impact of what has happened home for Rowan?

11. As Rowan struggles with her grief over her father's death, she repeatedly reflects on the difficulty of coming to terms with the "reason" her father killed himself. On page 189 she says, "They want a *reason*, an event, something they can pinpoint and steer clear of." Why do you think people have a need for this kind of "reason"? Do you think Rowan is correct that there isn't always a specific reason to point to?

12. Why do you think it's so important for Rowan and her mother to find the notes that Nick left them? When they do finally find the notes, do you think the one left for Rowan satisfies her? Why or why not?

13. On page 274, Eli tells Rowan that his father's secret for dealing with anything really difficult is to "Just keep breathing." What do you think this means? Do you think it's good advice? Why do you think it works, or doesn't work? Can you think of other ways to cope with difficult things that are similar?

14. As Rowan falls for Eli, she wonders, "I will never understand how life can rip your heart out with one hand and then give you a small, warm piece of it back with the other?" (p. 280) Do you think life is like this, in your experience? Can you think of an example from your own life that proves or disproves this idea?

15. As Rowan and her mother finally begin to get rid of some of Nick's stuff, Rowan says in her grief journal, "Without your stuff, you will really be gone." Why do you think this is? Do you agree with this? Why is it so difficult to finally get rid of Nick's possessions?

16. Throughout *Me Since You*, Rowan reflects on the coincidences that led to her father's death (for example, p. 220), and the "ripple effect" that Corey's suicide had. What do you think is truly meant by the "ripple effect"? Do you think that the coincidences in the novel are truly coincidences, or something more? Do you see the "ripple effect" in your own life?

Enhance Your Book Club

1. Throughout *Me Since You*, Laura Wiess uses epigraphs to enhance the meaning of certain chapters or passages, as well as the book as a whole. When Rowan's family is writing Nick's eulogy, her mother also uses an epigraph from *Bartlett's Quotations* to find a way to begin their tribute to Nick. Imagine you had to replace the epigraph at the beginning of the book—find a new quotation that you think represents a theme or idea from *Me Since You*. Share your choice with the group, and explain why you think it represents the novel and its ideas. If you don't have your own copy of *Bartlett's Quotations*, here are some online resources that can help get you started.

    http://www.bartleby.com/quotations
    http://www.quotationspage.com
    http://www.online-literature.com

2. Laura Wiess has written several other novels: *Ordinary Beauty, How It Ends, Such a Pretty Girl* and *Leftovers.* Check out one of these other excellent stories, and share your thoughts on it with your group. How did it change the way you thought about *Me Since You?* What are some of the themes of the book you chose that match up with

the themes of *Me Since You*? Did you see other similarities between the novels?

3. Join the conversation! www.laurawiess.com, http://www.facebook.com/pages/Laura-Wiess/163023280412622, and https://twitter.com/LauraWiess are great resources for more information on Laura Wiess's novels and a way to meet other fans of *Me Since You*. Share your favorite parts of *Me Since You* on Facebook or Twitter, and check out all the great information on LauraWiess.com!